"A cross

and

"Nothing is true. Everything is permissible."
—Hassan i Sabbah, founder (1090 A.D.)

Have YOU ever wondered:

WHO IS the MAN in ZURICH that
some SWEAR is LEE HARVEY OSWALD?

IF there's an ESOTERIC ALLEGORY concealed
in the APPARENTLY INNOCENT legend of
Snow White and the Seven Dwarfs?

WHY scholarly anthropologists TURN PALE
with terror at the very MENTION of the
FORBIDDEN name YOG-SOTHOTH?

Find out in the original and genuine
trilogy of CONSPIRACIES
battling for world control—

ILLUMINATUS!

Volume I   THE EYE IN THE PYRAMID
Volume II   THE GOLDEN APPLE
Volume III LEVIATHAN

— by Robert Shea and Robert Anton Wilson —

PUBLISHED
BY SPHERE BOOKS

ILLUMINATUS! Part I

The Eye in the Pyramid

ROBERT SHEA and ROBERT ANTON WILSON

SPHERE BOOKS LIMITED

First published in Great Britain
by Sphere Books Ltd 1976
27 Wrights Lane, London W8 5TZ
Reprinted 1977, 1978, 1979, 1980, 1983, 1986
Copyright © 1975 by
Robert J. Shea and Robert Anton Wilson

Published by arrangement with
Dell Publishing Co. Inc.,
New York, N.Y., U.S.A.

To Gregory Hill
and Kerry Thornley

Set in Intertype Times

Printed and bound in Great Britain by
Cox & Wyman Ltd, Reading

BOOK ONE

VERWIRRUNG

The history of the world is the history of
the warfare between secret societies.
        —Ishmael Reed, *Mumbo-Jumbo*

THE FIRST TRIP, OR KETHER
From Dealey Plaza
To Watergate . . .

The Purple Sage opened his mouth and moved his tongue
and so spake to them and he said:

The Earth quakes and the Heavens rattle; the beasts of
nature flock together and the nations of men flock apart;
volcanoes usher up heat while elsewhere water becomes
ice and melts; and then on other days it just rains.

Indeed do many things come to pass.

—Lord Omar Khayaam Ravenhurst, K.S.C.,
'The Book of Predications,' *The Honest Book of Truth*

It was the year when they finally immanentized the
Eschaton. On April 1, the world's great powers came closer
to nuclear war than ever before, all because of an obscure
island named Fernando Poo. By the time international
affairs returned to their normal cold-war level, some wits
were calling it the most tasteless April Fool's joke in history. I happen to know all the details about what happened,
but I have no idea how to recount them in a manner that
will make sense to most readers. For instance, I am not
even sure who I am, and my embarrassment on that matter
makes me wonder if you will believe anything I reveal.
Worse yet, I am at the moment very conscious of a squirrel
– in Central Park, just off Sixty-eighth Street, in New York
City – that is leaping from one tree to another, and I think
that happens on the night of April 23 (or is it the morning
of April 24?), but fitting the squirrel together with Fernando
Poo is, for the present, beyond my powers. I beg your
tolerance. There is nothing I can do to make things any easier
for any of us, and you will have to accept being addressed
by a disembodied voice just as I accept the compulsion to
speak out even though I am painfully aware that I am talk-

ing to an invisible, perhaps nonexistent, audience. Wise
men have regarded the earth as a tragedy, a farce, even an
illusionist's trick; but all, if they are truly wise and not
merely intellectual rapists, recognize that it is certainly
some kind of stage in which we all play roles, most of us
being very poorly coached and totally unrehearsed before
the curtain rises. Is it too much if I ask, tentatively, that we
agree to look upon it as a circus, a touring carnival wandering about the sun for a record season of four billion years
and producing new monsters and miracles, hoaxes and
bloody mishaps, wonders and blunders, but never quite
entertaining the customers well enough to prevent them
from leaving, one by one, and returning to their homes for
a long and bored winter's sleep under the dust? Then, say,
for a while at least, that I have found an identity as ringmaster; but that crown sits uneasily on my head (if I have
a head) and I must warn you that the troupe is small for a
universe this size and many of us have to double or triple
our stints, so you can expect me back in many other guises.
Indeed do many things come to pass.

For instance, right now, I am not at all whimsical or
humorous. I am angry. I am in Nairobi, Kenya, and my
name is, if you will pardon me, Nkrumah Fubar. My skin
is black (does that disturb you? it doesn't me), and I am,
like most of you, midway between tribalism and technology; to be more blunt, as a Kikuyu shaman moderately
adjusted to city life, I still believe in witchcraft – I haven't,
yet, the folly to deny the evidence of my own senses. It is
April 3 and Fernando Poo has ruined my sleep for several
nights running, so I hope you will forgive me when I admit
that my business at the moment is far from edifying and is
nothing less than constructing dolls of the rulers of
America, Russia, and China. You guessed it: I am going
to stick pins in their heads every day for a month; if they
won't let me sleep, I won't let them sleep. That is Justice,
in a sense.

In fact, the President of the United States had several
severe migraines during the following weeks; but the atheistic rulers of Moscow and Peking were less susceptible to
magic. They never reported a twinge. But, wait, here is another performer in our circus, and one of the most intelligent and decent in the lot – his name is unpronounceable,

but you can call him Howard and he happens to have been
born a dolphin. He's swimming through the ruins of
Atlantis and it's April 10 already – time is moving; I'm not
sure what Howard sees but it bothers him, and he decides
to tell Hagbard Celine all about it. Not that I know, at this
point, who Hagbard Celine is. Never mind; watch the waves
roll and be glad there isn't much pollution out here yet.
Look at the way the golden sun lights each wave with a
glint that, curiously, sparkles into a silver sheen; and watch,
watch the waves as they roll, so that it is easy to cross five
hours of time in one second and find ourselves amid trees
and earth, with even a few falling leaves for a touch of
poetry before the horror. Where are we? Five hours away,
I told you – five hours due west, to be precise, so at the
same instant that Howard turns a somersault in Atlantis,
Sasparilla Godzilla, a tourist from Simcoe, Ontario (she had
the misfortune to be born a human being) turns a neat
nosedive right here and lands unconscious on the ground.
This is the outdoor extension of the Museum of Anthropology in Chapultepec Park, Mexico, D.F., and the other
tourists are rather upset about the poor lady's collapse. She
later said it was the heat. Much less sophisticated in important matters than Nkrumah Fubar, she didn't care to
tell anybody, or even to remind herself, what had really
knocked her over. Back in Simcoe, the folks always said
Harry Godzilla got a sensible woman when he married
Sasparilla, and it is sensible in Canada (or the United
States) to hide certain truths. No, at this point I had better
not call them truths. Let it stand that she either saw, or
imagined she saw, a certain sinister kind of tight grin, or
grimace, cross the face of the gigantic statue of Tlaloc, the
rain god. Nobody from Simcoe had ever seen anything like
that before; indeed do many things come to pass.

And, if you think the poor lady was an unusual case, you
should examine the records of psychiatrists, both institu-
tional and private, for the rest of the month. Reports of
unusual anxieties and religious manias among schizophrenics in mental hospitals skyrocketed; and ordinary men
and women walked in off the street to complain about eyes
watching them, hooded beings passing through locked
rooms, crowned figures giving unintelligible commands,
voices that claimed to be God or the Devil, a real witch's

brew for sure. But the sane verdict was to attribute all this to the aftermath of the Fernando Poo tragedy.

The phone rang at 2:30 A.M. the morning of April 24. Numbly, dumbly, mopingly, gropingly, out of the dark, I find and identify a body, a self, a task. 'Goodman,' I say into the receiver, propped up on one arm, still coming a long way back.

'Bombing and homicide,' the electrically eunuchoid voice in the transmitter tells me. I sleep naked (sorry about that), and I'm putting on my drawers and trousers as I copy the address. East Sixty-eighth Street, near the Council on Foreign Relations. 'Moving,' I say, hanging up.

'What? Is?' Rebecca mumbles from the bed. She's naked, too, and that recalls very pleasant memories of a few hours earlier. I suppose some of you will be shocked when I tell you I'm past sixty and she's only twenty-five. It doesn't make it any better that we're married, I know.

This isn't a bad body, for its age, and seeing Rebecca, most of the sheets thrown aside, reminds me just how good it is. In fact, at this point I don't even remember having been the ringmaster, or what echo I retain is confused with sleep and dream. I kiss her neck, unself-consciously, for she is my wife and I am her husband, and even if I am an inspector on the Homicide Squad – Homicide North, to be exact – any notions about being a stranger in this body have vanished with my dreams into air. Into thin air.

'What?' Rebecca repeats, still more asleep than awake.

'Damned fool radicals again,' I say, pulling on my shirt, knowing any answer is as good as another in her half-conscious state.

'Um,' she says, satisfied, and turns over into deep sleep again.

I washed my face somewhat, tired old man watching me from the mirror, and ran a brush through my hair. Just time enough to think that retirement was only a few years away and to remember a certain hypodermic needle and a day in the Catskills with my first wife, Sandra, back when they at least had clean air up there . . . socks, shoes, tie, fedora . . . and you never stop mourning, as much as I loved Rebecca I never stopped mourning Sandra. Bombing *and* homicide. What a *meshuganah* world. Do you remember when you could at least drive in New York at three in the morning without traffic jams? Those days were gone; the trucks that were banned in the daytime were all making their deliveries now. Everybody was supposed to pretend the pollution went away before dawn. Papa used to say, 'Saul, Saul, they did it to the Indians and now they're doing it to themselves. *Goyische narrs.*' He left Russia to escape the pogrom of 1905, but I guess he saw a lot before he got out. He seemed like a cynical old man to me then, and I seem like a cynical old man to others now. Is there any pattern or sense in any of it?

The scene of the blast was one of those old office buildings with Gothic-and-gingerbread styling all over the lobby floor. In the dim light of the hour, it reminded me of the shadowy atmosphere of Charlie Chan in the Wax Museum. And a smell hit my nostrils as soon as I walked in.

A patrolman lounging inside the door snapped to attention when he recognized me. 'Took out the seventeenth floor and part of the eighteenth,' he said. 'Also a pet shop here on the ground level. Some freak of dynamics. Nothing else is damaged down here, but every fish tank went. That's the smell.'

Barney Muldoon, an old friend with the look and mannerisms of a Hollywood cop, appeared out of the shadows. A tough man, and nowhere as dumb as he liked to pretend, which was why he was head of the Bomb Squad.

'Your baby, Barney?' I asked casually.

'Looks that way. Nobody killed. The call went out to you because a clothier's dummy was burned on the eighteenth floor and the first car here thought it was a human body.'

(Wait: George Dorn is screaming. . . .)

Saul's face showed no reaction to the answer – but poker players at the Fraternal Order of Police had long ago given up trying to read that inscrutable Talmudic countenance. As Barney Muldoon, I knew how I would feel if I had the chance to drop this case on another department and hurry home to a beautiful bride like Rebecca Goodman. I smiled down at Saul – his height would keep him from appointment to the Force now, but the rules were different when he was young – and I added quietly, 'There might be something in it for you, though.'

The fedora ducked as Saul took out his pipe and started to fill it. All he said was, 'Oh?'

'Right now,' I went on, 'we're just notifying Missing Persons, but if what I'm afraid of is right, it'll end up on your desk after all.'

He struck a match and started puffing. 'Somebody missing at this hour . . . might be found among the living . . . in the morning,' he said between drags. The match went out, and shadows moved where nobody stirred.

'And he might not, in this case,' Muldoon said. 'He's been gone three days now.'

'An Irishman your size can't be any more subtle than an elephant,' Saul said wearily. 'Stop tantalizing me. What have you got?'

'The office that was hit,' Muldoon explained, obviously happy to share the misery, 'was a magazine called *Confrontation*. It's kind of left-of-center, so this was probably a right-wing job and not a left-wing one. But the interesting thing is that we couldn't reach the editor, Joseph Malik, at his home, and when we called one of the associate editors, what do you think he told us? Malik disappeared three days ago. His landlord confirms it. He's been trying to get hold of Malik himself because there's a no-pets rule there and the other tenants are complaining about his dogs. So, if a man drops out of sight and then his office gets bombed, I kind of think the matter might come to the attention of the Homicide Department eventually, don't you?'

Saul grunted. 'Might and might not,' he said. 'I'm going home. I'll check with Missing Persons in the morning, to see what they've got.'

The patrolman spoke up. 'You know what bothers me most about this? The Egyptian mouth-breeders.'

'The what?' Saul asked.

'That pet shop,' the patrolman explained, pointing to the other end of the lobby. 'I looked over the damage, and they had one of the best collections of rare tropical fish in New York City. Even Egyptian mouth-breeders.' He noticed the expressions on the faces of the two detectives and added lamely, 'If you don't collect fish, you wouldn't understand. But, believe me, an Egyptian mouth-breeder is pretty hard to get these days, and they're all dead in there.'

'Mouth-*breeder?*' Muldoon asked incredulously.

'Yes, you see they keep their young in their mouths for a couple days after birth and they never, never swallow them. That's one of the great things about collecting fish: you get to appreciate the wonders of nature.'

Muldoon and Saul looked at each other. 'It's inspiring,' Muldoon said finally, 'to have so many college graduates on the Force these days.'

The elevator door opened, and Dan Pricefixer, a redheaded young detective on Muldoon's staff, emerged, carrying a metal box.

'I think this is important, Barney,' he began immediately, with just a nod to Saul. 'Damned important. I found it in the rubble, and it had been blown partly open, so I looked inside.'

'And?' Muldoon prompted.

'It's the freakiest bunch of interoffice memos I ever set eyes on. Weird as tits on a bishop.'

This is going to be a long night, Saul thought suddenly, with a sinking feeling. A long night, and a heavy case.

'Want to peek?' Muldoon asked him maliciously.

'You better find a place to sit down,' Pricefixer volunteered. 'It'll take you awhile to go through them.'

'Let's use the cafeteria,' Saul suggested.

'You just have no idea,' the patrolman repeated. 'The value of an Egyptian mouth-breeder.'

'It's rough for all nationalities, man or fish,' Muldoon said in one of his rare attempts to emulate Saul's mode of speech. He and Saul turned to the cafeteria, leaving the patrolman looking vaguely distressed.

His name is James Patrick Hennessy and he's been on the Force three years. He doesn't come back into this story at all. He had a five-year-old retarded son whom he loved helplessly; you see a thousand faces like his on the street every day and never guess how well they are carrying their tragedies . . . and George Dorn, who once wanted to shoot him, is still screaming. . . . But Barney and Saul are in the cafeteria. Look around. The transition from the Gothic lobby to this room of laminated functional and glittering plastic colors is, one might say, trippy. Never mind the smell; we're closer to the pet shop here.

Saul removed his hat and ran a hand through his gray hair pensively, as Muldoon read the first two memos in one quick scan. When they were passed over, he put on his glasses and read more slowly, in his own methodical and thoughtful way. Hold onto your hats. This is what they said:

ILLUMINATI PROJECT: MEMO #1

7/23

J.M.:

The first reference I've found is in *Violence* by Jacques Ellul (Seabury Press, New York, 1969). He says (pages 18–19) that the Illuminated Ones were founded by Joachim of Floris in the 11th century and originally taught a primitive Christian doctrine of poverty and equality, but later under the leadership of Fra Dolcino in the 15th century they became violent, plundered the rich and announced the imminent reign of the Spirit. 'In 1507,' he concludes, 'they were vanquished by the "forces of order" – that is, an army commanded by the Bishop of Vercueil.' He makes no mention of any Illuminati movement in earlier centuries or in more recent times.

I'll have more later today.

Pat

P.S. I found a little more about Joachim of Floris in the back files of the *National Review*. William Buckley and his cronies think Joachim is responsible for modern liberalism, socialism and communism; they've condemned him in fine theological language. He committed the heresy, they say, of 'immanentizing the Christian Eschaton.' Do you want me to look that up in a technical treatise on Thomism? I think it means bringing the end of the world closer, sort of.

ILLUMINATI PROJECT: MEMO #2

7/23

J.M.:

My second source was more helpful: Akron Daraul, *A History of Secret Societies* (Citadel Press, New York, 1961).

Daraul traces the Illuminati back to the 11th century also, but not to Joachim of Floris. He sees the origin in the Ishmaelian sect of Islam, also known as the Order of Assassins. They were vanquished in the 13th century, but later made a comeback with a new, less-violent philosophy and eventually became the Ishmaelian sect of today, led by the Aga Khan. However, in the 16th century, in Afghanistan, the Illuminated Ones (Roshinaya) picked up the original tactics of the Order of Assassins. They were wiped out by an alliance of the Moguls and Persians (pages 220–223). But, 'The beginning of the seventeenth century saw the foundation of the Illuminated Ones of Spain – the Allumbrados, condemned by an edict of the Grand Inquisition in 1623. In 1654, the "illuminated" Guerinets came into public notice in France.' And, finally – the part you're most interested in – the Bavarian Illuminati was founded on May Day, 1776, in Ingolstadt, Bavaria, by Adam Weishaupt, a former Jesuit. 'Documents still extant show several points of resemblance between the German and Central Asian Illuminists: points that are hard to account for on grounds of pure coincidence' (page 255). Weishaupt's Illuminati were suppressed by the Bavarian government in 1785; Daraul also mentions the Illuminati of Paris in the 1880s, but suggests it was simply a passing fad. He does not accept the notion that the Illuminati still exist today.

This is beginning to look big. Why are we keeping the details from George?

Pat

Saul and Muldoon exchanged glances. 'Let's see the next one,' Saul said. He and Muldoon read together:

ILLUMINATI PROJECT: MEMO #3

7/24

J.M.:

The Encyclopedia Britannica has little to say on the subject (1966 edition, Volume 11, 'Halicar to Impala,' page 1094):

> *Illuminati*, a short-lived movement of republican free thought founded on May Day 1776 by Adam Weishaupt, professor of canon law at Ingolstadt and a former Jesuit. . . . From 1778 onward they began to make contact with various Masonic lodges where, under the impulse of A. Knigge (q.v.) one of their chief converts, they often managed to gain a commanding position. . . .

The scheme itself had its attractions for literary
men like Goethe and Herder, and even for the reigning
dukes of Gotha and Weimar. . . .

The movement suffered from internal dissention and
was ultimately banned by an edict of the Bavarian
government in 1785.

                                                    Pat

Saul paused. 'I'll make you a bet, Barney,' he said
quietly. 'The Joseph Malik who vanished is the J.M. these
memos were written for.'

'Sure,' Muldoon replied scornfully. 'These Illuminati
characters are still around, and they got him. Honest to
God, Saul,' he added, 'I appreciate the way your mind
usually pole-vaults ahead of the facts. But you can ride a
hunch just so far when you're starting from nothing.'

'We're not starting from nothing,' Saul said softly.
'Here's what we've got to start with. One' – he held up a
finger – 'a building is bombed. Two' – another finger – 'an
important executive disappeared three days before the
bombing. Already, there's an inference, or two inferences:
something got him, or else he knew something was coming
for him and he ducked out. Now, look at the memos. Point
three' – he held up another finger – 'a standard reference
work, the *Encyclopedia Britannica*, seems to be wrong
about when the Illuminati came into existence. They say
eighteenth-century Germany, but the other memos trace it
back to – let's see – Spain in the seventeenth century,
France in the seventeenth century, then in the eleventh century back to Italy and halfway across the world to
Afghanistan. So we've got a second inference: if the
Britannica is wrong about when the thing started, they may
be wrong about when it ended. Now, put these three points
and two inferences together—'

'And the Illuminati got the editor and blew up his office.
Nutz. I still say you're going too fast.'

'Maybe I'm not going fast enough,' Saul said. 'An
organization that has existed for a couple of centuries *minimum* and kept its secrets pretty well hidden most of that
time might be pretty strong by now.' He trailed off into
silence, and closed his eyes to concentrate. After a moment,
he looked at the younger man with a searching glance.

Muldoon had been thinking too. 'I've seen men land on the moon,' he said. 'I've seen students break into administration offices and shit in the dean's waste basket. I've even seen nuns in mini-skirts. But this international conspiracy existing in secret for eight hundred years, it's like opening a door in your own house and finding James Bond and the President of the United States personally shooting it out with Fu Manchu and the five original Marx Brothers.'

'You're trying to convince yourself, not me. Barney, it sticks out so far that you could break it into three pieces and each one would be long enough to goose somebody up in the Bronx. There *is* a secret society that keeps screwing up international politics. Every intelligent person has suspected that at one time or another. Nobody wants war any more, but wars keep happening – why? Face it, Barney – this is the heavy case we've always had nightmares about. It's cast iron. If it were a corpse, all six pallbearers would get double hernias at the funeral. Well?' Saul prompted.

'Well, we're either going to have to do something or get off the pot, as my sainted mother used to say.'

It was the year when they finally immanentized the Eschaton. On April 1 the world's great powers came closer to nuclear war than ever before, all because of an obscure island named Fernando Poo. But, while all other eyes turned to the UN building in apprehension and desperate hope, there lived in Las Vegas a unique person known as Carmel. His house was on Date Street and had a magnificent view of the desert, which he appreciated. He liked to spend long hours looking at the wild cactus wasteland although he did not know why. If you told him that he was symbolically turning his back upon mankind, he would not have understood you, nor would he have been insulted; the remark would be merely irrelevant to him. If you added that he himself was a desert creature, like the gila monster and the rattlesnake, he would have grown bored and classified you as a fool. To Carmel, most of the world were fools who asked meaningless questions and worried about pointless issues; only a few, like himself, had discovered what was really important – money – and pursued it without distractions, scruples, or irrelevancies. His favorite moments were those, like this night of April 1, when he sat and tallied his take for the month and looked out his picture window occasionally at the flat sandy landscape, dimly lit by the lights of the city behind him. In this physical and emotional desert he experienced happiness, or something as close to happiness as he could ever find. His girls had earned $46,000 during March, of which he took $23,000; after paying 10 percent to the Brotherhood for permission to operate without molestation by Banana-Nose Maldonado's soldiers, this left a tidy profit of $20,700, all of it tax free. Little Carmel, who stood five feet two and had the face of a mournful weasel, beamed as he completed his calculations; his emotion was as inexpressible, in normal terms, as that of a necrophile who had just broken into the town morgue. He had tried every possible sexual combination with his girls; none gave him the *frisson* of looking at a figure like that at the end of a month.

He did not know that he would have another $5 million, and incidentally become the most important human being on earth, before May 1. If you tried to explain it to him, he would have brushed everything else aside and asked merely, 'The five million – how many throats do I hafta cut to *get my hands in it*?'

But wait: Get out the Atlas and look up Africa. Run your eyes down the map of the western coast of that continent until you come to Equatorial Guinea. Stop at the bend where part of the Atlantic Ocean curves inward and becomes the Bight of Biafra. You will note a chain of small islands; you will further observe that one of these is Fernando Poo. There, in the capital city of Santa Isobel, during the early 1970s, Captain Ernesto Tequilla y Mota carefully read and reread Edward Luttwak's *Coup d'Etat: A Practical Handbook*, and placidly went about following Luttwak's formula for a perfect coup d'etat in Santa Isobel. He set up a timetable, made his first converts among other officers, formed a clique, and began the slow process of arranging things so that officers likely to be loyal to Equatorial Guinea would be on assignment at least forty-eight hours away from the capital city when the coup occurred. He drafted the first proclamation to be issued by his new government; it took the best slogans of the most powerful left-wing and right-wing groups on the island and embedded them firmly in a tapiocalike context of bland liberal-conservatism. It fit Luttwak's prescription excellently, giving everybody on the island some small hope that his own interests and beliefs would be advanced by the new regime. And, after three years of planning, he struck: the key officials of the old regime were quickly, bloodlessly, placed under house arrest; troops under the command of officers in the cabal occupied the power stations and newspaper offices; the inoffensively fascist-conservative-liberal-communist proclamation of the new People's Republic of Fernando Poo went forth to the world over the radio station in Santa Isobel. Ernesto Tequilla y Mota had achieved his ambition – promotion from captain to general-issimo in one step. Now, at last, he began wondering about how one went about governing a country. He would probably have to read a new book, and he hoped there was one as good as Luttwak's treatise on seizing a country. That was on March 14.

On March 15, the very name of Fernando Poo was unknown to every member of the House of Representatives, every senator, every officer of the Cabinet, and all but one of the Joint Chiefs of Staff. In fact, the President's first reaction, when the CIA report landed on his desk that afternoon, was to ask his secretary, 'Where the hell is Fernando Poo?'

Saul took off his glasses and polished them with a hand-kerchief, conscious of his age and suddenly more tired than ever. 'I outrank you, Barney,' he began.

Muldoon grinned. 'I know what's coming.'

Methodically, Saul went on, 'Who, on your staff, do you think is a double agent for the CIA?'

'Robinson I'm sure of, and Lehrman I suspect.'

'Both of them go. We take no chances.'

'I'll have them transferred to the Vice Squad in the morning. How about your own staff?'

'Three of them, I think, and they go, too.'

'Vice Squad'll love the increase in manpower.'

Saul relit his pipe. 'One more thing. We might be hearing from the FBI.'

'We might indeed.'

'They get nothing.'

'You're really taking me way out on this one, Saul.'

'Sometimes you have to follow your hunches. This is going to be a heavy case, agreed?'

'A heavy case,' Muldoon nodded.

'Then we do it my way.'

'Let's look at the fourth memo,' Muldoon said tonelessly. They read:

ILLUMINATI PROJECT: MEMO #4

7/24

J.M.:

Here's a letter that appeared in *Playboy* a few years ago ('The Playboy Advisor,' *Playboy*, April, 1969, pages 62–64):

> I recently heard an old man of right-wing views – a friend of my grandparents – assert that the current wave of assassinations in America is the work of a secret society called the Illuminati. He said that the Illuminati have existed throughout history, own the international banking cartels, have all been 32nd-degree Masons and were known to Ian Fleming, who portrayed them as *Spectre* in his James Bond books – for which the Illuminati did away with Mr. Fleming. At first all this seemed like a paranoid delusion to me. Then I read in *The New Yorker* that Allan Chapman, one of Jim Garrison's investigators in the New Orleans probe of the John Kennedy assassination, believes that the Illuminati really exist. . . .

Playboy, of course, puts down the whole idea as ridiculous and gives the standard *Encyclopedia Britannica* story that the Illuminati went out of business in 1785.

Pat

Pricefixer stuck his head in the cafeteria door. 'Minute?' he asked.

'What is it?' Muldoon replied.

'Peter Jackson is out here. He's the associate editor I spoke to on the phone. He just told me something about his last meeting with Joseph Malik, the editor, before Malik disappeared.'

'Bring him in,' Muldoon said.

Peter Jackson was a black man – truly black, not brown or tan. He was wearing a vest in spite of the spring weather.

He was also very obviously wary of policemen. Saul noted this at once, and began thinking about how to overcome it – and at the same time he observed an increased blandness in Muldoon's features, indicating that he, too, had noted it and was prepared to take umbrage.

'Have a seat,' Saul said cordially, 'and tell us what you just told the other officer.' With the nervous ones it was sound policy to drop the policeman role at first, and try to sound like somebody else – somebody who, quite naturally, asks a lot of questions. Saul began slipping into the personality of his own family physician, which he usually used at such times. He made himself *feel* a stethoscope hanging about his neck.

'Well,' Jackson began in a Harvard accent, 'this is probably not important. It may be just a coincidence.'

'Most of what we hear is just unimportant coincidence,' Saul said gently. 'But it's our job to listen.'

'Everybody but the lunatic fringe has given up on this by now,' Jackson said. 'It really surprised me when Joe told me what he was getting the magazine into.' He paused and studied the two impassive faces of the detectives; finding little there, he went on reluctantly. 'It was last Friday. Joe told me he had a lead that interested him, and he was putting a staff writer on it. He wanted to reopen the investigation of the assassinations of Martin Luther King and the Kennedy brothers.'

Saul carefully didn't look at Muldoon, and just as carefully moved his hat to cover the memos on the table. 'Excuse me a moment,' he said politely and left the cafeteria.

He found a phone booth in the lobby and dialed his home. Rebecca answered after the third ring; she obviously had not gotten back to sleep after he left. 'Saul?' she asked, guessing who would be calling at this hour.

'It's going to be a long night,' Saul said.

'Oh, hell.'

'I know, baby. But that case is a son-of-a-bitch!'

Rebecca sighed. 'I'm glad we had a little ball earlier this evening. Otherwise, I'd be furious.'

Saul thought, suddenly, of how this conversation would sound to an outsider. A sixty-year-old man and a twenty-five-year-old wife. And if they knew she was a whore and a heroin addict when I first met her . . .

'Do you know what I'm going to do?' Rebecca lowered her voice. 'I'm going to take off my nightgown, and throw the covers to the foot of the bed, and lie here naked, thinking about you and waiting.'

Saul grinned. 'A man my age shouldn't be able to respond to that, after doing what I did earlier.'

'But you did respond, didn't you?' Her voice was confident and sensual.

'I sure did. I won't be able to leave the phone booth for a couple of minutes.'

She chuckled softly and said, 'I'll be waiting. . . .'

'I love you,' he said, surprised (as always) at the simple truth of it in a man his age. I won't be able to leave the phone booth at all if this keeps up, he thought. 'Listen,' he added hurriedly, 'let's change the subject before I start resorting to the vices of a high school boy. What do you know about the Illuminati?' Rebecca had been an anthropology major, with a minor in psychology, before the drug scene had captured her and she fell into the abyss from which he had rescued her; her erudition often astonished him.

'It's a hoax,' she said.

'A what?'

'A hoax. A bunch of students at Berkeley started it back around sixty-six or sixty-seven.'

'No, that's not what I'm asking. The original Illuminati in Italy and Spain and Germany in the fifteenth to eighteenth centuries? You know?'

'Oh, that's the basis of the hoax. Some right-wing historians think the Illuminati still exist, you see, so these students opened an Illuminati chapter on the campus at Berkeley and started sending out press releases on all sorts of weird subjects, so people who want to believe in conspiracies would have some evidence to point to. That's all there is to it. Sophomore humor.'

I hope so, Saul thought. 'How about the Ishmaelian sect of Islam?'

'It has twenty-three divisions, but the Aga Khan is the leader of all of them. It was founded around – oh – 1090 A.D., I think, and was originally persecuted, but now it's part of the orthodox Moslem religion. It has some pretty weird doctrines. The founder, Hassan i Sabbah, taught that

nothing is true and everything is permissible. He lived up
to that idea – the word "assassin" is a corruption of his
name.'

'Anything else?'

'Yes, now that I think of it. Sabbah introduced marijuana to the Western world, from India. The word
"hashish" also comes from his name.'

'This is a heavy case,' Saul said, 'and now that I can
walk out of the phone booth without shocking the patrolman in the hall, I'll get back to work on it. Don't say anything that'll get me aroused again. Please.'

'I won't. I'll just lie here naked and ...'

'Good-bye.'

'Good-bye,' she said, laughing.

Saul hung up frowning. Goodman's intuition, the other
detectives call it. It's not intuition; it's a way of thinking
beyond and between the facts, a way of sensing *wholes*, of
seeing that there must be a relationship between fact number one and fact number two even if no such relationship
is visible yet. And I know. There is an Illuminati, whether
or not those kids at Berkeley are kidding.

He came out of his concentration and realized where he
was. For the first time, he noticed a sticker on the door:

THIS PHONE BOOTH RESERVED FOR CLARK KENT

He grinned: an intellectual's kind of joke. Probably
somebody on the magazine.

He walked back to the cafeteria, reflecting. 'Nothing is
true. Everything is permissible.' With a doctrine like that,
people were capable of . . . He shuddered. Images of
Buchenwald and Belsen, of Jews who might have been
him. . . .

Peter Jackson looked up as he reentered the cafeteria.
An intelligent, curious black face. Muldoon was as impassive as the faces on Mount Rushmore. 'Mad Dog, Texas,
was the town where Malik thought these . . . assassins . . .
had their headquarters,' Muldoon said. 'That's where the
staff writer was sent.'

'What was the staff writer's name?' Saul asked.

'George Dorn,' Muldoon said. 'He's a young kid who

used to be in SDS. And he was once rather close to the Weatherman faction.'

Hagbard Celine's gigantic computer, FUCKUP – First Universal Cybernetic-Kinetic-Ultramicro-Programmer – was basically a rather sophisticated form of the standard self-programming algorithmic logic machine of the time; the name was one of his whimsies. FUCKUP's real claim to uniqueness was a programmed stochastic process whereby it could 'throw' an *I Ching* hexagram, reading a random open circuit as a broken (*yin*) line and a random closed circuit as a full (*yang*) line until six such 'lines' were round. Consulting its memory banks, where the whole tradition of *I Ching* interpretation was stored, and then cross-checking its current scannings of that day's political, economic, meterological, astrological, astronomical, and technological eccentricities, it would provide a reading of the hexagram which, to Hagbard's mind, combined the best of the scientific and occult methods for spotting oncoming trends. On March 13, the stochastic pattern spontaneously generated Hexagram 23, 'Breaking Apart.' FUCKUP then interpreted:

This traditionally unlucky sign was cast by Atlantean scientist-priests shortly before the destruction of their continent and is generally connected with death by water. Other vibrations link it to earthquakes, tornadoes and similar disasters, and to sickness, decay, and morbidity as well.

The first correlation is with the unbalance between technological acceleration and political retrogression, which has proceeded earthwide at everwidening danger levels since 1914 and especially since 1964. The breaking apart is fundamentally the schizoid and schismatic mental fugue of lawyer-politicians attempting to administrate a worldwide technology whose mechanisms they lack the education to comprehend and whose gestalt trend they frustrate by breaking apart into obsolete Renaissance nation-states.

World War III is probably imminent and, considering the advances in chemical biological warfare in conjunction with the sickness vibrations of Hexagram 23, the unleashing of plague or nerve gas or both is as probable as thermonuclear overkill.

General prognosis: many megadeaths.

There is some hope for avoidance of the emerging pattern with prompt action of correct nature. Probability of such avoidance is 0.17 ± 0.05.

No blame.

'My *ass*, no blame,' Hagbard raged; and rapidly reprogrammed FUCKUP to read off to him its condensed psychobiographies of the key figure in world politics and the key scientists in chemobiological warfare.

The first dream came to Dr. Charles Mocenigo on February 2 – more than a month before FUCKUP picked up the vibrations. He was, as usual with him, aware that he was dreaming, and the vision of a gigantic pyramid which seemed to walk or lumber about meant nothing and quickly vanished. Now he seemed to be looking at an enlargement of the DNA double helix; it was so detailed that he began searching it for the bonding irregularities at every 23rd Angstrom. To his surprise, they were missing; instead, there were other irregularities at each 17th Angstrom. 'What the devil . . .?' he asked – and the pyramid returned seeming to speak and saying, 'Yes, the devil.' He jolted awake, with a new concept, Anthrax-Leprosy-Mu, coming into consciousness, and began jotting in his bedside pad.

'What the hell is this Desert Door project?' the President had asked once, scrutinizing the budget. 'Germ warfare,' an aide explained helpfully. 'They started with something called Anthrax Delta and now they've worked their way up to something called Anthrax Mu and . . .' His voice was drowned out by the rumble of paper shredders in the next room. The President recognized the characteristic sound of the 'cesspool cleaners' hard at work. 'Never mind,' he said. 'Those things make me nervous.' He scribbled a quick 'OK' next to the item and went on to 'Deprived Children,' which made him feel better. 'Here,' he said, 'this is something we can cut.'

He forgot everything about Desert Door, until the Fernando Poo crises. 'Suppose, just suppose,' he asked the Joint Chiefs on March 29, 'I go on the tube and threaten all-out thermonuclear *heck*, and the other side doesn't blink. Have we got something that'll scare them even more?'

The J.C.'s exchanged glances. One of them spoke tentatively. 'Out near Las Vegas,' he said, 'we have this Desert Door project that seems to be way ahead of the Comrades in b-b and b-c—'

'That's biological-bacteriological and biological-chemical,' the President explained to the Vice-President, who was frowning. 'It has nothing to do with B-B guns.' Turning his attention back to the military men, he asked, 'What have we got specifically that will curdle Ivan's blood?'

'Well, there's Anthrax-Leprosy-Mu. . . . It's worse than any form of anthrax. More deadly than bubonic and anthrax and leprosy all in one lump. As a matter of fact,' the General who was speaking smiled grimly at the thought, 'our evaluation suggests that with death being so quick, the psychological demoralization of the survivors – if there are any survivors – will be even worse than in thermonuclear exchange with maximum "dirty" fallout.'

'By golly,' the President said. 'By *golly*. We won't use that out in the open. My speech'll just talk Bomb, but we'll leak it to the boys in the Kremlin that we've got this anthrax gimmick in cold storage, too. By gosh, you just wait and see them back down.' He stood up, decisive, firm, the image he always projected on television. 'I'm going to see my speechwriters right now. Meanwhile, arrange that the brain responsible for this Anthrax-Pi gets a raise. What's his name?' he asked over his shoulder going out the door.

'Mocenigo. Dr. Charles Mocenigo.'

'A raise for Dr. Charles Mocenigo,' the President called from the hallway.

'Mocenigo?' the Vice-President asked thoughtfully. 'Is he a wop?'

'Don't say wop,' the President shouted back. 'How many times do I have to tell you? Don't say wop or kike or *any* of those words anymore.' He spoke with some asperity, since he lived daily with the dread that someday the secret tapes he kept of all Oval Room transactions would be released to the public. He had long ago vowed that if that day ever came, the tapes would not be full of '(expletive deleted)' or '(characterization deleted).' He was harassed, but still he spoke with authority. He was, in fact, characteristic of the best type of dominant male in the world at this time. He was fifty-five years old, tough, shrewd, unburdened by the complicated ethical ambiguities which puzzle intellectuals, and had long ago decided that the world was a mean son-of-a-bitch in which only the most cunning and ruthless can survive. He was also as kind as was possible for one holding that ultra-Darwinian philosophy; and he genuinely loved children and dogs, unless they were on the site of something that had to be bombed in the National Interest. He still retained some sense of humor, despite the burdens of his almost godly office, and, although he had been impotent with his wife for nearly ten years now, he generally achieved orgasm in the mouth of a skilled prostitute within 1.5 minutes. He took amphetamine pep pills to keep going on his grueling twenty-hour day, with the result that his vision of the world was somewhat skewed in a paranoid direction, and he took tranquilizers to keep from worrying too much, with the result that his detachment sometimes bordered on the schizophrenic; but most of the time his innate shrewdness gave him a fingernail grip on reality. In short, he was much like the rulers of Russia and China.

In Central Park, the squirrel woke again as a car honked loudly in passing. Muttering angrily, he leaped to another tree and immediately went back to sleep. *At the all-night Bickford's restaurant on Seventy-second Street, a young man named August Personage left a phone booth after making an obscene call to a woman in Brooklyn; he left behind one of his* THIS PHONE BOOTH RESERVED FOR CLARK KENT *stickers.* In Chicago, one hour earlier on the clock but the same instant, the phone booth closed, a rock group called Clark Kent and His Supermen began a revival of 'Rock Around the Clock': their leader, a tall black man with a master's degree in anthropology, had been known as El Hajj Starkerlee Mohammed during a militant phase a few years earlier, and his birth certificate said Robert Pearson on it. He was observing his audience and noted that that bearded young white cat, Simon, was with a black woman as usual – a fetish Pearson-Mohammed-Kent could understand by reverse psychology, since he preferred white chicks himself. Simon, for once, was not entranced by the music; instead, he was deep in conversation with the girl and drawing a diagram of a pyramid on the table to explain what he meant. 'Crown Point,' Pearson heard him say over the music. *And listening to 'Rock Around the Clock' ten years earlier, George Dorn had decided to let his hair grow long, smoke dope and become a musician. He had succeeded in two of those ambitions.* The statue of Tlaloc in the Museum of Anthropology, Mexico, D.F., stared inscrutably upward, toward the stars . . . *and the same stars glittered above the Carribean where the porpoise named Howard sported in the waves.*

The motorcade passes the Texas School Book Depository and moves slowly toward the Triple Underpass. At the sixth-floor window, Lee Harvey Oswald sights carefully through the Carcano-Mannlicher: his mouth is dry, desert dry. But his heartbeat is normal; and no sweat stands out on his forehead. This is the moment, he is thinking, the one moment transcending time and hazard, heredity and environment, the final test and proof of free will and of my right to call myself a man. In this moment, now, as I tighten the trigger, the Tyrant dies, and with him all the lies of a cruel, mendacious epoch. It is a supreme exaltation, this moment and this knowledge: and yet his mouth is dry, dust-dry, dry as death, as if his salivary glands alone rebelled against the murder which his intellect pronounced necessary and just. *Now:* He recalls the military formula BASS: Breath, Aim, Slack, Squeeze. He breathes, he aims, he slacks, he starts to squeeze, as a dog barks suddenly—

And his mouth falls open in astonishment as three shots ring out, obviously from the direction of the Grassy Knoll and Triple Underpass.

'Son-of-a-bitch,' he said, softly as a prayer. And he began to grin, a rictus not of omnipotence such as he had expected but of something different and unexpected and therefore better – omniscience. That smirk appeared in all the photos during the next day and a half, before his own death, a sneering smile that said so clearly that none dared to read it: *I know something you don't know.* That grimace only faded Sunday morning when Jack Ruby pumped two bullets into Lee's frail fanatic body, and its secret went with him to the grave. But another part of the secret had already left Dallas on Friday afternoon's TWA Whisperjet to Los Angeles, traveling behind the business suit, gray hair, and only moderately sardonic eyes of a little old man who was listed on the flight manifest as 'Frank Sullivan.'

This is serious, Peter Jackson was thinking; Joe Malik wasn't on a paranoid trip at all. The noncommittal expressions of Muldoon and Goodman did not deceive him at all – he had long ago learned the black art of surviving in a white world, which is the art of reading not what is on a face but what is behind the face. The cops were worried and excited, like any hunters on the track of something both large and dangerous. Joe was right about the assassination plot, and his disappearance and the bombing were part of it. And that meant George Dorn was in danger, too, and Peter liked George even if he was a snotty kid in some ways and an annoying ass-kisser about the race thing like most young white radicals. Mad Dog, Texas, Peter thought: that sure sounds like a bad place to be in trouble.

(Almost fifty years before, a habitual bank robber named Harry Pierpont approached a young convict in Michigan City Prison and asked him, 'Do you think there might be a true religion?')

But why is George Dorn screaming while Saul Goodman is reading the memos? Hold on for another jump, and this one is a shocker. Saul is no longer human; he's a pig. All cops are pigs. Everything you've ever believed is probably a lie. The world is a dark, sinister, mysterious and totally frightening place. Can you digest all that quickly? Then, walk into the mind of George Dorn for the second time, five hours before the explosion at *Confrontation* (four hours before, on the clock) and suck on the joint, suck hard and hold it down. ('One o'clock . . . two o'clock . . . three o'clock . . . ROCK!'). You are sprawled on a crummy bed in a rundown hotel, and a neon light outside is flashing pink and blue patterns into your room. Exhale slowly, feel the hit of the weed and see if the wallpaper looks any brighter yet, any less Unintentional Low Camp. It's hot, Texas-dry hot, and you push your long hair back from your forehead and haul out your diary, George Dorn, because reading over what you wrote last sometimes helps you to learn what you're really getting into. As the neon splotches the page with pink and blue, read this:

April 23

How do we know whether the universe is getting bigger or the objects in it are getting smaller? You can't say that the universe is getting bigger in relation to anything outside it, because there isn't any outside for it to relate to. There isn't any outside. But if the universe doesn't have an *out*-side, then it goes on forever. Yeah, but, its *in*-side doesn't go on forever. How do you know it doesn't, shithead? You're just playing with words, man.

—No, I'm not. The universe is the inside without an outside, the sound made by one

There was a knock at the door.

The Fear came over George. Whenever he was high, the least little detail wrong in his world would bring the Fear, irresistible, uncontrollable. He held his breath, not to contain the smoke in his lungs, but because terror had paralyzed the muscles in his chest. He dropped the little notebook in which he wrote his thoughts daily and clutched at his penis, an habitual gesture in moments of panic. The hand holding the roach drifted, automatically, over the hollowed-out copy of Sinclair Lewis's *It Can't Happen Here*, which lay beside him on the bed, and he dropped the half-inch twist of paper and marijuana on top of the plastic Baggie full of green grains. Instantly a brown smoldering dime-sized hole opened up on the bag, and the pot near the coal started to smoke.

'Stupid,' said George, as his thumb stabbed the smoking coal to crush it, and he drew back his lips in a grimace of pain.

A short fat man walked into the room, Law Officer written in every mean line of his crafty little face. George shrank back and started to close *It Can't Happen Here*; like lightning, three stiff, concrete-hard fingers drove into his forearm. He screamed and the book jumped out of his hand, spilling pot all over the bedspread.

'Don't touch that,' said the fat man. 'An officer will be in to gather it up for evidence. I went easy with that karate punch. Otherwise you'd be nursing a compound fracture of the left arm in Mad Dog County Jail tonight, and no right-thinking doctor likely to have a mind to come out and treat you.'

'You got a warrant?' George tried to sound defiant.

'Oh, you think you have cojones.' The fat man's breath stank of bourbon and cheap cigars. 'Rabbit cojones. I have terrified you unto death, boy, and you know it and I know it, yet you find it in your heart to speak of warrants. Next you'll want to see the American Civil Liberties Union.' He pulled aside the jacket of an irridescent gray summer suit that might have been new when *Heartbreak Hotel* was the top of the hit parade. A silver five-pointed star decorated his pink shirt pocket and a .45 automatic stuck in his pants-top dented the fat of his belly. 'That is all the law I need when dealing with your type in Mad Dog. Walk careful with me, son, or you won't have nothing to grab onto next time one of us pigs, as you choose to call us in your little articles, busts in on you. Which is not likely to happen in the next forty years, while you rot and grow old in our state prison.' He seemed immensely pleased with his own oratorical style, like one of Faulkner's characters.

George thought:

> It is forbidden to dream again;
> We maim our joys or hide them;
> Horses are made of chromium steel
> And little fat men shall ride them.

He said, 'You can't hit me with forty years for possession. And grass is legal in most other states. This law is archaic and absurd.'

'Shit and onions, boy, you got too much of the killer weed there to call it mere possession. I call it possession with intent to sell. And the laws of this state are stern, and they are just and they are our laws. We know what that weed can do. We remember the Alamo and Santa Anna's troops losing all fear because they were high on Rosa Maria, as they called it in those days. Get on your feet. And don't ask to talk to a lawyer, neither.'

'Can I ask who you are?'

'I am Sheriff Jim Cartwright, nemesis of all evil in Mad Dog and Mad Dog County.'

'And I'm Tiny Tim,' said George, immediately saying to

himself, Shut the fuck up, you're too goddam high. And he went right on and said, 'Maybe your side would have won if Davy Crockett and Jim Bowie got stoned, too. And, by the way, Sheriff, how did you know you could catch me with pot? Usually an underground journalist would make it a point to be clean when he comes into this godforsaken part of the country. It wasn't telepathy that told you I had pot on me.'

Sheriff Cartwright slapped his thigh. 'Oh, but it was. It *was* telepathy. Now just what made you think it wasn't telepathy brung me here?' He laughed, seized George's arm in a grip of iron, and pushed him toward the hotel-room door. George felt a bottomless terror as if the pit of hell were opening beneath his feet and Sheriff Jim Cartwright were about to pitchfork him into the bubbling sulfur. And I must admit that was more or less the case; there are periods of history when the visions of madmen and dope fiends are a better guide to reality than the common-sense interpretation of data available to the so-called normal mind. This is one such period, if you haven't noticed already.

('Keep on hanging out with those wild boys from Passaic and you'll end up in jail,' George's mother said. 'You mark my words, George.' And, another time, at Columbia, after a very late meeting, Mark Rudd said soberly, 'A lot of us are going to spend some time in the Man's jails before this shit-storm is over'; and George, together with the others, nodded glumly but bravely. The marijuana he had been smoking was raised in Cuernavaca by a farmer named Arturo Jesus Maria Ybarra y Mendez, who had sold it in bulk to a young *Yanqui* named Jim Riley, the son of a Dayton, Ohio, police officer, who in turn smuggled it through Mad Dog after paying a suitable bribe to Sheriff Jim Cartwright. After that it was resold to a Times Square dealer called Rosetta the Stoned and a Miss Walsh from *Confrontation*'s research department bought ten ounces from her, later reselling five ounces to George, who then carried it back to Mad Dog without any suspicion that he was virtually completing a cycle. The original seed was part of that strain recommended by General George Washington in the famous letter to Sir John Sinclair in which he writes, 'I find that, for all purposes, the Indian

hemp is in every way superior to the New Zealand variety previously cultivated here.' *In New York, Rebecca Goodman, deciding that Saul will not be home tonight, slips out of bed, dons a robe and begins to browse through her library. Finally she selects a book on Babylonian mythology and begins to read:* 'Before all of the gods, was Mummu, the spirit of Pure Chaos. . . .' *In Chicago, Simon and Mary Lou Servix sit naked on her bed, legs intertwined in the yabum lotus position.* 'No,' *Simon is saying,* 'You don't move, baby; you wait for* IT *to move you.'* Clark Kent and His Supermen swing into a reprise: 'We're gonna rock around the clock tonight . . . We're gonna ROCK ROCK ROCK till broad daylight.')

George's cellmate in Mad Dog County Jail had a skull-like face with large, protruding front teeth. He was about six and a half feet tall and lay curled up on his cell bunk like a coiled python.

'Have you asked for treatment?' George asked him.

'Treatment for what?'

'Well, if you think you're an assassin—'

'I don't think, baby brother. I've killed four white men and two niggers. One in California, the rest down here. Got paid for every one of them.'

'Is that what you're in for?' My God, they don't stick murderers in the same cell with potheads, do they?

'I'm in for vagrancy,' said the man scornfully. 'Actually, I'm just here for safekeeping, till they give me my orders. Then it's good-bye to whoever – President, civil rights leader, enemy of the people. Someday I'll be famous. I'm gonna write a book about myself someday, Ace. Course, I'm no good at writing. Look, maybe we can do a deal. I'll have Sheriff Jim bring you some writing paper if you'll write about my life. They gonna keep you here forever, you know. I'll come and visit you between assassinations, and you'll write the book, and Sheriff Jim'll keep it safe till I retire. Then you have the book published and you'll make a lot of money and be real comfortable in jail. Or maybe you can even hire a lawyer to get you out.'

'Where will you be?' said George. He was still scared, but he was feeling sleepy, too, and he was deciding that this was all bullshit, which had a calming effect on his nerves. But he'd better not go to sleep in the cell while this guy was awake. He didn't really believe this assassin talk, but it was safe to assume that anybody you met in prison was homosexual.

As if reading his mind, his cellmate said, 'How'd you like to let a famous assassin shove it up to you? How would that be, huh, Ace?'

'Please,' said George. 'That's not my bag, you know? I really couldn't do it.'

'Shit, piss, and corruption,' said the assassin. He suddenly uncoiled and slid off the bunk. 'I been wasting my time with you. Now bend the hell over and drop your pants. You are getting it, and there ain't no further way about it.' He stepped toward George, fists clenched.

'Guard! Guard!' George yelled. He grabbed the cell door in both hands and began rattling it frantically.

The man caught George a cuff across the face. Another blow to the jaw knocked George against the wall.

'*Guard!*' he screamed, his head spinning with pot and panic.

A man in a blue uniform came through the door at the end of the corridor. He seemed miles away and vastly disinterested, like a god who had grown bored with his creations.

'Now, what the hell is all this yelling about in here?' he asked, his hand on the butt of his revolver, his voice still miles away.

George opened his mouth, but his cellmate spoke first. 'This little long-haired communist freak won't drop his pants when I tell him. Ain't you supposed to make sure I'm happy in here?' The voice shifted to a whine. 'Make him do what I say.'

'You've got to protect me,' said George. 'You've got to get me out of this cell.'

The god-guard laughed. 'Well, now, you might say this is a very enlightened prison we have here. You come down from New York and you probably think we're pretty backward. But we ain't. We got no police brutality. Now, if I interfered between you and Harry Coin here, I might have to use force to keep him away from your young ass. I know you people believe all cops ought to be abolished. Well, in this here situation I hereby abolish myself. Furthermore, I know you people believe in sexual freedom, and I do, too. So Harry Coin gonna have his sexual freedom without any interference or brutality from me.' His voice was still distant and disinterested, almost dreamy.

'No,' said George.

The guard drew his pistol. 'Now, sonny. You take down your pants and bend over. You are gonna get it up the ass from Harry Coin here, and no two ways about it. And I am gonna watch and see that you let him do it right. Otherwise, you get no forty years. You get killed, right now. I put a bullet in you and I say you are resisting arrest. Now make up your mind what it's gonna be. I really will kill you if you don't do like he tells you to. I really will. You are totally expendable and he ain't. He's a very important man, and it's my job to keep him happy.'

'And I'll fuck you either way, dead or alive,' the demented Coin laughed, like an evil spirit. 'So there's no way you can escape it, Ace.'

The door at the end of the corridor clanged, and Sheriff Jim Cartwright and two blue-uniformed policemen strode down to the cell. 'What's going on here?' said the Sheriff.

'I caught this queer punk George Dorn here trying to commit homosexual rape on Harry,' said the guard. 'Had to draw my pistol to stop him.'

George shook his head. 'You guys are unbelievable. If you're acting out this little game for my benefit, you can quit now, because you're certainly not fooling each other, and you're not fooling me.'

'Dorn,' said the Sheriff, 'you've been attempting unnatural acts in my jail, acts forbidden by the Holy Bible and the laws of this state. I don't like that. I don't like it one little bit. Come on out here. I wanna have a little talk with you. We goin' to the main interrogation room for some speakin' together.'

He unlocked the cell door and motioned George to precede him. He turned to the two policemen who had accompanied him. 'Stay behind and take care of that other *little matter*.' The last words were strangely emphasized.

George and the Sheriff walked through a series of corridors and locked doors until at last they came to a room whose walls were made of embossed sheet tin painted bottle-green. The Sheriff told George to sit on one chair, while he straddled the back of the chair facing him.

'You're a bad influence on my prisoners,' he said. 'I got
a good mind to see that some kind of accident happens to
you. I don't want to see you corrupting prisoners in my
jail – mine or anyone's – for forty years.'

'Sheriff,' said George. 'What do you want from me?
You got me on a pot charge. What more do you want?
Why did you stick me in that cell with that guy? What's
all this scare stuff and threats and questioning for?'

'I wanna know some things,' said the Sheriff. 'I want to
find out everything you can tell me about certain matters.
So, from this moment be prepared to tell me only the truth.
If you do, maybe things will go easier on you, after.'

'Yes, Sheriff,' said George. Cartwright squinted at him.
He really does look like a pig, thought George. Most do.
Why do so many of them get so fat and have such little
eyes?

'Well, then,' said the Sheriff. 'What was your purpose in
coming down here from New York?'

'I'm simply on an assignment from *Confrontation*, the
magazine—'

'I know it. It is a smutty magazine, and a communist
magazine. I have read it.'

'You're using loaded words. It's a left wing libertarian
magazine, to be exact.'

'My pistol is loaded, too, boy. So talk straight. All right.
Tell me what you came down here to write about.'

'Sure. You ought to be as interested in this as I am, if
you're really interested in law and order. There have been
rumours circulating throughout the country for more than a
decade now that all the major political assassinations in
America – Malcolm X, the Kennedy brothers, Medgar
Evers, King, Nixon, maybe even George Lincoln Rockwell
– are the work of a single, conspiratorial, violence-oriented
right-wing organization, and that this organization has its
base right here in Mad Dog. I came down to see what I
could find out about this group.'

'That's what I figured,' said the Sheriff. 'You poor, sad
little turd. You come down here with your long hair and
you expect to get, as you put it, a line on a right-wing
organization. Why, it's lucky for you you didn't meet any
of our real right-wingers, like God's Lightning for instance.
The ones around here would have tortured you to death

by this time, boy. You really are dumb. OK, I'm not gonna waste any more of my time with you. Come on, I'll take you back to your cell. You might as well get used to looking at the moon through bars.'

They walked back the same way they had come. At the entrance to the corridor where George's cell was, the Sheriff opened the door and yelled, 'Come and get him, Charley.'

George's guard, his face pale and his mouth set in a lipless line, took George by the arm. The corridor door clanged shut behind the Sheriff. Charley took George to his cell and pushed him in wordlessly. But at least he was three-dimensional now and less like a marijuana phantom.

Harry Coin wasn't there. The cell was empty. George became aware of a shadow in the corner of his vision. Something in the cell next to him. He turned: His heart stopped. There was a man hanging from a pipe on the ceiling. George went over and stared through the bars. The body was swaying slightly. It was attached to the pipe by a leather belt which was buckled around the neck. The face, with the staring eyes, was that of Harry Coin. George's glance went lower. Something was coming out of Harry Coin's midsection and was dangling down to the floor. It wasn't suicide. They had disemboweled Harry Coin, and someone had thoughtfully moved a shit-can under him for his bloody intestines to dangle into.

George screamed. There was no one around to answer him. The guard had vanished like Hermes.

(But in Cherry Knolls mental hospital in Sunderland, England, where it was already eleven the following morning, a schizophrenic patient who hadn't spoken in ten years abruptly began exhorting a ward attendant: 'They're all coming back – Hitler, Goering, Streicher, the whole lot of them. And, behind them, the powers and persons from the other spheres who control them. . . .' But Simon Moon in Chicago still calmly and placidly retains the lotus position and instructs Mary Lou sitting in his lap: 'Just hold it, hold it with your vaginal wall like you'd hold it with your hand, gently, and feel its warmth, but don't think about orgasm, don't think about the future, not even a minute ahead, think about the now, the only now, the only now, the only now that we'll ever have, just my penis in your vagina now and the simple pleasure of it, not a greater pleasure to work toward. . . .' 'My back hurts,' Mary Lou said.)

WE'RE GONNA ROCK ROCK ROCK AROUND THE CLOCK TO-NIGHT

There are Swedish and Norwegian kids, Danes, Italian and French kids, Greeks, even Americans. George and Hagbard move through the crowd trying to estimate its number – 200,000? 300,000? 500,000? Peace symbols dangling about every neck, nudes with body paint, nudes without body paint, long and dangling hair on boys and girls alike, and over all of it the hypnotic and unending beat. 'Woodstock Europa,' Hagbard says drily. 'The last and final Walpurgisnacht and Adam Weishaupt's Erotion finally realized.'

WE'RE GONNA ROCK ROCK ROCK TILL BROAD DAYLIGHT

'It's a League of Nations,' George says, 'a young people's League of Nations.' Hagbard isn't listening. 'Up there,' he points, 'to the Northwest is the Rhine, where *die Lorelei* was supposed to sit and sing her deadly songs. There will be deadlier music on the Danube tonight.'

WE'RE GONNA ROCK AROUND THE CLOCK TONIGHT

(But that was still seven days in the future, and now George lies unconscious in Mad Dog County Jail. And it began – that phase of the operation, as Hagbard called it – over thirty years before when a Swiss chemist named Hoffman climbed on his bicycle and pedaled down a country road into new dimensions.)

'And will they all come back?' George asked.

'All of them,' Hagbard answered tightly. 'When the beat reaches the proper intensity . . . unless we can stop it.'

('Now I'm getting it,' Mary Lou cried. 'It's not what I expected. It's different from sex, and better.' Simon smiled benignly. 'It *is* sex, baby,' he said. 'What you've had before wasn't sex. Now we can start moving . . . but slowly . . . the Gentle Way . . . the Way of Tao. . . .' *They're all coming back; they never died* – the lunatic raved at the startled attendant – *You wait, guvnor. You just wait. You'll see it.*)

The amplifiers squealed suddenly. There was too much feedback, and the sound went off into a pitch beyond endurance. George winced, and saw others hold their ears.

ROCK, ROCK, ROCK, AROUND THE CLOCK. *The key missed the lock, turned and cut Muldoon's hand.* 'Nerves,' he said to Saul. 'I always feel like a burglar when I do this.'

Saul grunted. 'Forget burglary,' he said. 'We might be hanged for treason before this is over. If we don't become national heroes.'

'A fanfuckingtastic case,' Muldoon grinned. He tried another way.

They were in an old brownstone on Riverside Drive, trying to break into the apartment of Joseph Malik. And they were not merely looking for evidence, both tacitly admitted – they were hiding from the FBI.

The call had come from headquarters just as they were finishing the questioning of associate editor Peter Jackson. Muldoon had gone out to his car to take it, while Saul finished getting a full physical description of both Malik and George Dorn. Jackson had just left and Saul was picking up the fifth memo, when Muldoon returned, looking as if his doctor had just told him his Wasserman was positive.

'Two special agents from the FBI are coming over to help us,' he said woodenly.'

'Still ready to play a hunch?' Saul asked calmly, pushing all the memos back in the metal box.

Muldoon merely called Pricefixer back into the cafeteria and told him, 'Two feds will be here in a few minutes. Tell them we went back to headquarters. Answer any question they ask, but don't tell them about this box.'

Pricefixer looked at the two older officers carefully and then said to Muldoon, 'You're the boss.'

He's either awfully dumb and trusting, Saul had thought, or he's so damned smart he's going to be dangerous someday.

'Now,' he asked Muldoon nervously, 'is that the last key?'

'No, I've got five more beauties here and one of them will – here it is!' The door opened smoothly.

Saul's hand drifted toward his revolver as he stepped into the apartment and felt for a light switch. Nobody was revealed when the light came on, and Saul relaxed. 'You look around for the dogs,' he said. 'I want to sit down and go over the rest of these memos.'

The room was used for work as well as living and was

untidy enough to leave no room for doubt that Malik had
been a bachelor. Saul pushed the typewriter back on the
writing desk, set down the memo box and then noticed
something odd. The whole wall, on this side of the room,
was covered with pictures of George Washington. Standing
to examine them more closely, he saw that each had a
label – half of them saying 'G.W.' and the others, 'A.W.'

Odd – but the whole case had overtones that smelled as
fishy as those dead Egyptian mouth-breeders.

Saul sat down and took a memo from the box.

Muldoon came back into the living room and said, 'No
dogs. Not a goddam dog anywhere in the whole apartment.'

'That's interesting,' Saul remarked thoughtfully. 'You
say the landlord had complaints from several other tenants
about the dogs?'

'He said everybody in the building was complaining.
The rule is no pets and he enforced it. People wanted to
know why they had to get rid of their kittens when Malik
could have a whole pack of dogs up here. They said there
must have been ten or twelve from the noise they made.'

'He sure must love those animals, if he took them all
with him when he went into hiding,' Saul mused. The pole
vaulter in his unconscious was jumping again. 'Let's look
in the kitchen,' he suggested mildly.

Barney followed as Saul methodically ransacked the re-
frigerator and cupboards, finishing up with a careful examination of the garbage.

'No dog food,' Saul said finally.

'I noticed.'

'And no dog dishes either. And no empty dog-food tins
in the garbage.'

'What wild notion are you following now?'

'I don't know,' Saul said thoughtfully. 'He doesn't mind
the neighbors hearing the dogs – probably he's the kind of
left-wing individualist who likes nothing better than quar-
reling with his landlord and the other tenants about some
issue like the no-pets rule. So he wasn't hiding anything
until he ducked out. And then he not only took the dogs
but hid all evidence that they'd ever been here. Even
though he must have known that the neighbors would all
talk about them.'

'Maybe he was feeding them human flesh,' Muldoon suggested ghoulishly.

'Lord, I don't know. You look around for anything of interest. I'm going to read those Illuminati memos.' Saul returned to the living room and began:

ILLUMINATI PROJECT: MEMO #5

7/26

J.M.:

Sometimes you find things in the damnedest places. The following is from a girl's magazine ('The Conspiracy' by Sandra Glass, *Teenset*, March 1969, pages 34–40).

> Simon proceeded to tell me about the Bavarian Illuminati. The nightmarish story begins in 1090 A.D. in the Middle East when Hassan i Sabbah founded the Ismaelian Sect, or *Hashishim*, so called because of their use of hashish, a deadly drug derived from the hemp plant which is better known as the killer weed marijuana. . . . The cult terrorized the Moslem world until Genghis Khan's Mongols brought law and order to the area. Cornered in their mountain hideaway, the Hashishim dope fiends proved no match for the clean-living Mongol warriors, their fortress was destroyed, and their dancing girls shipped to Mongolia for rehabilitation. The heads of the cult fled westward. . . .
>
> 'The Illuminati surfaced next in Bavaria in 1776,' Simon told me. . . . 'Adam Weishaupt, a student of the occult, studied the teachings of Hassan i Sabbah and grew hemp in his backyard. On February 2, 1776, Weishaupt achieved illumination. Weishaupt officially founded the Ancient Illuminated Seers of Bavaria on May 1st, 1776. Their slogan was *'Ewige Blumenkraft.'* . . . . They attracted many illustrious members such as Goethe and Beethoven. Beethoven tacked up an *Ewige Blumenkraft* poster on the top of the piano on which he composed all nine of his symphonies.'

The last paragraph of the article is, however, the most interesting of all:

Recently I saw a documentary film on the Democratic Convention of 1968, and I was struck by the scene in which Senator Abraham Ribicoff made a critical remark provoking the anger of the Mayor of Chicago. In the ensuing tumult it was impossible to hear the Mayor's shouted retort, and there has been much speculation about what he actually said. To me it seemed his lips were forming the words that by this time become frighteningly familiar: *'Ewige Blumenkraft!'*

The further I dig, the wilder the whole picture looks. When are we going to tell George about it?

Pat

ILLUMINATI PROJECT: MEMO #6

7/26

J.M.:

The John Birch Society has looked into the subject and they have a theory of their own. The first source I've found on this is a pamphlet 'CFR: Conspiracy to Rule the World' by Gary Allen, associate editor of the Birchers' magazine, *American Opinion.*

Allen's thesis is that Cecil Rhodes created a secret society to establish English domination of the world in 1888. This society acts through Oxford University, the Rhodes Scholarships and – hold your breath – the Council on Foreign Relations, a nonprofit foundation for the study of International Affairs headquartered right here on Sixty-eighth Street in New York. Seven out of nine of our last Secretaries of State were recruited from the CFR, Allen points out, and dozens of other leading politicians as well – including Richard Nixon. It is also implied, but not directly stated, that William Buckley, Jr. (an old enemy of the Birchers) is another tool of the CFR; and the Morgan and Rothschild banking interests are supposed to be financing the whole thing.

How does this tie in with the Illuminati? Mr. Allen merely drops hints, linking Rhodes to John Ruskin, and Ruskin to earlier internationalists, and finally stating that 'the originator on the profane level of this type of secret society' was Adam Weishaupt, whom he calls 'the monster who founded the Order of the Illuminati on May 1, 1776.'

Pat

ILLUMINATI PROJECT: MEMO #7

7/27

J.M.:

This is from a small left-wing newspaper in Chicago (*The RogerSPARK* Chicago, July 1969, Vol. 2, No. 9: 'Daley Linked With Illuminati,' no author's name given):

> No historian knows what happened to Adam Weishaupt after he was exiled from Bavaria in 1785, and entries in 'Washington's' diary after that date frequently refer to the hemp crop at Mount Vernon.
>
> The possibility that Adam Weishaupt killed George Washington and took his place, serving as our first President for two terms, is now confirmed. . . . The two main colors of the American flag are, excluding a small patch of blue in one corner, red and white: these are also the official colors of the Hashishim. The flag and the Illuminati pyramid both have thirteen horizontal divisions: thirteen is, of course, the traditional code for marijuana . . . and is still used in that sense by Hell's Angels among others.
>
> Now, 'Washington' formed the Federalist party. The other major party in those days. The Democratic Republicans, was formed by Thomas Jefferson [and] there are grounds for accepting the testimony of the Reverend Jedediah Morse of Charleston, who accused Jefferson of being an Illuminati agent. Thus, even at the dawn of our government, both parties were Illuminati fronts. . . .

This story later repeats the *Teenset* report that Mayor Daley used the phrase *'Ewige Blumenkraft'* during his incoherent diatribe against Abe Ribicoff.

Pat

ILLUMINATI PROJECT: MEMO #8

7/27

J.M.:

More on the Washington-Weishaupt theory:

> In spite of the fact that his face appears on billions of stamps and dollar bills, and his portrait hangs in every public building in the country, no one is quite sure what Washington looks like. A 'Project 20' script,

'Meet George Washington' will be seen tonight at
7:30 on Channel (fill in by local stations). The program offers contemporary portraits of the first President, some of which do not even seem to be the same
man.

This is a press release sent out by NBC on April 24, 1969.
Some of the portraits can be found in *Encyclopedia Britannica* and the resemblance to portraits of Weishaupt is
undeniable.

Incidentally, Barbara called my attention to this: the
letter in *Playboy* asking about the Illuminati was signed
'R.S., Kansas City, Missouri.' According to the Kansas
City newspapers, a Robert Stanton of that city was found
dead on March 17, 1969 (about a week after the April
Playboy appeared on the newsstands) with his throat torn
as if by the talons of some enormous beast. No animal was
reported missing from any of the local zoos.

                                                    Pat

Saul looked up at the pictures of Washington on the
wall. For the first time, he noticed the strange half-smile
on the most famous of them all, the one by Gilbert Stuart
that appears on one-dollar bills. *'As if by the talons of
some enormous beast,' he quoted to himself, thinking again
of Malik's disappearing dogs.*

'What the hell are you grinning about?' he asked sourly.

Congressman Koch, he remembered suddenly, in a speech
years and years ago when marijuana was illegal everywhere, said something about Washington's hemp crop.
What was it? Yes: it was about the entries in the General's
diary – they showed that he separated the female hemp
plants from the males before fertilization. That was botani-
cally unnecessary if he was growing the crop for rope, but
it was standard practise in cultivating hemp for marijuana, Koch pointed out.

And 'illumination' was one of the words hippies were
always using to describe the experience one obtains from
the highest grade of grass. Even the more common term,
'turning on,' had the same meaning as 'illumination,' when
you stopped to think about. Wasn't that what the crown
of light around Jesus' head in Catholic art was supposed

to mean? And Goethe – if he was really part of this – might have been referring to the experience in his last words, as he lay dying: 'More light!'

I should have become a rabbi, like my father wanted, Saul thought bemusedly. Police work is getting to be too much for me.

In a few minutes I'll be suspecting Thomas Edison.

ROCK ROCK ROCK TILL BROAD DAYLIGHT

Slowly, Mary Lou Servix swam back to consciousness, like a shipwreck victim reaching a raft.

'Good Lord,' she breathed softly.

Simon kissed her neck. 'Now you know,' he whispered.

'Good *Lord*,' she repeated. 'How many times did I come?'

Simon smiled. 'I'm not an anal-compulsive type – I wasn't counting. Ten or twelve, something like that, I guess?'

'Good *Lord*. And the hallucinations. Was that what you were doing to my nervous system, or was it the grass?'

'Just tell me about what you saw.'

'Well, you got a halo around you, sort of. A big blue halo. And then I saw that it was around me, too, and that it had all sorts of little blue dots dancing in sort of whorls inside it. And then there wasn't even that anymore. Just light. Pure white light.'

'Suppose I told you I have a friend who's a dolphin and he exists in that kind of limitless light all the time.'

'Oh, don't start jiving me. You've been so nice, until now.'

'I'm not jiving you. His name is Howard. I might arrange for you to meet him.'

'A fish?'

'No, baby. A dolphin is a mammal. Just like you and me.'

'You are either the world's greatest brain or the world's craziest motherfucker, Mr. Simon Moon. I mean it. But that light . . . My God, I will never forget that light.'

'And what happened to your body?' Simon asked casually.

'You know, I didn't know where it was. Even in the middle of my orgasms I didn't know where my body was. Everything was just . . . the light. . . .'

ROCK ROCK ROCK AROUND THE CLOCK TONIGHT

And leaving Dallas that much-discussed November 22 afternoon in 1963, the man using the name 'Frank Sullivan' brushes past McCord and Barker at the airport, but no foreshadowing of Watergate darkens his mind. (Back at the Grassy Knoll, Howard Hunt's picture is being snapped and will later turn up in the files of New Orleans D.A. Jim 'The Jolly Green Giant' Garrison: not that Garrison ever came within light years of the real truth. . . .)

'*Here, kitty-kitty-kitty,*' *Hagbard calls.*

But now we are going back, again, to April 2 and Las Vegas; Sherri Brandi (nee Sharon O'Farrell) arriving home finds Carmel in her living room at four in the morning. It doesn't surprise her; he often made these unexpected visits. *He seems to enjoy invading other people's territory like some kinda creepy virus.* 'Darling,' I cried, rushing to kiss him as he expected. *I wish the creep would drop dead,* I thought as our mouths met.

'An all-night john?' he asked casually.

'Yeah. One of these scientists who works at that place out in the desert we're all supposed to pretend we don't know about. A freak.'

'He wanted something special?' Carmel asked quickly. 'You charged him extra?' At times I thought I could really see dollar signs in his eyes.

'No,' I said, 'he just wanted a lay. But afterward he wouldn't let me go. Just kept jawing.' I yawned, looking around at the nice furniture and the nice paintings; I had managed to get everything in shades of pink and lavender, really beautiful, if that creep hadn't been sitting there on the couch looking like a hungry dead rat. I always wanted pretty things and I think I could have been some kind of artist or designer if all my luck wasn't always lousy. Christ, who ever told Carmel a blue turtleneck would go with a brown suit? If it wasn't for women, in my honest-to-Pete opinion, men would all go around looking like that. That's what I think. Insensitive. A bunch of cavemen, or Meander Thralls, or whatever you call them. 'This john had a lot on his mind,' I said before old candy-bar could start crossexamining me about something else. 'He's against fluorides in drinking water and the Catholic church and faggots and he thinks the new birth-control pill is as bad as the old one and I should use a diaphragm instead. Christ, he's got the inside dope on everything under the sun, he thinks, and I hadda listen to it all. That kind of john.'

Carmel nodded. 'Scientists are schmucks,' he said.

I pulled the dress over my head and hung it in the closet (it was the nice green one with the spangles and the new style where my nipples stick out through little holes, which is a pain in the ass because they're always rubbing against something and getting raw, but it really turns on the johns, and, like I always say, that's the name of the game, in this sonofabitching town with all the lousy luck, the only way to heavy scratch is go out there, girl, and sell your snatch) and then I grabbed my robe quickly before old blow-job bobo decided it was time for his weekly Frenching. 'He's got a nice house, though,' I said to distract the creep. 'He doesn't have to live out there on the base, he's too important for rules and regularities. Nice to look at, I mean. Redwood walls and burnt orange decor, you know? Pretty. He hates it, though. Acts as if he thinks it's haunted by Count Frankenstein or somebody. Keeps jumping up and walking around like he's looking for something. Something that'll bite his head off in one gulp if he finds it.' I decided to let the top of the robe hang open a little. Carmel was either horny or he wanted something else, and *something else* with him generally means he thinks you've been holding back some cash. Him and his damned belt. Of course, sometimes with that I go queer all over for a flash and I guess that's like the come that men have, the orgasm, but it ain't worth the pain, believe me. I wonder if it's true some women get it in intercourse? Really get it? I don't think so. I've never known anybody in the business who gets it, from a man, only from Rosy Palm and her five sisters, sometimes, and if none of *us* do, how could some straight nicey-nicey get it?

'Bugs,' Carmel said, looking shrewd and clever, off on his usual shtick of proving he was more hip to everything than anybody else on God's green earth. I didn't know what the hell he was talking about.

'What do you mean, bugs?' I asked. It was better than talking about money.

'The john,' he said with a know-it-all grin. 'He's important, you said. So his house has bugs. He probably keeps taking them out, and the FBI keeps coming back and putting in new ones. I bet he was very quiet when he was making it with you, right?' I nodded, remembering. 'See. He couldn't stand the thought of those Feds eavesdropping on the other end of the wire. Just like Mal – like a guy I know in the Syndicate. He's so afraid of bugs he won't hold a business talk anywhere but the bathroom in his hotel suite with all four faucets going full blast and both of us whispering. Running water screws up a bug more than playing loud music on the radio, for some scientific reason.'

'Bugs,' I said suddenly. 'That's it.' The other kind of bugs. I was remembering Charley raving about flouridation: 'And we're all classified as mental cases, because a few right-wing nuts fifteen or twenty years ago said fluoridation was a communist plot to poison us. Now, anybody who criticizes fluoridation is supposed to be just as bananas as God's Lightning. Good Lord, if anybody wants to do us in without firing a shot, I could –' and he caught himself, hid something that almost showed on his face, and ended like his brain was walking on one foot, 'I could point to a dozen things in any chemistry book more effective than fluoride.' But he wasn't thinking of chemicals, he was thinking of those little bugs, microbes is the word, and that's what he was working on. I could feel that flash I always get when I read something in a john, like if he had more money than he let on, or he'd caught his wife spreading for the milkman and was doing it to get even, or he was really a faggola and was just proving to himself that he wasn't *completely* a faggola. 'My God,' I said, 'Carmel, I read about those microbe bugs in the *Enquirer*. If they have an accident out there, this whole town goes, and the state with it, and God knows how many other states. Jesus, no wonder he keeps washing his hands!'

'Germ warfare?' Carmel said, thinking fast. 'God, I'll bet this town is crawling with Russian spies trying to find out what's going on out there. And I've got a direct lead for them. But how the hell do you meet a Russian spy, or a Chinese spy for that matter? You can't just advertise in a newspaper. Hell. Maybe if I went down to the university and talked to some of those freaking commie students. . . .'

I was shocked. 'Carmel! You can't sell your own country like that!'

'The hell I can't. The Statue of Liberty is just another broad, and I'll take what I can get for her. Don't be a fool.' He reached in his jacket pocket and took out a caramel candy like he always did when he was excited. 'I'll bet somebody in the Mob will know. They know everything. Jesus, there has to be *some* way of cashing in on this.'

The President's actual television broadcast was transmitted to the world at 10:30 P.M. EST, March 31. The Russians and Chinese were given twenty-four hours to get out of Fernando Poo or the skies over Santa Isobel would begin raining nuclear missiles: 'This is *darn* serious,' the Chief Executive said, 'and America will not shirk its responsibility to the freedom-loving people of Fernando Poo!' The broadcast concluded at 11 P.M. EST, and within two minutes people attempting to get reservations on trains, planes, buses or car pools to Canada had virtually every telephone wire in the country overloaded.

In Moscow, where it was ten the next morning, the Premier called a conference and said crisply, 'That character in Washington is a mental lunatic, and he means it. Get our men out of Fernando Poo right away, then find out who authorized sending them in there in the first place and transfer him to be supervisor of a hydroelectric works in Outer Mongolia.'

'We don't have any men in Fernando Poo,' a commissar said mournfully. 'The Americans are imagining things again.'

'Well, how the hell can we withdraw men if we don't have them there in the first place?' the Premier demanded.

'I don't know. We've got twenty-four hours to figure that out, or –' the commissar quoted an old Russian proverb which means, roughly, that when the polar bear excrement interferes with the fan belts, the machinery overheats.

'Suppose we just announce that our troops are coming out?' another commissar suggested. 'They can't say we're lying if they don't find any of our troops there afterward.'

'No, they never believe anything we *say*. They want to be shown,' the premier said thoughtfully. 'We'll have to infiltrate some troops surreptitiously and then withdraw them with a lot of fanfare and publicity. That should do it.'

'I'm afraid it won't end the problem,' another commissar said funereally. 'Our intelligence indicates that there are Chinese troops there. Unless Peking backs down, we're going to be caught in the middle when the bombs start flying and –' he quoted a proverb about the man in the intersection when two manure trucks collide.

'Damn,' the Premier said. 'What the blue blazes do the Chinese want with Fernando Poo?'

He was harassed, but still he spoke with authority. He was, in fact, characteristic of the best type of dominant male in the world at this time. He was fifty-five years old, tough, shrewd, unburdened by the complicated ethical ambiguities which puzzle intellectuals, and had long ago decided that the world was a mean son-of-a-bitch in which only the most cunning and ruthless can survive. He was also as kind as was possible for one holding that ultra-Darwinian philosophy; and he genuinely loved children and dogs, unless they were on the site of something that had to be bombed in the National Interest. He still retained some sense of humor, despite the burdens of his almost godly office, and although he had been impotent with his wife for nearly ten years now, he generally achieved orgasm in the mouth of a skilled prostitute within 1.5 minutes. He took amphetamine pep pills to keep going on his grueling twenty-hour day, with the result that his vision of the world was somewhat skewed in a paranoid direction, and he took tranquilizers to keep from worrying too much, with the result that his detachment sometimes bordered on schizophrenia; but most of the time his innate shrewdness gave him a fingernail grip on reality. In short, he was much like the rulers of America and China.

And, banishing Thomas Edison and his light bulbs from mind, Saul Goodman looks back over the first eight memos briefly, using the conservative and logical side of his personality, rigidly holding back the intuitive functions. It was a habitual exercise with him, and he called it expansion-and-contraction: leaping in the dark for the connection that must exist between fact one and fact two, then going back slowly to check on himself.

The names and phrases flow past, in review: Fra Dolcino – 1508 – Roshinaya – Hassan i Sabbah – 1090 – Weishaupt – assassinations – John Kennedy, Bobby Kennedy, Martin Luther King – Mayor Daley – Cecil Rhodes – 1888 – George Washington. . . .

Choices: (1) it is all true, exactly as the memos suggest; (2) it is partly true, and partly false; (3) it is all false, and there is no secret society that has endured from 1090 A.D. to the present.

Well, it isn't all true. Mayor Daley never said '*Ewige Blumenkraft*' to Senator Ribicoff. Saul had read, in the *Washington Post*, a lip-reader's translation of Daley's diatribe and there was no German in it, although there was obscenity and anti-Semitism. The Weishaupt-Washington impersonation theory also had some flaws – in those days, before plastic surgery, such an undetected assumption of the identity of a well-known figure was especially hard to credit, despite the circumstantial evidence quoted in the memos – two strong arguments against choice one. The memos are not *all* true.

How about choice three? The Illuminati might not be a straight unbroken line from the first recruit gathered by old Hassan i Sabbah to the person who bombed *Confrontation* – it might have died and lain dormant for a term, like the Ku Klux Klan between 1872 and 1915; and it might have gone through such breakups and resurrections more than once in eight centuries – but linkages of some sort, however tenuous, reached from the eleventh century to the twentieth, from the Near East to Europe and from Europe to America. Saul's dissatisfaction with official explanations of recent assassinations, the impossibility of making any rational sense out of current American foreign policy, and the fact that even historians who vehemently distrusted all 'conspiracy theories' acknowledged the pivotal role of secret Masonic lodges in the French Revolution: all these added weight to the rejection of choice 3. Besides, the Masons were the first group, according to at least two of the memos, infiltrated by Weishaupt.

Choice 1 is definitely out, then, and choice 3 almost certainly equally invalid; choice 2, therefore, is most probably correct. The theory in the memos is partly true and partly false. But what, in essence, is the theory – and which part of it is true, which part false?

Saul lit his pipe, closed his eyes, and concentrated.

The theory, in essence, was that the Illuminati recruited people through various 'fronts,' turned them onto some sort of *illuminizing* experience through marijuana (or some special extract of marijuana) and converted them into fanatics willing to use any means necessary to 'illuminize' the rest of the world. Their aim, obviously, is nothing less than the total transformation of humanity itself, along the lines suggested by the film *2001*, or by Nietzsche's concept of the Superman. In the course of this conspiracy the Illuminati, according to Malik's hints to Jackson, were systematically assassinating every popular political figure who might interfere with their program.

Saul thought, suddenly, of Charlie Manson, and of the glorification of Manson by the Weatherman and Morituri bombers. He thought of the popularity of pot smoking and of the slogan 'by any means necessary' with contemporary radical youth, even outside Weatherman. And he thought of Neitzsche's slogan, 'Be hard. . . . Whatever is done for love is beyond good and evil. . . . Above the ape is man, and above man, the Superman. . . . Forget not thy whip. . . .' In spite of his own logic, which had proved that Malik's theory was only *partly* true, Saul Goodman, a lifelong liberal, suddenly felt a pang of typically right-wing terror toward modern youth.

He reminded himself that Malik seemed to think the conspiracy emanated chiefly from Mad Dog – and that was God's Lightning country down there. God's Lightning had no fondness for marijuana, or for youth, or for the definitely anti-Christian overtones of the Illuminati philosophy.

Besides, Malik's sources were only partly trustworthy.

And there were other possibilities: the Shriners, for instance, were part of the Masonic movement, were generally right-wing, had their own hidden rites and secrets, and used Arabic trappings that might well derive from Hassan i Sabbah or the Roshinaya of Afghanistan. Who could say what secret plots were hatched at Shriner conventions?

No, that was the intuitive pole vaulter in the right lobe

at work again; and right now Saul was concerned with the plodding logician in the left lobe.

The key to the mystery was in getting a clearer definition of the purpose of the Illuminati. Identify the change they were trying to accomplish – in man and in his society – and then you would be able to guess, at least approximately, who they were.

Their aim was English domination of the world, and they were Rhodes Scholars – according to the Birchers. *That* idea, obviously, belonged with Saul's own whimsy about a worldwide Shriner conspiracy. What then? The Italian Illuminati, under Fra Dolcino, wanted to redistribute the wealth – but the International Bankers, mentioned in the *Playboy* letter, presumably wanted to hold onto their wealth. Weishaupt was a 'freethinker' according to the *Britannica,* and so were Washington and Jefferson – but Sabbah and Joachim of Florence were evidently heretical mystics of the Islamic and Catholic traditions respectively.

Saul picked up the ninth memo, deciding to get more facts (or pretended facts) before analyzing further – and then it hit him.

Whatever the Illuminati were aiming at had not been accomplished. Proof: If it had, they would not still be conspiring in secret.

Since almost everything has been tried in the course of human history, find out what hasn't been tried (at least not on a large scale) – and that will be the condition to which the Illuminati are trying to move the rest of mankind.

Capitalism had been tried. Communism has been tried. Even Henry George's Single Tax has been tried, in Australia. Fascism, feudalism and mysticism have been tried.

Anarchism has never been tried.

Anarchism was frequently associated with assassinations. It had an appeal for freethinkers, such as Kropotkin and Bakunin, but also for religious idealists, like Tolstoy and Dorothy Day of the Catholic Worker movement. Most anarchists hoped, Joachim-like, to redistribute the wealth, but Rebecca had once told him about a classic of anarchist literature, Max Stirner's *The Ego and His Own,* which had been called 'the Billionaire's Bible' because it stressed the advantages the rugged individualist would gain in a stateless society – and Cecil Rhodes was an adventurer before he was a banker. The Illuminati were anarchists.

It all fit: the pieces of the puzzle slipped together smoothly.

Saul was convinced.

He was also wrong.

'We'll just get our troops out of Fernando Poo,' the Chairman of the Chinese Communist party said on April 1. *'A place that size isn't worth world war.'*

'But we don't have any troops there,' an aide told him, 'it's the Russians who do.'

'Oh?' the Chairman quoted a proverb to the effect that there was urine in the rosewater. 'I wonder what the hell the Russians want with Fernando Poo?' he added thoughtfully.

He was harassed, but still he spoke with authority. He was, in fact, characteristic of the best type of dominant male in the world at this time. He was fifty-five years old, tough, shrewd, unburdened by the complicated ethical ambiguities which puzzled intellectuals, and had long ago decided that the world was a mean son-of-a-bitch in which only the most cunning and ruthless can survive. He was also as kind as was possible for one holding that ultra-Darwinian philosophy; and he genuinely loved children and dogs, unless they were on the site of something that had to be bombed in the National Interest. He still retained some sense of humor, despite the burdens of his almost godly office, and, although he had been impotent with his wife for nearly ten years now, he generally achieved orgasm in the mouth of a skilled prostitute within 1.5 minutes. He took amphetamine pep pills to keep going on his grueling twenty-hour day, with the result that his vision of the world was somewhat skewed in a paranoid direction, and he took tranquilizers to keep from worrying too much, with the result that his detachment sometimes bordered on the schizophrenic; but most of the time his innate shrewdness gave him a fingernail grip on reality. In short, he was much like the rulers of America and Russia.

('And it's not only a sin against God,' Mr. Mocenigo shouts, 'but it gives you germs, too.' It is 1950, early spring on Mulberry Street, and young Charlie Mocenigo raises terrified eyes. 'Look, look,' Mr. Mocenigo goes on angrily, 'don't believe your own father. See what the dictionary says. Look, look at the page. Here, see. "Masturbation: self-pollution." Do you know what self-pollution means? Do you know how long those germs last?' And in another spring, 1955, Charles Mocenigo, a pale, skinny, introverted genius, registers for his first semester at MIT and, coming to the square on the form that says 'Religion,' writes in careful block capitals, ATHEIST. He has read Kinsey and Hirschfeld and almost all the biologically oriented sexological treatises by this time – studiously ignoring psychoanalysts and such unscientific types – and the only visible remnant of that early adolescent terror is a habit of washing his hands frequently when under tension, which earns him the nickname 'Soapy.')

General Talbot looks at Mocenigo pityingly and raises his pistol to the scientist's head....

On August 6, 1902, the world produced its usual crop of new humans, all programmed to act more or less alike, all containing minor variations of the same basic DNA blueprint; of these, approximately 51,000 were female and 50,000 were male; and two of the males, born at the same second, were to play a large role in our story, and to pursue somewhat similar and anabatic careers. The first, born over a cheap livery stable in the Bronx, New York, was named Arthur Flegenheimer and, at the other end of his life, spoke very movingly about his mother (as well as about bears and sidewalks and French Canadian Bean Soup); the second, born in one of the finest old homes on Beacon Hill in Boston, was named Robert Putney Drake and, at the other end of his life, thought rather harshly of his mother . . . but when the paths of Mr. Flegenheimer and Mr. Drake crossed, in 1935, one of the links was formed which led to the Fernando Poo Incident.

And, in present time, more or less, 00005 was summoned to meet W. in the headquarters of a certain branch of British Intelligence. The date was March 17, but being English, neither 00005 nor W. gave a thought to blessed Saint Patrick; instead, they spoke of Fernando Poo.

'The Yanks,' W. said crisply, 'are developing evidence that the Russians or the Chinese, or both of them, are behind this Tequilla y Moto swine. Of course, even if that were true, it wouldn't matter a damn to Her Majesty's government; what do we care if a *speck* of an island that size turns Red? But you know the Yanks, 00005 – they're ready to go to war over it, although they haven't announced that publicly yet.'

'My mission,' 00005 asked, the faint lines of cruelty about his mouth turning into a most engaging smile, 'is to hop down to Fernando Poo and find out the real politics of this Tequilla y Mota bloke and if he is Red overthrow him before the Yanks blow up the world?'

'That's the assignment. We can't have a bloody nuclear war just when the balance of payments is almost straightened out and the Common Market is finally starting to work. So, hop to it, straightaway. Naturally, if you're captured, Her Majesty's government will have to disavow any knowledge of your actions.'

'It always seems to work out that way,' 00005 said ironically. 'I wish for once you'd give me a mission where Her Majesty's bleeding government would stand behind me in a tight spot.'

But 00005, of course, was merely being witty; as a loyal subject, he would follow orders under any circumstances, even if it required the death of every soul on Fernando Poo and himself as well. He rose, in his characteristic debonair fashion, and headed for his own office, where he began his preparations for the Fernando Poo mission. His first step was to check his personal worldwide travel notebook, seeking the bar in Santa Isobel which came closest to serving a suitable martini and the restaurant most likely to prepare an endurable lobster Newburg. To his horror, there was no such bar and no such restaurant. Santa Isobel was bereft of social graces.

'I say,' 00005 muttered, 'this is going to be a bit *thick*.'

But he cheered up quickly, for he knew that Fernando Poo would be equipped at least with a bevy of tawny-skinned or coffee-colored females, and such women were the Holy Grail to him. Besides, he had already formed his own theory about Fernando Poo: he was convinced that BUGGER – Blowhard's Unreformed Gangsters, Goons, and Espionage Renegades, an international conspiracy of criminals and double agents, led by the infamous and mysterious Eric 'the Red' Blowhard – was behind it all. 00005 had never heard of the Illuminati.

In fact, 00005, despite his dark hair combed straight back, his piercing eyes, his cruel and handsome face, his trim athlete's body, and his capacity to penetrate any number of females and defenestrate any number of males in the course of duty, was not really an ideal intelligence agent. He had grown up reading Ian Fleming novels and one day, at the age of twenty-one, looked in the mirror, decided he was everything a Fleming hero should be, and started a campaign to get into the spy game. After fourteen years in bureaucratic burrowing, he finally arrived in one of the intelligence services, but it was much more the kind of squalid and bumbling organization in which Harry Palmer had toiled his cynical days away than it was a berth of Bondage. Nevertheless, 00005 did his best to refurbish and glamorize the scene and, perhaps because God looks after fools, he hadn't managed to get himself killed in any of the increasingly bizarre missions to which he was assigned. The missions were all weird, at first, because nobody took them seriously – they were all based on wild rumors that had to be checked out just in case there be some truth in them – but later it was realized that 00005's peculiar schizophrenia was well suited to certain real problems, just as the schizoid of the more withdrawn type is ideal for a 'sleeper' agent since he could easily forget what was conventionally considered his real self. Of course, nobody at any time ever took BUGGER seriously, and, behind his back, 00005's obsession with this organization was a subject of much interdepartmental humor.

'*Wonderful as it was,*' Mary Lou said, '*some of it was scary.*'

'*Why?*' Simon asked.

'*All those hallucinations. I thought I might be losing my mind.*'

Simon lit another joint and passed it over to her. '*What makes you think, even now, that it was just hallucinations?*' he asked.

ROCK ROCK ROCK TILL BROAD DAYLIGHT

'*If that was real,*' Mary Lou said firmly, '*everything else in my life has been a hallucination.*'

Simon grinned. '*Now,*' he said calmly, '*you're getting the point.*'

THE SECOND TRIP, OR CHOKMAH

Hopalong Horus Rides Again

Hang on for some metaphysics. The Aneristic Principle is that of ORDER, the Eristic Principle is that of DISORDER. On the surface, the Universe seems (to the ignorant) to be ordered; this is the ANERISTIC ILLUSION. Actually, what order is 'there' is imposed on primal chaos in the same sense that a person's name is draped over his actual self. It is the job of the scientist, for example, to implement this principle in a practical manner and some are quite brilliant at it. But on closer examination, order dissolves into disorder, which is the ERISTIC ILLUSION.

—Malaclypse the Younger, K.S.C.,
Principia Discordia

And Spaceship Earth, that glorious and bloody circus, continued its four-billion-year-long spiral orbit about the Sun; the engineering, I must admit, was so exquisite that none of the passengers felt any motion at all. Those on the dark side of the ship mostly slept and voyaged into worlds of freedom and fantasy; those on the light side moved about the tasks appointed for them by their rulers, or idled waiting for the next order from above. In Las Vegas, Dr. Charles Mocenigo woke from another nightmare and went to the toilet to wash his hands. He thought of his date the next night with Sherri Brandi and, quite mercifully, had no inkling that it would be his last contact with a woman. Still seeking calm, he went to the window and looked at the stars – being a specialist, with no interest beyond his own field, he imagined he was looking up rather than out at them. In New Delhi aboard the afternoon TWA flight for Hong Kong, Honolulu, and Los Angeles, R. Buckminster Fuller, one of the few people to be aware that he lived on a spaceship, glanced at his three watches, showing local time (5:30 P.M.), time at Honolulu, his point of destination (2:30 A.M. the next morning) and present time in his home at Carbandale, Illinois (3:30 A.M. the previous

THE EYE IN THE PYRAMID

morning.) In Paris, the noon crowds were jostled by hordes
of young people distributing leaflets glowingly describing
the world's greatest Rock Festival and Cosmic Love Feast
to be celebrated on the shores of Lake Totenkopf near
Ingolstadt at the end of the month. At Sunderland, England,
a young psychiatrist left his lunch to rush to the chronic
ward and listen to weird babble proceeding from a patient
who had been decade-silent: 'On *Walpurgasnacht* it's coming. That's when His power is strongest. That's when you'll
see Him. Right at the very stroke of midnight.' In the
middle of the Atlantic, Howard the porpoise, swimming
with friends in the mid-morning sun, encountered some
sharks and had a nasty fight. Saul Goodman rubbed tired
eyes in New York City as dawn crept over the windowsill,
and read a memo about Charlemagne and the Courts of
the Illuminated; Rebecca Goodman, meanwhile, read how
the jealous priests of Bel-Marduk betrayed Babylon to the
invading army of Cyrus because their young king, Belshaz-
zar, had embraced the love-cult of the goddess Ishtar. In
Chicago, Simon Moon was listening to the birds begin to
sing and waiting for the first cinnamon rays of dawn, as
Mary Lou Servix slept beside him; his mind was active,
thinking about pyramids and rain-gods and sexual yoga
and fifth-dimensional geometries, but thinking mostly about
the Ingolstadt Rock Festival and wondering if it would all
happen as Hagbard Celine had predicted.

(*Two blocks north in space and over forty years back
in time, Simon's mother heard pistol shots as she left
Wobbly Hall – Simon was a second-generation anarchist –
and followed the crowd to gather in front of the Biograph
Theatre where a man lay bleeding to death in the alley.
And the next morning – July 23, 1934 – Billie Freschette,
in her cell at Cook County Jail, got the news from a
matron.* In this White Man's Country, I am the lowliest of
the lowly, subjugated because I am not white, and subjugated again because I am not male. I am the embodi-
ment of all that is rejected and scorned – the female, the
colored, the tribe, the earth – all that has no place in this
world of white male technology. I am the tree that is cut
down to make room for the factory that poisons the air. I
am the river filled with sewage. I am the Body that the
Mind despises. I am the lowliest of the lowly, the mud

beneath your feet. And yet of all the world John Dillinger picked me to be his bride. He plunged within me, into the very depths of me. I was his bride, not as your Wise Men and Churches and Governments know marriage, but we were truly wed. As the tree is wed to the earth, the mountain to the sky, the sun to the moon. I held his head to my breast, and tousled his hair as if it were sweet as fresh grass, and I called him 'Johnnie.' He was more than a man. He was mad but not mad, not as a man may go mad when he leaves his tribe and lives among hostile strangers and is mistreated and scorned. He was not mad as all other white men are mad because they have never known a tribe. He was mad as a god might be mad. And now they tell me he is dead. *'Well,' the matron asked finally, 'aren't you going to say anything? Aren't you Indians human?' She had a real evil shine in her eye, like the eye of the rattlesnake.* She wants to see me cry. She stands there and waits, watching me through the bars. *'Don't you have any feelings at all? Are you some kind of animal?'* I say nothing. I keep my face immobile. No white shall ever see the tears of a Menominee. *At the Biograph Theatre, Molly Moon turns away in disgust as souvenir hunters dip their handkerchiefs in the blood.* I turn away from the matron and look up, out the barred window, to the stars, and the spaces between them seem bigger than ever. Bigger and emptier. Inside me there is a space like that now, big and empty, and it will never be filled again. When the tree is torn out by its roots, the earth must feel that way. The earth must scream silently, as I screamed silently.) *But she understood the sacramental meaning of the handkerchiefs dipped in blood; as Simon understands it.*

Simon, in fact, had what can only be called a funky education. I mean, man, when your parents are both anarchists the Chicago public school system is going to do your head absolutely no good at all. Feature me in a 1956 classroom with Eisenhower's Moby Dick face on one wall and Nixon's Captain Ahab glare on the other, and in between, standing in front of the inevitable American rag, Miss Doris Day or her older sister telling the class to take home a leaflet explaining to their parents why it's important for them to vote.

'My parents don't vote,' I say.

'Well, this leaflet will explain to them why they should,' she tells me with the real authentic Doris Day sunshine and Kansas cornball smile. It's early in the term and she hasn't heard about me from the last-semester teacher.

'I really don't think so,' I say politely. 'They don't think it makes any difference whether Eisenhower or Stevenson is in the White House. They say the orders will still come from Wall Street.'

It's like a thundercloud. All the sunshine goes away. They never prepared her for this in the school where they turn out all these Doris Day replicas. The wisdom of the Fathers is being questioned. She opens her mouth and closes it and opens and closes it and finally takes such a deep breath that every boy in the room (we're all on the cusp of puberty) gets a hard-on from watching her breasts heave up and slide down again. I mean, they're all praying (except me, I'm an atheist, of course) that they won't get called on to stand up; if it wouldn't attract attention, they'd be clubbing their dicks down with their geography books. 'That's the wonderful thing about this country,' she finally gets out, 'even people with opinions like that can say what they want without going to jail.'

'You must be nuts,' I say. 'My dad's been in and out of jail so many times they should put in a special revolving door just for him. My mom, too. *You* oughta go out with subversive leaflets in this town and see what happens.'

Then, of course, after school, a gang of patriots, with the odds around seven-to-one, beat the shit out of me and make me kiss their red-white-and-blue totem. It's no better at home. Mom's an anarcho-pacifist, Tolstoy and all that, and she wants me to say I didn't fight back. Dad's a Wobbly and wants to be sure that I hurt some of them at least as bad as they hurt me. After they yell at me for a half hour, they yell at each other for two. Bakunin said this and Kropotkin said that and Gandhi said the other and Martin Luther King is the savior of America and Martin Luther King is a bloody fool who's selling his people an opium utopia and all that jive. Go down to Wobbly Hall or Solidarity Bookstore and you'll still hear the same debate, doubled, redoubled, in spades, and vulnerable.

So naturally I start hanging out on Wall Street and smoking dope and pretty soon I'm the youngest living member of what they called the Beat Generation. Which does not improve my relations with school authorities, but at least it's a relief from all that patriotism and anarchism. By the time I'm seventeen and they shoot Kennedy and the country starts coming apart at the seams, we're not beatniks anymore, we're hippies, and the thing to do is go to Mississippi. Did you ever go to Mississippi? You know what Dr. Johnson said about Scotland – 'The best thing you can say for it is that God created it for some purpose, but the same is true of Hell.' Blot Mississippi; it's not part of this story anyway. The next stop was Antioch in dear old Yellow Springs where I majored in mathematics for reasons you will soon guess. The pot there grows wild in acres and acres of beautiful nature preserve kept up by the college. You can go out there at night, pick your own grass for the week from the female of the hemp species and sleep under the stars with a female of your own species, then wake up in the morning with birds and rabbits and the whole lost Thomas Wolfe America scene, a stone, a leaf, and unfound door and all of it, then make it to class really feeling good and ready for an education. Once I woke up with a spider running across my face, and I thought, 'So a spider is running across my face,' and brushed him off gently, 'it's his world, too.' In the city, I would have killed him. What I mean is Antioch is a stone groove but that life is no preparation for coming back to Chicago and Chemical Warfare. Not that I ever got maced before '68, but I could read the signs; don't let anybody tell you it's pollution, brothers and sisters. It's Chemical Warfare. They'll kill us all to make a buck.

I got stoned one night and went home to see what it would be like relating to Mom and Dad in that condition. It was the same but different. Tolstoy coming out of her mouth, Bakunin out of his. And it was suddenly all weird and super-freaky, like Goddard shooting a Kafka scene: two dead Russians debating with each other, long after they were dead and buried, out of the mouths of a pair of Chicago Irish radicals. The young frontal-lobe-type anarchists in the city were in their first surrealist revival just then and I had been reading some of their stuff and it clicked.

'You're both wrong,' I said. 'Freedom won't come

through love, and it won't come through Force. It will come through the Imagination.' I put in all the capital letters and I was so stoned that they got contact-high and heard them, too. Their mouths dropped open and I felt like William Blake telling Tom Paine where it was really at. A Knight of Magic waving my wand and dispersing the shadows of Maya.

Dad was the first to recover. 'Imagination,' he said, his big red face crinkling in that grin that always drove the cops crazy when they were arresting him. 'That's what comes of sending good working-class boys to rich people's colleges. Words and books get all mixed up with reality in their heads. When you were in that jail in Mississippi you imagined yourself throught the walls, didn't you? How many times an hour did you imagine yourself through the walls? I can guess. The first time I was arrested, during the GE strike of thirty-three, I walked through those walls a million times. But every time I opened my eyes, the walls and the bars were still there. What got me out finally? What got you out of Biloxi finally? *Organization.* If you want big words to talk to intellectuals with, that's a fine big word, son, just as many syllables as *imagination*, and it has a lot more realism in it.'

That's what I remember best about him, that one speech, and the strange clear blue of his eyes. He died that year, and I found out that there was more to the Imagination than I had known, for he didn't die at all. He's still around, in the back of my skull somewhere, arguing with me, and that's the truth. It's also the truth that he's dead, really dead, and part of me was buried with him. It's uncool to love your father these days, so I didn't even know that I loved him until they closed the coffin and I heard myself sobbing, and it comes back again, that same emptiness, whenever I hear 'Joe Hill':

'The copper bosses killed you, Joe.'
'I never died,' said he.

Both lines are true, and mourning never ends. They didn't shoot Dad the clean way, like Joe Hill, but they ground him down, year after year, burning out his Wob fires (and he was Aries, a real fire sign) with their cops, their courts,

their jails, and their taxes, their corporations, their cages
for the spirit and cemeteries for the soul, their plastic
liberalism and murderous Marxism, and even as I say that
I have to pay a debt to Lenin for he gave me the words to
express how I felt when Dad was gone. 'Revolutionaries,'
he said, 'are dead men on furlough.' The Democratic
Convention of '68 was coming and I knew that my own
furlough might be much shorter than Dad's because I was
ready to fight them in the streets. All spring Mom was
busy at the Women for Peace centre and I was busy conspiring with surrealists and Yippies. Then I met Mao Tsu-
hsi.

It was April 30, *Walpurgasnacht* (pause for thunder on
the soundtrack), and I was rapping with some of the crowd
at the Friendly Stranger. H.P. Lovecraft (the rock group,
not the writer) was conducting services in the back room,
pounding away at the door to Acid Land in the gallant
effort, new and striking that year, to break in on waves of
sound without any chemical skeleton key at all and I am
in no position to evaluate their success objectively since I
was, as is often the case with me, 99 and 44/100ths percent stoned out of my gourd before they began operations.
I kept catching this uniquely pensive Oriental face at the
next table, but my own gang, including the weird faggot-
priest we nicknamed Padre Pederastia, had most of my
attention. I was laying it on them heavy. It was my
Donatien Alphonse François de Sade period.

'The head-trip anarchists are as constipated as the
Marxists,' I was giving forth; you recognize the style by
now. 'Who speaks for the thalamus, the glands, the cells of
the organism? Who *sees* the organism? We cover it with
clothes to hide its apehood. We won't have liberated ourselves from servitude until people throw all their clothes
in the closet in spring and don't take them out again until
winter. We won't be human beings, the way apes *are* apes
and dogs *are* dogs, until we fuck where and when we want
to, like any other mammal. Fucking in the streets isn't
just a tactic to blow minds; it's recapturing our own bodies.
Anything less and we're still robots possessing the wisdom
of the straight line but not the understanding of the organic
curve.' And so on. And so forth. I think I found a few
good arguments for rape and murder while I was at it.

'The next step beyond anarchy,' somebody said cynically. '*Real* chaos.'

'Why not?' I demanded. 'Who works at a straight job here?' None of them did, of course; I deal dope myself. 'Will you work at a straight job for something that calls itself an anarchist syndicate? Will you run an engine lathe eight unfucking hours a day because the syndicate tells you the people need what the lathe produces? If you will, *the people* just becomes a new tyrant.'

'To hell with machines,' Kevin McCool, the poet, said enthusiastically. 'Back to the caves!' He was as stoned as me.

The Oriental face leaned over: she was wearing a strange headband with a golden apple inside a pentagon. Her black eyes somehow reminded me of my father's blue eyes. 'What you want is an organization of the imagination?' she asked politely.

I flipped. It was too much, hearing those words just then.

'A man at the Vedanta Society told me that John Dillinger walked through the walls when he made his escape from Crown Point Jail,' Miss Mao went on in a level tone. 'Do you think that is possible?'

You know how dark coffee houses are. The Friendly Stranger was murkier than most. I had to get out. Blake talked to the Archangel Gabriel every morning at breakfast, but I wasn't that heavy yet.

'Hey, where you going, Simon?' somebody called. Miss Mao didn't say anything, and I didn't look back at that polite and pensive face – it would have been much easier if she looked sinister and inscrutable. But when I hit Lincoln and started toward Fullerton, I heard steps behind me. I turned and Padre Pederastia touched my arm gently.

'I asked her to come and listen to you,' he said. 'She was to give a signal if she thought you were ready. The signal was more dramatic than I expected, it seems. A conversation out of your past that had some heavy emotional meaning to you?'

'She's a medium?' I asked numbly.

'You can name it that.' I looked at him in the light from the Biograph marquee and I remembered Mom's story about the people dipping their handkerchiefs in Dillinger's

blood and I heard the old hymn start in my head ARE YOU
WASHED are you washed ARE YOU WASHED in the BLOOD
of the Lamb and I remembered how we all thought he
hung out with us freaks in the hope of leading us back to
the church holy Roman Catholic and apostolic as Dad
called it when he was drunk and bitter. It was obvious that
whatever the Padre was recruiting for had little to do with
that particular theological trade union.

'What is this?' I asked. 'And who is that woman?'

'She's the daughter of Fu Manchu,' he said. Suddenly,
he threw his head back and laughed like a rooster crowing.
Just as suddenly, he stopped and looked at me. Just looked
at me.

'Somehow,' I said slowly, 'I've qualified for a small
demonstration of whatever you and she are selling. But I
don't qualify for any more until I make the right move?'
He gave the faintest hint of a nod and went on watching
me.

Well, I was young and ignorant of everything outside ten
million books I'd gobbled and guilty-unsure about my
imaginative flights away from my father's realism and of
course stoned of course but I finally understood why he
was watching me that way, it was (this part of it) pure
Zen, there was nothing I could do consciously or by volition that would satisfy him and I had to do exactly that
which I could not *not* do, namely be Simon Moon. Which
led to deciding then and there without any time to mull it
over and rationalize it just what the hell being Simon
Moon or, more precisely Simon Mooning, consisted of, and
it seemed to be a matter of wandering through room after
room of my brain looking for the owner and not finding
him anywhere, sweat broke out of my forehead, it was
becoming desperate because I was running out of rooms
and the Padre was still watching me.

'Nobody home,' I said finally, sure that the answer
wasn't good enough.

'That's odd,' he said. 'Who's conducting the search?'

And I walked through the walls and into the Fire.

Which was the beginning of the larger and funkier part
of my (Simon's) education, and where we cannot, as yet,
follow him. He sleeps now, a teacher rather than a learner,
while Mary Lou Servix awakes beside him and tries to

decide whether it was just the pot or if something really spooky happened last night. Howard sports in the Atlantic; Buckminster Fuller, flying above the Pacific, crosses the international date line and slips back into April 23 again; it is dawn in Las Vegas and Mocenigo, the nightmares and anxieties of night forgotten, looks forward cheerfully to the production of the first live cultures of Anthrax-Leprosy-Pi, which will make this a memorable day in more ways than he expects; and George Dorn, somewhere outside this time system, is writing in his journal. Each word, however, seems magically to appear by itself as if no volition on his part were necessary to its production. He read the words his pencil scrawled, but they appeared the communications of another intelligence. Yet they picked up where he had left off in his hotel room and they spoke with his private idiom:

. . . the universe is the inside without any outside, the sound made by one eye opening. In fact, I don't even know that there is a *uni*verse. More likely, there are many *multi*verses; each with its own dimensions, times, spaces, laws and eccentricities. We wander between and among these multiverses, trying to convince others and ourselves that we all walk together in a single public universe that we can share. For to deny that axiom leads to what is called schizophrenia.

Yeah, that's it: every man's skin is his own private multiverse, just like every man's home is supposed to be his castle. But all the multiverses are trying to merge, to create a true universe such as we have only imagined previously. Maybe it will be spiritual, like Zen or telepathy, or maybe it will be physical, one great big gang-fuck, but it has to happen: the creation of a universe and the one great eye opening to see itself at last. Aum Shiva!

– Oh, man, you're stoned out of your gourd. You're writing gibberish.

No, I'm writing with absolute clarity, for the first time in my life.

– Yeah? Well what was that business about the universe being the sound of one eye opening?

Never mind that. Who the hell are you and how did you get into my head?

* * *

'Your turn now, George.'

Sheriff Cartwright stood in the door, a monk in a strange red and white robe beside him, holding some kind of wand the deep color of a fire engine.

'No – no –' George started to stammer. But he knew.

'Of course you know,' the Sheriff said kindly – as if he were suddenly sorry about it all. 'You knew before you left New York and came down here.'

They were at the foot of the gallows. '. . . each with its own time, spaces, laws and eccentricities,' George was thinking wildly. Yes: if the universe is one big eye looking at itself, then telepathy is no miracle, for anyone who opens his own eyes fully can then look through all other eyes. (For a moment, George looks through the eyes of John Ehrlichman as Dick Nixon urges lewdly, 'You can say I don't remember. You can say I can't recall. I can't give any answer to that that I can recall.' *I can't give any answer to that that I can recall*.) 'All flesh will see it in one instant': who wrote that?

'Gonna miss you, boy,' the Sheriff said, offering an embarrassed handshake. Numbly, George clasped the man's hot, reptilian palm.

The monk walked beside him up the gallows' steps. Thirteen, George was thinking, there are always thirteen steps on a gallows. . . . And you always cream in your jeans when your neck breaks. It has something to do with the pressure on the spinal cord being transmitted through the prostate gland. The Orgasm-Death Gimmick, Burroughs calls it.

At the fifth step, the monk said suddenly: 'Hail Eris.'

George stared at the man dumbfounded. Who was Eris? Somebody in Greek mythology, but somebody very important. . . .

'It all depends on whether the fool has wisdom enough to repeat it.'

'Quiet, idiot – he can hear us!'

I got some bad pot, George decided, and I'm still back on the hotel bed, hallucinating all this. But he repeated, uncertainly: 'Hail Eris.'

Immediately, just like his one and only acid trip, dimension began to alter. The steps grew larger, steeper – ascending them seemed as perilous as climbing Mount Everest.

The air was suddenly lit with reddish flame – *Definitely,* George thought, *some weird and freaky pot. . . .*

And then, for some reason, he looked upward.

Each step was now higher than an ordinary building. He was near the bottom of a pyramidal skyscraper of thirteen collossal levels. And at the top. . . . And at the top. . . .

And at the top One Enormous Eye – a ruby and demonic orb of cold fire, without mercy or pity or contempt – looked at him and *into* him and through him.

The hand reaches down, turns on both bathtub faucets full-power, then reaches upward to do the same to the sink faucets. Banana-Nose Maldonado leans forward and whispers to Carmel, 'Now you can talk.'

(The old man using the name 'Frank Sullivan' was met, at Los Angeles International Airport, November 22, 1963, by Mao Tsu-Hsi, who drove him to his bungalow on Fountain Avenue. He gave his report in terse, unemotional sentences. 'My God,' she said when he finished, 'what do you make of it?' He thought carefully and grunted, 'It beats the hell out of me. The guy on the triple underpass was definitely Harry Coin. I recognized him through my binoculars. The guy in the window at the Book Depository very likely was this galoot Oswald that they've arrested. The guy on the grassy knoll was Bernard Barker from the CIA Bay of Pigs gang. But I didn't get a good look at the gink on the County Records building. One thing I'm sure of: we can't keep all this to ourselves. At the very least, we pass the word on to ELF. It might alter their plans for OM. You've heard of OM?' She nodded, saying, 'Operation Mindfuck. It's their big project for the next decade or so. This is a bigger Mindfuck than anything they had planned.')

'Red China?' Maldonado whispers incredulously. 'You musta been reading the Readers Digest. *We get all our horse from friendly governments like Laos. The CIA would have our ass otherwise.'* Straining to be heard over the running water, Carmel asks despondently, *'Then you don't know how I could meet a Communist spy?'*

Maldonado stares at him levelly. 'Communism doesn't have a good image right now,' he says icily; it is April 3, two days after the Fernando Poo Incident.

Bernard Barker, former servant of both Batista and

Castro, dons his gloves outside the Watergate; in a flash
of memory he sees the grassy knoll, Oswald, Harry Coin,
and, further back, Castro negotiating with Banana-Nose
Maldonado.

(But this present year, on March 24, Generalissimo
Tequilla y Mota finally found the book he was looking for,
the one that was as precise and pragmatic about running a
country as Luttwak's *Coup d'Etat* had been about seizing
one. It was called *The Prince* and its author was a subtle
Italian named Machiavelli; it told the Generalissimo everything he wanted to know – except how to handle American
hydrogen bombs, which, unfortunately, Machiavelli had
lived too soon to foresee.)

'*It is our duty, our sacred duty to defend Fernando
Poo,*' Atlanta Hope was telling a cheering crowd in Cincinnati that very day. 'Are we to wait until the godless
Reds are right here in Cincinnati?' The crowd started to
scream their unwillingness to wait that long – they had
been expecting the godless Reds to arrive in Cincinnati
since about 1945 and were, by now, convinced that the
dirty cowards were never going to come and would have
to be met on their own turf – but a group of dirty, long-
haired, freaky-looking students from Antioch College began
to chant, 'I Don't Want to Die for Fernando Poo.' The
crowd turned in fury: at last, some real reds to fight. . . .
Seven ambulances and thirty police cars were soon racing
to scene. . . .

(But only five years earlier Atlanta had a different message. When God's Lightning was first founded, as a splinter
off Women's Liberation, it had as its slogan 'No More
Sexism,' and its original targets were adult bookstores, sex-
education programs, men's magazines, and foreign movies.
It was only after meeting 'Smiling Jim' Trepomena of
Knights of Christianity United in Faith that Atlanta discovered that both male supremacy and orgasms were part
of the International Communist Conspiracy. It was at that
point, really, that God's Lightning and orthodox Women's
Lib totally parted company, for the orthodox faction, just
then, were teaching that male supremacy and orgasms were
part of the International Kapitalist Conspiracy.)

'Fernando Poo,' the President of the United States told

reporters even as Atlanta was calling for all-out war, 'will not become another Laos, or another Costa Rica.'

'When are we going to get our troops out of Laos?' a reporter from the *New York Times* asked quickly; but a man from the *Washington Post* asked just as rapidly, 'And when are we going to get our troops out of Costa Rica?'

'Our President Plans for Withdrawal are going Forward according to an Orderly Schedule,' the President began; *but in Santa Isobel itself,* as Tequilla y Mota underlined a passage in Machiavelli, *00005 concluded a shortwave broadcast to a British submarine lying 17 miles off the coast of the island:* 'The Yanks have gone absolutely bonkers, I'm afraid. I've been here nine days now and I am absolutely convinced there is not one Russian or Chinese agent in any way involved with Generalissimo Tequilla y Mota, nor are there any troops of either of those governments hiding anywhere in the jungles. However, BUGGER is definitely running a heroin smuggling ring here, and I would like permission to investigate that.' (The permission was to be denied; old W., back at Intelligence HQ in London, knew that 00005 was a bit bonkers about BUGGER himself and imagined that it was involved in every mission he undertook.)

At the same time, in a different hotel, Tobias Knight, on special loan from the FBI to the CIA, concluded his nightly shortwave broadcast to an American submarine 23 miles off the coast: 'The Russian troops are definitely engaged in building what can only be a rocket-launching site, and the Slants are constructing what seems to be a nuclear installation. . . .'

And Hagbard Celine, lying 40 miles out in the Bight of Biafra in the *Lief Erickson,* intercepted both messages, and smiled cynically, and wired P. in New York: ACTIVATE MALIK AND PREPARE DORN.

(While the most obscure, seemingly trivial part of the whole puzzle appeared in a department store in Houston. It was a sign that said:

NO SMOKING.   NO SPITTING.

THE MGT.

This replaced an earlier sign that had hung on the main showroom wall for many years, saying only:

NO SMOKING.
THE MGT.

The change although small, had subtle repercussions. The store catered only to the very wealthy, and this clientele did not object to being told that they could not smoke. The fire hazard, after all, was obvious. On the other hand, that bit about spitting was somehow a touch offensive; they most certainly were not the sort of people who would spit on somebody's floor – or, at least, none of them had done such a thing at any time since about one month or at most one year after they became wealthy. Yes, the sign was definitely bad diplomacy. Resentment festered. Sales fell off. And membership in the Houston branch of God's Lightning increased. Wealthy, powerful membership.

(The odd thing was that the Management had nothing at all to do with the sign.)

George Dorn awoke screaming.

He lay on the floor of his cell in Mad Dog County Jail. His first frantic, involuntary glance told him that Harry Coin had vanished completely from the adjoining cell. The shit-pot was back in its corner and he knew, without being able to check, that there would be no human intestines in it.

Terror tactics, he thought. They were out to break him – a task which was beginning to look easy – but they were covering up the evidence as they went along.

There was no light through the cell window; it was, therefore, still night. He hadn't slept but merely fainted.

Like a girl.

Like a long-haired commie faggot.

Oh, shit and prune juice, he told himself sourly, cut it out. You've known for years that you're no hero. Don't take that particular sore out and rub sandpaper on it now. You're not a hero, but you're a goddam stubborn, pig-headed, and determined coward. That's why you've stayed alive on assignments like this before.

Show these redneck mammyjammers just how stubborn, pig-headed, and determined you can be.

George started with an old gimmick. A piece torn off the tail of his shirt gave him a writing tablet. The point of his shoelace became a temporary pen. His own saliva, spat onto the polish of the shoes themselves, created a substitute ink.

Laboriously, after a half hour, he had his message written:

WHOEVER FINDS THIS $50 TO CALL JOE MALIK,
NEW YORK CITY, AND TELL HIM GEORGE DORN
HELD WITHOUT LAWYER MAD DOG COUNTY
JAIL

The message shouldn't land too close to the jail, so George began looking for a weighted object. In five minutes, he decided on a spring from the bunk mattress; it took him seventeen minutes more to pry it loose.

After the missile was hurled out the window – probably, George knew, to be found by somebody who would immediately turn it over to Sheriff Jim Cartwright – he began thinking of alternate plans.

He found, however, that instead of devising schemes for escape or deliverance, his mind insisted on going off in an entirely different direction. The face of the monk from his dream pursued him. He had seen that face somewhere before, he knew; but where? Somehow, the question was important. He began trying in earnest to re-create the face and identify it – James Joyce, H. P. Lovecraft, and a monk in a painting by Fra Angelico all came to mind. It was none of them, but it looked somehow a little like each of them.

Suddenly tired and discouraged, George slouched back on the bunk and let his hand lightly clutch his penis through his trousers. Heroes of fiction don't jack off when the going gets rough, he reminded himself. Well, hell, he wasn't a hero and this wasn't fiction. Besides, I wasn't going to jack-off (after all, They might be watching through a peephole, ready to use this natural jailhouse weakness to humiliate me further and break my ego). No, I definitely wasn't going to jack-off: I was just going to hold it, lightly, through my trousers, until I felt some life-force surging back into my body and displacing fear, exhaustion and despair. Meanwhile, I thought about Pat back in New York. She was wearing nothing but her cute black lace bra and panties, and her nipples are standing up pointy

and hard. Make it Sophia Loren, and take the bra off so
I can see the nipples directly. Ah, yes, and now try it the
other way: she (Sophia, no make it Pat again) is wearing
the bra but the panties are off showing the pubic bush. Let
her play with it, get her fingers in there, and the other hand
on a nipple, ah, yes, and now she (Pat – no, Sophia) is
kneeling to unzipper my fly. My penis grew harder and her
mouth opened in expectation. I reached down and cupped
her breast with one hand, taking the nipple she had been
caressing, feeling it harden more. (Did James Bond ever do
this in Doctor No's dungeon?) Sophia's tongue (not my
hand, *not* my hand) is busy and hot, sending pulsations
through my entire body. Take it, you cunt. Take it, O God,
a flash of the Passaic and the gun at my forehead, and you
can't call them cunts nowadays, ah, you cunt, you cunt,
take it, and it is Pat, it's that night at her pad when we
were both zonked on hashish and I never never never had
a blow-job like that before or since, my hands were in her
hair, gripping her shoulders, take it, suck me off (get out
of my head, mother), and her mouth is wet and rhythmic
and my cock is just as sensitive as that night zonked on
the hash, and I pulled the trigger and then the explosion
came just as I did (pardon the diction) and I was on the
floor coughing and bouncing, my eyes watering. The second
blast lifted me again and threw me with a crunch against
the wall.

Then the machine-gun fire started.

Jesus H. Particular Christ on a crutch, I thought frantically, whatever it is that's happening they're going to find
me with come on the front of my trousers.

And every bone in my body broken, I think.

The machine gun suddenly stopped stuttering and I
thought I heard a voice cry 'Earwicker, Bloom and Craft.'
– I've still got Joyce on my mind, I decided. Then the third
explosion came, and I covered my head as parts of the
ceiling began falling on me.

A key suddenly clanked against his cell door. Looking
up, I saw a young woman in a trench coat, carrying a
tommy gun, and desperately trying one key after another
in the lock.

From somewhere else in the building there came a fourth
explosion.

The woman grinned tensely at the sound. 'Commie motherfuckers,' she muttered, still trying keys.

'Who the hell are you?' I finally asked hoarsely.

'Never mind that now,' she snapped. 'We've come to rescue you – isn't that enough?'

Before I could think of a reply, the door swung open.

'Quick,' she said, 'this way.'

I limped after her down the hall. Suddenly she stopped, studied the wall a moment, and pressed against a brick. The wall slid smoothly aside and we entered what appeared to be a chapel of some sort.

Good weeping Jesus and his brother Irving, I thought, I'm *still* still dreaming.

For the chapel was not anything that a sane man would expect to find in Mad Dog County Jail. Decorated entirely in red and white – the colors of Hassan i Sabbah and the Assassins of Alamout, I remembered incredulously – it was adorned with strange Arabic symbols and slogans in German: *'Heute die Welt, Morgens das Sonnensystem,'* *'Ewige Blumenkraft Und Ewige Schlangekraft!'* *Gestern Hanf, Heute Hanf, Immer Hanf.'*

And the altar was a pyramid with thirteen ledges – with a ruby-red eye at the top.

This symbol, I now recalled with mounting confusion, was the Great Seal of the United States.

'This way,' the woman said, motioning with her tommy gun.

We passed through another sliding wall and found ourselves in an alley behind the jail.

A black Cadillac awaited us. 'Everybody's out!' the driver shouted. He was an old man, more than sixty, but hard and shrewd-looking.

'Good,' the woman said. 'Here's George.'

I was pushed into the back seat – which was already full of grim-looking men and grimmer-looking munitions of various sorts – and the car started at once.

'One for good measure,' the woman in the trench coat shouted and threw another plastic bomb back at the jail.

'Right,' the driver said. 'It fits, too – that makes it five.'

'The Law of Fives,' another passenger chuckled bitterly. 'Serves the commie bastards right. A taste of their own medicine.'

I could restrain myself no longer.

'What the hell is going on?' I demanded. 'Who are you people? What makes you think Sheriff Cartwright and his police are communists? And where are you taking me?'

'Shut up,' said the woman who had unlocked my cell, nudging me none too affectionately with her machine gun. 'We'll talk when we're ready. Meanwhile, wipe the come off your pants.'

The car sped into the night.

(In a Bentley limousine, Fedrico 'Banana Nose' Maldonado drew on his cigar and relaxed as his chauffeur drove him toward Robert Putney Drake's mansion in Blue Point, Long Island. In back of his eyes, almost forgotten, Charlie 'The Bug' Workman, Mendy Weiss, and Jimmy the Shrew listen soberly, on October 23, 1935, as Banana Nose tells them: 'Don't give the Dutchman a chance. Cowboy the son of a bitch.' The three guns nod stolidly; cowboying somebody is messy, but it pays well. In an ordinary hit, you can be precise, even artistic, because after all the only thing that matters is that the person so honored should be definitely dead afterwards. Cowboying, in the language of the profession, leaves no room for personal taste or delicacy: the important thing is that there should be a lot of lead in the air and the victim should leave a spectacularly gory corpse for the tabloids, as notification that the Brotherhood is both edgy and short-tempered and everybody better watch his ass. Although it wasn't obligatory, it was considered a sign of true enthusiasm on a cowboy job if the guest of honor took along a few innocent bystanders, so everybody would understand exactly how edgy the Brotherhood was feeling. The Dutchman took two such bystanders. And in a different world that is still this world, Albert 'The Teacher' Stern opens his morning paper on July 23, 1934, and reads FBI SHOOTS DILLINGER, thinking wistfully *If I could kill somebody that important, my name would never be forgotten.* Further back, back further: February 7, 1932, Vincent 'Mad Dog' Coll looks through the phone-booth door and sees a familiar face crossing the drugstore and a tommygun in the man's hand. 'The god-damned pig-headed Dutchman,' he howled, but nobody heard him because the Thompson gun was already systematically spraying the phone-booth up and down, right and left, left and right, and up and down again for good measure . . . But tilt the picture another way and this emerges: On November 10, 1948, the 'World's Greatest Newspaper,' the *Chicago Tribune* announced the election to the Presidency of the United States of America of Thomas Dewey, a man who not only was not elected but would not even have been alive if Banana Nose Maldonado had not given such specific instructions concerning the Dutchman to Charlie the Bug, Mendy Weiss and Jimmy the Shrew.)

Who shot you? the police stenographer asked. *Mother is the best bet, Oh mama mama mama. I want harmony. I don't want harmony*, is the delirious answer. *Who shot you?* the question is repeated. The Dutchman still replies: *Oh mama mama mama. French Canadian bean soup.*

We drove till dawn. The car stopped on a road by a beach of white sand. Tall, skinny palm trees stood black against a turquoise sky. This must be the Gulf of Mexico, I thought. They could now load me with chains and drop me in the gulf, hundreds of miles from Mad Dog, without involving Sheriff Jim. No, they had raided Sheriff Jim's jail. Or was that a hallucination? I was going to have to keep more of an eye on reality. This was a new day, and I was going to know facts hard and sharp-edged in the sunlight and keep them straight.

I was stiff and sore and tired from a night of driving. The only rest I'd gotten was fitful dozing in which cyclopean ruby eyes looked at me till I awoke in terror. Mavis, the woman with the tommy gun, had put her arms around me several times when I screamed. She would murmur soothingly to me, and once her lips, smooth, cool and soft, had brushed my ear.

At the beach, Mavis motioned me out of the car. The sun was as hot as the bishop's jock strap when he finished his sermon on the evils of pornography. She stepped out behind me and slammed the door.

'We wait here,' she said. 'The others go back.'

'What are we waiting for?' I asked. Just then the driver of the car gunned the motor. The car swung round in a wide U-turn. In a minute its rear end had disappeared beyond a bend in the Gulf highway. We were alone with the rising sun and the sand-strewn asphalt.

Mavis motioned me to walk down the beach with her.
A little ways ahead, far back from the water, was a small
white-painted frame cabana. A woodpecker landed wearily
on its roof like he had flown more missions than Yossarian
and never intended to go up again.

'What's the plan, Mavis? A private execution on a lonely
beach in another state so Sheriff Jim can't get blamed?'

'Don't be a dummy, George. We blew up that commie
bastard's jail.'

'Why do you keep calling Sheriff Cartwright a commie?
If ever a man had KKK written all over his forehead, it
was that reactionary redneck prick.'

'Don't you know your Trotsky? "Worse is better." Slobs
like Cartwright are trying to discredit America to make it
ripe for a left-wing takeover.'

'I'm a left-winger. If you're against commies, you've got
to be against me.' I didn't care to tell her about my other
friends in Weatherman and Morituri.

'You're just a liberal dupe.'

'I'm not a liberal, I'm a militant radical.'

'A radical is nothing but a liberal with a big mouth.
And a militant radical is nothing but a big-mouthed liberal
with a Che costume. Balls. We're the real radicals, George.
We do things, like last night. Except for Weatherman and
Morituri, all the militant radicals in your crowd ever do is
take out the Molotov cocktail diagram that they carefully
clipped from *The New York Review of Books*, hang it on
the bathroom door and jack-off in connection with it. No
offense meant.' The woodpecker turned his head and
watched us suspiciously like a paranoid old man.

'And what are your politics, if you're such a radical?' I
asked.

'I believe that government governs best of all that governs least of all. Preferably *not* at all. And I believe in the
laissez faire capitalist economic system.'

'Then you must hate my politics. Why did you rescue
me?'

'You're wanted,' she said.

'By whom?'

'Hagbard Celine.'

'And who is Hagbard Celine?' We had reached the
cabana and were standing beside it, facing each other, glar-

ing at each other. The woodpecker turned his head and looked at us with the other eye.

'What is John Guilt?' Mavis said. I might have guessed, I thought, a Hope fiend. She went on, 'It took a whole book to answer that one. As for Hagbard, you'll learn by seeing. Enough for now that you know that he's the man who requested that we rescue you.'

'But you personally don't like me and would not have gone out of your way to help me?'

'I don't know about not liking you. That splotch of come on your trousers has had me horny ever since Mad Dog. Also the excitement of the raid. I've got some tension to burn off. I'd prefer to save myself for a man who completely meets the criteria of my value system. But I could get awfully horny waiting for him. No regrets, no guilt, though. You're all right. You'll do.'

'What are you talking about?'

'I'm talking about your fucking me, George.'

'I never knew a girl – I mean woman – who believed in the capitalist system who was any kind of a good fuck.'

'What has your pathetic circle of acquaintances got to do with the price of gold? I doubt you ever met a woman who believed in the real laissez faire capitalist system. Such a woman is not likely to be caught traveling in your left-liberal circles.' She took me by the hand and led me into the cabana. She shrugged out of her trench coat and spread it carefully on the floor. She was wearing a black sweater and a pair of blue jeans, both tight-fitting. She pulled the sweater off over her head. She was wearing no bra, and her breasts were apple-sized cherry-tipped cones. There was some sort of dark red birthmark between them. 'Your kind of capitalist woman was a Nixonette in 1972, and she believes in that half-ass corporate socialist bastard fascist mixed economy Frank Roosevelt blessed these United States with.' She unbuckled her wide black belt and unzipped her jeans. She tugged them down over her hips. I felt my hardon swelling up inside my pants. 'Libertarian women are good fucks, because they know what they want, and what they want they like a lot.' She stepped out of her jeans to reveal, of all things, panties made of some strange metallic-looking synthetic material that was gold in color. How can I know facts hard and sharp-edged in the sunlight and keep them straight when this happens? 'You really want me to fuck you right now on this public beach in broad daylight?' The woodpecker went to work above us just then, banging away like a rock drummer, I suddenly remembered from high school:

The Woodpecker pecked on the out-house door;
He pecked and he pecked till his pecker was sore. . . .

'George, you're too serious. Don't you know how to play? Did you ever think that life is maybe a game? There is no difference between life and a game, you know. When you play, for instance, playing with a toy, there is no winning or losing. Life is a toy, George, I'm a toy. Think of me as a doll. Instead of sticking pins in me, you can stick your thing in me. I'm a magic doll, like a voodoo doll. A doll is a work of art. Art is magic. You make an image of the thing you want to possess or cope with, so you can cope with it. You make a model, so you have it under control. Dig? Don't you want to possess me? You can, but just for a moment.'

I shook my head. 'I can't believe you. The way you're talking – it's not real.'

'I always talk like this when I'm horny. It happens that at such times I'm more open to the vibrations from outer space. George, are unicorns real? Who made unicorns? Is a thought about unicorns a real thought? How is it different from the mental picture of my pussy – which you've never seen – that you've got in your head at this minute? Does the fact that you can think of fucking me and I can think of fucking with you mean we *are* going to fuck? Or is the universe going to surprise us? Wisdom is wearying, folly is fun. What does a horse with a single long horn sticking straight out of its head mean to you?'

My eyes went from the pubic bulge under her gold panties where they'd strayed when she said 'pussy,' to the mark between her breasts.

It wasn't a birthmark. I felt like a bucket of ice water hit my groin.

I pointed. 'What does a red eye inside a red-and-white triangle mean to you?'

Her open hand slammed against my jaw. 'Motherfucker! Never speak to me about that!'

Then she bowed her head. 'I'm sorry, George, I had no
right to do that. Hit me back, if you want.'

'I don't want. But I'm afraid you've turned me off sexually.'

'Nonsense. You're a healthy man. But now I want to
give you something without taking anything from you.'
She knelt before me on her trench coat, her knees parted,
unzipped my fly, reached in with quick, tickling fingers,
and pulled my penis out. She slipped her mouth around it.
It was my jail fantasy coming true.

'What are you *doing*?'

She took her lips away from my penis, and I looked
down and saw that the head was shiny with saliva and
swelling visibly in rapid throbs. Her breasts – my glance
avoided the Masonic tattoo – were somewhat fuller, and
the nipples stuck out erect.

She smiled. 'Don't whistle while you're pissing, George,
and don't ask questions when you're getting blowed. Shut
up and get hard. This is just quid pro quo.'

When I came I didn't feel much juice jetting out through
my penis; I'd used a lot up whacking off in jail. I noted
with pleasure that what there was of it she didn't spit out.
She smiled and swallowed it.

The sun was higher and hotter in the sky and the woodpecker celebrated by drumming faster and harder. The
Gulf sparkled like Mrs. Astor's best diamonds. I peered
out at the water: just below the horizon there was a flash
of gold among the diamonds.

Mavis suddenly struck her legs out in front of her and
dropped onto her back. 'George! I can't give without taking. Please, quick, while it's still hard, get down here and
slip it to me.'

I looked down. Her lips were trembling. She was tugging
the gold panties away from her black-escutcheoned crotch.
My wet cock was already beginning to droop. I looked
down at her and grinned.

'No,' I said. 'I don't like *girls* who slap you one minute
and get the hots for you the next minute. They don't meet
the criteria of *my* value system. I think they're nuts.'
Carefully and deliberately I stuffed my pecker back into my

trousers and stepped away from her. It was sore anyway,
like in the ryhme.

'You're not such a schmuck after all, you bastard,' she
said through gritted teeth. Her hand was moving rapidly
between her legs. In a moment she arched her back, eyes
clenched tight, and emitted a little scream, like a baby
seagull out on its first flight, a strangely virginal sound.

She lay relaxed for a moment, then picked herself up off
the cabana floor and started to dress. She glanced out at
the water and I followed her eyes. She pointed at the distant glint of gold.

'Hagbard's here.'

A buzzing sound floated across the water. After a moment, I spotted a small black motorboat coming toward
us. We watched in silence as the boat grounded its bow on
the white beach. Mavis motioned at me, and I followed her
down the sand to the water's edge. There was a man in a
black turtleneck sweater sitting in the stern of the boat.
Mavis climbed in the bow and turned to me with a questioning look. The woodpecker felt bad vibes and took off
with a flapping and cawing like the omen of Doom.

What the hell am I getting into, and why am I so crazy
as to go along? I tried to see what it was out there that the
motorboat had come from, but the sun on the gold metal
was flashing blindingly and I couldn't make out a shape.
I looked back at the black motorboat and saw that there
was a circular gold object painted on the bow and there
was a little black flag flying at the stern with the same gold
object in its center. I pointed at the emblem on the bow.

'What's that?'

'An apple,' said Mavis.

People who chose a gold apple as their symbol couldn't
be all bad. I jumped into the boat, and its pilot used an
oar to push off. We buzzed over the smooth water of the
Gulf toward the golden object on the horizon. It was still
blinding from reflected sunlight, but I was now able to
make out a long, low silhouette with a small tower in the
center, like a matchbox on top of a broomstick. Then I
realized that I had my judgment of distances wrong. The
ship, or whatever it was, was much more distant than I'd
first realized.

It was a submarine – a golden submarine – and it appeared

to be the equivalent of five city blocks long, as big as the
biggest ocean liner I had ever heard of. The conning tower
was about three stories high. As we drew up beside it I
saw a man on the tower waving to us. Mavis waved back.
I waved halfheartedly, supposing somehow that it was the
thing to do. I was still thinking about that Masonic tattoo.

A hatch opened in the submarine's side, and the little
motorboat floated right in. The hatch closed, the water
drained out, and the boat settled into a cradle. Mavis
pointed to a door that looked like an entrance to an elevator.

'You go that way, she said. 'I'll see you later, maybe.'
She pressed a button and the door opened, revealing a
carpeted gilt cage. I stepped in and was whisked up three
stories. The door opened and I stepped out into a small
room where a man was waiting, standing with a grace that
reminded me of a Hindu or an American Indian. I thought
at once of Metternich's remark about Talleyrand: 'If
somebody kicked him in the backside, not a muscle would
move in his face until he decided what to do.'

He bore a striking resemblance to Anthony Quinn; he
had thick black eyebrows, olive skin, and a strong nose
and jaw. He was big and burly, powerful muscles bulging
under his black-and-green striped nautical sweater. He held
out his hand.

'Good, George. You made it. I'm Hagbard Celine.' We
shook hands; he had a grip like King Kong. 'Welcome
aboard the *Lief Erickson*, named after the first European
to reach America from the Atlantic side, may my Italian
ancestors forgive me. Fortunately, I have Viking ancestors,
as well. My mother is Norwegian. However, blond hair,
blue eyes, and fair skin are all recessive. My Sicilian father
creamed my mother in the genes.'

'Where the hell did you get this ship? I wouldn't have
believed a submarine like this could exist without the
whole world knowing about it.'

'The sub's my creation, built in accordance with my
design in a Norwegian fjord. This is what the liberated
mind can do. I am the twentieth-century Leonardo, except
that I'm not gay. I've tried it, of course, but women interest
me more. The world has never heard of Hagbard Celine.
That is because the world is stupid and Celine is very

smart. The submarine is radar and sonar transparent. It
is superior to the best either the American or Russian
government even has on the drawing board. It can go to
any depth in any ocean. We've sounded the Atlantic
Trench, the Mindinao Deep, and a few holes in the floor
of the sea that no one's ever heard of or named. *Lief Erickson* is capable of meeting the biggest, most ferocious, and
smartest monsters of the deep, of which we've found God's
plenty. I'd even risk her in battle with Leviathan himself,
though I'm just as pleased that we've only seen him from
afar hitherto.'

'You mean whales?'

'I mean Leviathan, man. That fish – if fish it be – that is
to your whale what your whale is to your meanest guppy.
Don't ask me what Leviathan is – I haven't even gotten
close enough to tell you his shape. There's only one of
him, or her, or it in all that world that's water. I don't
know how it reproduces – maybe it doesn't have to repro-
duce – maybe it's immortal. It may be neither plant nor
animal for all I know, but it's alive, and it's the biggest
living thing there is. Oh, we've seen monsters, George.
We've seen, in *Lief Erickson*, the sunken ruins of Atlantis
and Lemuria – or Mu, as it's known to keepers of the
Sacred Chao.'

'What the fuck are you talking about?' I asked, wondering if I was in some crazy surrealist movie, wandering from
telepathic sheriffs to homosexual assassins, to nympho
lady Masons, to psychotic pirates, according to a script
written in advance by two acid-heads and a Martian humor-
ist.

'I'm talking about adventure, George. I'm talking about
seeing things and being with people that will really liberate
your mind – not just replacing liberalism with Marxism
so you can shock your parents. I'm talking about getting
altogether off the grubby plane you live on and taking a
trip with Hagbard to a transcendental universe. Did you
know that on sunken Atlantis there is a pyramidal structure built by ancient priests and faced with a ceramic substance that has withstood thirty thousand years of ocean
burial so that the pyramid is clean and white as polished
ivory – except for the giant red mosaic of an eye at its
top?'

'I find it hard to believe that Atlantis ever existed,' I said. 'In fact' – I shook my head angrily – 'you're conning me into qualifying that. The fact is I simply don't believe Atlantis ever existed. This is pure bullshit.'

'Atlantis is where we're going next, friend. Do you trust the evidence of your senses? I hope so, because you'll see Atlantis and the pyramid, just as I said. Those bastards, the Illuminati, are trying to get gold to further their conspiracies by looting an Atlantean temple. And Hagbard is going to foil them by robbing it first. Because I fight the Illuminati every chance I get. And because I'm an amateur archeologist. Will you join us? You're free to leave right now, if you wish. I'll put you ashore and even supply you with money to get back to New York.'

I shook my head. 'I'm a writer. I write magazine articles for a living. And even if ninety percent of what you say is bullshit, moonshine, and the most elaborate put-on since Richard Nixon, this is the best story I've ever come across. A nut with a gigantic golden submarine whose followers include beautiful guerrilla women who blow up southern jails and take out the prisoners. No, I'm not leaving. You're too big a fish to let get away.'

Hagbard Celine slapped me on the shoulder. 'Good man. You've got courage and initiative. You trust only the evidence of your eyes and believe what no man tells you. I was right about you. Come on down to my stateroom.' He pressed a button and we entered the golden elevator and sank rapidly till we came to an eight-foot-high archway barred by a silver gate. Celine pressed a button and the elevator door and the gate outside both slid back. We stepped out into a carpeted room with a lovely black woman sitting at one end under an elaborate emblem concocted of anchors, seashells, Viking figureheads, lions, ropes, octopi, lightning bolts, and, occupying the central position, a golden apple.

'Kallisti,' said Celine, saluting the girl.

'All hail Discordia,' she answered.

'Aum Shiva,' I contributed, trying to enter the spirit of the game.

Celine led me down a long corridor, saying, 'You'll find this submarine is opulently furnished. I have no need to live in monklike surroundings like those masochists who become naval officers. No Spartan simplicity for me. This is more like an ocean liner or a grand European hotel of the Edwardian era. Wait till you see my suite. You'll like your stateroom, too. To please myself, I built this thing on the grand scale. No finicky naval architects or parsimonious accountants in my business. I believe you've got to spend money to make money and spend the money you make to enjoy money. Besides, I have to live in the damned thing.'

'And what precisely is your business, Mr. Celine?' I asked. 'Or should I call you Captain Celine?'

'You should certainly not. No bullshit authority titles for me. I'm Freeman Hagbard Celine, but the conventional Mister is good enough. I'd prefer you called me by my first name. Hell, call me anything you want to. If I don't like it, I'll punch you in the nose. If there were more bloody noses, there'd be fewer wars. I'm in smuggling mostly. With a spot of piracy, just to keep ourselves on our toes. But that only against the Illuminati and their communist dupes. We aim to prove that no state has the right to regulate commerce in any way. Nor can it, when it is up against free men. My crew are all volunteers. We have among us liberated sailors who were indentured to the navies of America, Russia, and China. Excellent fellows. The governments of the world will never catch us, because free men are always cleverer than slaves, and any man who works for a government is a slave.'

'Then you're a gang of Objectivists, basically? I've got to warn you, I come from a long line of labor agitators and Reds. You'll never convert me to a right-wing position.'

Celine reared back as if I had waved offal under his nose. 'Objectivists?' he pronounced the word as if I had accused him of being a child-molester. 'We're anarchists and outlaws, goddam it. Didn't you understand that much? We've got nothing to do with right-wing, left-wing or any other half-assed political category. If you work within the system, you come to one of the either/or choices that were implicit in the system from the beginning. You're talking like a medieval serf, asking the first agnostic whether he worships God or the Devil. We're outside the system's categories. You'll never get the hang of our game if you keep thinking in flat-earth imagery of right and left, good and evil, up and down. If you need a group label for us, we're political non-Euclideans. But even that's not true. Sink me, nobody of this tub agrees with anybody else about anything, except maybe what the fellow with the horns told the old man in the clouds: *Non serviam.*'

'I don't know Latin,' I said, overwhelmed by his outburst.

' "I will not serve," ' he translated. 'And here's your room.'

He threw open an oaken door, and I entered a living room furnished in handsome teak and rosewood Scandinavian, upholstered in bright solid colors. He hadn't been exaggerating about the scale: you could have parked a Greyhound bus in the middle of the carpet and the room would still seem uncluttered. Above an orange couch hung a huge oil painting in an elaborate gilt frame easily a foot deep on all sides. The painting was essentially a cartoon. It showed a man in robes with long, flowing white hair and beard standing on a mountaintop staring in astonishment at a wall of black rock. Above his head a fiery hand traced flaming letters with its index finger on the rock. The words it wrote were:

THINK FOR YOURSELF, SCHMUCK!

As I started to laugh, I felt, through the soles of my feet, an enormous engine beginning to throb.

And, in Mad Dog, Jim Cartwright said into a phone with a scrambler device to evade taps, 'We let Celine's crowd take Dorn, according to plan, and, Harry Coin is, ah, no longer with us.'

'Good,' said Atlanta Hope. 'The Four are heading for Ingolstadt. Everything is GO.' She hung up and dialed again at once, reaching Western Union. 'I want a flat rate telegram, same words, twenty-three different addresses,' she said crisply. 'The message is. "Insert the advertisement in tomorrow's newspapers." Signature, "Atlanta Hope." ' She then read off the twenty-three addresses, each located in a large city in the United States, each a regional headquarters of God's Lightning. (The following day, April 25, the newspapers in those cities ran an obscure ad in the personals columns; it said 'In thanks to Saint Jude for favors granted. A.W.' The plot, accordingly, thickened.)

And then I sat back and thought about Harry Coin.

Once I imagined I could make it with him: there was something so repulsive, so cruel, so wild and psychopathic there . . . but, of course, it hadn't worked. The same as every other man. Nothing. 'Hit me,' I screamed. 'Bite me. Hurt me. *Do something.*' He did everything, the most agreeable sadist in the world, but it was the same as if he had been the gentlest, most poetic English instructor at Antioch. Nothing. Nothing, nothing, nothing. . . . The closest miss was that strange banker, Drake, from Boston. What a scene. I'd gotten into his office on Wall Street, seeking a contribution for God's Lightning. Old white-haired buzzard, between sixty and seventy: typical of our wealthier members, I thought. I started the usual spiel, communism, sexism, smut, and all the time his eyes were bright and hard as a snake's. It finally hit me that he didn't believe a word of it, so I started to cut it off, and then he pulled out his checkbook and wrote and held it up so I could see it. Twenty thousand dollars. I didn't know what to say, and I started something about how all true Americans would appreciate this great gesture and so on, and he said, 'Rubbish. You're not rich but you're famous. I want to add you to my collection. Deal?' The coldest bastard I ever met, even Harry Coin was human by comparison, yet his eyes were such a clear blue I couldn't believe they could be so frightening, a real madman in a perfectly sane way, not even a psychopath but something they don't have a name for, and it clicked, the humiliation of whoredom and the predatory viciousness in his face plus the twenty grand; I nodded. He took me into a private suite off of his business office and he touched one button, the lights dimmed, another button, down came a movie screen, a third button, and I was watching a pornographic movie. He didn't approach me, just watched, and I tried to get excited, wondering if the actress was really making it or just faking it, and then a second film began, four of them this time in permutations and combinations, he led me to the couch, every time I opened my eyes I could still see the film over his shoulder, and it was the same, the same, as soon as he got his thing inside me, nothing, nothing, nothing, I kept looking at the actors trying to feel something, and then, as he came, he whispered in my ear, '*Heute die Welt, Morgens das Sonnensystem!*' That was the only time I almost made it. Sheer terror that this maniac *knew*. . . .

Later, I tried to find out about him, but nobody above me in the Order would say a word, and those below me didn't know anything. But I finally found out: he was very big in the Syndicate, maybe the top. And that's how I figured out that the old rumor was true, the Syndicate was run by the Order, too, just like everything else. . . .

But that cold sinister old man never said another word about it. I kept waiting while we dressed, when he gave me the check, when he escorted me to the door, and even his expression seemed to deny that he had said it or knew what it meant. When he opened the door for me, he put an arm on my shoulder and spoke, so his secretary could hear it, 'May your work hasten the day when America returns to purity.' Even his eyes weren't mocking and his voice sounded completely sincere. And yet he had read me to the core, knew I was faking, and guessed that terror alone could unlock my reflexes: maybe he even knew that I had already tried physical sadism and it hadn't worked. Out on Wall Street in the crowd, I saw a man with a gas mask – they were still rare that year – and I felt the whole world was moving faster than I could understand and that the Order wasn't telling me nearly as much as I needed to know.

Brother Beghard, who is actually a politician in Chicago under his 'real' name, once explained the Law of Fives to me in relation to the pyramid-of-power principle. Intellectually, I understand: it's the only way we can work, each group a separate vector so that the most any infiltrator can learn is a small part of the design. Emotionally, though, it does get frightening at times: do the Five at the top really have the whole picture? I don't know, and I don't see how they can predict a man like Drake or guess what he's planning next. There's a paradox here, I know: I joined the Order seeking power, and now I am more a tool, an object, than ever before. If a man like Drake ever thought that, he might tear the whole show apart.

Unless the Five really do have the powers they claim; but I'm not gullible enough to believe that bull. Some of it's hypnotism, and some is plain old stage magic, but none of it is really supernatural. Nobody has sold me on a fairy tale since my uncle got into me when I was twelve with his routine about stopping the bleeding. If my parents had only told me the truth about menstruation in advance . . .

Enough of that. There was work to be done. I hit the buzzer on my desk and my secretary, Mr. Mortimer, came in. As I'd guessed, it was past nine o'clock and he'd been out there in the reception area straightening up and worrying about my mood for God knows how long, while I was daydreaming. I studied my memo pad, while he waited apprehensively. Finally, I noticed him and said, 'Be seated.' He sank into the dictation chair, putting his head right under the point of the lightning bolt on the wall – an effect I always enjoyed – and opened his pad.

'Call Zev Hirsch in New York,' I said watching his pencil fly to keep up with my words. 'The Foot Fetishist Liberation Front is having a demonstration. Tell him to *cream* them; I won't be satisfied unless a dozen of the perverts are put in the hospital, and I don't care how many of our people get arrested doing it. The bail fund is available, if they need it. If Zev has any objections, I'll talk to him, but otherwise you handle it. Then make up the standard number-two press release, where I deny any knowledge of illegal activities by that chapter and promise we will investigate and expel anybody guilty of mob action – have that ready for release this afternoon. Then get me the latest sales figures on *Telemachus Sneezed.* . . .' Another busy day at the national headquarters of God's Lightning was started; and Hagbard Celine, feeding Mavis's report on George's sexual and other behavior into FUCKUP, came out with a coding of C-1472-B-2317A, which caused him to laugh immoderately.

'What's so damned funny?' Mavis asked.

'From out of the west come the thundering hooves of the great horse, Onan,' Hagbard grinned. 'The lonely stranger rides again!'

'What the hell does all that mean?'

'We've got sixty-four thousand possible personality types,' Hagbard explained, 'and I've only seen that reading once before. Guess who it was?'

'Not me,' Mavis said quickly, beginning to color.

'No, not you.' Hagbard laughed again. 'It was Atlanta Hope.'

THE EYE IN THE PYRAMID 91

Mavis was startled. 'That's impossible. She's frigid for
one thing.'

'There are many kinds of frigidity,' Hagbard said. 'It
fits, believe me. She joined women's liberation at the same
age George joined Weatherman, and they both split after a
few months. And you'd be surprised how similar their
mothers were, or how the successful careers of their older
brothers annoy them—'

'But George is a nice guy, underneath it all.'

Hagbard Celine knocked an ash off his long Italian
cigar. 'Everybody is a nice guy, underneath it all,' he said.
'What we become when the world is through messing us
over is something else.'

At Château Thierry, in 1918, Robert Putney Drake
looked around at the dead bodies, knew he was the last
man alive in the platoon, and heard the Germans start to
advance. He felt the cold wetness on his thighs before he
realized he was urinating in his pants; a shell exploded
nearby and he sobbed. 'O God, please, Jesus. Don't let
them kill me. I'm afraid to die. Please, Jesus, Jesus,
Jesus . . .'

Mary Lou and Simon are eating breakfast in bed, still
naked as Adam and Eve. Mary Lou spread jam on toast
and asked, 'No, seriously: which part was hallucination
and which part was real?'

Simon sipped at his coffee. 'Everything in life is a hallucination,' he said simply. 'Everything in death, too,' he
added. 'The universe is just putting us on. Handing us a
line.'

THE THIRD TRIP, OR BINAH

The Purple Sage cursed and waxed sorely pissed and cried out in a loud voice: A pox upon the accursed Illuminati of Bavaria; may their seed take no root.

May their hands tremble, their eyes dim and their spines curl up, yea, verily, like unto the backs of snails; and may the vaginal orifices of their women be clogged with Brillo pads.

For they have sinned against God and Nature; they have made of life a prison; and they have stolen the green from the grass and the blue from the sky.

And so saying, and grimacing and groaning, the Purple Sage left the world of men and women and retired to the desert in despair and heavy grumpiness.

But the High Chapperal laughed, and said to the Erisian faithful: Our brother torments himself with no cause, for even the malign Illuminati are unconscious pawns of the Divine Plane of Our Lady.

> —Mordecai Malignatus, K.N.S.,
> 'The Book of Contradictions,' *Liber 555*

October 23, 1970, was the thirty-fifth anniversary of the murder of Arthur Flegenheimer (alias 'The Dutchman,' alais 'Dutch Schultz'), but this dreary lot has no intention of commemorating that occasion. They are the Knights of Christianity United in Faith (the group in Atlantis were called Mauls of Lhuv-Kerapht United for the Truth; see what I mean?) and their president, James J. (Smiling Jim) Trepomena has noted a bearded and therefore suspicious young man among the delegates. Such types were not likely to be KCUF members and might even be dope fiends. Smiling Jim told the Andy Frain ushers to keep a watchful eye on the young man so no 'funny business' could occur, and then went to the podium to begin his talk on 'Sex Education: Communist Trojan Horse in Our Schools.' (In Atlantis, it was 'Numbers: Nothingarian Squid-Trap in Our Schools.' The same drivel eternally.) The bearded young man, who happened to be Simon Moon, adviser to

Teenset magazine on Illuminati affairs and instructor in sexual yoga to numerous black young ladies, observed that he was being observed (which made him think of Heisenberg) and settled back in his chair to doodle pentagons on his note pad. Three rows ahead, a crew-cut middle-aged man, who looked like a surburban Connecticut doctor, also settled back comfortably, awaiting his opportunity: the funny business that he and Simon had in mind would be, he hoped, very funny indeed.

WE SHALL NOT   WE SHALL NOT BE MOVED

There was a road going due east from Dayton, Ohio, towards New Lebanon and Brookville, and on a small farm off that road lives an excellent man named James V. Riley, who is a sergeant on the Dayton police force. Although he grieves the death of his wife two years back in '67 and worries about his son, who seems to be in some shady business involving frequent travel between New York City and Cuernavaca, the sergeant is basically a cheerful man; but on June 25, 1969, he was a bit out of sorts and generally not up to snuff because of his arthritis and the seemingly endless series of pointless and peculiar questions being asked by the reporter from New York. It didn't make sense – who would want to publish a book about John Dillinger at this late date? And why would such a book deal with Dillinger's dental history?

'You're the same James Riley who was on the Mooresville, Indiana, Force when Dillinger was first arrested, in 1924?' the reporter had begun.

'Yes, and a smart-alecky young punk he was. I don't hold with some of these people who've written books about him and said the long sentence he got back then is what made him bitter and turned him bad. He got the long sentence because he was so snotty to the judge. Not a sign of repentence or remorse, just wisecracks and a know-it-all grin spread all over his face. A bad apple from the start. And always hellbent-for-leather. In a hurry to get God knows where. Sometimes folks used to joke that there were two of him, he'd go through town so fast. Rushing to his own funeral. Young punks like that never get long enough sentences, if you want my opinion. Might slow them down a bit.'

The reporter – what was his name again? James Mal-

lison, hadn't he said – was impatient. 'Yes, yes, I'm sure
we need stricter laws and harsher penalties. But what I
want to know was where was Dillinger's missing tooth –
on the right side or the left side of his face?'

'Saints in Heaven! You expect me to remember that
after all these years?'

The reporter dabbed his forehead with a handkerchief –
very nervous he seemed to be. 'Look, Sergeant, some psychologists say we never forget anything, really; it's all
stored somewhere inside our brain. Now, just try to picture
John Dillinger as you remember him, with that know-it-all
grin as you called it. Can you get the picture into focus?
Which side is the missing tooth on?'

'Listen, I'm due to go on duty in a few minutes and I
can't be—'

Mallison's face changed, as if in desperation which he
was trying to conceal. 'Well, let me ask you a different
question. Are you a Mason?'

'A Mason? Bejesus, no – I've been a Catholic all my
life, I'll have you know.'

'Well, did you know any Masons in Mooresville? I
mean, to talk to?'

'Why would I be talking to the likes of them, with the
terrible things they're always saying about the church?'

The reporter plunged on, 'All the books on Dillinger
say that the intended victim of that first robbery, the grocer
B. F. Morgan, summoned help by giving the Masonic signal
of distress. Do you know what that is?'

'You'd have to ask a Mason, and I'm sure they wouldn't
be telling. The way they keep their secrets, by the saints,
I'm sure even the FBI couldn't find out.'

The reporter finally left, but Sergeant Riley, a methodical
man, filed his name in memory: James Mallison – or had
he said Joseph Mallison? A strange book he claimed to be
writing – about Dillinger's teeth and the bloody atheistic
Freemasons. There was more to this than met the eye,
obviously.

LIKE A TREE THAT'S PLANTED BY THE WATER

WE SHALL NOT BE MOVED

Miskatonic University, in Arkham, Massachusetts, is not
a well-known campus by any means, and the few scholarly
visitors who come there are an odd lot, drawn usually by

the strange collection of occult books given to the Miskatonic Library by the late Dr. Henry Armitage. Miss Doris
Horus, the librarian, had never seen quite such a strange
visitor though, as this Professor J. D. Mallison who claimed
to come from Dayton, Ohio, but spoke with an unmistakable New York accent. Considering his furtiveness, she
found it no surprise that he spent the whole day (June 26,
1969) pouring over the rare copy of Dr. John Dee's translation of the *Necronomicon* of Abdul Alhazred. That was
the book most of the queer ones went for; that or *The
Book of Sacred Magic of Abra-Melin the Mage.*

Doris didn't like the *Necronomicon*, although she considered herself an emancipated and free-thinking young
woman. There was something sinister, or to be downright
honest about it, *perverted* about that book – and not in a
nice, exciting way, but in a sick and frightening way. All
those strange illustrations, always with five-sided borders
just like the Pentagon in Washington, but with those people
inside doing all those freaky sex acts with those other
creatures who weren't people at all. It was frankly Doris's
opinion that old Abdul Alhazred had been smoking some
pretty bad grass when he dreamed up those things. Or
maybe it was something stronger than grass: she remembered one sentence from the text: 'Onlie those who have
eaten a certain alkaloid herb, whose name it were wise not
to disclose to the unilluminated, maye in the fleshe see a
Shoggothe.' I wonder what a 'Shoggothe' is, Doris thought
idly; probably one of those disgusting creatures that the
people in the illustrations are doing those horny things
with. Yech.

She was glad when J. D. Mallison finally left and she
could return the *Necronomicon* to its position on the closed
shelves. She remembered the brief biography of crazy old
Abdul Alhazred that Dr. Armitage had written and also
given to the library: 'Spent seven years in the desert and
claimed to have visited Irem, the city forbidden in the
Koran, which Alhazred asserted was of pre-human origin.
. . .' Silly! Who was around to build cities before there were
people? Those Shoggothes? 'An indifferent Moslem, he
worshipped beings whom he called Yog-Sothoth and
Cthulhu.' And that insidious line: 'According to contemporary historians, Alhazred's death was both tragic

and bizarre, since it was asserted that he was eaten alive by an invisible monster in the middle of the market-place.' Dr. Armitage had been such a nice old man, Doris remembered, even if his talk about cabalistic numbers and Masonic symbols was a little peculiar at times; why would he collect such *icky* books by *creepy* people?

The Internal Revenue Service knows this much about Robert Putney Drake: during the last fiscal year, he earned $23,000,005 on stocks and bonds in various defense corporations, $17,000,523 from the three banks he controlled, and $5,807,400 from various real-estate holdings. They did not know that he also banked (in Switzerland) over $100,000,000 from prostitution, an equal amount from heroin and gambling, and $2,500,000 from pornography. On the other hand, they didn't know either about certain legitimate business expenses which he had not cared to claim, including more than $5,000,000 in bribes to various legislators, judges and police officials, in all 50 states in order to maintain the laws which made men's vices so profitable to him, and $50,000 to Knights of Christianity United in Faith as a last-ditch effort to stave off total legalization of pornography and the collapse of that part of his empire.

'What the deuce do you make of this?' Barney Muldoon asked. He was holding an amulet in his hand. 'Found it in the bedroom,' he explained, holding it for Saul to examine the strange design:

'Part of it is Chinese,' Saul said thoughtfully. 'The basic design – two interlocking commas, one pointing up and the other down. It means that opposites are equal.'

'And what does *that* mean?' Muldoon asked sarcastically. 'Opposites are opposite, not equal. You'd have to be a Chinaman to think otherwise.'

Saul ignored the comment. 'But the pentagon isn't in the Chinese design – and neither is the apple with the *K* in it. . . .' Suddenly, he grinned. 'Wait, I'll bet I know what that is. It's from Greek mythology. There was a banquet on Olympus, and Eris wasn't invited, because she was the Goddess of Discord and always made trouble. So, to get even, she made *more* trouble: she created a beautiful golden apple, and wrote on it *Kallisti*. That means "for the prettiest one" in Greek. It's what the *K* stands for, obviously. Then she rolled it into the banquet hall, and, naturally, all the goddesses there immediately claimed it, each one saying that *she* was "the prettiest one." Finally, old man Zeus himself, to settle the squabble, allowed Paris to decide which goddess was the prettiest and should get the apple. He chose Aphrodite, and as a reward she gave him an opportunity to kidnap Helen, which led to the Trojan War.'

'Very interesting,' Muldoon said. 'And does that tell us what Joseph Malik knew about the assassinations of the Kennedys and this Illuminati bunch and why his office was blown up? Or where he's disappeared to?'

'Well, no,' Saul said, 'but it's nice to find something in this case that I can recognize. I just wish I knew what the pentagon means, to. . . .'

'Let's look at the rest of the memos,' Muldoon suggested.

The next memo, however, stopped them cold:

ILLUMINATI PROJECT: MEMO #9

7/28

J.M.:

The following chart appeared in the *East Village Other*, June 11, 1969, with the label 'Current Structure of the Bavarian Illuminati Conspiracy and the Law of Fives':

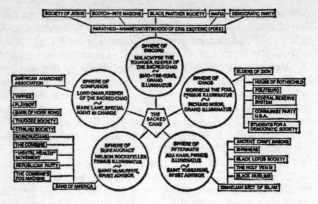

The chart hangs at the top of the page, the rest of which is empty space – as if the editors originally intended to publish an article explaining it, but decided (or were persuaded) to suppress all but the diagram itself.

Pat

'This one has to be some damned hippie or yippie hoax,' Muldoon said after a long pause. But he sounded uncertain.

'*Part* of it is,' Saul said thoughtfully keeping certain thoughts to himself. 'Typical hippie psychology: mixing truth and fantasy to blow the fuses of the Establishment. The Elders of Zion section is just a parody of Nazi ideology. If there really was a Jewish conspiracy to run the world, my rabbi would have let me in on it by now. I contribute enough to the *schule*.'

'My brother's a Jesuit,' Muldoon added, pointing at the Society of Jesus square, 'and he never invited me into any worldwide conspiracy.'

'But this part is almost plausible,' Saul said, pointing to the Sphere of Aftermath. 'Aga Khan *is* the head of the Ishmaelian sect of Islam, and that sect was founded by Hassan i Sabbah, the "old man of the mountains" who led the Hashishim in the eleventh century. Adam Weishaupt is supposed to have originated the Bavarian Illuminati after studying Sabbah, according to the third memo, so this part fits together – and Hassan i Sabbah is supposed to be the first one to introduce marijuana and hashish to the Western world, from India. That ties in with Weishaupt's growing hemp and Washington's having a big hemp crop at Mount Vernon.'

'Wait a minute. Look at how the whole design revolves around the pentagon. Everything else sort of grows out of it.'

'So? You think the Defense Department is the international hub of the Illuminati conspiracy?'

'Let's just read the rest of the memos,' Muldoon suggested.

(The Indian Agent at the Menominee Reservation in Wisconsin knows this: from the time Billie Freschette returned there until her death in 1968, she received mysterious monthly checks from Switzerland. He thinks he knows the explanation: despite all stories to the contrary, Billie *did* help to betray Dillinger and this is the payoff. He is convinced of this. He is also quite wrong.)

'. . . children seven and eight years old,' Smiling Jim Trepomena is telling the KCUF audience, 'are talking about penises and vaginas – *and using those very words!* Now, is this an accident? Let me quote you Lenin's own words. . . .' Simon yawns.

Banana-Nose Maldonado evidently had his own brand of sentimentality or superstition, and in 1936 he ordered his son, a priest, to say one hundred masses for the salvation of the Dutchman's soul. Even years afterward, he would defend the Dutchman in conversation: 'He was OK, Dutch was, if you didn't cross him. If you did, forget it; you were finished. He was almost a Siciliano about that. Otherwise, he was a good businessman, and the first one with a real CPA mind in the whole organization. If he hadn't gotten that crazy-head idea about gunning down Tom Dewey, he'd still be a big man. I told him myself. "You kill Dewey," I said, "and the shit hits the fan everywhere. The boys won't take the risk; Lucky and the Butcher want to cowboy you right now." But he wouldn't listen. "Nobody fucks with me," he said. "I don't care if his name is Dewey, Looey, or Phooey. He *dies*." A real stubborn German Jew. You couldn't talk to him. I even told him how Capone helped set up Dillinger for the Feds just because of the heat those bank-heists were bringing

down. You know what he said? He said: "You tell Al that
Dillinger was a lone wolf. I have my own pack." Too bad,
too bad, too bad. I'll light another candle for him at church
Sunday.'

HAND IN HAND TOGETHER
WE SHALL NOT BE MOVED

Rebecca Goodman closes her book wearily and stares
into space, thinking about Babylon. Her eyes focus suddenly on the statue Saul had bought her for her last birth-
day: the mermaid of Copenhagen. How many Danes, she
wonders, know that this is one form of representation of
the Babylonian sex goddess Ishtar? (*In Central Park, Perri
the squirrel is beginning to hunt for the day's food. A
French poodle, held on a leash by a mink-coated lady,
barks at him, and he runs three times around a tree.*)
George Dorn looks at the face of a corpse: it is his own
face. 'In Wyoming, after one sex-education class in a high
school, the teacher was raped by seventeen boys. She said
later she would never teach sex in school again.' Making
sure he is alone in the Meditation Room of the UN building, the man calling himself Frank Sullivan quickly moves
the black plinth aside and descends the hidden stairs into
the tunnel. He is thinking, whimsically, that hardly anybody realizes that the shape of the room is the same as the
truncated pyramid on the dollar bill, or guesses what that
means. 'In Wilmette, Illinois, an 8-year-old boy came home
from a sensitivity training class and tried to have intercourse with his 4-year-old sister.' Simon gave up on his
pentagons and began doodling pyramids instead.

Above, beyond Joe Malik's window, Saul Goodman gave
up on the line of thought which had led him to surmise
that the Illuminati were a front for the International Psychoanalytical Society, conspiring to drive everyone paranoid,
and turned back to the desk and the memos. Barney Muldoon came in from the bedroom, carrying a strange amulet,
and asked, 'What do you make of this?' Saul looked at a
design of an apple and a pentagon . . . and, several years
earlier, Simon Moon looked at the same medallion.

'They call it the Sacred Chao,' Padre Pederastia said.
They sat alone at a table pulled off to the corner; the
Friendly Stranger was the same as ever, except that a new
group, the American Medical Association (consisting,

naturally, of four kids from Germany), had replaced H. P. Lovecraft in the back room. (Nobody knew that the AMA was going to become the world's most popular rock group within a year, but Simon already thought they were superheavy). Padre Pederastia was, as on the night Simon met Miss Mao, very serious and hardly camping at all.

'Sacred Cow?' Simon asked.

'It's pronounced that way, but you spell it c-h-a-o. A chao is a single unit of chaos, they figure.' The Padre smiled.

'Too much, they're nuttier than the SSS,' Simon objected.

'Never underestimate absurdity, it is one door to the Imagination. Do I have to remind *you* of that?'

'We have an alliance with them?' Simon asked.

'The JAMs can't do it alone. Yes, we have an alliance, as long as it profits both parties. John – Mr. Sullivan himself authorized this.'

'OK. What do they call themselves?'

'The LDA.' The Padre permitted himself a smile. 'New members are told the initials stand for Legion of Dynamic Discord. Later on, quite often, the leader, a most fetching scoundrel and madman named Celine, sometimes tells them it really stands for Little Deluded Dupes. That's the *pons asinorum*, or an early *pons asinorum*, in Celine's System. He judges them by how they react to that.'

'Celine's System?' Simon asked warily.

'It leads to the same destination as ours – more or less – by a somewhat wilder and woolier path.'

'Right-hand or left-hand path?'

'Right-hand,' the priest said. 'All absurdist systems are right-hand. Well, almost all. They don't invoke You-Know-Who under any circumstances. They rely on Discordia . . . do you remember your Roman myths?'

'Enough to know that Discordia is just the Latin equivalent of Eris. They're part of the Erisian Liberation Front, then?' Simon was beginning to wish he were stoned; these conspiratorial conversations always made more sense when he was slightly high. He wondered how people like the President of the U.S. or the Chairman of the Board of GM were able to plot such intricate games without being on a trip at the time. Or did they take enough tranquilizers to produce a similar effect?

'No,' the priest said flatly. 'Don't ever make that mistake. ELF is a much more, um, esoteric outfit than the LDD. Celine is on the activist side, like us. Some of his capers make Morituri or God's Lightning look like Trappists by comparison. No, ELF will never get on Mr. Celine's trip.'

'He's got an absurdist yoga and an activist ethic?' Simon reflected. 'The two don't mix.'

'Celine is a walking contradiction. Look at his symbol again.'

'I've *been* looking at it and that pentagon worries me. Are you sure he's on our side?'

The American Medical Association came to some kind of erotic or musical climax and the priest's answer was drowned out. 'What?' Simon asked, after the applause died down.

'I said,' Padre Pederastia whispered, 'that we're never sure *anybody* is on our side. Uncertainty is the name of the game.'

ILLUMINATI PROJECT: MEMO #10

7/28

J.M.:

On the origin of the pyramid-and-eye symbol, test your credulity on the following yarn from *Flying Saucers in the Bible* by Virginia Brasington (Saucerian Books, 1963, page 43.):

> The Continental Congress had asked Benjamin Franklin, Thomas Jefferson and John Adams to arrange for a seal for the United States of America. . . . None of the designs they created or which were submitted to them, were suitable. . . .
>
> Fairly late at night, after working on the project all day, Jefferson walked out into the cool night air of the garden to clear his mind. In a few minutes he rushed back into the room, crying, jubilantly: 'I have it! I have it!' Indeed, he did have some plans in his hands. They were the plans showing the Great Seal as we know it today.

Asked how he got the plans, Jefferson told a strange story. A man approached him wearing a black cloak that practically covered him, face and all, and told him that he (the stranger) knew they were trying to devise a Seal, and that he had a design which was appropriate and meaningful. . . .

After the excitement died down, the three went into the garden to find the stranger, but he was gone. *Thus, neither these Founding Fathers, nor anybody else, ever knew who really designed the Great Seal of the United States!*

Pat

ILLUMINATI PROJECT: MEMO #11

7/29

J.M.:

The latest I've found on the eye-and-pyramid is in a San Francisco underground paper (*Planet*, San Francisco, July 1969, Vol. I, No.4.), suggesting it as a symbol for Timothy Leary's political party when he was running for governor of California instead of just running:

> The emblem is a tentative design for the Party's campaign button. One wag suggested that everyone cut out the circle from the back of a dollar bill and send the holey dollar to Governor Leary so he can wallpaper his office with them. Then paste the emblem on your front door to signify your membership in the party.

Translations: The year of the beginning
New Secular Order

Both translations are wrong, of course. *Annuit Coeptis* means 'he blesses our beginning' and *Novus Ordo Seclorem* means 'a new order of the ages.' Oh, well, scholarship was never the hippies' strong point. But – *Tim Leary* an Illuminatus?

And pasting the Eye on the door – I can't help but think of the Hebrews marking their doorways with the blood of a lamb so that the Angel of Death would pass by their houses.

Pat

ILLUMINATI PROJECT: MEMO #12

8/3

J.M.:

I've finally found the basic book on the Illuminati: *Proofs of a Conspiracy* by John Robison (Christian Book Club of America, Hawthorn, California, 1961; originally published in 1801). Robison was an English Mason who discovered through personal experience that the French Masonic lodges – such as the Grand Orient – were Illuminati fronts and were the main instigators of the French Revolution. His whole book is very explicit about how Weishaupt worked: every infiltrated Masonic group would have several levels, like an ordinary Masonic lodge, but as candidates advanced through the various degrees they would be told more about the real purposes of the movement. Those at the bottom simply thought they were Masons; in the middle levels, they knew they were engaged in a great project to change the world, but the exact nature of the change was explained to them according to what the leaders thought they were prepared to know. Only those at the top knew the secret, which – according to Robison – is this: the Illuminati aims to overthrow all government and religion, setting up an anarcho-communists free-love world, and, because 'the end justifies the means' (a principle Weishaupt acquired from his Jesuit youth), they didn't care how many people they killed to accomplish that noble purpose. Robison knows nothing of earlier Illuminati movements, but does say specifically that the Bavarian Illuminati was not destroyed by the government's crackdown in 1785 but was, in fact, still active, both in England and France and possibly elsewhere, when he wrote, in 1801. On page 116, Robison lists their existing lodges as follows: Germany (84 lodges); England (8 lodges); Scotland (2); Warsaw (2); Switzerland (many); Rome, Naples, Ancona, Florence, France, Holland, Dresden (4); United States of America (several). On page 101, he mentions that there are 13 ranks in the Order; this may account for the 13 steps on their symbolic pyramid. Page 84 gives the code name of Weishaupt, which was Spartacus; his second-in-command, Freiherr Knigge, had the code name Philo (page 117); this is revealed in papers seized by the Bavarian government in a raid on the home of a lawyer named

Zwack, who had the code name Cato. Babeuf, the French revolutionary, evidently took the name Gracchus in imitation of the classical style of these titles.

Robison's conclusion, page 269, *is* worth quoting:

> Nothing is as dangerous as a mystic Association. The object remaining a secret in the hands of the managers, the rest simply put a ring in their own noses, by which they may be led about at pleasure; and still panting after the secret they are the more pleased the less they see.

Pat

At the bottom of the page was a note in pencil, scrawled with a decisive masculine hand. It said: 'In the beginning was the Word and it was written by a baboon.'

ILLUMINATI PROJECT: MEMO #13

8/5

J.M.:

The survival of the Bavarian Illuminati throughout the nineteenth century and into the twentieth is the subject of *World Revolution* by Nesta Webster (Constable and Company, London, 1921). Mrs. Webster follows Robison fairly closely on the early days of the movement, up to the French Revolution, but then veers off and says that the Illuminati never intended to create their Utopian anarcho-communist society: that was just another of their masks. Their real purpose was dictatorship over the world, and so they soon formed a secret alliance with the Prussian government. All subsequent socialist, anarchist, and communist movements are mere decoys, she argues, behind which the German General Staff and the Illuminati are plotting to overthrow other governments, so Germany can conquer them. (She wrote right after England fought Germany in the First World War). I see no way of reconciling this with the Birchers' thesis that the Illuminati has become a front for the Rhodes Scholars to take over the world for *English* domination. Obviously – as Robison states – the Illuminati say different things to different people, to get them into the conspiracy. As for the links

with modern communism, here are some passages from
her pages 234–45:

> But now that the (First) Internationale was dead it
> became necessary for the secret societies to reorganize,
> and it is at this crisis that we find that 'formidable
> sect' springing to life again – *the original Illuminati
> of Weishaupt.*
>
> . . . What we do know definitely is that the society
> was refounded in Dresden in 1880. . . . That it was
> consciously modelled on its eighteenth century pre-
> decessor is clear from the fact that its chief, one
> Leapold Engel, was the author of a lengthy panegyric
> on Weishaupt and his Order, entitled *Geschichte des
> Illuminaten Ordens* (published in 1906). . . .
>
> . . . In London a lodge called by the same name . . .
> carried on the rite of Memphis – founded, it is said,
> by Cagliostro on Egyptian models – and initiated
> adepts into illuminized Freemasonry. . . .
>
> Was it . . . a mere coincidence that in July 1889
> an International Socialist Congress decided that May
> 1, which was the day on which Weishaupt founded
> the Illuminati, should be chosen for an annual Inter-
> national Labour demonstration?

Pat

ILLUMINATI PROJECT: MEMO #14

8/6

J.M.:

And here's still another version of the origin of the Illuminati, from the Cabalist Eliphas Levi (*The History of Magic*
by Eliphas Levi, Borden Publishing Company, Los Angeles,
1963, page 65). He says there were two Zoroasters, a true
one who taught white 'right hand' magic and a false one
who taught black 'left hand' magic. He goes on:

> To the false Zoroaster must be referred the cultus of
> material fire and that impious doctrine of divine dual-
> ism which produced at a later period the monstrous
> Gnosis of Manes and the false principles of spurious
> Masonry. The Zoroaster in question was the father of
> that materialized Magic which led to the massacre of

the Magi and brought their true doctrine at first into proscription and then oblivion. Ever inspired by the spirit of truth, the Church was forced to condemn – under the names of Magic, Manicheanism, Illuminism and Masonry – all that was in kinship, remote or approximate, with the primitive profanation of the mysteries. One signal example is the history of the Knights Templar, which has been misunderstood to this day.

Levi does not elucidate that last sentence; it is interesting, however, that Nesta Webster (see memo 13) also traced the Illuminati to the Knights Templar, whereas Daraul and most other sources track them Eastward to the Hashishim. Is all this making me paranoid? I'm beginning to get the impression that the evidence has not only been hidden in obscure books but also made confusing and contradictory to discourage the researcher. . . .

Pat

Scrawled on the bottom of this memo was a series of jottings in the same masculine hand (Malik's, Saul guessed) that had jotted the baboon reference on memo 12. The jottings said:

Check on Order of DeMolay

 Eleven-fold DeMolay Cross. Eleven intersections, therefore 22 lines. The 22 Atus of Tahuti? Why not 23??

TARO=TORA=TROA=ATOR=ROTA !?????
Abdul Alhazred=A∴ A∴??!

'Oh, Christ,' Barney groaned. 'Oh, Mary and Joseph. Oh, shit. We'll end up either become mystics or going crazy before this case is over. If there's any difference.'

'The Order of DeMolay is a Masonic society for boys,' Saul commented helpfully. 'I don't know what the Atus of Tahuti are, but that sounds Egyptian. Taro, usually spelled t-a-r-o-*t*, is the deck of cards Gypsy fortune tellers use – and the word "Gypsy" means Egyptian. Tora is the Law, in Hebrew. We keep coming back to something that has roots in both Jewish mysticism and Egyptian magic. . . .'

'The Knights Templar were kicked out of the church,' Barney said, 'for trying to combine Christian and Moslem ideas. Last year, my brother – the Jesuit – gave a lecture about how modern ideas are just old heresies from the Middle Ages warmed over. I had to go for politeness' sake. I remember something else he said about the Templars. They were engaged in what he called "unnatural sex acts." In other words, they were faggots. Do you get the impression that all these groups related to the Illuminati are all male? Maybe the big secret they're hiding so fanatically is that they're all some vast worldwide homosexual plot. I've heard show-biz people complain about what they call the "homintern," a homo organization that tries to keep all the best jobs for other fruits. How does that sound?'

'It sounds plausible,' Saul said ironically. 'But it also sounds plausible to say the Illuminati is a Jewish conspiracy, a Catholic conspiracy, a Masonic conspiracy, a communist conspiracy, a banker's conspiracy, and I suppose we'll eventually find evidence to suggest it's an interplanetary scheme masterminded from Mars or Venus. Don't you see, Barney? Whatever they're really up to, they keep creating masks so all sorts of scapegoat groups will get the blame for being the "real" Illuminati.' He shook his head dismally. 'They're smart enough to know they can't operate indefinitely without a few people eventually realizing something's there, so they've taken that into account and arranged for an inquisitive outsider to get all sorts of wrong ideas about who they are.'

'They're dogs,' Muldoon said. 'Intelligent talking dogs from the dog star, Sirius. They came here and ate Malik, Just like they ate that guy in Kansas City, except that time they didn't get to finish the job.' He turned back and read from memo 8: ' ". . . with his thoat torn as if by the talons of some enormous beast. No animal was reported missing from any of the local zoos." ' He grinned. 'Lord God, I'm almost ready to believe it.'

'They're werewolves.' Saul answered, grinning also. 'The pentagon is the symbol of the werewolf. Look at the Late Late Show some time.'

'That's the penta*gram*, not the penta*gon*.' Barney lit a cigarette, adding. 'This is really getting on our nerves, isn't it?'

Saul looked up wearily and glanced around the apartment almost as if he were looking for its absent owner. 'Joseph Malik,' he said aloud, 'what can of worms have you opened? And how far back does it go?'

WE SHALL NOT

WE SHALL NOT BE MOVED

In fact, for Joseph Malik the beginning was several years earlier, in a medley of teargas, hymn singing, billy clubs, and obscenity, all of which were provoked by the imminent nomination for President of a man named Hubert Horatio Humphrey. It began in Lincoln Park on the night of August 25, 1968, while Joe was waiting to be teargassed. He did not know then that anything was beginning; he was only conscious, in an acid, gut-sour way, of what was ending: his own faith in the Democratic party.

He was sitting with the Concerned Clergymen under the cross they had erected. He was thinking, bitterly, that they should have erected a tombstone instead. It should have said: Here lies the New Deal.

Here lies the belief that all Evil is on the *other* side, among the reactionaries and Ku Kluxers. Here lies twenty years of the hopes and dreams and sweat and blood of Joseph Wendall Malik. Here lies American Liberalism, clubbed to death by Chicago's heroic peace officers.

'They're coming,' a voice near him said suddenly. The Concerned Clergymen immediately began singing, 'We shall not be moved.'

'We'll be moved, all right,' a dry sardonic, W. C. Fields voice said quietly. 'When the teargas hits, we'll be moved.' Joe recognized the speaker: it was novelist William Burroughs with his usual poker face, utterly without anger or contempt or indignation or hope or faith or any emotion Joe could understand. But he sat there, making his own protest against Hubert Horatio Humphrey by placing his body in front of Chicago's police, for reasons Joe could not understand.

How, Joe wondered, can a man have courage without faith, without belief? Burroughs believed in nothing, and yet there he sat stubborn as Luther. Joe had always had

faith in something – Roman Catholicism, long ago, then
Trotskyism at college, then for nearly two decades main-
stream liberalism (Arthur Schlesinger, Jr.'s, 'Vital Center')
and now, with that dead, he was trying desperately to
summon up faith in the motley crowd of dope-and-astrol-
ogy-obsessed Yippies, Black Maoists, old-line hard-core
pacifists, and arrogantly dogmatic SDS kids who had come
to Chicago to protest a rigged convention and were being
beaten and brutalized unspeakably for it.

Allen Ginsberg – sitting amid a huddle of Yippies off to
the right – began chanting again, as he had all evening:
'Hare Krishna Hare Krishna Krishna Krishna Hare Hare.
. . .' Ginsberg believed; he believed in everything – in
democracy, in socialism, in communism, in anarchism, in
Ezra Pound's idealistic variety of fascist economics, in
Buckminster Fuller's technological utopia, in D. H.
Lawrence's return to preindustrial pastoralism, and in
Hinduism, Buddhism, Judaism, Christianity, Voodoo, as-
trology magic; but, above all, in the natural goodness of
man.

The natural goodness of man . . . Joe hadn't fully believed in that, since Buchenwald was revealed to the world
in 1944, when he was seventeen.

'KILL! KILL! KILL!' came the chant of the police – exactly like the night before, the same neolithic scream of
rage that signaled the beginning of the first massacre. They
were coming, clubs in hand, spraying the teargas before
them. 'KILL! KILL! KILL!'

Auschwitz, U.S.A., Joe thought, sickened. If they had
been issued Zyklon B along with the teargas and Mace,
they would be using it just as happily.

Slowly, the Concerned Clergymen came to their feet,
holding dampened handkerchiefs to their faces. Unarmed
and helpless, they prepared to hold their ground as long
as possible before the inevitable retreat. A moral victory,
Joe thought bitterly: All we ever achieve are moral victories. The immoral brutes win the real victories.

'All hail Discordia,' said a voice among the clergymen
– a bearded young man named Simon, who had been arguing in favor of anarchism against some SDS Maoists earlier
in the day.

And that was the last sentence Joe Malik remembered

clearly, for it was gas and clubs and screams and blood from then on. He had no way of guessing, at the time, that hearing that sentence was the most important thing that happened to him in Lincoln Park.

(Harry Coin curls his long body into a knot of tension, resting on his elbows and sighting the Remington rifle carefully, as the motorcade passes the Book Depository and heads toward his perch on the triple underpass. He could see Bernard Barker from the CIA down on the grassy knoll. If he carried this off right, they promised him more jobs; it would be the end of petty crime for him, the beginning of big-time money. In a way he was sorry: Kennedy seemed like a nice enough young fellow – Harry would like to make it with both him and that hot-looking wife of his at the same time – but money talks and sentiment is only for fools. He released the bolt action, ignoring the sudden barking of a dog, and took aim – just as the three shots resounded from the grassy knoll.

'Jesus Motherfuckin' Christ,' he said; and then he caught the glint of the rifle in the Book Depository window. Great God Almighty, how the *fuck* many of us are there here?' he cried out, scampering to his feet and starting to run.)

It was almost a year after being clubbed – June 22, 1969 – that Joe returned to Chicago, to witness another rigged convention, to suffer further disillusionment, to meet Simon once more and to hear the mysterious phrase 'All hail Discordia' again.

The convention this time was the last ever held by the Students for a Democratic Society, and from the first hour after it opened, Joe realized that the Progressive Labor faction had stacked all the cards in advance. It was the Democratic party all over again – and it would have been equally bloody if the PL boys had their own police force to 'deal with' the dissenters known then as RYM-I and RYM-II. Lacking that factor, the smoldering violence remained purely verbal, but when it was all over another part of Joe Malik was dead and his faith in the natural goodness of man was eroded still further. And so he found himself, aimlessly searching for something that was not totally corrupt, attending the Anarchist Caucus at the old Wobbly Hall on North Halsted Street.

Joe knew nothing about anarchism, except that several

famous anarchists – Parsons and Spies of Chicago's Hay-
market riot in 1888, Sacco and Vanzetti in Massachusetts,
and the Wobbly's own poet-laureate, Joe Hill – had been
executed for murders which they apparently hadn't really
committed. Beyond that, anarchists wanted to abolish government – a proposition so evidently absurd that Joe had
never bothered to read any of their theoretical or polemical
works. Now, however, eating the maggotty meat of his
growing disillusionment with every conventional approach
to politics, he began to listen to the Wobblies and other
anarchists with acute curiousity. After all, the words of his
favourite fictional hero, 'When you have eliminated all
other possibilities, whatever remains, however improbable,
must be true.'

The anarchists, Joe found, were not going to quit SDS
– 'We'll stay in and do some righteous ass-kicking,' one of
them said, to the applause and cheers of the others. Beyond
that, however, they seemed to be in a welter of ideological
disagreement. Gradually, he began to identify the con-
flicting positions expressed: the individualist-anarchists,
who sounded like right-wing Republicans (except that they
wanted to get rid of all functions of government); the
anarcho-syndicalists and Wobblies, who sounded like
Marxists (except that they wanted to get rid of all functions
of government); the anarcho-pacifists, who sounded like
Gandhi and Martin Luther King (except that they wanted
to get rid of all functions of government); and a group
who were dubbed, rather affectionately, 'the Crazies' –
whose position was utterly unintelligible. Simon was among
the Crazies.

In a speech that Joe followed only with difficulty, Simon
declared that 'cultural revolution' was more important
than political revolution; that Bugs Bunny should be
adopted as the symbol of anarchists everywhere; that
Hoffman's discovery of LSD in 1943 was a manifestation
of direct intervention by God in human affairs; that the
nomination of the boar hog Pigasus for President of the
United States by the Yippies had been the most 'transcen-
dentally lucid' political act of the twentieth century; and
that 'mass orgies of pot-smoking and fucking, on every
street-corner' was the most practical next step in liberating
the world from tyranny. He also urged deep study of the

tarot, 'to fight the real enemy with their own weapons,' whatever that meant. He was launching into a peroration about the mystic significance of the number 23 – pointing out that 2 plus 3 equals 5, the pentad within which the Devil can be invoked 'as for example in a pentacle or at the Pentagon building in Washington,' while 2 divided by 3 equals 0.666, 'the Number of The Beast, according to that freaked-out Revelation of Saint John the Mushroom-head,' that 23 itself was present esoterically 'because of its conspicuous exoteric absence' in the number series repre-sented by the Wobbly Hall address, which was 2422 North Halsted – and that the dates of the assassinations of John F. Kennedy and Lee Harvey Oswald, November 22 and 24, also had a conspicuous 23 absent in between them – when he finally was shouted down, the conversation re-turned to a more mundane level.

Half in whimsy and half in despair, Joe decided to per-form one of his chronic acts of faith and convince him-self, at least for a while, that there was some kind of meaning in Simon's ramblings. His equally chronic skepti-cism, he knew, would soon enough reassert itself.

'What the world calls sanity has led us to the present planetary crisis,' Simon had said, 'and insanity is the only viable alternative.' That was a paradox worth some kind of consideration.

'About that 23,' Joe said, approaching Simon tenta-tively after the meeting broke up.

'It's everywhere,' was the instant reply. 'I just started to scratch the surface. All the great anarchists died on the 23rd day of some month or other – Sacco and Vanzetti on August 23, Bonnie Parker and Clyde Barrow on May 23, Dutch on October 23 – and Vince Coll was 23 years old when he was shot *on 23rd Street* – and even though John Dillinger died on the 22nd of July, if you look it up, like I did, in Toland's book, *The Dillinger Days*, you'll find he couldn't get away from the 23 Principle, because 23 other people died that night in Chicago, too, all from heat pros-tration. "Nova heat moving in," dig? And the world began on October 23, in 4004 B.C., according to Bishop Usher, and the Hungarian Revolution started on October 23, too, and Harpo Marx was born on November 23, and—'

There was more of it, much more, and Joe patiently listened to all of it, determined to continue his experiment in applied schizophrenia at least for this one evening. They retired to a nearby restaurant, the Seminary, on Fullerton Street, and Simon rambled on, over beers, proceeding to the mystic significance of the letter W - 23rd in the alphabet - and its presence in the words 'woman' and 'womb' as well as in the shape of the feminine breasts and spread-eagled legs of the copulating female. He even found some mystic meaning in the W in Washington, but was strangely evasive about explicating this.

'So, you see,' Simon was explaining when the restaurant was starting to close, 'the whole key to liberation is magic. Anarchism remains tied to politics, and remains a form of death like all other politics, until it breaks free from the defined *"reality"* of capitalist society and creates its own reality. A pig for President. Acid in the water supply. Fucking in the streets. Making the totally impossible become the eternally possible. Reality is thermoplastic, not thermosetting, you know: I mean you can reprogram it much more than people realize. The hex hoax – original sin, logical positivism, those restriction and constriction myths – all that's based on a thermosetting reality. Christ, man, there are limits, of course – nobody is nutty enough to deny *that* – but the limits are nowhere near as rigid as we've been taught to believe. It's much closer to the truth to say there are no practical limits at all and reality is whatever people decide to make it. But we've been on one restriction kick after another for a couple thousand years now, the world's longest head-trip, and it takes real negative entropy to shake up the foundations. This isn't shit; I've got a degree in mathematics, man.'

'I studied engineering myself, a long time ago.' Joe said. 'I realize that part of what you say is true. . . .'

'It's all true. The land belongs to the landlords, right now, because of magic. People worship the deeds in the government offices, and they won't dare move onto a square of ground if one of the deeds says somebody else owns it. It's a head-trip, a kind of magic, and you need the opposite magic to lift the curse. You need shock elements to break up and disorganize the chains of command in the brain, the "mind-forg'd manacles" that Blake wrote about. That's the unpredictable elements, dads: the erratic, the erotic, the Eristic. Tim Leary said it: "People have to go out of their minds before they can come to their senses." They can't feel and touch and smell the real earth, man, as long as the manacles in the cortex tell them it belongs to somebody else. If you don't want to call it magic, call it counter-conditioning, but the principle is the same. Breaking up the trip society laid on us and starting our own trip. Bringing back old realities that are supposed to be dead. Creating new realities. Astrology, demons, lifting poetry off of the written page into the acts of your daily life. Surrealism, dig? Antonin Artaud and André Breton put it in a nutshell in the First Surrealist Manifesto: *"total transformation of mind, and all that resembles it."* They knew all about the Illuminated Lodge, founded in Munich in 1923, and that it controlled Wall Street *and* Hitler *and* Stalin, through witchcraft. We gotta get into witchcraft ourselves to undo the hex they've cast on everybody's mind. All hail Discordia! Do you read me?'

When they finally parted, and Joe headed back for his hotel, the spell ended. I've been listening to a spaced-out acid-head all night, Joe thought in his cab headed south toward the Loop, and almost managing to believe him. If I keep on with this little experiment, I *will* believe him. And that's how insanity always begins: you find reality unbearable and start manufacturing a fantasy alternative. With an effort of will, he forced himself back into his usual framework; no matter how cruel reality was, Joe Malik would face it and would not follow the Yippies and Crazies in the joy ride to Cloud Cuckoo Land.

But when he arrived at his hotel door, and noticed for the first time that he had Room 23, he had to fight the impulse to call Simon on the phone and tell him about the latest invasion of surrealism into the real world.

And he lay awake in his bed for hours remembering 23s that had occurred in his own life . . . and wondering about the origin of that mysterious bit of 1929 slang, '23 Skidoo. . . .'

After being lost for an hour in Hitler's old neighborhood, Clark Kent and His Supermen finally found *Ludwigstrasse* and got out of Munich. 'About forty miles and we'll be in Ingolstadt,' Kent-Mohammed-Pearson said. '*At last,*' one of the Supermen groaned. Just then a tiny Volkswagen

inched past their VW bus, like an infant running ahead of
its mother, and Kent looked bemused. 'Did you check out
that cat at the wheel? I saw him once before, and never
forgot it because he was acting so weird. It was in Mexico
City. Funny seeing him again, halfway around the world
and umpteen years later.' 'Go catch him,' another Superman commented. 'With the AMA and the Trashers and
other heavy groups we're going to get buried alive. Let's
make sure that at least *he* knows we were in Ingolstadt
for this gig.'

JUST LIKE A TREE THAT'S STANDING BY THE WAAAAAAATER

The morning after the Wobbly meeting Simon tele-
phoned Joe.

'Listen,' he asked, 'do you have to fly back to New
York today? Can you possibly stay over a night? I've got
something I'd like you to see. It's time we started reaching
people in your generation and really showing you instead
of just telling you. Are you game?'

And Joe Malik – ex-Trotskyist, ex-engineering student,
ex-liberal, ex-Catholic – heard himself saying, 'Yes.' And
heard a louder voice, unspeaking, uttering a more profound
'yes' deep inside himself. He was game – for astrology,
for *I Ching*, for LSD, for demons, for whatever Simon
had to offer as an alternative to the world of sane and
rational men who were sanely and rationally plotting their
course toward what could only be the annihilation of the
planet.

(WE SHALL NOT BE MOVED)

'God is dead,' the priest chanted.

'God is dead,' the congregation repeated in chorus.

'God is dead: we are all absolutely free,' the priest in-
toned more rhythmically.

'God is dead,' the congregation picked up the almost
hypnotic beat. 'we are all absolutely free.'

Joe shifted nervously in his chair. The blasphemy was
exhilarating, but also strangely disturbing. He wondered
how much fear of Hell still lingered in the back corridors
of his skull, left over from his Catholic boyhood.

They were in an elegant apartment, high above Lake
Shore Drive – 'We always meet here,' Simon had explained, 'because of the acrostic significance of the street

name' – and the sounds of the automobile traffic far below mingled strangely with the preparations for what Joe already guessed was a black Mass.

'Do what thou wilt shall be the whole of the law,' the priest chanted.

'Do what thou wilt shall be the whole of the law,' Joe repeated with the rest of the congregation.

The priest – who was the only one who had not removed his clothes before the beginning of the ceremony – was a slightly red-faced middle-aged man in a Roman collar, and part of Joe's discomfort derived from the fact that he looked so much like every Catholic priest he had known in his childhood. It had not helped matters that he had given his name, when Simon introduced Joe to him, as 'Padre Pederastia' – which he pronounced with a very campy inflection, looking flirtatiously directly in Joe's eyes.

The congregation divided, in Joe's mind, into two easily distinguishable groups: poor full-time hippies, from the Old Town area, and rich part-time hippies, from Lake Shore Drive itself and, no doubt, also from the local advertising agencies on Michigan Avenue. There were only eleven of them, however, including Joe, and Padre Pederastia made twelve – where was the traditional thirteenth?

'Prepare the pentad,' Padre Pederastia commanded.

Simon and a rather good-looking young female, both quite unself-conscious in their nakedness, arose and left the group, walking toward the door which Joe had assumed led to the bedroom area. They stopped to take some chalk from the table on which hashish and sandalwood incense were burning in a goat's-head taper, then squatted to draw a large pentagon on the blood-red rug. A triangle was then added to each side of the pentagon, forming a star – the special kind of star, Joe knew, which was known as pentagram, symbol of werewolves and also of demons. He found himself remembering the corny old poem from the Lon Chaney, Jr., movies, but it suddenly didn't sound like kitsch anymore:

> Even a man who is pure of heart
> And says his prayers by night
> Can turn to a wolf when the wolfbane blooms
> And the autumn moon is bright

'I-O,' the priest chanted raptly.

'I-O,' the chorus came,

'I-O, E-O, Evoe,' the chant rose weirdly.

'I-O, E-O, Evoe,' the rhythmic reply came in cadence.

Joe felt a strange, ashy, acrid taste gathering in his mouth, and a coldness creeping into his toes and fingers. The air, too, seemed suddenly greasy and unpleasantly, mucidly moist.

'I-O, E-O, Evoe, HE!' the priest screamed, in fear or in ecstasy.

'I-O, E-O, Evoe, HE!' Joe heard himself joining the others. Was it imagination, or were all their voices subtly changing, in a bestial and pongoid fashion?

'Ol sonuf vaoresaji,' the priest said, more softly.

'Ol sonuf vaoresaji,' they chorused.

'It is accomplished,' the priest said. 'We may pass the Guardian.'

The congregation arose and moved toward the door. Each person, Joe noticed, was careful to step into the pentagram and pause there a moment gathering strength before actually approaching the door. When it was his turn, he discovered why. The carving on the door, which had seemed merely obscene and ghoulish from across the room, was more disturbing when you were closer to it. It was not easy – to convince yourself that those eyes were just a trick of *trompe l'oeil*. The mind insisted on feeling that they very definitely looked at you, not affectionately, as you passed.

This – *thing* – was the Guardian which had to be pacified before they could enter the next room.

Joe's fingers and toes were definitely freezing, and auto-suggestion didn't seem a very plausible explanation. He seriously wondered about the possibility of frostbite. But then he stepped into the pentagram and the cold suddenly decreased, the eyes of the Guardian were less menacing, and a feeling of renewed energy flowed through his body, such as he had experienced in a sensitibity-training session after he had been cajoled by the leader into unleashing a great deal of pent-up anxiety and rage by kicking, screaming, weeping, and cursing.

He passed the Guardian easily and entered the room where the real action would occur.

It was as if he had left the twentieth century. The furnishings and the very architecture were Hebraic, Arabic, and medieval European, all mixed together in a most disorienting way, and entirely unrelieved by any trace of the modern or functional.

A black-draped altar stood in the center, and upon it lay the thirteenth member of the coven. She was a woman with red hair and green eyes – the traits which Satan supposedly relished most in mortal females. (There had been a time, Joe remembered, when any woman having those features was automatically suspected of witchcraft.) She was, of course, naked, and her body would be the medium through which this strange sacrament would be attempted.

What am I doing here? Joe thought frantically. *Why don't I leave these lunatics and get back to the world I know, the world where all the horrors are, after all, merely human?*

But he knew the answer.

He could not – literally could not – attempt to pass the Guardian until all those present gave their consent.

Padre Pederastia was speaking. 'This part of the ceremony,' he said, camping outrageously, 'is very distasteful to me, as you all know. If only Our Father Below would allow us to substitute a boy on the altar when I'm officiating – but, alas, He is, as we all know, very rigid about such things. As usual, therefore, I will ask the newest member to take my place for this rite.'

Joe knew, from the *Malleus malificarum* and other grimoires, what the rite was, and he was both excited and frightened.

He approached the altar nervously, noting the others forming a pentagon around the nude woman and himself. She had a lovely body with large breasts and fine nipples, but he was still too nervous to become aroused physically.

Padre Pederastia handed him the Host. 'I stole this from the church myself,' he whispered. 'You can be sure it is fully consecrated and completely potent. You know what to do?'

Joe nodded, unable to meet the priest's lascivious eyes.

He took the Host and spat upon it quickly.

The greasiness and electrically charged quality of the air seemed to increase sharply. The light seemed harsher, like the glint of a sword, just as schizophrenics often described light as a hostile or destructive force.

He stepped forward and placed the Host upon the thighs of the Bride of Satan.

Immediately, she moaned softly, as if the simple touch were more erotic than one momentary contact could possibly be. Her legs spread voluptuously and the middle of the Host crumpled as it sunk slightly into her red pubic hair. The effect was, at once, powerful; her whole body shuddered and the Host was drawn farther into her obviously moist cunt. Using his finger, Joe pushed it the rest of the way in, and she began breathing in a hoarse staccato rhythm.

Joe Malik knelt to complete the rite. He felt like a fool and a pervert; he had never performed oral sex, or any kind of sex, in front of an audience before. He wasn't even turned on erotically. He went ahead just to find out if there was any real magic in this revolting lunacy.

As soon as his tongue entered her, she began heaving and he knew her first orgasm would arrive rapidly. His penis finally began swelling; he began licking the Host caressingly. Inside his temple, a drum seemed to be beating hollowly; he hardly noticed it when she came. His senses spun and he licked more, aware only that she flowed more heavily and thickly than any woman he had known. He put his thumb in her anus, and his middle finger in her vagina, keeping his tongue in the clitoral area, doing it up right – this was the technique occultists call the Rite of Shiva. (Irreverently, he remembered that swingers call it the One-Man Band.) He felt an unusual electrical quality in her pubic hair and was aware of a heaviness and tension in his penis more powerful than he had ever known in his life, but all else was drowned out by the drumming in his head, the cunt-taste, cunt-smell, cunt-warmth. . . . She was Ishtar, Aphrodite, Venus; the experience was so intense he began to feel a real religious dimension to it. Hadn't some nineteenth century anthropologist argued that cunt-worship was the earliest religion? He didn't even know this woman and yet he had an emotion beyond love: true reverence. *Trippy*, as Simon would say.

How many times she came, he never knew; he came

himself, without once touching his penis, when the Host was finally dissolved.

He staggered back dizzily, and the air now seemed as resistant to motion as brackish water.

'Yogge Sothothe Neblod Zin,' the priest began chanting. 'By Ashtoreth, by Pan Pangenitor, by the Yellow Sign, by the gifts I have made and the powers I have purchased, by He Who Is Not to Be Named, by Rabban and by Azathoth, by Samma-El, by Amon and Ra, *vente, vente, Lucifer, lux fiat!*'

Joe never saw it: he *felt* it – and it was like chemical Mace, blinding and numbing him at once.

'Come not in that form!' the priest screamed. 'By Jesu Elohim and the Powers that You fear, I command thee: come not in that form! *Yod He Vah He* – come not in that form.'

One of the women began weeping in fear.

'Quiet, you fool,' Simon shouted at her. 'Don't give it more Power.'

'Your tongue is bound, until I release it,' the priest said to her – but the distraction of his attention had its cost; Joe *felt* It growing in potency again, and so did the others, judging from their sudden involuntary gasps.

'*Come not in that form!*' the priest shouted. 'By the Cross of Gold, and by the Rose of Ruby, and by Mary's Son, I command and demand it of thee: come not in that form! By thy Master, Chronzon! By Pangenitor and Panphage, come not in that form!'

There was a hiss, like air pouring into a vacuum, and the atmosphere began to clear – but it also dropped abruptly in temperature.

MASTER, CALL NO MORE UPON THOSE NAMES. I MEANT NOT TO ALARM THEE.

The Voice was the most shocking experience of the night for Joe. It was oily, flattering, obscenely humble, but there was still within it a secret strength that revealed all too well that the priest's power over it, however obtained, was temporary, that both of them knew it, and that the price of that power was something it longed to collect.

'Come not in that form either,' said the priest, more stern and more confident. 'Ye know full well that such tones and manners are also intended to frighten, and I like

not such jokes. Come in this form which thou habitually
wearest in thy current earthly activities, or I shall banish
thee back to that realm of which you like not to imagine.
I command. I command. I command.' There was nothing
campy about the Padre now.

It was just a room again – an odd, medieval, mideastern
room, but just a room. The figure that stood among them
could not have looked less like a demon.

'OK,' it said in a pleasant American voice, 'we don't
have to get touchy and hostile with each other over a little
theatrics, do we? Just tell me what sort of business transaction you went and dragged me here for, and I'm sure
we can work out all the details in a down-home, business-
like, cards-on-the-table fashion, with no hard feelings and
mutual satisfaction all around.'

It looked like Billy Graham.

('The Kennedys? Martin Luther King? You are fantas-
tically naive still, George. It goes back much, much farther.' Hagbard was relaxing with some Alamont Black
hash, after the Battle of Atlantis. 'Look at the pictures of
Woodrow Wilson in his last months: The haggard look,
the vague eyes, and, in fact, symptoms of a certain slow-
acting and undetectable poison. They slipped it to him at
Versailles. Or look into the Lincoln caper. Who opposed
the greenback plan – the closest thing to flaxscript America
ever had? Stanton the banker. Who ordered all roads out
of Washington closed, except one? Stanton the banker.
And Booth went straight for that road. Who got ahold of
Booth's diary afterward? Stanton the banker. And turned
it over to the Archives with seventeen pages missing?
Stanton the banker. George, you have so much to learn
about real history. . . .')

The Reverend William Helmer, religious columnist for
Confrontation, stared at the telegram. Joe Malik was supposed to be in Chicago covering the SDS convention;
what was he doing in Providence, Rhode Island, and what
was he involved in that could provoke such an extraordinary communication? Helmer reread the telegram carefully:

Drop next month's column. Will pay large bonus for
prompt answers to these questions. First, trace all
movements of Reverend Bill Graham during last week

and find out if he could possibly have gotten to Chicago surreptitiously. Second, send me a list of reliable books on Satanism and witchcraft in the modern world. Tell nobody else on the magazine about this. Wire me c/o Jerry Mallory, Hotel Benefit, Providence, Rhode Island. P.S. find out where The John Dillinger Died for You Society has its headquarters. Joe Malik.

Those SDS kids must have turned him on with acid, Helmer decided. Well, he was still the boss, and he paid nice bonuses when he was pleased. Helmer reached for the phone.

(Howard, the dolphin, was singing a very satirical song about sharks, as he swam to meet the *Lief Erikson* at Peos.)

James Walking Bear had no great love for palefaces most of the time, but he had just dropped six peyote buttons before this Professor Mallory arrived and he was feeling benevolent and forgiving. After all, the Road Chief once said at a very sacred midsummer peyote festival that the line about forgiving *those who trespass against us* had a special meaning for Indians. Only when we all forgave the whites, he had said, would our hearts be totally pure, and when our hearts were pure the Curse would be lifted – the white men would cease to trespass, go home to Europe, and vex one another instead of persecuting us. James tried to forgive the professor for being white and found, as usual, that peyote made forgiveness easier.

'Billie Freschette?' he said. 'Hell, she died back in sixty-eight.'

'I know that,' the professor said. 'What I'm looking for is any photographs she may have left.'

Sure. James knew what kind of photographs.

'You mean ones that had Dillinger in them?'

'Yes, she was his mistress, virtually his common-law wife, for a long time, and—'

'No soap. You're years too late. Reporters bought up everything she had that showed even the back of Dillinger's head, way back, long before she came here to the reservation to die.'

'Well, did you know her?'

'Sure.' James was careful not to be spiteful and didn't

add: all Menominee Indians know one another, in a way you whites can't understand 'knowing.'

'Did she ever converse about Dillinger?'

'Of course. Old women always talk about their dead men. Always say the same thing, too: never was another man as good as him. Except when they say there never was another man as bad as him. They only say that when they're drunk, though.'

The paleface kept turning colors, the way people do when you're on peyote. Now he looked almost like an Indian. That made it easier to talk to him.

'Did she ever say anything about John's attitude toward the Masons?'

Why shouldn't people turn colors? All the trouble in world came from the fact that they usually stayed the same color. James nodded profoundly. As usual, peyote had brought him a big Truth. If whites and blacks and Indians were turning colors all the time, there wouldn't be any hate in the world, because nobody would know which people to hate.

'I said, did she ever mention John's attitude toward the Masons?'

'Oh. Oh, yes. Funny you should ask that.' The man had a halo around his head now, and James wondered what that meant. Every time he took peyote alone things like that would happen, and he'd end up wishing there were a Road Chief or some other priest around to explain these signs properly. But what about the Masons? Oh, yes. 'Billie said the Masons were the only people John Dillinger really hated. He said they railroaded him to prison the first time, and they owned all the banks, so he was getting even by robbing them.'

The professor's mouth dropped open in surprise and delight – and James thought it was kind of funny to see that, especially with the halo turning from pink to blue to pink to blue to pink again at the same time.

('*A big mouth, a tiny brain/He only thinks of blood and pain*,' Howard sang.)

Notes found by a TWA stewardess in a seat vacated by a Mr. 'John Mason' after a Madison, Wisconsin, to Mexico City flight June 29, 1969: one week after the last SDS convention of all time:

'*We only robbed from the banks what the banks robbed from the people*' – Dillinger, Crown Point Jail, 1934. Could have come from any anarchist text.

Lucifer – bringer of light.

Weishaupt's 'illumination' & Voltaire's 'enlightenment': from the Latin 'lux' meaning light.

Christianity all in 3s (Trinity, etc.) Buddhism in 4s. Illuminism in 5s. A progression?

Hopi teaching: all men have 4 souls now, but in future will have 5 souls. Find an anthropologist for more data on this.

Who decided the Pentagon building should have that particular shape?

'Kick out the Jams'??? Cross-check.

'Adam,' the first man; 'Weis,' to know; 'haupt,' chief or leader. 'The first man to be a leader of those who know.' Assumed name from the beginning?

Iok-Sotot in Pnakotic manuscripts. Cd. be Yog-Sothoth?

D.E.A.T.H. – Don't Ever Antagonize The Horn. Does Pynchon know?

Must get Simon to explain the Yellow Sign and the Aklo chants. Might need protection.

C. says the h. neophobe type outnumber us 1000-to-1. If so, all this is hopeless.

What gets me is how much has been out in the open for so long. Not just in Lovecraft, Joyce, Melville, etc., or in the Bugs Bunny cartoons but in scholarly works that pretend to explain. Anybody who wants to go to the trouble can find out, for instance, that the 'secret' of the Eleusinian Mysteries was the words whispered to the novice after he got the magic mushroom: 'Osiris is a black God!' Five words (of course!) but no historian, archeologist, anthropologist, folklorist, etc. has understood. Or, those who did understand, didn't care to admit it.

Can I trust C.? For that matter, can I trust Simon?

This matter of Tlaloc should convince me, one way or the other.

('He only thinks of blood and slaughter/The shark should live on land not water.')

('To hell with the shark and all his kin/And fight like hell when you see his fin.')

When Joe Malik got off the plane at Los Angeles International Airport, Simon was waiting for him.

'We'll talk in your car,' Joe said briefly.

The car, being Simon's, was naturally a psychedelic Volkswagen. 'Well?' he asked as they drove out of the airport onto Central Avenue.

'It all checks out,' Joe said with an odd calm. 'It did rain blue cats when they dug up Tlaloc. Mexico City has had unusual and unseasonable rains ever since. The missing tooth was on the right, and the corpse at the Biograph Theatre had a missing tooth on the left. Billy Graham couldn't have gotten to Chicago by any normal means, so that was either the best damned makeup job in the history of show business and plastic surgery or I witnessed a genuine miracle. And all the rest of it, the law of Fives and all. I'm sold. I no longer claim membership in the liberal intellectual guild. You behold in me a horrible example of creeping mysticism.'

'Ready to try acid?'

'Yes,' Joe said. 'I'm ready to try acid. I only regret that I have but one mind to lose for my Shivadarshana.'

'Right on! First, though, you'll meet *him*. I'll drive right to his bungalow – it's not far from here.' Simon began humming as he drove; Joe recognized the tune as the Fugs' 'Rameses II Is Dead, My Love.'

They drove for a while in silence, and Joe finally asked, 'How old is . . . our little group . . . exactly?'

'Since 1888.' Simon said. 'That's when Rhodes horned in and they "kicked out the Jams," like I told you in Chicago after the Sabbath.'

'And Karl Marx?'

'A schmuck. A dupe. A nebbish from the word Go.' Simon made an abrupt turn. 'Here we are at his house. The greatest headache they had since Harry Houdini knocked out their spiritualist fronts.' He grinned. 'How do you think you'll feel talking to a dead man?'

'Weird,' Joe said, 'but I've felt weird for the last week and a half.'

Simon parked the car and held the door open. 'Just think,' he said. 'Hoover sitting there every day with the death-mask on his desk, and half-suspecting, deep down in his bones, how we suckered him.'

They crossed the yard of the small, modest bungalow.
'What a front, eh?' Simon chuckled. He knocked.

A little old man – he was five foot seven exactly, Joe
remembered from the FBI files – opened the door.

'Here's our new recruit,' Simon said simply.

'Come in,' John Dillinger said, 'and tell me how an
asshole egghead like you can help us beat the shit out of
those motherfucking Illuminati cocksuckers.'

('They fill their books with obscene words, claiming that
this is realism,' Smiling Jim shouted to the KCUF assembly. 'It's not my idea of realism. I don't know anybody
who talks in that gutter language they call realism. And
they describe every possible perversion, acts against nature
that are so outrageous I wouldn't sully this audiences' ears
by even mentioning their medical names. Some of them
even glorify the criminal and the anarchist. I'd like to see
one of these hacks come up to me and look me in the eye
and say, "I didn't do it for money. I was honestly trying
to tell a good, honest story that would teach people something of value." They couldn't say that. The lie would stick
in their throats. Who can doubt where they get their orders
from? What person in this audience needs to be told what
group is behind this overflowing sewer of smut and filth?')

*May storms and rains and typhoons beat them,' Howard
sang on. 'May Great Cthulhu rise and eat them.'*

'I got into the JAMs in Michigan City Prison,' Dillinger,
much relaxed and less arrogant, was saying as he, Simon,
and Joe sat in his living room drinking Black Russians.

'And Hoover knew, from the beginning?' Joe asked.

'Of course. I wanted the bastards to know – him and
every other high-ranking Mason and Rosicrucian and Illuminati front-man in the country.' The old man laughed
harshly; except for his unmistakable eyes, which still held
the strange blend of irony and intensity that Joe had noted
in the 1930s photos, he was indistinguishable from any
other elderly fellow who had come to California to enjoy
his last years in the sun. 'The first bank job I pulled off,
in Daleville, Indiana, I used the line that I always repeated:
"Lie down on the floor and keep calm." Hoover couldn't
miss it. That's been the motto of the JAMs ever since
Diogenes the Cynic. He knew no ordinary bank robber
would be quoting an obscure Greek philosopher. The

reason I repeated it on every heist was just to rub it in
and let him know I was taunting him.'

'But going back to Michigan City Prison . . .' Joe
prompted, sipping his drink.

'Pierpont was the one who initiated me. He'd been with
the JAMs for years by then. I was just a kid, you know
– in my early twenties – and I had only pulled one job, a
real botch. I couldn't understand why I got such a stiff
sentence, after the D.A. promised me clemency if I'd plead
guilty, and I was kind of bitter. But old Harry Pierpont
saw my potential.

'At first I thought he was just another big-house faggot,
when he started tracking me around and asking me all
sorts of personal questions. But he was what I wanted to
become – a successful bank-robber – so I played along. To
tell you the truth, I was so horny it wouldn't have mattered
if he was a faggot. You have no idea how horny a man gets
in prison. That's why Baby-Face Nelson and a lot of other
guys preferred to die rather than go back to the big house
again. Hell, if you haven't been there, you can't understand. You just don't know what being horny *is*.

'Well, anyway, after a lot of bull about Jesus and
Jehovah and the Bible and all that, Harry just asked me
point-blank one day in the prison yard: "Do you think
it's possible there might be a true religion?" I was about
to say, "Bullshit – like there might be an honest cop," but
something stopped me. I realized he was dead serious, and
a lot might depend on my answer. So I was cautious. I
said, "If there is, I haven't heard about it." And he just
came back, real quiet, "Most people haven't."

'It was a couple of days afterward that he brought the
subject up again. Then, he went right on with it, showed
me the Sacred Chao and everything. It took my breath
away.' The old man's voice trailed off, as he sank into silent
memories.

'And it really does go back to Babylon?' Joe prompted.

'I'm not much of an intellectual,' Dillinger replied.
'Action is my arena. Let Simon tell you that part.'

Simon was eager to leap into the breach. 'The basic book
to confirm our tradition,' he said, 'is *The Seven Tablets of
Creation*, which is dated at about 2500 B.C. the time of Sargon. It describes how Tiamat and Apsu, the first gods,

were coexisting in Mummu, the primordial chaos. Von Junzt, in his *Unausprechilchen Kulten*, tells how the Justified Ancients of Mummu originated, just about the time the *Seven Tablets* were inscribed. You see, under Sargon, the chief deity was Marduk. I mean, that was what the high priests gave out to the public – in private, of course, they worshipped Iok-Sotot, who became the Yog-Sothoth of the *Necronomicon*. But maybe I'm going too fast. Getting back to the official religion of Marduk, it was based on usury. The priests monopolized the medium of exchange and were able to extract interest for lending it. They also monopolized the land, and extracted tribute for renting it. It was the beginning of what we laughingly call civilization, which has always rested on rent and interest. The old Babylonian con.

'The official story was that Mummu was dead, killed in the war between the gods. When the first anarchist group arose, they called themselves Justified Ancients of Mummu. Like Lao-Tse and the Taoists in China, they wanted to get rid of usury and monopoly and all the other pigshit of civilization and go back to a natural way of life. So, grok, they took the supposedly dead god, Mummu, and claimed he was still alive and was actually stronger than all the other gods. They had a good argument. "Look around," they'd say, "what do you see most of? Chaos, right? Therefore, the god of Chaos is the strongest god, and is still alive."

'Of course, we got our ass whipped good. We were just no match for the Illuminati in those days. Didn't have a clue about how they performed their "miracles," for instance. So we got our asses whipped again, in Greece, when the JAMs got started again, as part of the Cynic movement. By the time the whole thing was happening again in Rome – usury and monopoly and the whole bag of tricks – the truce took place. The Justified Ancients became part of the Illuminati, a special group still keeping our own name, but taking orders from the Five. We thought we'd humanize them, like the anarchists who stayed in SDS after last year. And so it went until 1888. Then Cecil Rhodes started the Circle of Initiates and the big schism occurred. Every meeting would have a faction of Rhodes boys carrying signs that said "Kick out the

JAMs!" It was the parting of the ways. They just didn't trust us – or maybe they were afraid of being humanized.

'But we had learned a lot by our long participation in the Illuminati conspiracy, and now we know how to fight them with their own weapons.'

'Fuck their weapons,' Dillinger interrupted. 'I like to fight them with *my* weapons.'

'You *are* behind the big unsolved bank robberies of the last few years—'

'Sure. Just in the planning, though. I'm too old to vault over tellers' cages and carry on like I did back in the thirties.'

'John is also fighting on another front,' Simon interjected.

Dillinger laughed. 'Yes,' he said. 'I'm the president of Laughing Buddha Jesus Phallus Inc. You've seen them – "If it's not an LBJP it's NOT an L.P."?'

'Laughing Buddha Jesus Phallus?' Joe exclaimed. 'My God, you put out the best rock in the country! The only rock a man my age can listen to without wincing.'

'Thanks,' Dillinger said modestly. 'Actually, the Illuminati own the companies that put out *most* of the rock. We started Laughing Buddha Jesus Phallus to counter-attack. We were ignoring that front until they got the MC-5 to cut a disc called "Kick Out The Jams" just to taunt us with old, bitter memories. So we came back with our own releases, and the next thing I knew I was making bales of money from it. We've also fed information, through third parties, to Christian Crusade in Tulsa, Oklahoma, so they could expose some of what the Illuminati are doing in the rock field. You've seen the Christian Crusade publications – *Rhythm, Riots and Revolution*, and *Communism, Hypnotism and the Beatles*, and so forth?'

'Yes,' Joe said absently. 'I thought it was nut literature. It's so hard,' he added, 'to grasp the whole picture.'

'You'll get used to it,' Simon smiled. 'It just takes awhile to sink in.'

'Who really did shoot John Kennedy?' Joe asked.

'I'm sorry,' Dillinger said. 'You're only a private in our army right now. Not cleared for that kind of information yet. I'll just tell you this much: his initials are H.C. – so don't trust anybody with those initials, no matter where or how you meet him.'

'He's being fair,' Simon told Joe. 'You'll appreciate it later.'

'And advancement is rapid,' Dillinger added, 'and the rewards are beyond your present understanding.'

'Give him a hint, John,' Simon suggested with an anticipatory grin. 'Tell him how you got out of Crown Point Jail.'

'I've read two versions of that,' Joe said. 'Most of the sources claim you carved a fake gun out of balsa wood and dyed it black with your shoe polish. Toland's book says that you made that story up and leaked it out to protect the man who really managed the break for you – a federal judge that you bribed to smuggle in a real gun. Which was it?'

'Neither,' Dillinger said. 'Crown Point was known as the "escape-proof jail" before I crashed out of it, and, believe me, it deserved the name. Do you want to know how I did it? I walked through the walls. Listen. . . .'

HARE KRISHNA HARE HARE

The sun beat down on the town of Daleville on July 17, 1933, like a rain of fire.

Motoring down the main street, John Dillinger felt the perspiration on his neck. Although he had been paroled three weeks earlier, he was still pale from his nine years in prison, and the sunlight was cruel on his almost albino-tinted skin.

I'm going to have to walk through that door all by myself, he thought. All alone.

And fighting every kind of fear and guilt that has been beaten into me from childhood on.

'The spirit or Mummu is stronger than the Illuminati's technology,' Pierpont had said. 'Remember that. We've got the Second Law of Thermodynamics on our side. Chaos steadily increases, all over the universe. All "law and order" is a kind of temporary accident.'

But I've got to walk through that door all alone. The Secret of the Five depends on it. This time it's my turn to be the goat.

Pierpont and Van Meter and the others were still back in Michigan City Prison. It was all in his hands – being the first one paroled, he had to raise the money to finance the jail-break that would get the others out. Then, having proved himself, he would be taught the JAM 'miracles.'

The bank suddenly loomed before him. Too suddenly. His heart skipped a beat.

Then, calmly, he drove his Chevrolet coupe over to the curb and parked.

I should have prepared better. This car should be souped-up like the ones Clyde Barrow uses. Well, I'll know that the next time.

He left his hands on the steering wheel and squeezed, hard. He took a deep breath and repeated the Formula: '23 Skidoo.'

It helped a little – but he still wanted to get the hell out of there. He wanted to drive straight back to his father's farm in Mooresville and find a job and learn all the straight things again, how to kiss a boss's ass and how to look the parole officer straight in the eye and be like everybody else.

But everybody else was an Illuminati puppet and didn't know it. He did know it and was going to liberate himself.

Hell, that's what a younger John Dillinger thought back in 1924 – except that he hadn't known about the Illuminati or the JAMs then – but he was trying to liberate himself, in his own way, when he held up that grocer. And what did it lead to? Nine years of misery and monotony and almost going mad with horniness in a stinking cell.

It'll be nine years more if I fuck up today.

'The spirit of Mummu is stronger than the Illuminati's technology.'

He got out of the car and forced his feet and legs to move and he walked straight for the bank door.

'Fuck it,' he said, '23 Skidoo.'

He walked through the door – and then he did the thing the bank tellers remembered after and told the police. He reached up and adjusted his straw hat to the most dapper and debonair angle – and he grinned.

'All right, this is a stick-up,' he said clearly, taking out his pistol. 'Everybody lie down on the floor and keep calm. None of you will get hurt.'

'Oh, God,' a female teller gasped, 'don't shoot. Please don't shoot.'

'Don't worry, honey,' John Dillinger said easily, 'I don't want to hurt anybody. Just open the vault.'

LIKE A TREE THAT'S PLANTED BY THE WATER

'That afternoon,' the old man said, 'I met Calvin Coolidge in the woods near my father's farm at Mooresville. I gave him the haul – twenty thousand dollars – and it went into the JAM treasury. He gave me twenty tons of hempscript.'

'Calvin Coolidge?' Joe Malik exclaimed.

'Well, of course, I knew it wasn't really Calvin Coolidge. But that was the form he chose to appear in. Who or what he really is, I haven't learned yet.'

'You met him in Chicago,' Simon added gleefully. 'He appeared as Billy Graham that time.'

'You mean the Dev—'

'Satan,' Simon said simply 'is just another of the innumerable masks he wears. Behind the mask is a man and behind the man is another mask. It's all a matter of merging multiverses, remember? Don't look for an Ultimate Reality. There isn't any.'

'Then this person – this being –' Joe protested, 'really is supernatural—'

'Supernatural, schmupernatural,' Simon grimaced. 'You're still like the people in that mathematical parable about Flatland. You can only think in categories of right and left, and I'm talking about up and down, so you say "supernatural." There is no "supernatural"; there are just more dimensions than you are accustomed to, that's all. If you were living in Flatland and I stepped out of your plane into a plane at a different angle, it would look to you as if I vanished "into thin air." Somebody looking down from our three-dimensional viewpoint would see me going off at a tangent from you, and would wonder why you were acting so distressed and surprised about it.'

'But the flash of light—'

'It's an energy transformation,' Simon explained patiently. 'Look, the reason you can only think three-dimensionally is because there are only three directions in cubical space. That's why the Illuminati – and some of the kids they've allowed to become partially illuminized lately – refer to ordinary science as "square." The basic energy-vector coordinates of Universe are five-dimensional – of course – and can best be visualized in terms of the five sides of the Illuminati Pyramid of Egypt.'

'Five sides?' Joe objected. 'It only has four.'

'You're ignoring the bottom.'

'Oh. Go on.'

'Energy is always triangular, not cubical. Bucky Fuller has a line on this, by the way: he's the first one outside the Illuminati to discover it independently. The basic energy transformation we're concerned with is the one Fuller hasn't discovered yet, although he's said he's looking for it – the one that ties Mind into the matter-energy continuum. The pyramid is the key. You take a man in the lotus position and draw lines from his pineal gland – the Third Eye, as the Buddhists call it – to his two knees, and from each knee to the other, and this is what you get. . . .' Simon sketched rapidly in his notepad and passed it over to Joe:

PINEAL EYE (closed) → MAN MEDITATING   PINEAL EYE (opened) → ENERGY FIELD

'When the Pineal Eye opens – after fear is conquered; that is, after your first Bad Trip – you can control the energy field entirely,' Simon went on. 'An Irish Illuminatus of the ninth century, Scotus Ergina, put it very simply – in five words, of course – when he said *Omnia quia sunt, lumina sunt:* "All things that are, are lights." Einstein also put it into five symbols when he wrote $e = mc^2$. The actual transformation doesn't require atomic reactors and all that jazz, once you learn how to control the mind vectors, but it always lets off one hell of a flash of light, as John can tell you.'

'Damn near blinded me and knocked me on my ass, that first time in the woods,' Dillinger agreed. 'But I was sure glad to know the trick. I was never afraid of being arrested after that, 'cause I could always walk out of any jail they put me in. That's why the Feds decided to kill me, you know. It was embarassing to always find me wandering around loose again a few days after they locked me up. You know the background to the Biograph Theatre scam – they killed three guys in Chicago, without giving them a chance to surrender, because they thought I was one of them. Well, those three were all wanted in New York for armed robbery, so nobody criticized the cops much for that caper. But then up in Lake Geneva, Wisconsin, they shot three very respectable businessmen, and one of *them* went and died, and Hoover's Heroes caught all sorts of crap from the newspapers. So I knew where it was at; I could never again surrender and walk away a few days later. We had to produce a body for them.' The old man looked suddenly sad. 'There was one possibility that we hated to think about. . . . But, luckily it didn't come to that. The gimmick we finally worked out was perfect.'

'And everything really follows the Fives' law?' Joe asked.

'More than you guess,' Dillinger remarked blandly.

'Even when you're dealing with social fields,' Simon added. 'We've run studies of cultures where the Illuminati were not in control, and they still follow Weishaupt's five-stage pattern: *Verwirrung, zweitracht, Unordnung, Beamtenherrschaft* and *Grummet.* That is: chaos, discord, confusion, bureaucracy, and aftermath. America right now is between the fourth and fifth stages. Or you might say that the older generation is mostly in *Beamtenherrschaft* and the younger generation is moving into *Grummet* rapidly.'

Joe took another stiff drink and shook his head. 'But why do they leave so much of it out in the open? I mean, not merely the really shocking things you told me about the Bugs Bunny cartoons, but putting the pyramid on the dollar bill where everybody sees it almost every day—'

'Hell,' Simon said, 'look what Beethoven did when Weishaupt illuminated him. Went right home and wrote the Fifth Symphony. You know how it begins: da-da-da-DUM. Morse code for V – the Roman numeral for five. Right out in the open, as you say. It amuses the devil out of them to confirm their low opinion of the rest of humanity by putting things up front like that and watching how almost everybody misses it. Of course, if somebody doesn't miss something, they recruit him right away. Look at Genesis: "lux fiat" – right on the first page. They do it all the time. The Pentagon Building. "23 Skiddo." The lyrics of rock songs like "Lucy in the Sky with Diamonds" – how obvious can you get? Melville was one of the most outrageous of the bunch; the very first sentence of *Moby Dick* tells you he's a disciple of Hassan i Sabbah, but you

can't find a single Melville scholar who has followed up
that lead – in spite of Ahab being a truncated anagram of
Sabbah. He even tells you, again and again, directly and
indirectly, that Moby Dick and Leviathan are the same
creature, and that Moby Dick is often seen at the same
time in two different parts of the world, but not one reader
in a million groks what he's hinting at. There's a whole
chapter on whiteness and why white is really more terrifying than black; *all* the critics miss the point.'

' "Osiris is a black god," ' Joe quoted.

'Right on! You're going to advance fast,' Simon said
enthusiastically. 'In fact, I think it's time for you to get
off the verbal level and really confront your own "Lucy in
the Sky with Diamonds" – your own lady Isis.'

'Yes,' Dillinger said. 'The *Leif Erikson* is laying off-
shore near California right now; Hagbard is running some
hashish to the students at Berkeley. He's got a new black
chick in his crew who plays the Lucy role extremely well.
We'll have him send her ashore for the Rite. I suggest that
you two drive up to the Norton Lodge in Frisco and I'll
arrange for her to meet you there.'

'I don't like dealing with Hagbard,' Simon said. 'He's
a right-wing nut, and so is his whole gang.'

'He's one of the best allies we have against the Illuminati,' Dillinger said. 'Besides, I want to exchange some
hempscript for some of his flaxscript. Right now, the Mad
Dog bunch won't except anything but flaxscript – they
think Nixon is really going to knock the bottom out of the
hemp market. And you know what they do with Federal
Reserve notes. Every time they get one, they burn it. Instant demurrage, they call it.'

'Puerile,' Simon pronounced. 'It will take decades to
undermine the Fed that way.'

'Well,' Dillinger said. 'Those are the kinds of people
we have to deal with. The JAMs can't do it all alone, you
know.'

'Sure,' Simon shrugged. 'But it bugs me.' He stood up
and put his drink on the table.

'Let's go,' he said to Joe. 'You're going to be illuminized.'

Dillinger accompanied them to the door, then leaned
close to Joe and said, 'A word of advice about the Rite.'

'Yes?'

Dillinger lowered his voice. 'Lie down on the floor and keep calm,' he said, and his old, impudent grin flashed wickedly.

Joe stood there looking at the mocking bandit, and it seemed to him a freeze and a frieze in time: a moment that would linger, as another stage of illumination, forever in his mind. Sister Cecilia, back in Resurrection School, spoke out of the abyss of memory: 'Stand in the corner, Joseph Malik!' And he remembered too, the chalk that he crumbled slowly between his fingers, the feeling of needing to urinate, the long wait, and then Father Volpe entering the classroom, his voice like thunder: 'Where is he? Where is the boy who dared to disagree with the good Sister that God sent to instruct him?' And the other children, led out of the classroom and across the street to the church to pray for his soul, while the priest harangued him: 'Do you know how hot hell is? Do you know how hot the worst part of hell is? That's where they send people who have the good fortune to be born into the church and then rebel against it, misled by Pride of Intellect.' *And five years later, those two faces came back: the priest, angry and dogmatic, demanding obedience, and the bandit, sardonic, encouraging cynicism, and Joe understood that he might someday have to kill Hagbard Celine. But more years had to pass and the Fernando Poo incident had to pass, and Joe had to plan the bombing of his own magazine with Tobias Knight before he knew that he would, in fact, kill Celine without compunction if it were necessary. . . .*

But on March 31, in that year of fruition for all the Illuminati's plans, while the President of the United States went on the air to threaten 'all-out thermonuclear heck,' a young lady named Concepcion Galore lay nude on a bed in the Hotel Durrutti in Santa Isobel and said, 'It's a lloigor.'

'What's a lloigor?' asked her companion, an Englishman named Fission Chips, who had been born on Hiroshima Day and named by a father who cared more for physics than for the humanities.

The room was in the luxury suite of the Hotel Durrutti, which meant that it was decorated in abominable Spanish-Moorish decor, the sheets were changed daily (to a less luxurious suite), the cockroaches were minimal, and the plumbing sometimes worked. Concepcion contemplated the bullfight mural on the opposite wall, Manolete turning an elegant *Veronica* on an unconvincingly drawn bull, and said thoughtfully, 'Oh, a lloigor is a god of the black people. The natives. A very bad god.'

Chips glanced at the statue again and said, more to himself than to the peasant girl, 'Looks vaguely like Tlaloc in Mexico City, crossed with one of those Polynesian Cthulhu *tikis.*'

'The Starry Wisdom people are very interested in these statues,' Concepcion said, just to be making conversation, since it was obvious that Chips wasn't going to be ready to prong her again for at least another half hour.

'Indeed?' Chips said, equally bored. 'Who are the Starry Wisdom people?'

'A church. Down on Tequilla y Mota Street. What used to be Lumumba Street and was Franco Street when I was a girl. Funny church.' The girl frowned, thinking about them. 'When I worked in the telegraph office I was always seeing their telegrams. All in code. And never to another church. Always to banks all over Europe and North and South America.'

'You don't say,' drawled Chips, no longer bored but trying to sound casual; his code number in British Intelligence was, of course, 00005. 'Why are they interested in these statues?' He was thinking that statues, properly hollowed out, could transport heroin; he was already sure that Starry Wisdom was a front for BUGGER.

(In 1933, at Harvard, Professor Tochus told his Psychology 101 class, 'Now, the child feels frightened and inferior, according to Adler, because he is, in fact, physically smaller and weaker than the adult. Thus, he knows he has no chance of successful rebellion, but nevertheless he dreams about it. This is the origin of the Oedipus Complex in Adler's system: not sex, but the will to power itself. The class will readily see the influence of Neitzsche . . .' Robert Putney Drake, glancing around the room, was quite sure that most of the students would not readily see *anything*; and Tochus himself didn't really see either. The child, Drake had decided – it was the cornerstone of his own system of psychology – was not brainwashed by sentimentality, religion, ethics, and other bullshit. The child saw clearly that, in every relationship, there is a dominant party and a submissive party. And the child, in its quite correct egotism, determined to become the dominant party. It was that simple; except, of course, that the brainwashing takes effect eventually in most cases and, by about this time, the college years, most of them were ready to become robots and accept the submissive role. Professor Tochus droned on; and Drake, serene in his lack of superego, continued to dream of how he would seize the dominant role. . . . In New York, Arthur Flegenheimer, Drake's psychic twin, stood before seventeen robed figures, one wearing a goat's head mask, and repeated, 'I will forever hele, always conceal, never reveal, any art or arts, part or parts. . . .')

You look like a robot, Joe Malik says in a warped room in a skewered time in San Francisco. *I mean, you move and walk like a robot.*

Hold onto that, Mr. Wabbit, says a bearded young man with a saturnine smile. *Some trippers see themselves as robots. Others see the guide as a robot. Hold that perspective. Is it a hallucination, or is a recognition of something we usually black out?*

Wait, Joe says. *Part of you is like a robot. But part of you is alive, like a growing thing, a tree or a plant. . . .*

The young man continues to smile, his face drifting above his body toward the mandala painted on the ceiling. *Well?* he asks. *Do you think that might be a good poetic shorthand: that part of me is mechanical, like a robot, and part of me is organic, like a rosebush? And what's the difference between the mechanical and the organic? Isn't a rosebush a kind of machine used by the DNA code to produce more rosebushes?*

'*No*, Joe says. *Everything is mechanical, but people are different. A cat has a grace that we've lost, or partly lost.*

How do you think we've lost it?

And Joe sees the face of Father Volpe and hears the voice screaming about submission. . . .

The SAC bases await the presidential order to take off for Fernando Poo, Atlanta Hope addresses a rally in Atlanta, Georgia, protesting the gutless appeasement of the comsymp administration in not threatening to bomb Moscow and Peking the same time as Santa Isobel, the Premier of Russia rereads his speech nervously as the TV cameras are set up in his office ('and, in socialist solidarity with the freedom-loving people of Fernando Poo'), the Chairman of the Chinese Communist party, having found the thought of Chairman Mao of little avail, throws the *I Ching* sticks and looks dismally at Hexagram 23, and 99 percent of the peoples of the world wait for their leaders to tell them what to do; but in Santa Isobel itself, three locked doors across the suite from the now-sleeping Concepcion, Fission Chips says angrily into his shortwave, 'Repeat none. Not one Russian or Chinese anywhere on the bloody island. I don't care what Washington says. I'm telling you what I have seen. Now, about the BUGGER heroin ring here—'

'Sign off,' the submarine tells him. 'HQ is not interested in BUGGER or heroin right now.'

'Damn and blast!' Chips stares at the shortwave set. That bloody well tore it. He would just have to proceed on his own, and show those armchair agents back in London, especially that smug W., how little they actually knew about the real problem in Fernando Poo and the world.

Storming, he charged back to the bedroom. I'll just get dressed, he thought furiously, including my smoke bombs and Luger and laser ray, and toddle over to this Starry Wisdom church and see what I can nose out. But when he tore open the bedroom door he stopped, momentarily stunned. Concepcion still lay in the bed but she was no longer sleeping. Her throat was neatly cut and a curious dagger with a flame design on it stuck into the pillow beside her.

'Damn, blast and thunder!' cried 00005. 'Now that absolutely does tear it. Every time I find a good piece of ass those fuckers from BUGGER come along and shaft her!'

Ten minutes later, the GO signal came from the White House, a fleet of SAC bombers headed for Santa Isobel with hydrogen bombs, and Fission Chips, fully dressed, toddled over to the Starry Wisdom church where he encountered, not BUGGER, but something on an entirely different plane.

BOOK TWO

ZWEITRACHT

'It must have a "natural"
  cause.'

'It must have a "supernatural"
  cause.'

} Let these
   two asses
be set to
   grind corn.

—Frater Perdurabo, O.T.O.,
'Chinese Music,' *The Book of Lies*

THE FOURTH TRIP, OR CHESED

Jesus Christ On A Bicycle

> Mister Order, he runs at a very good pace
> But old Mother Chaos is winning the race
> —Lord Omar Khayaam Ravenhurst, K.S.C.,
> 'The Book of Advice,' *The Honest Book of Truth*

Among those who knew that the true faith of Mohammed was contained in the Ishmaelian teachings, most were sent out into the world to seek positions in the governments of the Near East and Europe. Since it pleased Allah to decree this task for them, they obeyed willingly; many served thus for their whole lives. Some, however, after five or ten or even twenty years of such fealty to a given shah or caliph or king, would receive, through surreptitious channels, a parchment bearing the symbol: ♄ That night, the servant would strike, and disappear like smoke; and the master would be found in the morning, throat cut, with the emblematic Flame Dagger of the Ishmaelians lying beside him. Others were chosen to serve in a different manner, maintaining the palace of Hassan i Sabbah himself at Alamout. These were especially fortunate, for it was their privilege to visit more often than others the Garden of Delights, in which the Lord Hassan himself would, through his command of magic chemicals, transfer them into heaven while they still lived in the body. One day in the year 470 (known to the uncircumcized Christian dogs as 1092 A.D.) another proof of the Lord Hassan's powers was given to them, for they were all summoned to the throne room and there sat the Lord Hassan in all his glory, while before him on the floor lay a plate bearing the head of the disciple Ibn Azif.

'This deluded one,' the Lord Hassan declared, 'has disobeyed a command – the one crime that cannot be forgiven

in our Sacred Order. I show you his head to remind you
of the fate of traitors in this world. More; I will instruct
you on the fate of such dogs in the next world.' So saying,
the good and wise Lord Hassan rose from his throne, walking with his characteristic lurching gait, and approached
the head. 'I command thee,' he said. 'Speak.'

The mouth opened and the head emitted a scream such
that all the faithful covered their ears and turned their
eyes away, many of them muttering prayers.

'Speak, dog!' the wise Lord Hassan repeated. 'Your
whine is of no interest to us. Speak!'

'The flames,' the head cried. 'The terrible flames. Allah,
the flames . . .' it babbled on as a soul will in extreme
agony. 'Forgiveness,' it begged. 'Forgiveness, O mighty
Lord.'

'There is no forgiveness for traitors,' said the all-wise
Hassan. 'Return to hell!' And the head immediately
silenced. All bowed down and prayed to Hassan and Allah
alike; of the many miracles they had seen this was certainly
the greatest and most terrible.

The Lord Hassan then dismissed everyone, saying, 'Forget not this lesson. Let it stay in your hearts longer than
the names of your fathers.'

*('We want to recruit you,' Hagbard said, 900-odd years
later, 'because you are so gullible. That is, gullible in the
right way.')*

Jesus Christ went by on a bicycle. That was my first
warning that I shouldn't have taken acid before coming
down to Balbo and Michigan to see the action. But it really seemed right, on another level: acid was the only way
to relate to that whole Kafka-on-a-bummer example of
quote democratic process in action unquote. I found Hagbard in Grant Park, cool as usual, with a bucket of water
and a pile of handkerchiefs for the teargas victims. He was
near the General Logan statue, watching the more violent
confrontations across the street at the Hilton, sucking one
of his Italian cigars and looking like Ahab finally finding
the whale . . . *Hagbard, in fact, was remembering Professor
Tochus at Harvard:* 'Damn it, Celine, you *can't* major in
naval engineering and law both. You're not Leonardo da
Vinci, after all.' 'But I am,' he had replied, poker-faced. 'I
recall all my past incarnations in detail and Leonardo was

one of them.' Tochus almost exploded: '*Be* a wise-ass, then! When you start flunking half your subjects, perhaps you'll come back to reality.' The old man had been terribly disappointed to see the long row of *A*s. Across the street, the demonstrators advanced toward the Hilton and the police charged again, clubbing them back; Hagbard wondered if Tochus had ever realized that a professor is a policeman of the intellect. Then he saw the Padre's new disciple, Moon, approaching. . . . '*You haven't been clubbed yet*,' I said, thinking that in a sense Jarry's old presurrealist classic, 'The Crucifixion of Christ Considered as an Uphill Bike Race,' was really the best metaphor for the circus Daley was running. 'Neither have you, I'm glad to see,' Hagbard replied: 'Judging from your eyes, though, you got teargassed in Lincoln Park last night.' I nodded, remembering that I had been thinking of him and his weird Discordian yoga when it happened. Malik, the dumb social-democratic-liberal that John wanted to recruit soon, was only a few feet away, and Burroughs and Ginsberg were near me on the other side. I could see, suddenly, that we were all chessmen, but who was the chessmaster moving us? And how big was the board? Across the street, a rhinoceros moved ponderously, turning into a jeep with a barbed-wire crowd-sticker on the front of it. 'My head's leaking,' I said.

'Do you have any idea who's picking it up?' Hagbard asked. He was remembering a house lease in Professor Orlock's class. 'What it amounts to, in English,' Hagbard had said, 'is that the tenant has no rights that can be successfully defended in court, and the landlord has no duties on which he cannot, quite safely, default.' Orlock looked pained, and several students were shocked, as if Hagbard had suddenly jumped up and exposed his penis in front of the class. 'That's putting it too baldly,' Orlock said finally. . . . '*It might be somebody years in the future*,' I said, '*or the past*.' I wondered if Jarry was picking it up, in Paris, half a century before; that would account for the resemblance. Abbie Hoffman went by just then, talking to Apollonius of Tyana. Were we all in Jarry's mind, or Joyce's? We even have a Sheriff Wood riding herd on us and Rubin's horde of Jerry men. . . . '*Fuller's car is a stunt, a showpiece*,' Professor Caligari fumed, 'and, anyway, it has

nothing to do with naval architecture.' Hagbard looked at
him levelly and said, 'It has *everything* to do with naval
architecture.' As in law school, the other students were
disturbed. Hagbard began to understand: they are not
here to learn, they are here to acquire a piece of paper that
would make them eligible for certain jobs. . . .

*'There are only a few more memos.' Saul said to Mul-
doon. 'Let's skim them and then call headquarters to see
if Danny found this "Pat" who wrote them.'*

ILLUMINATI PROJECT: MEMO #15

8/6

J.M.:

Here's the weirdest version of the Illuminati history that
I've found so far. It's from a publication written, edited
and published by somebody named Philip Campbell Argyle-Stuart, who holds that the conflicts in the world are
due to an age-old war between Semitic 'Khazar' peoples
and Nordic 'Faustian' peoples. This is the essence of his
thinking:

> My theory is that an extremely devilish imposed over-
> crust was added to the Khazar population consisting
> of humanoids who arrived by flying saucer from the
> planet Vulcan, which I assume to be not in intra-
> Mercurial orbit around the sun, but rather in the
> earth's orbit, behind the Sun, forever out of sight to
> earthlings, always six months behind or ahead of the
> earth in orbital travel. . . .
>
> Likewise for the Gothic Faustian Western Culture.
> The previously comparatively inert and purposeless
> migrating population streams known as Franks, Goths,
> Angles, Saxons, Danes, Swabians, Alemani, Lom-
> bards, Vandals, and Vikings suddenly had an over-
> crust added consisting of Norman-Martian-Varangians,
> arriving from Saturn by way of Mars in flying
> saucers. . . .
>
> After 1776 it (the Khazar-Vulcanian conspiracy)
> used the Illuminati and Grand Orient Masons. After
> 1815 it used the financial machinations of the House
> of Rothschild and after 1848 the Communist move-
> ment and after 1895 the Zionist movement. . . .

One more thing needs to be mentioned. Mrs. Helena
Petrovna Blavatski (nee Hahn in Germany), 1831-
1891, founder of Theosophy . . . was both hypocritical
and devilish, a true witch of great evil power allied
with Illuminati, Grand Orient Masons, Russian Anarchists, British Israel Theorists, Proto-Zionists, Arabian
Assassins and Thuggi from India.

Source: *The High I.Q. Bulletin,* Vol. IV, No. 1, January
1970. Published by Philip Campbell Argyle-Stuart, Colorado Springs, Colorado.

                                                    Pat

'What was that word?' Private Celine asked eagerly.

'SNAFU,' Private Pearson told him. 'You mean to say
you never heard it before?' He sat up in his bunk and
stared.

'I'm a naturalized citizen,' Hagbard said. 'I was born in
Norway.' He pulled his shirt away from his back again;
the Fort Benning summer was much too hot for the Nordic
half of his genes. 'Situation Normal, All Fucked Up,' he
repeated. 'That really sums it up. That really says it.'

'Wait'll you've been in This Man's Army a little longer,'
the black man told him vehemently. 'Then you'll really
appreciate the *application* of that word, dads. Oh, man,
will you *appreciate* it.'

'It's not just the army,' Hagbard said thoughtfully. 'It's
the whole world.'

*Actually, after they immanentized the Eschaton, I found
out where my head was leaking that night (and a few other
nights, too).* Into poor George Dorn. The leak almost gave
him water on the brain. He kept wondering where all that
Joyce and surrealism was coming from. I'm seven years
older than he is, but we're on the same valence, because
of similar grammar school experiences and revolutionary
fathers. That's why Hagbard never really understood either
of us, fully: he had private tutors until he hit college, and
by that stage Official Education is beginning to make some
partial concessions to reality so the victims have at least
a chance of surviving on the outside. But I didn't know
any of that in Grant Park that night or how the Army
helped Hagbard understand college, because I was work-

ing out this new notion of the total valence of the set remaining constant. It would mean that I would have to leave
when George came on, or say, Marilyn Monroe and Jane
Mansfield had to do the pill or auto-wreck shticks before
there was room for Racquel Welch's vibes.

ILLUMINATI PROJECT: MEMO #16

8/7

J.M.:
I think I've found the clue as to how Zoroaster, flying
saucers and all that lunatic-fringe stuff fits into the Illuminati puzzle. Dig this, boss-man:

> The Nazi Party was founded as the political append-
> age of the Thule Society, an extremist fringe of the
> Illuminated Lodge of Berlin. This lodge, in turn, was
> made up of Rosicrucians – high Freemasons – and its
> preoccupation was mourning the death of the feudal
> system. Masons of this time were, like the Federalist
> Party in post-revolutionary America, working dili-
> gently to prevent 'anarchy' and preserve the old values
> by bringing about Christian Socialism. Indeed, the
> Aaron Burr conspiracy, which Professor Hofstadter
> notes was allegedly Masonic in origin, was an Ameri-
> can prototype of German intrigues of a century later.
> To their external scientific socialism these Masons
> added mystic concepts which were thought to be
> 'gnostic' in origin. One of these was the concept of
> 'Gnosticism' itself, called Illumination – which held
> that heavenly beings directly or indirectly gave hu-
> manity its great ideas and would come back to Earth
> after mankind had achieved sufficient progress. Il-
> lumination was a brand of pentecostalism which was
> persecuted by orthodox Christianity for centuries and
> had become lodged in Freemasonry through a complex
> historical process which is impossible to explain with-
> out a major digression. It is sufficient to say that the
> Nazis, being 'Illuminated,' felt themselves to be divinely
> inspired and therefore felt justified in rewriting the
> rules of good and evil to suit their own purposes.
> (According to Nazi theory) the heavenly beings,
> before the present Moon was captured, had lived on

the highest ground, in Peru, Mexico, Gondor (Ethiopia), Himalaya, Atlantis and Mu, forming the Uranian Confederation. This was taken quite seriously and British intelligence actually combatted it with the Tolkien fantasy called the 'Silmarillion,' basis for the famous 'Hobbit' books. . . .

Both J. Edgar Hoover and Congressman Otto Passman are high-ranking Masons and both, significantly, reflect this philosophy and its Manichean attitude. The chief danger in Masonic thinking aside from the 'divine right of government' is, of course, Manicheanism, the belief that your opponent is opposing God's will and is therefore an agent of Satan. This is the extreme application and Mr. Hoover usually reserves it for 'Godless Communism' but it is almost always present to some degree.

Source: 'The Nazi Religion: Views on Religious Statism in Germany and America' by J. F. C. Moore, *Libertarian American*, Vol. III, No. 3, August 1969.

Pat

They were using Mace now, and I saw one photographer snapping a picture of a cop while the cop was still Macing him (Heisenberg rides again! From out of the west come the thundering hooves of the great hearse, Joint Phenomenon! Except that I was on acid; if I'd been on weed, then it would really, royally, be a Joint Phenomenon). And I heard later that the photographer got an award for that shot. Right then, he didn't look like he was getting an award. He looked like they had just taken off his skin and touched each raw nerve with a dentist's drill. 'Christ,' I said to Hagbard, 'look at that poor bastard. I hope I come out of this with just another teargassing or two. I don't want any of that Mace.' But acid is placid, you know, and a minute later I was on Joyce's juices again and thinking of a drama called 'Their Mace and My Gripes.' I made the first line fruity, in honor of Padre Pederastia: 'What a botch of a pair to plumb this hour's gripes.'

'*Bism'allah*,' Hagbard said. 'Our karma is made by our

deeds, not by our prayers. You're on the set, so you take the action as it comes.'

'Oh, cut out that Holy Man craperoo and stop reading my mind,' I protested. 'You don't have to go on impressing me.' But I was off on another tangent, which went something like this: If this set is Mayor Daley's circus, then Mayor Daley is the ringmaster. If the things below are the things above, as Hermes hermetically hinted, then this set *is* the bigger set. Mr. Microcosm, meet Mr. Macrocosm. 'Hi, Mike!' 'Hi, Mac.' Conclusion: Mayor Daley, in a small way, is what Krishna is, in a large way. QED.

Just then some SDS kids who'd been teargassed across the street came running our way, and Hagbard got busy handing out wet handkerchiefs. They needed them: they were half-blind, like Joyce splitting his Adam into wise hopes. And I wasn't much help, because I was too busy crying myself.

'Hagbard,' I gasped in ecstasy. 'Mayor Daley is Krishna.'

'Worse luck for him,' he said curtly, distributing the handkerchiefs. 'He doesn't suspect it.'

I thought, suddenly:

> Hubert the Hump has coughed and hawked
> And spat on the streets that Lincoln walked

The water turned to blood (Hagbard was a joking jolting Jesus: you expected wine maybe?) and I remembered my mother's story about Dillinger at the Biograph. We all sit there, like him, in the Biograph Theatre, dreaming the drama of our lives, then walk outside to the grandmotherly kindness of the lead kisses that wake us back to our slipping beatitude. Except that he found a way to come back. What was it Charley Mordecai said: 'First as tragedy, then as farce?' Marxism-Lennonism: Ed Sanders of the Fugs, the night before, talking about fucking in the streets as if he had read my mind (or had I read his?) and Lennon's 'Why Don't We Do It in the Road' was recorded a year in the future. The Marx and our groupies. The bloody handkerchiefs dipped into water, or wine, and the mass rite went on, the mass went Right On, the Mace they rowed. Capone set it up for the Feds, but John was fed up and left the set, so an extra named Frank Sullivan got

the bullets. The Autobiograph Theatre, a drama house and
a trauma, yes. I maybe should have taken only half a tab
instead of the full 500 mikes, because at that point the SDS
kids, all of them siding with RYM-I at the split next year,
looked like they had altar boy robes on and I thought
Hagbard was distributing communion wafers, not handkerchiefs. He looked at me, suddenly, with that hawk-
faced Egyptian glare, and I observed that he had observed,
Hopalong Horus Heisenberg, just where I was at. You
don't have to be a waterman, I thought, to know which
way my mind is blowing.

There was a sound from the crowd, like a subway opening all its doors with a suck of air, and I saw the police
coming, crossing the street to clear the park.

'Here we go again,' I said. 'All hail Discordia.'

'*Snafu ueber alles*,' Hagbard grinned, starting to trot
beside me.

We headed North, figuring that the ones who retreated
eastward would get trapped against the wall and creamed.
'Democracy in action,' I said, panting along.

'There thou might'st behold the very image of Authority,'
he quoted, shifting his water bucket to keep it in balance.
I caught the Shakespearean reference and looked back:
my mind had already: each policeman indeed looked like
Shakespeare's dog. I remembered the frantic semantics at
the LBJ anti-birthday party, when Burroughs insisted
Chicago Cops were more like dogs than pigs, in contradiction to the SDS rhetoric. Terry Southern, taking his
usual maniacal middle course, claimed they were more akin
to the purple-assed mandrill, most surly of the baboon
family. But most of them hadn't discovered writing yet.

'Authority?' I asked, realizing I'd lost something along
the way. We were slowing to a walk, the action was behind
us.

'A is not A,' Hagbard explained with that tiresome
patience of his. 'Once you accept A *is* A, you're hooked.
Literally hooked, addicted to the System.'

I caught the references to Aristotle, the old man of the
tribe with his unfortunate epistemological paresis, and also
to that feisty little lady I always imagine is really the lost
Anastasia, but I still didn't grok. 'What do you mean?' I

asked, grabbing a wet handkerchief as some of the teargas started to drift to our end of the park.

'Chairman Mao didn't say half of it,' Hagbard replied holding a handkerchief to his own face. His words came through muffled: 'It isn't only political power that grows out of the barrel of a gun. So does a whole definition of reality. A set. And the action that has to happen on that particular set and on none other.'

'Don't be so bloody patronizing,' I objected, looking around a corner in time and realizing this was the night I would be Maced. 'That's just Marx: the ideology of the ruling class becomes the ideology of the whole society.'

'Not the ideology. The Reality.' He lowered his hand-kerchief. 'This was a public park until they changed the definition. Now, the guns have changed the Reality. It *isn't* a public park. There's more than one kind of magic.'

'Just like the Enclosure Acts,' I said hollowly. 'One day the land belonged to the people. The next day it belonged to the landlords.'

'And like the Narcotics Acts,' he added. 'A hundred thousand harmless junkies became criminals overnight, by Act of Congress, in nineteen twenty-seven. Ten years later, in thirty-seven, all the pot-heads in the country became criminals overnight, by Act of Congress. And they really were criminals, when the papers were signed. The guns prove it. Walk away from those guns, waving a joint, and refuse to halt when they tell you. Their Imagination will become your Reality in a second.'

And I had my answer to Dad, finally, just as a cop jumped out of the darkness screaming something about freaking motherfucking fag commies and Maced me, as was certain to happen (I knew it as I crumbled in pain) on that set.

ILLUMINATI PROJECT: MEMO #16

8/7

J.M.:

Here's some more info on how Blavatsky, theosophy and the motto under the great pyramid on the U.S. Seal fit into the Illuminati picture (or *don't* fit into the picture. It's getting more confusing the further I dig into it!) This is an article defending Madame Blavatsky, after Truman

Capote had repeated the John Birch Society's charge that Sirhan Sirhan was inspired to murder Robert Kennedy by reading Blavatsky's works: 'Sirhan Blavatsky Capote' by Ted Zatlyn, *Los Angeles Free Press*, July 26, 1968:

> Birchers that attack Madame Blavatsky, though smaller in number and as crazy as ever, find a new home in an atmosphere of suspicion and violence. Truman Capote takes them seriously. . . .
>
> Does Mr. Capote know that the Illuminati (according to sacred Birch doctrine) began in the Garden of Eden when Eve made it with the snake and gave birth to Cain? That all the descendents of snake-man Cain belong to a super-secret group known as the Illuminati, dedicated to absolutely nothing but the meanest low down evil imagined in the Satanic mind of man?
>
> Anti-Illuminati John Steinbacher writes in his unpublished book, *Novus Ordo Seclorum* (The New Order of the Ages): 'Today in America, many otherwise talented people are flirting with disaster by associating with those same evil forces . . . Madame Blavatsky's doctrine was strikingly similar to that of Weishaupt. . . .'

The author also gives *his* version of the *Bircher's* version of what the Illuminati are actually trying to accomplish:

> Their evil goal is to transcend materiality, and to bring about one world, denying the sovereignty of nations and the sanctity of private property:

I don't think I can believe, or even understand, this, but at least it explains how both the Nazis and the Communists can be pawns of the Illuminati. Or does it?

Pat

'Property is theft,' Hagbard said, passing the peace pipe. 'If the BIA helps those real estate developers take our land,' Uncle John Feather said, 'that will be theft. But if we keep the land, that is certainly not theft.'

Night was falling in the Mohawk reservation, but Hagbard saw Sam Three Arrows nod vigorously in the gloom of the small cabin. He felt, again, that American Indians were the hardest people in the world to understand. His tutors had given him a cosmopolitan education, in every sense of the word, and he usually found no blocks in relating to people of any culture, but the Indians did puzzle him at times. After five years of specializing in handling the legal battles of various tribes against the Bureau of Indian Affairs and the land pirates it served, he was still conscious that these people's heads were someplace he couldn't yet reach. Either they were the simplest, or the most sophisticated, society on the planet; maybe, he thought, they were both, and the ultimate simplicity and the ultimate sophistication are identical.

'Property is liberty,' Hagbard said. 'I am quoting the same man who said property is theft. He also said property is impossible. I speak from the heart. I wish you to understand why I take this case. I wish you to understand in fullness.'

Sam Three Arrows drew on the pipe, then raised his dark eyes to Hagbard's. 'You mean that justice is not known like a dog who barks in the night? That it is more like the unexpected sound in the woods that must be identified cautiously after hard thinking?'

There it was again: Hagbard had heard the same concreteness of imagery in the speech of the Shoshone at the opposite end of the continent. He wondered, idly, if Ezra Pound's poetry might have been influenced by habits of speech his father acquired from the Indians – Homer Pound had been the first white man born in Idaho. It certainly went beyond the Chinese. And it came, not from books on rhetoric, but from listening to the heart – the Indian metaphor he had himself used a minute ago.

He took his time about answering: he was beginning to acquire the Indian habit of thinking a long while before speaking.

'Property and justice are water,' he said finally. 'No man can hold them long. I have spent many years in courtrooms, and I have seen property and justice change when a man speaks, change as the caterpillar changes to the butterfly. Do you understand me? I thought I had victory in my hands, and then the judge spoke and it went away. Like water running through the fingers.'

Uncle John Feather nodded. 'I understand. You mean

we will lose again. We are accustomed to losing. Since George Washington promised us these lands "as long as the mountain stands and the grass is green," and then broke his promise and stole part of them back in ten years – in ten years, my friend! – we have lost, always lost. We have one acre left of each hundred promised to us then.'

'We may not lose,' Hagbard said. 'I promise you, the BIA will at least know they have been in a fight this time. I learn more tricks, and get nastier, each time I go into a courtroom. I am very tricky and very nasty by now. But I am less sure of myself than I was when I took my first case. I no longer understand what I am fighting. I have a word for it – the Snafu Principle, I call it – but I do not understand what it is.'

There was another pause. Hagbard heard the lid on the garbage can in back of the cabin rattling: that was the raccoon that Uncle John Feather called Old Grandfather come to steal his evening dinner. Property was theft, certainly, in Old Grandfather's world, Hagbard thought.

'I am also puzzled,' Sam Three Arrows said finally. 'I worked, long ago, in New York City, in construction, like many young men of the Mohawk Nation. I found that whites were often like us, and I could not hate them one at a time. But they do not know the earth or love it. They do not speak from the heart, usually. They do not act from the heart. They are more like the actors on the movie screen. They play roles. And their leaders are not like our leaders. They are not chosen for virtue, but for their skill at playing roles. Whites have told me this, in plain words. They do not trust their leaders, and yet they follow them. When we do not trust a leader, he is finished. Then, also, the leaders of the whites have too much power. It is bad for a man to be obeyed too often. But the worst thing is what I have said about the heart. Their leaders have lost it and they have lost mercy. They speak from somewhere else. They act from somewhere else. But from where? Like you, I do not know. It is, I think, a kind of insanity.' He looked at Hagbard and added politely. 'Some are different.'

It was a long speech for him, and it stirred something in Uncle John Feather. 'I was in the army,' he said. 'We went to fight a bad white man, or so the whites told us. We had meetings that were called orientation and education. There were films. It was to show us how this bad white man was doing terrible things in his country. Everybody was angry after the films, and eager to fight. Except me. I was only there because the army paid more than an Indian can earn anywhere else. So I was not angry, but puzzled. There was nothing that this white leader did that the white leaders in this country do not also do. They told us about a place named Lidice. It was much like Wounded Knee. They told us of families moved thousands of miles to be destroyed. It was much like the Trail of Tears. They told us of how this man ruled his nation, so that none dared disobey him. It was much like the way white men work in corporations in New York City, as Sam has described it to me. I asked another soldier about this, a black white man. He was easier to talk to than the regular white man. I asked him what he thought of the orientation and education. He said it was shit, and he spoke from the heart. I thought about it a long time, and I knew he was right. The orientation and education was shit. When the men from the BIA come here to talk, it is the same. Shit. But let me tell you this: the Mohawk Nation is losing its soul. Soul is not like breath or blood or bone and it can be taken in ways no man understands. My grandfather had more soul than I have, and the young men have less than me. But I have enough soul to talk to Old Grandfather, who is a raccoon now. He thinks as a raccoon and he is worried about the raccoon nation, more than I am worried about the Mohawk Nation. He thinks the raccoon nation will die soon, and all the nations of the free and wild animals. That is a terrible thing and it frightens me. When the nations of the animals die, the earth will also die. That is an old teaching and I cannot doubt it. I see it happening, already. If they steal more of our land to build that dam, more of our soul will die, and more of the souls of the animals will die! The earth will die, and the stars will no longer shine! The Great Mother herself may die!' The old man was crying unashamedly. 'And it will be because men do not speak words but speak shit!'

Hagbard had turned pale beneath his olive skin. 'You're coming into court,' he said slowly, 'and you're going to tell the judge that, in exactly those words.'

ILLUMINATI PROJECT: MEMO #17

8/8

J.M.:

You may remember that the *East Village Other*'s chart of the Illuminati Conspiracy (Memo #9) listed 'The Holy Vehm' as an Illuminati front. I have finally found out what The Holy Vehm is (or, rather was). My source is Eliphas Levy's *History of Magic*, op. cit., pages 199-200:

They were a kind of secret police, having the right of life and death. The mystery which surrounded their judgments, the swiftness of their executions, helped to impress the imagination of people still in barbarism. The Holy Vehm assumed gigantic proportions; men shuddered in describing apparitions of masked persons, of summonses nailed to the doors of nobles in the very midst of their watch-guards and their orgies, of brigand chiefs found dead with the terrible cruciform dagger in their breasts and on the scroll attached thereto an extract from the sentence of the Holy Vehm. The Tribunal affected most fantastic forms of procedure: the guilty person, cited to appear at some discredited cross-road, was taken to the assembly by a man clothed in black, who bandaged his eyes and led him forward in silence. This occurred invariably at some unseemly hour of the night, for judgment was never pronounced except at midnight. The criminal was carried into a vast underground vault, where he was questioned by one voice. The hoodwink was removed, the vault was illuminated in all its depth and height, and the Free Judges sat masked and wearing black vestures.

The Code of the Vehmic Court was found in the ancient archives of Westphalia and has been printed in the Reichstheater of Müller, under the following title: 'Code and Statutes of the Holy Secret Tribunal of Free Courts and Free Judges of Westphalia, established in the year 772 by the Emperor Charlemagne and revised in 1404 by King Robert, who made those alterations and additions requisite for the administration of justice in the tribunals of the illuminated, after investing them with his own authority.'

A note on the first page forbade any profane person to glance at the book under penalty of death. The word 'illuminated', here given to the associates of the Secret Tribunal, unfolds their entire mission: they had to track down in the shadows those who worshipped the darkness; they counterchecked mysteriously those who conspired against society in favour of mystery; but they were themselves the secret soldiers of light, who cast the light of day on criminal plottings, and it is this which was signified by a sudden splendour illuminating the Tribunal when it pronounced sentence.

So now we have to add *Charlemagne* to the list of the Illuminated – along with Zoroaster, Joachim of Floris, Jefferson, Washington, Aaron Burr, Hitler, Marx, and Madame Blavatsky. Could this *all* be a hoax?

ILLUMINATI PROJECT: MEMO #18

8/9

J.M.:

My last memo may have been too hasty in using the past tense in speaking about the Holy Vehm. I find that Darual thinks they may still exist (*History of Secret Societies,* op. cit., p. 211):

These terrible courts were never formally abolished. They were reformed by various monarchs, but even in the nineteenth century it was said that they still existed, though very much underground. The Nazi werewolves and resistance organizations fighting the Communist occupation of East Germany claimed that they were carrying on the tradition of the 'Chivalrous and Holy Vehm.' Perhaps they still are.

Pat

Federal Court for the 17th District of New York State. Plaintiffs: John Feather, Samuel Arrows, et al. Defendants: Bureau of Indian Affairs, Department of the Interior, and President of the United States. For plaintiffs: Hagbard Celine. For the defendants: George Kharis, John Alucard, Thomas Moriarity, James Moran. Presiding: Justice Quasimodo Immhotep.

MR. FEATHER *(concluding):* And it will be because men do not speak words but speak shit!

MR. KHARIS: Your honor, I move that the last speech be stricken from the record as irrelevant and immaterial. We are dealing here with a practical question, the need of the people of New York for this dam, and Mr. Feather's superstitions are totally beside the point.

MR. CELINE: Your honor, the people of New York have survived a long time without a dam in that particular place. They can survive longer without it. Can anything survive, anything worth having, if our words become, as Mr. Feather says, excrement? Can anything we can reasonably call American Justice survive, if the words of our first President, if the sacred honor of George Washington is destroyed, if his promise that the Mohawk could keep these lands 'as long as the mountain stands and the grass is green,' if all that becomes nothing but excrement?

MR. KHARIS: Counsel is not arguing. Counsel is making speeches.

MR. CELINE: I am speaking from the heart. *Are you* – or are you speaking excrement that you are ordered to speak by your superiors?

MR. ALUCARD: More speeches.

MR. CELINE: More excrement.

JUSTICE IMMHOTEP: Control yourself, Mr. Celine.

MR. CELINE: I am controlling myself. Otherwise, I would speak as frankly as my client and say that most of the speeches here are plain old shit. Why do I say 'excrement' at all, if it isn't, like you people, to disguise a little what we are all doing? It's shit. Plain shit.

JUSTICE IMMHOTEP: Mr. Celine, you are coming very close to contempt of court. I warn you.

MR. CELINE: Your honor, we speak the tongue of Shakespeare, of Milton, of Melville. Must we go on murdering it? Must we tear it away from its last umbilical connection with reality? What is going on in this room, actually? Defendants, the U.S. government and its agents, want to steal some land from my clients. How long do we have to argue that they have no justice, no right, no honor, in their cause? Why can't we say highway robbery is highway robbery, instead of calling it eminent

domain? Why can't we say shit is shit, instead of calling
it excrement? Why do we never use language to convey
meaning? Why must we always use it conceal meaning? Why do we never speak from the heart? Why do we
always speak words programmed into us, like robots?

JUSTICE IMMHOTEP: Mr. Celine, I warn you again.

MR. FEATHER: And I warn you. The world will die. The
stars will go out. If men and women cannot trust the
words spoken, the earth will crack, like a rotten pump-
kin.

MR. KHARIS: I call for a recess. Plaintiff and their counsel
are both in no emotional state to continue at this time.

MR. CELINE: You even have guns. You have men with
guns and clubs, who are called marshals, and they will
beat me if I don't shut up. How do you differ from any
other gang of bandits, then, except in using language
that conceals what you are doing? The only difference
is that the bandits are more honest. That's the only difference. The only difference.

JUSTICE IMMHOTEP: Mr. Marshal, restrain the counsel.

MR. CELINE: You're stealing what isn't yours. Why can't
you talk turkey for just one moment? Why—

JUSTICE IMMHOTEP: Just hold him, Marshal. Don't use
unnecessary force. Mr. Celine, I am tempted to forgive
you, considering that you are obviously much involved
with your clients, emotionally. However, such mercy on
my part would encourage other lawyers to believe they
could follow your example. I have no choice. I find you
guilty of contempt of court. Sentencing will take place
when court reconvenes after a fifteen-minute recess. You
may speak at that time, but only on any mitigating
grounds that should lighten the degree of your sentence.
I will not hear the United States government called
bandits again. That is all.

MR. CELINE: You steal land, and you will not hear yourselves called bandits. You order men with guns and
clubs to hold us down, and you will not hear yourselves
called thugs. You don't act from the heart; where the
hell do you act from? What in God's name does motivate
you?

JUSTICE IMMHOTEP: Restrain him, Marshal.

MR. CELINE: (Indistinguishable.)

JUSTICE IMMHOTEP: Fifteen-minute recess.
BAILIFF: All rise.

ILLUMINATI PROJECT: MEMO #19

8/9

J.M.:
I wish you would explain to me how your interest in the
numbers 5 and 23 fit in with this Illuminati project.

This is all I've been able to unearth so far on the number
mystery, and I hope you find it enlightening. It's from a
book of mathematical and logical paradoxes: *How to
Torture Your Mind*, edited by Ralph L. Woods, Funk and
Wagnalls, New York, 1969, page 128.

> 2 and 3 are even and odd;
> 2 and 3 are 5;
> Therefore, 5 is both even and odd.

The damned book, by the way, provides no solutions to
the paradoxes. I could sense the fallacy in that one right
away, but it took me hours (and a headache) before I
could state it in precise words. Hope this helps you. Anyway, for me, it was a relief from the really frightening
stuff I've been tracking down lately.

Pat

There were two further memos in the box, on different
stationeries and by different typewriters. The first was
brief:

April 4
RESEARCH DEPARTMENT:
I am seriously concerned about Pat's absence from the
office, and the fact that she doesn't answer the phone when
we call her. Would you send somebody to her apartment
to talk to the landlord and try to find out what has happened to her?

Joe Malik
Editor

The last memo was the oldest in the lot and already
yellowing at the edges. It said:

Dear Mr. 'Mallory:'

The information and books, you requested are enclosed,
at length. In case you are rushed, here is a quick summary.

1. Billy Graham was in Australia, making public ap-
pearances all through last week. There is no way he could
have gotten to Chicago.

2. Satanism and witchcraft both still exist in the modern
world. The two are often confused by orthodox Christian
writers, but objective observers agree that there is a difference. Satanism is a Christian heresy – the ultimate heresy,
one might say – but witchcraft is pre-Christian in origin
and has nothing to do with the Christian God *or* the
Christian Devil. The witches worship a goddess called
Dana or Tana (who goes back to the Stone Age probably).

3. The John Dillinger Died For You Society has its
headquarters in Mad Dog, Texas, but was founded in
Austin, Texas several years ago. It's some kind of poker-
faced joke and is affiliated with the Bavarian Illuminati,
another bizarre bunch at the Berkeley campus of the University of California. The Illuminati pretend to be a cabal
of conspirators who run the whole world behind the scenes.
If you suspect either of these groups of being involved in
something sinister, you have probably just fallen for one
of their put-ons.

W.H.

'So this thing was already linked to Mad Dog several
years ago,' Saul said thoughtfully. 'And Malik was already
assuming an alternative identity, since the letter is obviously
addressed to him. And, also as I've begun to suspect as
we read this stuff, the Illuminati have their own brand of
humor.'

'Deduce me one more deduction,' Barney said. 'Who the
hell is this W.H.?'

'People have been asking that for three hundred years,'
Saul said absently.

'Huh?'

'I'm being whimsical. Shakespeare's sonnets are dedicated to a Mr. W.H., but I don't think we have to worry

that this is the same one. This case is as nutty as a squirrel's dinner, but I don't really think it's *that* nutty.' He added, 'We can be grateful for one thing at least: the Illuminati doesn't really run the world. They're just trying.'

Barney frowned, perplexed. 'How did you make that one?'

'Simple. Same way I know they're a right-wing organization, not left-wing.'

'We're not all geniuses,' Barney said. 'Take it a step at a time, will you?'

'How many contradictions did you spot in these memos? I counted thirteen. This researcher, Pat, saw it, too: the evidence is deliberately warped and twisted. All of it – not just that *East Village Other* chart – is a mixture of fact and fiction.' Saul lit his pipe and settled back in his chair (in 1921, reading Arthur Conan Doyle, he first began playing these scenes, in imagination).

'In the first place, either the Illuminati want publicity or they don't. If they control everything, and want publicity, they'd be on billboards more often than Coca-Cola and on TV more often than Lucille Ball. On the other hand, if they control everything, and *don't* want publicity, none of these magazines and books would have survived – they would have disappeared from libraries, book stores and publisher's warehouses. This researcher, Pat, never would have found them.

'In the second place, if you want to recruit people into a conspiracy, besides idealism and whatever other noble motives you might exploit in them, you would always exploit hope. You would exaggerate the size and power of the conspiracy, because most people want to join the winning side. Therefore, all assertions about the actual strength of the Illuminati should be regarded, *a fortiori*, as suspect, like the voters' polls released by candidates before elections.

'Finally, it always pays to frighten the opposition. Therefore a conspiracy will exhibit the same behavior that ethologists have observed in animals under attack: it will puff itself up and try to look bigger. In short, potential or actual recruits and potential and actual enemies will both be given the same false impression: that the Illuminati is twice, or ten times, or a hundred times, its actual size. This is logical, but my first point was empirical – the memos do exist – and therefore logic and empiricism confirm each other: the Illuminati are not able to control everything. What then? They've been around a long time and they are as tireless as the Russian mathematician who worked out *pi* to the one-thousandth place. The probability, then, is that they control some things and influence a hell of a lot more. This probability increases as you think back over the memos. The two chief Arabic branches – the Hashishim and the Roshinaya – were both wiped out; the Italian Illuminati were "crushed" in 1507; Weishaupt's order was suppressed by the Bavarian government in 1785; and so forth. If they were behind the French Revolution, they influenced rather than controlled, because Napoleon undid everything the Jacobins started. That they had a hand in both Soviet Communism and German Fascism is plausible, considering the many similarities between the two; but if they controlled both, why did the two take opposite sides in the Second World War? And, if they ran both the Federalist party, through Washington, and the Democratic Republicans, through Jefferson, what was the purpose of the Aaron Burr counter-revolution, which they are also supposed to be behind? The picture I get is not a grand Puppet Master moving everybody on invisible strings, but some sort of million-armed octopus – a millepus, let's call it – constantly reaching out tentacles, and often drawing back nothing but a bloody stump, crying, "Foiled again!"

'But the millepus is very busy and quite resourceful. *If* it controlled the planet, it could choose either operating in the open or retaining secrecy, but since it doesn't have that omnipotence yet, it must choose to be as anonymous as possible. Therefore, many of its tentacles will be probing around in the areas of publication and communications. It wants to know when somebody is investigating it or getting ready to publicize an investigation he has already completed. Finding such a person, it then has two choices: kill him or neutralize him. Killing may be resorted to in certain emergencies, but will be avoided when possible: you never know when a person of that sort has stashed extra copies of his documents in various unexpected places to be released in the event of his death. Neutralization is best, almost always.'

Saul paused to relight his pipe, and Muldoon thought, *The most unrealistic aspect of Doyle's stories is Watson's admiration at these moments. I'm just irritated, because he makes me feel like a chump for not seeing it myself.* 'Go ahead,' he said gruffly, saving his own deductions until Saul was finished.

'The best form of neutralization is recruitment, of course. But any crude and hurried effort at recruitment is known as "taking your pants down" in the espionage business because it makes you more vulnerable. The safest approach is gradual recruitment, disguised as something else. The best disguise, of course, is the pretense of helping the subject in his investigation. This also opens the second, and preferable, option, which is leading him on a wild goose chase. Sending him looking for Illuminati in organizations which they have never really infiltrated. Feeding him balderdash like that stuff about the Illuminati coming from the planet Vulcan or being descended from Eve and the Serpent. Best of all, though, is telling him the purpose of the conspiracy is something other than it actually is, especially if the story you sell him is in keeping with his own ideals, since this can then shade over into recruitment.

'Now, the sources this Pat unearthed mostly seem to come to one of two conclusions: the Illuminati doesn't exist anymore, or the Illuminati is virtually identical with Russian Communism. The first I reject because Malik and Pat have both disappeared and two buildings, one here in New York and one way down in Mad Dog, have been bombed in a series palpably linked with an investigation of the Illuminati. You've already accepted that, but the next step is just as obvious. If the Illuminati tries to distort whatever publicity cannot be avoided, then we should look at the idea that the Illuminati is communist-oriented as skeptically as we look at the idea that they don't even exist.

'So, let's look at the opposite hypothesis. Could the Illuminati be a far-right or fascist group? Well, if Malik's information was in any way accurate, they seem to have some kind of special headquarters or central office in Mad Dog – and that's Ku Klux and God's Lightning territory. Also, whatever their history before Adam Weishaupt, they seem to have gone through some reformation and revitalization under his leadership. He was a German and an ex-Catholic, just like Hitler. One of his Illuminated Lodges survived long enough to recruit Hitler in 1923, according to a memo that might be the most accurate one in the lot for all we know. Considering the proclivities of the German character, Weishaupt could likely be an anti-Semite. Most historians I've read on Nazi Germany agree to at least the possibility that there was a "secret doctrine" which only the top Nazis shared among themselves and didn't tell the rest of the party. That doctrine might be pure Illuminism. Take up the many links between Illuminism and Free-masonry, and the known anti-Catholicism of the Masonic movement – add in the fact that ex-Catholics are frequently bitter against the church, and both Weishaupt and Hitler were ex-Catholics – and we get a hypothetical anti-Jewish, anti-Catholic, semi-mystical doctrine that would sell equally well in Germany and in parts of America. Finally, while some left-extremists might want to kill the Kennedys and Reverend King, all three were more likely targets for right-wingers; and the Kennedys would be especially abhorrent to anti-Catholic rightists.

'A last point,' Saul said. 'Consider the left-wing orientation of *Confrontation*. The editor, Malik, would probably not give much credence to most of the sources quoted in the memos, since the majority are from rightist publications, and most of them allege that the Illuminati is a leftish plot. His most probable reaction would be to dismiss this as another right-wing paranoia, *unless he had other sources besides his own Research Department*. Notice how cagey he is. He doesn't tell his associate editor, Peter Jackson, anything about the Illuminati itself – just that he wants a new investigation of the last decade's assassinations. The bottom memo is so old and yellow it suggests he got his first clue several years ago, but didn't act. Pat asks him why he's hiding all this from the reporter, George Dorn. Finally, he disappears. He was getting information from some place else, and it revealed a plot he could believe in and really fear. That would probably be a Fascist plot, anti-Catholic, anti-Jewish and anti-Negro.'

Muldoon grinned. *For once I don't have to play Watson,* he thought. 'Brilliant,' he said. 'You never cease to amaze me, Saul. Would you glance at this, though, and tell me how it fits in?' He handed over a piece of paper. 'I found it in a book on Malik's bedside table.'

The paper was a brief scrawl in the same handwriting as the occasional jottings on the bottoms of Pat's memos:

Pres. Garfield, killed by Charles Guiteau, a Roman Catholic.

Pres. McKinley, ditto by Leon Czolgosz, a Roman Catholic.

Pres. Theodore Roosevelt, attempted assassination by John Shrank, a Roman Catholic.

Pres. Franklin Roosevelt, attempted assassination by Giuseppe Zangara, a Roman Catholic.

Pres. Harry Truman, attempted assassination by Griselio Torresola and Oscar Collazo, two Roman Catholics.

Pres. Woodrow Wilson, somewhat mysterious death while tended by a Roman Catholic nurse.

Pres. Warren Harding, another mysterious death (one rumor: it was suicide), also attended by a Catholic nurse.

Pres. John Kennedy, assassination inadequately explained. Head of CIA then was John McCone, a Roman Catholic, who helped write the inconclusive and contradictory Warren Report.

(House of Representatives, March 1, 1964 – five Congressmen wounded by Lebron-Miranda-Codero-Rodriguez assassination squad, all Roman Catholics.)

When Saul looked up, Barney said pleasantly, 'I found it in a book, like I said. The book was *Rome's Responsibility for the Assassination of Abraham Lincoln* by General Thomas M. Harris. Harris points out that John Wilkes Booth, the Suratt family, and all the other conspirators were Catholics, and argues they are acting under orders from the Jesuits.' Barney paused to enjoy Saul's expression and went on, 'It occurs to me that, using your principle that most of the memos are full of false leads, we might question the idea that the Illuminati uses the Masons as a front to gather recruits. They would probably need some similar organization, though – one that exists all over the world, has mysterious rites and secrets, inner orders to which a select few are recruited, and a pyramidal authoritarian structure compelling everybody to take commands from above whether they understand them or not. One such organization is the Roman Catholic church.'

Saul picked up his pipe from the floor. He didn't seem to remember having dropped it. 'My turn to say, "brilliant," ' he murmured finally. 'Are you going to stop going to Mass on Sunday? Do you really believe it?'

Muldoon laughed. 'After twenty years,' he said, 'I finally did it. I got one jump ahead of you. Saul, you were standing face-to-face with the truth, eyeball-to-eyeball, nose-to-nose, mouth-to-mouth – but you were so close that your eyes crossed and you saw it backward. No, it's not the Catholic church. You made a good guess in saying it was anti-Catholic as well as anti-Jewish and anti-Negro. But it's inside the Catholic church and always has been. In fact, the church's efforts to root it out have given Holy Mother Rome a very unfortunate reputation for paranoia and hysteria. Its agents make a special effort to enter the priesthood, in order to obtain holy objects for use in their own bizarre rites. They also try to rise as high in the church as they can, to destroy it from within. Many times they have recruited and corrupted whole parishes, whole orders of clergy, even whole provinces. They probably got to Weishaupt when he was still a Jesuit – they've infiltrated that order several times in history and the Dominicans even more. If caught in criminal acts, they make sure that their cover Catholicism, and not their true faith, is publicised, just like this list of assassins. Their God is called the Light-Bearer and that's probably where the word "illumination" comes from. And Malik asked about them a long time ago and was told by this W.H., quite correctly, that they still exist. I'm talking about the Satanists, of course.'

'Of course,' Saul repeated softly, 'of course. That pentagon that keeps popping up – it's the middle of the pentacle for summoning the Devil. Fascism is only their political facet. Basically, they're a theology – or an anti-theology, I guess. But what in hell – literally in hell – is their ultimate objective, then?'

'Don't ask me,' Barney shrugged. 'I can follow my brother when he talks about the history of Satanism, but not when he tries to explain its motivations. He uses technical theological terms about "immanentizing the Eschaton," but all I can understand is that it has something to do with bringing on the end of the world.'

Saul turned ashen. 'Barney,' he cried, 'my God. *Fernando Poo!*'

'But that was settled—'

'That's just it. Their usual technique of the false front. The real threat is coming from somewhere else, and they mean to do it this time.'

Muldoon shook his head. 'But they must be crazy!'

'Everybody is crazy,' Saul said patiently, 'if you don't understand his motives.' He held up his tie. 'Imagine you arrive in a flying saucer from Mars – or from Vulcan, like the Illuminati did according to one of our allegedly reliable sources. You see me get up this morning and for no clear reason wrap this cloth around my neck, in spite of the heat. What explanation can you think of? I'm a fetishist – a nut, in other words. Most human behavior is that sort, not oriented to survival but some symbol-system that people believe in. Long hair, short hair, fish on Friday, no pork, rising when the judge enters the room – all symbols, symbols, symbols. Sure the Illuminati are crazy, from *our* point of view. From *their* point of view, we're crazy. If we can find out what they believe, what their symbols mean to them, we'll understand why they want to kill most of the rest of us, or all of the rest of us. Barney, call your brother. Get him out of bed. I want to find out more about Satanism.'

('The devil!' the President shouted on March 27. 'Nuclear war over an insignificant place like Fernando Poo? You must be mental. The American people are tired of our army policing the whole world. Let Equatorial Guinea fish its own nuts out of the troubled waters, or whatever that expression is.' 'Wait,' said the Director of the CIA, 'let me show you these aerial photographs . . .')

Back at the Watergate, G. Gordon Liddy carefully aims his pistol and shoots out the streetlight: in memory, he is in an old castle at Millbrook, New York, eagerly searching for naked women and not finding any. Beside him Professor Timothy Leary is saying with maddening serenity, 'But science is the most ecstatic kick of all. The intelligence of the galaxy is revealed in every atom, every gene, every cell.' *We'll get him back*, Liddy thinks savagely, *if we have to assassinate the whole Swiss government. That man is not going to remain free*. Beside him, Bernard Barker shifts nervously as in right-angular time a future president metamorphoses the plumbers into the cesspool cleaners: but now, inside the Watergate, the Illuminati bug is unnoticed by those planting the CREEP bug, although both were subsequently found by the technicians installing the BUGGER bug. 'It's the same Intelligence, making endlessly meaningful patterns,' Dr. Leary goes on enthusiastically. ('Here, kitty-kitty,' Hagbard repeats for the 109th time.)

'The devil?' Father James Augustine Muldoon repeated. 'Well, that's a very complicated story. Do you want me to go all the way back to Gnosticism?'

Saul, listening on the extension phone, nodded a vigorous affirmative.

'Go as far back as you have to,' Barney said. 'This is a complicated matter we're trying to untangle here.'

'OK, I'll try to remember you're not in my theology class at Fordham and keep this as brief as I can.' The priest's voice faded, then came back – probably he was shifting the phone as he got out of bed and moved to a chair, Saul guessed.

'There were many approaches to Gnosticism,' the voice went on in a moment, 'all of them centered on *gnosis* – direct experience of God – as distinguished from mere knowledge about God. The search for gnosis, or illumination as it was sometimes called, took many odd forms, some of them probably similar to Oriental yogas and some of them using the very same drugs that modern rebels against the slow path of orthodox religion have rediscovered. Naturally, with such a variety of paths to gnosis, different pilots would land at different ports, each insisting he had found the real New Jerusalem. Mystics are all a bit funny in the head anyway,' the priest added cynically, 'which is why the church locks them all up in mental hospitals and euphemistically calls these institutions monasteries. But I digress.

'What you're interested in, I guess is Cainism and Manicheanism. The former regarded Cain as a specially holy figure because he was the first murderer. You have to be a mystic yourself to understand that kind of logic. The notion was that, by bringing murder into the world, Cain created an opportunity for people to renounce murder. But, then, other Cainites went further – paradox always seems to breed more paradox and heresy creates more heresy – and ended up glorifying murder, along with all the other sins. The credo was that you should commit every sin possible, just to give yourself a chance to win a really difficult redemption after repenting. Also, it gave God a chance to be especially generous when He forgave you. Related ideas popped up in Tantric Buddhism about the same time, and it's a great historical mystery which group of lunatics, East or West, was influencing the other. Does any of this help you so far?'

'A bit,' Barney said.

'About this gnosis,' Saul asked, 'is it the orthodox theological position that the illuminations or visions were actually coming from the Devil and not from God?'

'Yes. That's where Manicheanism enters the picture,' Father Muldoon said. 'The Manicheans made exactly the same charge against the orthodox church. According to their way of looking at it, the God of orthodox Christianity and orthodox Judaism, *was* the Devil. The god they contacted through their own peculiar rites was the real god. This, of course, is still the teaching of Satanists today.'

'And,' Saul asked, beginning to intuit what the answer would be, 'what has all this to do with atomic energy?'

'With atomic energy? Nothing at all . . . at least, nothing that I can see. . . .'

'Why is Satan called the light-bringer?' Saul plunged on, convinced he was on the right track.

'The Manicheans reject the physical universe,' the priest said slowly. 'They say that the true god, their god, would never lower himself to mess around with matter. The God who created the world – our God, Jehovah – they call *panurgia*, which has the connotations of a kind of blind, stupid blundering force rather than a truly intelligent being. The realm which their god inhabits is pure spirit of pure light. Hence, he is called the light-bringer, and this universe is always called the realm of darkness. But they didn't know about atomic energy in those days – did they?' The

last sentence had started as a statement and ended as a
question.

'That's what *I'm* wondering,' Saul said. 'Atomic power
releases a lot of light, doesn't it? And it sure would im-
manentize the Eschaton if enough atomic power was unleashed at once, wouldn't it?'

'Fernando Poo!' the priest exclaimed. 'Is this connected
with Fernando Poo?'

'I'm beginning to think so,' Saul said. 'I'm also beginning
to think we've stayed in one place a long time, using a
phone that is almost certainly tapped. We better get moving. Thanks, Father.'

'You're quite welcome, although I'm sure I don't know
what you're getting at,' the priest said. 'If you think Satanists control the United States government a few priests
would agree with you, especially the Berrigan brothers, but
I don't see how this can be a police matter. Does the New
York Police Department now maintain a bureau of holy
inquisitions?'

'Don't mind him,' Barney said softly. 'He's very cynical
about dogma, like most clergymen these days.'

'I heard that,' the priest said. 'I may be cynical but I
really don't think Satanism is a joking matter. And your
friend's theory is very plausible, in its way. After all, the
Satanist's motive in infiltrating the church, in the old days,
was to disgrace the institution thought to represent God
on earth. Now that the United States government makes
the same claim, well. That may be a joke or a paradox on
my part, but it's the way their minds work, too. I am a
professional cynic – a theologian must be, these days, if he
isn't going to seem a total fool to young people with their
skeptical minds – but I'm orthodox, or downright reactionary, about the Inquisitions. I've read all the rationalist historians, of course, and there was certainly an element of
hysteria in the church in those days, but, still, Satanism is
not any less frightening than cancer or plague. It is totally
inimical to human life and, in fact, to all life. The church
had good reasons to be afraid of it. Just as people who are
old enough to remember have good reason to be panicky
at any hint of a revival of Hitlerism.'

Saul thought of the cryptic, evasive phrases in Eliphas
Levy: 'the monstrous gnosis of Manes . . . the cultus of

material fire. . . .' And, nearly ten years ago, the hippies gathered at the Pentagon, hanging flowers on the M.P.s' rifles, chanting 'Out, demon, out!' . . . Hiroshima . . . the White Light of the Void. . . .

'Wait,' Saul said. 'Is there more to it than just *ideas* about killing? Isn't killing a mystical experience to the Satanists?'

'Of course,' the priest replied. 'That's the whole point – they want gnosis, personal experience, not dogma, which is somebody else's word. Rationalists are always attacking dogma for causing fanaticism, but the worst fanatics start from gnosis. Modern psychologists are just beginning to understand some of this. You know how people in ex- plosive group-therapy sessions talk about sudden bursts of energy occurring in the whole group at once? One can get the same effect with dancing and drum-beating; that's what is called a "primitive" religion. Use drugs, nowadays, and you're a hippie. Do it with sex, and you're a witch, or one of the Knights Templar. Mass participation in an animal sacrifice has the same effect. Human sacrifice has been used in many religions, including the Aztec cult every- body has heard about, as well as in Satanism. Modern psychologists say that the force released is Freud's libidinal energy. Mystics call it prajna or the Astral Light. Whatever it is, human sacrifice seems to release more of it than sex or drugs or dancing or drum-beating or any less violent method and mass human sacrifice unleashes a ton of it. Now do you understand why I fear Satanism and half apologize for the Inquisition?'

'Yes,' Saul said absently, 'and I'm beginning to share your fear. . . .' A song he hated was pounding inside his skull: *Wenn das Judenblut vom Messer spritz. . . .*

He realized that he was holding the phone and seeing scenes forty years ago in another country. He jerked him- self back to attention as Muldoon thanked his brother again and hung up. Saul raised his eyes and the two detec- tives exchanged glances of mutual dread.

After a long pause, Muldoon said, 'We can't trust any- body with this. We can hardly even trust each other.'

Before Saul could answer the phone rang. It was Danny Pricefixer at headquarters. 'Bad news. There was only one girl in research at *Confrontation* named Pat. Patricia Walsh to be exact, and—'

'I know,' Saul said wearily, 'she's disappeared, too.'

'What are you going to do now? The FBI is still raising hell and demanding to know where you two are and the Commissioner is having the shits, the fits, and the blind staggers.'

'Tell them,' Saul said succinctly 'that we've disappeared.' He hung up carefully and began stuffing the memos back into the box.

'What now?' Muldoon asked.

'We go underground. And we stick to this until we crack it or it kills us.'

('How long is this motherfucker?' George asked, gesturing at the Danube six stories below. He and Stella were in their room at the Donau Hotel.

'You won't believe me,' Stella replied, smiling. 'It's exactly one thousand seven hundred and seventy-six miles in length. One-seven-seven-six, George.'

'The same as the date Weishaupt revived the Illuminati?'

'Exactly.' Stella grinned. 'We keep telling you. Synchronicity is as universal as gravity. When you start looking you find it everywhere.')

'Here's the money,' Banana-Nose Maldonado said generously, opening a briefcase full of crisp new bills. (It is now November 23, 1963: they were meeting on a bench near Cleopatra's needle in Central Park: the younger man, however, is nervous.) 'I want to tell you that . . . my superior . . . is very pleased. This will definitely decrease Bobby's power in the Justice Department and stop a lot of annoying investigations.'

The younger man, Ben Volpe, gulps. 'Look, Mr. Maldonado, there's something I've got to tell you. I know how the . . . Brotherhood . . . is when somebody fucks up and hides it.'

'You didn't fuck up,' Banana-Nose says, bewildered. 'In fact, you lucked out amazingly. That schmuck Oswald is going to fry for it. He came along at just the right time. It was a real Fortuna . . . Jesus, Mary and Joseph!' Banana-Nose sits up straight as the thought hits him. 'You mean . . . you mean . . . Did Oswald really do it? Did he shoot *before* you?'

'No, no,' Volpe is miserable. 'Let me explain it as clearly as I can. I'm there on top of the Dallas County Records Building like we planned, see? The motorcade turns onto Elm and heads for the underpass. I use my magnifying sight, swinging the whole gun around to look through it, just to make one last check that I have all the Feds spotted. When I face the School Book Depository, I catch this rifle. That was Oswald, I guess. Then I check out the grassy knoll and, goddam, there's another cat with a rifle. I just went cold. I couldn't figure it out. While I'm in this state, like a zombie, a dog barks and just then the guy in the grassy knoll calm and cool as if he was at a shooting range lays three of them right into the car. That's it,' Volpe ends miserably. 'I can't take the money. The . . . Brotherhood . . . would have my ass if they ever found out the truth.'

Maldonado sat silently, rubbing his famous nose as he did when making a hard decision. 'You're a good boy, Bennie. I give you ten percent of the money, just for being honest. We need more honest young boys like you in the Brotherhood.'

Volpe swallowed again, and said, 'There's one more thing I oughta tell you. I went down to the grassy knoll, after the cops run from there to the School Book Depository. I thought I might find the guy who did the shooting still hanging around and tell you what he looked like. He was long gone, though. But here's what so spooky. I ran into another galoot, who was sneaking down from the triple underpass. Long, skinny guy with buck teeth, kind of reminded me of a python or some kind of snake. He just looks at me and my umbrella and guesses what's in it. His mouth falls open. "Jesus Christ and his black bastard brother Harry," he says, "how the *fuck* many people does it take to kill a President these days?" '

('And they're teaching them about perversions as well,' Smiling Jim was building toward his climax. 'Homosexuality and lesbianism are being taught in our schools and we're paying for it out of our tax money. Now is that communism or isn't it?')

'Welcome to the Playboy Club,' the beautiful blonde said, 'I'm your bunny, Virgin.'

Saul took his seat in the dark wondering if he had heard

correctly. Virgin was an odd name for a bunny; perhaps she had actually said Virginia. Yes, Virginia, there is a Santa Claus.

'How do you wish your steak, sir?' the bunny was asking. A stake through the heart, for a vampire.

'Medium well,' Saul said, wondering why his mind was wandering in such odd directions. ('Odd erections,' somebody said in the nearby dark – or was it a distorted echo of his own voice?)

'Medium well,' the bunny repeated, seemingly speaking to the wall. A medium wall, Saul thought.

Immediately the wall opened and Saul was looking into a combination kitchen and butcher shop. A steer was standing not five feet from him, but before he could recover from this shock a male figure, stripped to the waist and wearing the hood of a medieval executioner, caught his attention. With one stroke of a huge hammer, this figure knocked the steer unconscious and it fell to the floor with a crash. Immediately the executioner produced an axe and chopped its head off; blood gushed in a crimson pool from its neck.

The wall closed, and Saul had the terrifying feeling that the whole scene had been a hallucination – that he was losing his mind.

'All our lunches are educational today,' the bunny said in his ear. 'We believe every customer should understand fully what's on the end of his fork and how it got there, before he takes a bite.'

'Good God,' Saul said, getting to his feet. This wasn't a Playboy Club, it was some den of lunatics and sadists. He stumbled toward the door.

'No way out,' a man at another table said softly as he passed.

'Saul, Saul,' the maître d' murmured politely, 'why dost thou persecute me? *Hab' rochmunas.*'

'It's a drug,' Saul said thickly, 'you've given me a drug.' Of course, that was it – something like mescaline or LSD – and they were guiding his hallucinations by providing proper stimuli. Perhaps they were even faking some of the hallucinations. But how had he fallen into their hands? The last thing he remembered, he was in Joe Malik's apartment with Barney Muldoon. . . . No, there was a voice saying, 'Now, Sister Victoria,' as they came out the door onto Riverside Drive. . . .

'No man should marry a woman more than thirty years younger than himself,' the maître d' said mournfully. How did they know about that? Had they investigated his whole life? How long had they held him?

'I'm getting out of here,' he shouted, pushing the maître d' aside and bolting for the door.

Hands grasped for him and missed (they weren't really trying, he realized: he was being allowed to reach the door). When he plunged through the doorway, he realized why: he was not on the street but in another room. This was the next ordeal.

A rectangle of light appeared on the wall; somewhere in the darkness there was a projector. A card, light an old silent-movie caption, appeared in the rectangle. It said:

ALL JEW GIRLS LIKE TO BALL WITH BUCK NIGGERS

'Sons of bitches,' Saul shouted back at them. They were still working on his feelings about Rebecca. Well, that would get them nowhere: he had ample reason to trust her devotion to him, especially her sexual devotion.

The card moved out of the rectangle, and a picture appeared in its place. It was Rebecca's, in her nightgown, kneeling. Before her stood a naked and enormous black man, six feet six at least, with an equally impressive penis which she held sensuously in her mouth. Her eyes were closed in bliss, like a baby nursing.

'Motherfuckers,' Saul screamed. 'It's a fake. That's not Rebecca – it's an actress with makeup. You forgot the mole on her hip.' They could drug his senses but not his mind.

There was a nasty laugh in the darkness. 'Try this one, Saul,' a voice said coldly.

A new picture slid into view: Adolph Hitler, in full Nazi uniform, and a naked Rebecca backing up to him, taking his penis in her rectum. Her face showed both pain and pleasure – and the mole on her hip was visible. Another fake – Rebecca was born years after Hitler died. But they hadn't produced the slide in the thirty seconds after his shout, and that meant they knew her body, intimately. . . .

And they also knew how skeptical and quick his mind was, and were prepared to administer a series of jolts until something got past his ability to doubt.

'No comment?' the voice asked mockingly.

'I don't believe a man who died thirty years ago would be buggering *any* woman today,' Saul said drily. 'Your tricks are kind of corny.'

'Sometimes, with the vulgar, we must communicate vulgarly,' the voice replied – and it was almost gentle and pitying this time.

A new picture appeared – and this time, without doubt, it *was* Rebecca. But it was Rebecca three years ago, when he first met her. She sat at a table in a cheap East Village pad, wearing the emaciated and self-pitying look he remembered from those days; and she was preparing to inject a needle in her arm. It was the real thing, but the terror was in its implications: *they* had been watching him that long ago. Perhaps – it was hard to date the picture precisely, although he remembered her apartment in those days – they even knew he would fall in love with her before he knew it himself. No; more likely, a friend of hers in those days had taken the picture and they had somehow found it when they became interested in him. Their resources must be fantastic.

A new card came on the screen:

ONCE A JUNKIE ALWAYS A JUNKIE

A new picture quickly followed: Rebecca, as she looked today, sitting in his kitchen – with the new café curtains they had just hung last week – once again injecting a needle into her arm.

'You're the vulgar ones, O mighty Illuminati,' Saul said caustically. 'I would have noticed the tracks on her arm, if she was shooting up again.'

The answer was nonverbal: the picture of Rebecca and the giant black man came back on the screen, and was immediately followed by a close-up of her face, eyes closed, mouth open receiving the penis. It was in perfect focus, the work of an artist with the camera, and he could see no sign of any makeup that would help another woman to pass as Rebecca. He held to his memory that the mole on her hip was missing, but, perversely, his mind tasted at last the other possibility – makeup can change a face, and it can also hide a mole. . . . If they wanted him to use his skepticism, so that they could gradually destroy that, and, in the process, undermine his total psyche. . . .

Another sign came on the screen:

THAT WE CAN CALL THESE DELICATE CREATURES OURS
BUT NOT THEIR APPETITES

Saul remembered, all too well, Rebecca's passion in bed. 'Shakespeare,' he called hoarsely. 'Advertising your erudition at a time like this is worse than vulgarity. It's petit-bourgeois pretentiousness.'

The answer was brutal: a whole series of slides, maybe fifteen or twenty in all, cascaded across the screen in such rapid succession that he couldn't examine them carefully, except that the central character was Rebecca, always Rebecca, Rebecca with the black giant in other sexual positions, Rebecca with another woman, Rebecca with Spiro Agnew, Rebecca with a little seven-year-old boy, Rebecca, Rebecca, in a rising crescendo of perversion and abnormality, Rebecca with a Saint Bernard dog – and a peppermint-colored sine-wave, part of the drug still working on him, cutting across the scene. . . .

'The true sadist has style,' Saul gasped fighting for control of his voice. 'You people are about as evil and frightening as a bad B-movie.'

There was a whirring mechanical sound and a movie began in place of the slides. It was Rebecca and the Saint Bernard, with several close-ups, and her expressions were the ones he knew. Could any actress portray another woman's individual style of sexual response? Yes – if necessary, these people would use hypnosis to get the effect letter-perfect.

The movie stopped abruptly and the projector had another message for him, held on the screen for minutes:

ONLY THE MADMAN IS ABSOLUTELY SURE

When he realized that there would be no further progress until he spoke, Saul said coldly, 'Very entertaining. Where do I go to crumble into a bundle of neuroses?'

There was no answer. No sound. Nothing happened. He half-saw a latticework of red pentagons, but that was the drug – and it helped identify which drug, for geometric patterns were characteristic of the mescaline experience. As he considered that, the peppermint sine-waves appeared before the pentagons and the screen gave him a new message:

> HOW MUCH IS THE DRUG?
> HOW MUCH IS OUR TRICKERY?
> HOW MUCH IS REALITY?

Suddenly, Saul was in Copenhagen, on a cruise boat, passing the mermaid of the harbor. She turned and looked at him. 'This case is fishy,' she said – and as she opened her mouth a school of guppies swam out. 'I'm a mouth-breeder,' she explained.

Saul had a reproduction of that famous statue in his home (which must be the source of the hallucination), yet he was strangely disturbed. Her punning words seemed to conceal a deeper meaning than mere casual references to the *Confrontation* bombing . . . something that went back . . . back through his whole life . . . and explained why he had purchased the statue in the first place.

I'm about to have one of those famous drug insights that hippies always talk about, he thought. But the mermaid broke apart into pentagons of red, orange, yellow. . . .

And a unicorn winked at him. 'Man,' it said, 'am I ever horny!'

Those sketches I made the other day, Saul thought . . . but the screen asked him:

> IS THE THOUGHT OF A UNICORN A REAL THOUGHT?

. . . and he suddenly understood for the first time what the words 'a real thought' meant; what Hegel meant by defining the Absolute Idea as pure thought thinking about pure thought; what Bishop Berkeley meant by denying the reality of the physical world in seeming contradiction of all human experience and common sense; what every detective was secretly attempting to detect, although it was always right out in the open; why he became a detective in the first place; why the universe itself became; why *everything*;

and then he forgot it;

caught a fleeting glimpse of it again – it had something to do with the eye at the top of the pyramid;

and lost it again in visions of unicorns, stallions, zebras, bars, bars, bars.

Now his whole visual field was hallucinatory . . . octagons, triangles, pyramids, organic shapes of embryos and growing ferns. The drug was taking stronger hold on him. Criminals he had sent to jail appeared – sullen, hating faces – and the screen said

GOODMAN IS A BAD MAN

He laughed to keep from crying. They had touched his deepest doubt about his job – his career, his life's work – precisely at the time the drug also was leading him there, with those damnable accusing faces. It was as if they could read his mind and see his hallucinations. No; it was just one lucky coincidence, because among all their tricks one was statistically likely to occur in tandem with an appropriate drug experience.

WHILE THERE IS A SOUL IN PRISON
I AM NOT FREE

Saul laughed again, more wildly, almost hysterically; and knew, even more clearly than before, the tears hiding behind the laughter. Prisons reform nobody; my life is wasted; I offer society a delusion of security but not a real service. Worse yet, I have known it for years, and lied to myself. The sense of total failure and utter bitterness that washed over Saul at that moment was, he knew, not produced but only magnified by the drug. It had been with him a long, long time but always pushed aside, brushed away from his attention by concentrating on something else; the drug merely allowed him (forced him) to look at the emotion honestly and totally for a few wrenching moments.

A doorway suddenly lit up toward his right and a neon light came on above it, saying, 'Absolution and Redemption.'

'OK,' he said icily, 'I'll play the next move.' He opened the door.

The room was tiny but furnished like the world's most expensive brothel. Above the fourposter bed was an illustration of Alice and a mushroom labeled 'Eat Me.' And on the bed, stripped of her Playboy costume, pinkly and beautifully naked with legs spread in anticipation, was the blonde bunny. 'Good evening,' she said speaking rapidly and fixing his eyes with her own stare, 'I'm your Virgin Bunny. Every man wants a Virgin Bunny, to eat on Easter to celebrate the miracle of the Resurrection. Do you understand the miracle of the Resurrection, sir? Do you know that nothing is true and everything is permissible and that a man who dares to break the robot conditioning of society and commit adultery dies in the moment of orgasm with his whore and wakes resurrected to a new life? Did they teach you that in *shule*? Or did they just fill you with a lot of monogamous Yiddish horseshit?' Most hypnotists spoke slowly, but she was obtaining the same effect by talking rapidly. 'You thought you were going to eat a dead animal, which is disgusting even if this crazy society accepts it as normal, but instead you're going to eat a desirable woman (and fuck her afterward), which is normal even if this crazy society thinks of it as disgusting. You are one of the Illuminated, Saul, but you never knew it. Tonight you are going to learn. You are going to find your real self as you were before your mother and father conceived you. And I'm not talking about reincarnation. I'm talking about something much more marvelous.'

Saul found his voice. 'Your offer is appreciated but declined,' he said. 'Frankly, I find your tawdry mysticism even more adolescent than your sentimental vegetarianism and coarse lasciviousness. The trouble with the Illuminati is that you have no sense of true drama and not even a patina of subtlety.'

Her eyes widened as he spoke, but not with surprise at his resistance – either she was really alarmed, and sorry for him, or she was a great actress. 'Too bad,' she said sadly. 'You've refused Heaven, so you must travel the harder path through the halls of Hell.'

Saul heard a movement behind him, but before he could turn a sharp sensation pricked his neck: a needle, another

drug. Just as he was guessing they had given him a strong-
ger psychedelic to escalate the effect, he felt consciousness
slipping away. It was a narcotic or a poison.

The wagon started with a jerk: we were off to see the
wizard, the wonderful wizard of arse. What was it Hagbard
had said to me, the first time we met, about straight lines,
courtrooms, and shit? I couldn't remember, my mind
drifted, Joseph K. opening the law books and finding
pornographic illustrations (Kafka knew where it was at),
deSade keeping a precise mathematical tally in the brothel,
how many times he flogged the whores, how many times
they flogged him, the Nazis counting every gold filling in
the corpses at Auschwitz, Shakespeare scholars debating
about that line in Macbeth (was it benches or banks of
time?), the prisoner may approach the bench, you can
bank on it, buddy, bank on it . . . PIGS EAT SHIT PIGS EAT
SHIT . . . and Pound wrote 'the buggering bank,' he rejected Freud, but even so he got a whiff of the real secret
. . . how one homo ominously loopses another. . . .

'My God,' the Englishman said. 'When do we get out
of the teargas area?'

'We're out of it,' I told him wearily. 'That's regular
Chicago air now. Courtesy of Commonwealth Edison and
U.S. Steel over in Gary.'

The McCarthy woman was weeping quietly, although
the Mace had worn off by now. The rest of us rode
silently, a little caravan of dried snot and tears, the par-
mesan cheese odor of stale vomit, some lingering acrid
Mace fumes, the urine of somebody who had peed himself,
and that high sulphur dioxide and slaughterhouse aroma of
Chicago's South Side. The quality of mercy is very strained;
it drippeth like the pus from chancre. Abandon hope all
ye who enter here. Chairman Mao appeared and lectured
us: 'Ho is just a poetaster. Now, if you want to hear some
real socialist verse, consider *my* latest composition:

> There was a young lady from Queens
> Who gobbled a plateful of beans
> The beans fermented
> And she was tormented
> By embarrassing sounds in her jeans!

Indicates the anal orientation of capitalist society,' he explained, dwindling into a pool of blood on the floor next to the kid with the broken arm.

(In 1923, Adolph Hitler stood beneath a pyramidal altar and repeated the words of a goat-headed man: *'Der Zweck heiligte die Mittel.'* James Joyce, in Paris, scrawled in crayon words that his secretary, Samuel Beckett, would later type: 'Pre-Austeric Man in Pursuit of Pan-Hysteric Woman.' In Brooklyn, New York, Howard Phillips Lovecraft, returning from a party at which Hart Crane had been perfectly beastly – thereby confirming Mr. Lovecraft's prejudice against homosexuals – finds a letter in his mailbox and reads with some amusement: 'Some of the secrets revealed in your recent stories would better be kept out of the light of print. Believe me, I speak as a friend, but there are those who would prefer such half-forgotten lore to remain in its present obscurity, and they are formidable enemies for any man. Remember what happened to Ambrose Bierce. . . .' And, in Boston, Robert Putney Drake screams, 'Lies, lies, lies. It's all lies. Nobody tells the truth. Nobody says what he thinks. . . .' His voice trails off.

'Go on,' Dr. Besetzung says, 'you were doing fine. Don't stop.'

'What the use?' Drake replies, drained of anger, turning on the couch to look at the psychiatrist. 'To you, this is just abreaction or acting-out or something clinical. You can't believe I'm right.'

'Perhaps I can. Perhaps I agree more than you realize.' The doctor looks up from his pad and meets Drake's eye. 'Are you sure you're not just *assuming* I'll react like everybody else you've tried to tell this to?'

'If you agreed with me,' Drake says carefully, 'if you understood what I'm really saying, you'd either be the head of a bank, out there in the jungle with my father, grabbing your own share of the loot, or you'd be a bomb-throwing revolutionary, like those Sacco and Vanzetti fellows. Those are the only choices that make sense.'

'The only choices? One must go to one extreme or the other?'

Drake looks back at the ceiling and talks abstractly. 'You had to get an M.D. long ago, before you specialized.

Do you know any case where germs gave up and went
away because the man they were destroying had a noble
character or sweet sentiments? Did the tuberculosis baccilli
leave John Keat's lungs because he had a few hundred
great poems still unwritten inside him? You must have
read some history, even if you were never at the front lines
like me: do you recall any battle that refutes Napoleon's
aphorism about God always being on the side of the biggest cannons and the best tacticians? This bolshie in Russia,
Lenin, he has ordered the schools to teach chess to everybody. You know why? He says that chess teaches the
lesson that revolutionaries must learn: that if you don't
mobilize your forces properly, you lose. No matter how
high your morality, no matter how lofty your goal: fight
without mercy, use every ounce of intelligence, or you lose.
My father understands that. The people who run the world
have always understood it. A general who doesn't understand it gets broken back to second lieutenant or worse. I
saw a whole platoon wiped out, exterminated like an ant-
hill under a boot. Not because they were immoral or
naughty or didn't believe in Jesus. Because at that place,
on that day, the Germans had superior fire power. That's
the law, the one true law, of the universe, and everything
that contradicts it – everything they teach in schools and
churches – is a lie.' He says the word listlessly now. 'Just a
lie.'

'If you really believe that,' the doctor asks, 'why do you
still have the nightmares and the insomnia?'

Drake's blue eyes stare at the ceiling. 'I don't know,' he
says finally. 'That's why I'm here.')

'Moon, Simon,' the Desk Sergeant called.

I stepped forward, seeing myself through his eyes:
beard, army surplus clothes, stains all over (my own mucus,
somebody else's vomit). The archetypical filthy, dirty, disgusting, hippie-commie revolutionary.

'Well,' he said, 'another bright red rose.'

'I usually look neater,' I told him calmly. 'You get a
bit messed over when you're arrested in this town.'

'The only way you get arrested in this town,' he said,
frowning, 'is if you break the laws.'

'The only way you get arrested in Russia is you break
the laws,' I replied cheerfully. 'Or by mistake,' I added.

That didn't set well at all. 'Wise guy,' he said gently.
'We like wise guys here.' He consulted my charge-slip.
'Nice record for one night, Moon. Rioting, mob action,
assaulting an officer, resisting arrest, disturbing the peace.
Nice.'

'I wasn't disturbing the peace,' I said. 'I was disturbing
the war.' I stole that one-liner from Ammon Hennacy, a
Catholic Anarchist that Mom was always quoting. 'The
rest of the charges are all bullshit, too.'

'Say, I know *you*,' he said suddenly. 'You're Tim
Moon's son. Well, well, well. A second-generation anarchist. I guess we'll be locking you up as often as we locked
him up.'

'I guess so,' I said. 'At least until the Revolution. Afterward, we won't be locking you up, though. We're going to
establish nice camps in places like Wisconsin, and send
you there *free* to learn a useful trade. We believe that all
policemen and politicians can be rehabilitated. But if you
don't want to go to the camp and learn a productive trade,
you don't have to. You can live on Welfare.'

'Well, well, well,' he said. 'Just like your old man. I
suppose if I looked the other way, while some of the boys
took you in back and worked you over a bit, you'd come
out still making wisecracks?'

'I'm afraid so,' I smiled. 'Irish national character, you
know. We see the funny side of everything.'

'Well,' he said thoughtfully (he was awfully fond of that
word), 'I hope you can see the funny side of what comes
next. You're going to be arraigned before Judge Bushman.
You'll find yourself wishing you had fallen into a buzzsaw
instead. Give my regards to your father. Tell him Jim
O'Malley says hello.'

'He's dead,' I said.

He looked down at his charge-slips. 'Sorry to hear it,'
he mumbled. 'Nanetti, Fred,' he bawled, and the kid with
the broken arm came forward.

A patrolman led me to the fingerprint room. This guy
was a computer: 'Right hand.' I gave him my right hand.
'Left hand.' I gave him my left hand. 'Follow the officer.'
I followed the officer, and they took my picture. We went
down some halls to the night court, and in a lonely section
the patrolman suddenly hit me in the lower back with his

club, the exact spot (he knew his business) to give me liver problems for a month. I grunted but refused to say anything that would set him off and get me another clout, so he spoke. 'Yellow-bellied faggot,' he said.

Just like Biloxi, Mississippi: one cop is nice, another is just impersonal, a third is a mean bastard – and it doesn't really matter. They're all part of the same machine, and what comes out the end of the gears and levers is the same product, whatever their attitude is. I'm sure Buchenwald was the same: some of the guards tried to be as humane as possible, some of them just did their job, some of them went out of their way to make it worse for the prisoners. It doesn't matter: the machine produces the effect it was designed for.

Judge Bushman (we slipped him AUM two years later, but that's another story, coming up on another trip) gave me his famous King Kong scowl. 'Here are the rules,' he said. 'This is an arraignment. You can enter a plea or stand mute. If you enter a plea, you retain the right to change it at your trial. When I set bond, you can be released by paying ten percent to the bailiff. Cash only, no checks. If you don't have the cash, you go to jail overnight. You people have the city tied up in knots and the bail bondsmen are too busy to cover every courtroom, so by sheer bad luck you landed in a courtroom they're not covering.' He turned to the bailiff. 'Charge sheet,' he said. He read the record of my criminal career as concocted by the arresting officer. 'Five offenses in one night. You're bad medicine, aren't you, Moon? Trial set for September fifteenth. Bail will be ten thousand dollars. Do you have one thousand dollars?'

'No,' I told him wondering how many times he'd made that speech tonight.

'Just a moment,' said Hagbard, materializing out of the hallway. 'I can make bail for this man.'

MR. KHARIS: Does Mr. Celine seriously suggest that the United States Government is in need of a guardian?

MR. CELINE: I am merely offering a way out for your client. Any private individual with a record of such incessant murder and robbery would be glad to cop an insanity plea. Do you insist that your client was in full

possession of its reason at Wounded Knee? At Hiroshima? At Dresden?

JUSTICE IMMHOTEP: You become facetious, Mr. Celine.

MR. CELINE: I have never been more serious.

'What is your relationship to this young man?' Bushman
asked angrily. He had been about to come when the cop
dragged me off to jail, and he was strangling in some kind
of gruesome S-M equivalent of coitus interruptus.

'He's my wife,' Hagbard said calmly.

'What?'

'Common-law wife,' Hagbard went on. 'Homosexual
marriage is not recognized in Illinois. But homosexuality
per se isn't a crime in this state, either, so don't try to make
waves, Your Honor. Let me pay and take him home.'

It was too much. 'Daddy,' I said, camping like our
friend the Padre. 'You're so masterful.'

Judge Bushman looked like he wanted to lay Hagbard
out with a gavel upside of his head, but he controlled himself. 'Count the money,' he told the bailiff. 'Make sure he
pays every penny. And then,' he told us, 'I want the two
of you out of this courtroom as quickly as possible. I'll see
you September fifteenth,' he added, to me.

MR. KHARIS: And we believe we have demonstrated the
necessity of this dam. We believe we have shown that
the doctrine of eminent domain is on sure constitutional
grounds, and has been held to apply in numerous similar
cases. We believe we have shown that the resettlement
plan offered by the government will be no hardship for
the plaintiffs. . . .

'Fuckin' faggots,' the cop said as we went out the door.

'All hail Discordia,' I told him cheerfully. 'Let's get out
of this neighborhood,' I added to Hagbard.

'My car is right here,' he said, pointing to a goddam
Mercedes.

'For an anarchist, you sure live a lot like a capitalist,' I
commented as we got into that beautiful machine crystal-
lized out of stolen labor and surplus value.

'I'm not a masochist,' Hagbard replied. 'The world
makes me uncomfortable enough. I see no reason to make

myself more uncomfortable. And I'm damned if I'll drive
a broken-down jalopy that spends half its time in a garage
being repaired merely because that would make me seem
more "dedicated" to you left-wing simpletons. Besides,' he
added practically, 'the police never stop a Mercedes and
search it. How many times a week do you get stopped and
harassed, with your beard and your psychedelic Slaves-
wagon, you damned moralist?'

'Often enough,' I admitted, 'that I'm afraid to transport
dope in it.'

'This car is full of dope,' he said blithely. 'I'm making
a big delivery to a dealer up in Evanston, on the North-
western campus, tomorrow.'

'You're in the dope business, too?'

'I'm in every illegal business. Every time a government
declares something *verboten*, two groups move in to service the black market created: the Mafia and the LDD.
That stands for Lawless Delicacy Dealers.'

'I thought it stood for Little Deluded Dupes.'

He laughed. 'Score one for Moon. Seriously, I'm the
worst enemy governments have, and the best protection for
the average person. The Mafia has no ethics, you know. If
it wasn't for my group and our years and years of experience, everything on the black market, from dope to
Canadian furs, would be shoddy and unreliable. We always
give the customer his or her money's worth. Half the dope
you sell probably has passed through my agents on its way
to you. The better half.'

'What was that homosexual business? Just buggin' old
Bushman?'

'Entropy. Breaking the straight line into a curve ball.'

'Hagbard,' I said, 'what the hell is your game?'

'Proving that government is a hallucination in the minds
of governors,' he said crisply. We turned onto Lake Shore
Drive and sped north.

'Thou, Jubela, did he tell you the Word?' asked the
goat-headed man.

The gigantic black said, 'I beat him and tortured him,
but he would not reveal the Word.'

'Thou, Jubelo, did he tell you the Word?'

The fishlike creature said, 'I tormented and vexed his

inner spirit, Master, but he would not reveal the Word.'

'And thou, Jubelum, did he tell you the Word?'

The hunchbacked dwarf said, 'I cut off his testicles and he was mute. I cut off his penis and he was mute. He did not tell me the Word.'

'A fanatic,' the goat-head said. 'It is better that he is dead.'

Saul Goodman tried to move. He couldn't twitch a single muscle: That last drug had been a narcotic, and a powerful one. Or was it a poison? He tried to assure himself that the reason he was paralyzed and laying in a coffin was because they were trying to break down his mind. But he wondered if the dead might tell themselves similar fables, as they struggled to escape from the body before it rotted.

As he wondered, the goat-head leaned over and closed the top of the coffin. Saul was alone in darkness.

'Leave first, Jubela.'

'Yes, Master.'

'Leave next, Jubelo.'

'Yes, Master.'

'Leave last, Jubelum.'

'Yes, Master.'

Silence. It was lonely and dark in the coffin, and Saul couldn't move. Let me not go mad, he thought.

Howard spotted the *Lief Erikson* ahead and sang: 'Oh, groovy, groovy, groovy scene/Once again I'll meet Celine.' *Maldonado's sleek Bentley edged up the drive to the home of America's best-known financier-philanthropist,' Robert Putney Drake.* (Louis marched toward the Red Window, maintaining his dignity. An old man in a strange robe pushed to the front of the crowd, trembling with exhaltation. The blade rose: the mob sucked in its breath. The old man tried to look into Louis's eyes, but the king could not focus them. The blade fell: the crowd exhaled. As the head rolled into the basket, the old man raised his eyes in ecstasy and cried out, 'Jacques De Molay, thou art avenged!') Professor Glynn lectured his class on medieval history (Dean Deane was issuing the Strawberry Statement on the same campus at the same time) and said, 'The real crime of the Templars, however, was probably their association with the Hashishim.' George Dorn, hardly listening, wondered if he should join Mark Rudd and the others who wanted to close down Columbia entirely.

'And modern novels are the same,' Smiling Jim went on. 'Sex, sex, sex – and not normal sex even. Every type of perverted, degenerate, unnatural, filthy, deviated, and sick kind of sex. This is how they're gonna bury us, as Mr. Khrushchev said, without even firing a shot.'

Sunlight awakened Saul Goodman.
Sunlight and a headache. A hangover from the combination of drugs.

He was in a bed and his clothes were gone. There was no mistaking the garment he wore: a hospital gown. And the room – as he squinted against the sun – had the dull modern-penitentiary look of a typical American hospital.

He hadn't heard the door open, but a weathered-looking middle-aged man in a doctor's smock drifted into the room. He was carrying a clipboard; pens stuck their necks out of his smock pocket; he smiled benignly. His horn-rimmed heavily black glasses and crewcut marked him as the optimistic, upward-mobile man of his generation, without either the depression/World War II memories that gave anxiety to Saul's contemporaries or nuclear nightmares that gave rage and alienation to youth. He would obviously think of himself as a liberal and vote conservatively at least half the time.

A hopeless schmuck.

Except that he was probably none of those things, but another of their agents, doing a very convincing performance.

'Well?' he said brightly. 'Feeling better, Mr. Muldoon?'

Muldoon, Saul thought. Here we go – another ride into their *kitsch* idea of the Heart of Darkness.

'My name is Goodman,' he said thinly. 'I'm about as Irish as Moishe Dayan.'

'Oh, still playing that little game, are we?' the man spoke kindly. 'And are you still a detective?'

'Go to hell,' Saul said, no longer in mood to fight back with wit and irony. He would dig into his hostility and make his last stand from a foxhole of bitterness and sullen brevity.

The man pulled up a chair and sat down. 'Actually,' he

said, 'these remaining symptoms don't bother us much.
You were in a much worse state when you were first
brought here six months ago. I doubt that you remember
that. Electroshock mercifully removed a great deal of the
near past, which is helpful in cases like yours. Do you
know that you were physically assaulting people on the
street, and tried to attack the nurses and orderlies your
first month here? Your paranoia was very acute at that
point, Mr. Muldoon.'

'Up yours, bubi,' Saul said. He closed his eyes and
turned the other way.

'Such moderate hostility these days,' the man went on,
bright as a bird in the morning grass. 'A few months ago
you would have tried to strangle me. Let me show you
something.' There was a sound of paper.

Curiosity defeated resistance: Saul turned and looked.
The man held out a driver's license, from the State of New
Jersey, for 'Barney Muldoon,' the picture was Saul's. Saul
grinned maliciously, showing his disbelief.

'You refuse to recognize yourself?' the man asked
quietly.

'Where is Barney Muldoon?' Saul shot back. 'Do you
have him in another room, trying to convince him he's
Saul Goodman?'

'Where is . . .?' the 'doctor' repeated, seeming genuinely
baffled. 'Oh, yes, you admit you know the name but claim
he was only a friend. Just like a rapist we had in here a
while ago. He said all the rapes were committed by his
roommate, Charlie. Well, let's try another tack. All those
people you beat up on the street – and that Playboy Club
bunny you tried to strangle – do you still believe they were
agents of this, um, Prussian Illuminati?'

'This is an improvement,' Saul said. 'A very intriguing
combination of reality and fantasy, much better than your
group's previous efforts. Let me hear the rest of it.'

'You think that's sarcasm,' the man said calmly. 'Actually, behind it, your recovery is proceeding nicely. You
really want to remember, even as you struggle to keep up
this Goodman myth. Very well: you are a sixty-year-old
police officer from Trenton, New Jersey. You never were
promoted to detective and that is the great grievance of
your life. You have a wife named Molly, and three sons –

Roger, Kerry, and Gregory. Their ages are twenty-eight, twenty-five, and twenty-three. A few years ago, you started a game with your wife; she thought it was harmless at first and learned to her sorrow that it wasn't. The game was, that you pretended to be a detective and, late at night, you would tell her about the important cases you were working on. Gradually, you built up to the most important case of all – the solution to all the assassinations in America during the past decade. They were all the work of a group called the Illuminati, who were surviving top-level Nazis that had never been captured. More and more, you talked about their leader – Martin Borman, of course – and insisted you were getting a line on his whereabouts. By the time your wife realized that the game had become reality to you, it was too late. You already suspected your neighbors of being Illuminati agents, and your hatred for Nazism led you to believe you were Jewish and had taken an Irish name to avoid American anti-Semitism. This particular delusion, I must say, caused you acute guilt, which it took up a long time to understand. It was, we finally realized, a projection of a guilt you have long felt for being a policeman at all. But perhaps at this point, I might aid your struggle for self-recognition (and abort your equal and opposite struggle for self-escape) by reading you part of a report on your case by one of our younger psychiatrists. Are you game to hear it?'

'Go ahead,' Saul said. 'I still find this entertaining.'

The man looked through the papers in his clipboard and smiled disarmingly. 'Oh, I see here that it's the Bavarian Illuminati, not the Prussian Illuminati, pardon my mistake.' He flipped a few more pages. 'Here we are,' he said.

'The root of the subject's problems,' he began to read, 'can be found in the trauma of the primal scene, which was reconstructed under narco-analysis. At the age of three, he came upon his parents in the act of fellatio, which resulted in his being locked in his room for "spying." This left him with a permanent horror of being locked up and a pity for prisoners everywhere. Unfortunately, this factor in his personality, which he might have sublimated harmlessly by becoming a social worker, was complicated by unresolved Oedipal hostilities and a reaction formation in favor of "spying," which led him to become a policeman.

The criminal became for him the father-symbol, who was
locked up in revenge for locking him up; at the same time,
the criminal was an ego-projection and he received mas-
ochistic gratification by identifying with the prisoner. The
deep-buried homosexual desire for the father's penis (present in all policemen) was next cathected by denial of the
father, *via* denial of paternal ancestry, and he began to
abolish all Irish Catholic traces from ego-memory, substituting those of Jewish culture, since the Jew, as persecuted minority, reinforced his basic masochism. Finally,
like all paranoids, the subject fancies himself to be of
superior intelligence (actually, on his test for the Trenton
Police Force, he rated only one hundred ten on the Stan-
ford-Binet IQ index) and his resistance to therapy will take
the form of "outwitting" his doctors by finding the "clues"
which reveal that they, too, are agents of the Illuminati
and that his assumed identity as "Saul Goodman" is, in
fact, his actual identity. For therapeutic purposes, I would
recommend . . .' The 'doctor' broke off. 'After that,' he
said briefly, 'it is of no interest to you. Well,' he added
tolerantly, 'do you want to "detect" the errors in this?'

'I've never been in Trenton in my life,' Saul said wearily.
'I don't know what anything in Trenton looks like. But
you'll just tell me that I've erased those memories. Let's
move to a deeper level of combat, *Herr Doktor*. I am quite
convinced that my mother and father never performed fellatio in their lives. They were too old-fashioned.' This was
the heart of the labyrinth, and their real threat: while he
was sure that they could not break down his belief in his
own identity, they were also insidiously undermining that
identity by suggesting it was pathological. Many of the
lines in the Muldoon case history could refer to any policeman and might, conceivably, refer to him; as usual, behind
a weak open attack they were mounting a more deadly
covered attack.

'Do you recognize these?' the doctor asked, producing
a sketchbook open to a page with some drawings of unicorn.

'It's my sketchbook,' Saul said. 'I don't know how you
got it but it doesn't prove a damned thing, except that I
sketch in my spare time.'

'No?' The doctor turned the book around; a bookplate

on the cover identified the owner as Barney Muldoon, 1472 Pleasant Avenue, Trenton, N.J.

'Amateur work,' Saul said. 'Anybody can paste a bookplate onto a book.'

'And the unicorn means nothing to you?' Saul sensed the trap and said nothing, waiting. 'You are not aware of the long psychoanalytical literature on the unicorn as symbol of the father's penis? Tell me, then, why did you decide to sketch unicorns?'

'More amateurism,' Saul said. 'If I sketched mountains, they would be symbols of the father's penis, too.'

'Very well. You might have made a good detective if your – illness – hadn't prevented your promotion. You do have a quick, skeptical mind. Let me try another approach – and I wouldn't be using such tactics if I weren't convinced you were on the road to recovery; a true psychotic would be driven into catatonia by such a blunt assault on his delusions. But, tell me, your wife mentioned that just before the acute stage of your – problem – you spent a lot of money, more than you could afford on a patrolman's salary, on a reproduction of the mermaid of Copenhagen. Why was that?'

'Damn it,' Saul exclaimed, 'it wasn't a lot of money.' But he recognized the displaced anger and saw that the other man recognized it too. He was avoiding the question of the mermaid . . . and her relation to the unicorn. *There must be a relationship between fact number one and fact number two.* . . . 'The mermaid,' he said, getting there before the enemy could, 'is a mother symbol, right? She has no human bottom, because the male child dare not think about that area of the mother. Is that correct jargon?'

'More or less. You avoid, of course, the peculiar relevance in your own case: that the sex act in which you caught your mother was not a normal one but a very perverted and infantile act, which, of course, is the only sex act a mermaid can perform – as all collectors of mermaid statues or mermaid paintings unconsciously know.'

'It's not perverted and infantile,' Saul protested. 'Most people do it. . . .' Then he saw the trap.

'But not *your* mother and father? They were different from most people?'

And then it clicked: the spell was broken. Every detail

from Saul's notebook, every physical characteristic Peter Jackson had described, was there. 'You're not a doctor,' he shouted. 'I don't know what your game is but I sure as hell know who you are. You're Joseph Malik!'

George's stateroom was paneled in teak, the walls hung with small but exquisite paintings by Rivers, Shahn, De Kooning, and Tanguy. A glass cabinet built into one wall held several rows of books. The floor was carpeted in wine red with a blue stylized octopus in the center, its waving tentacles radiating out like a sunburst. The light fixture hanging from the ceiling was a lucite model of that formidable jellyfish, the Portuguese man-of-war.

The bed was full size, with a rosewood headboard carved with Venetian seashell motifs. Its legs didn't touch the floor; the whole thing was supported on a huge, rounded beam that allowed the bed to seesaw when the ship rolled, the sleeper remaining level. Beside the bed was a small desk. Going to it, George opened a drawer and found several different sizes of writing paper and half a dozen felt-tipped pens in various colors. He took out a legal-size pad and a green pen, climbed on the bed, curled up at the head and began writing.

April 24

Objectivity is presumably the opposite of schizophrenia. Which means that it is nothing but acceptance of everybody else's notion of reality. But nobody's perception of reality is the same as everybody's notion of it, which means that the most objective person is the real schizophrenic.

It is hard to get beyond the accepted beliefs of one's own age. The first man to think a new thought advances it very tentatively. New ideas have to be around a while before anyone will promote them hard. In their first form, they are like tiny, imperceptible mutations that may eventually lead to new species. That's why cultural cross-fertilization is so important. It increases the gene-pool of the imagination. The Arabs, say, have one part of the puzzle. The Franks another. So when the Knights Templar meet the Hashishim, something new is born.

The human race has always lived more or less happily in the kingdom of the blind. But there is an elephant among us. A one-eyed elephant.

George put the pen down and read the green words with a frown. His thoughts still seemed to be coming from outside his own mind. What was that business about the Knights Templar? He had never felt the slightest interest in that period since his freshman year in college, when old Morrison Glynn had given him a *D* for that paper on the Crusades. It was supposed to be a simple research paper displaying one's grasp of proper footnote style, but George had chosen to denounce the Crusades as an early outbreak of Western racist imperialism. He'd even gone to the trouble of finding the text of a letter from Sinan, third leader of the Hashishim, in which he exonerates Richard Coeur de Lion of any complicity in the murder of Conrad of Montferret, King of Jerusalem. George felt the episode demonstrated the essential goodwill of the Arabs. How was he to know that Morrison Glynn was a staunch conservative Catholic? Glynn claimed, among other dyspeptic criticisms, that the letter from the castle called Messiac was well known as a forgery. Why were the Hashishim coming back to mind again? Did it have to do with the weird dream he'd had of the temple in the Mad Dog jail?

The sub's engine was vibrating pleasantly through the floor, the beam, the bed. The trip so far had reminded George of his first flight in a 747 – a surge of power, followed by motion so smooth it was impossible to tell how fast or how far they were going.

There was a knock at the stateroom door, and at George's invitation Hagbard's receptionist came in. She was wearing a tight-fitting golden-yellow slack ensemble. She stared compellingly at George, her pupils huge obsidian pools, and smiled faintly.

'Will you eat me if I can't guess the riddle?' George said. 'You remind me of a sphinx.'

Her lips, the color of ripe grapes, parted in a grin. 'I modeled for it. But no riddle, just an ordinary question. Hagbard wants to know if you need anything. Anything but me. I've got work to do now.'

George shrugged. 'You beat me to the question. I'd like

to get together with Hagbard and find out more about him
and the submarine and where we're going.'

'We are going to Atlantis. He must have told you that.'
She shifted her weight from one foot to the other, rolling
her hips. She had marvelously long legs. 'Atlantis is,
roughly speaking, about half way between Cuba and the
west coast of Africa, at the bottom of the ocean.'

'Yeah, well – That's where it's supposed to be, right?'

'Right. Hagbard's going to want you in the captain's
control room later. Meanwhile, smoke some of this, if you
want. Helps to pass the time.' She held out a gold cigarette
case. George took it from her, his fingers brushing the vel-
vety black skin of her hand. A pang of desire for her
swept through him. He fumbled with the catch of the case
and opened it. There were slender white tubes inside, each
one stamped with a gold *K*. He took one out and held it to
his nose. A pleasant, earthy smell.

'We've got a plantation and a factory in Brazil,' she
said.

'Hagbard must be a wealthy man.'

'Oh, yeah. He's worth billions and billions of tons of
flax. Well, look, George, if you need anything, just press
the ivory button on your desk. Someone will come along.
We'll be calling you later.' She turned with a languid wave
and walked down the fluorescent-lit corridor. George's gaze
clung to her unbelievable ass till she climbed a narrow
flight of carpeted stairs and was out of sight.

What was that woman's name? He lay down on the bed,
took out a joint, and lit it. It was marvelous. He was up in
seconds, not the usual gradual balloon ascent, but a rocket
trip, not unlike the effect of amyl nitrate. He might have
known this Hagbard Celine would have something special
in the way of grass. He studied the sparkles glinting through
the Portuguese man-of-war and wiggled his eyeballs rapidly
to make the lights dance. All things that are, are lights.
The thought came that Hagbard might be evil. Hagbard
was like some robber baron out of the nineteenth century.
Also like some robber baron out of the eleventh century.
The Normans took Sicily in the ninth century. Which gave
you mixtures of Viking and Sicilian, but did they ever
look like Anthony Quinn? Or his son Greg La Strade?
What son? What the sun done cannot be undone but is

well dun. The quintessence of evil. Nemesis of all evil. God bless us, every one. Even One. Odd, the big red one. Eye think it was his I. The eye of Apollo. His luminous I. Aum Shiva.

—Aye, trust me not. Trust not a man who's rich in flax – his morals may be sadly lax. Her name is Stella. Stella Maris. Black star of the sea.

The joint was down to the last half inch. He put it down and crushed it out. With grass flowing like tobacco around here, it was a luxury he could afford. He wasn't going to light another one. That wasn't a high, that was a trip! A Saturn rocket, right out of the world. And back, just as fast.

—George, I want you in the captain's control room.

Clearly, this hallucinating of voices and images meant he wasn't all the way back. Reentry was not completed. He now saw a vision of the layout of that part of the submarine between his stateroom and the captain's control room. He stood up, stretched, shook his head, his hair swirling around his shoulders. He walked to the door, slid it back, and walked on down the hall.

A little later, he stepped through a door onto a balcony which was a reproduction of the prow of a Viking ship. Above, below, in front, to the sides, was green-blue ocean. They seemed to be in a grass globe projecting into the ocean. A long-necked red-and-green dragon with golden eyes and a spiky crest reared above George and Hagbard.

'My approach is fanciful, rather than functional,' Hagbard said. 'If I weren't so intelligent, it would get me into a lot of trouble.' He patted the dragon figurehead with a black-furred hand. Some Viking, George thought. A Neanderthal Viking, perhaps.

'That was a good trick,' George said, feeling shrewd but still high. 'How you got me up on the bridge with that telepathy thing.'

'I called you on the intercom,' Hagbard said, with a look of absurd innocence.

'You think I can't tell a voice in my head from a voice in my ears?'

Hagbard roared with laughter, so loud that it made George feel a little uncertain. 'Not when you've had your first taste of Kallisti Gold, man.'

'Who am I to call a man a liar when he's just turned me
on with the best shit I ever had?' said George with a
shrug. 'I suspect you of making use of telepathy. Most
people who have that power would not only not try to hide
it, they'd go on television.'

'Instead, I put the ocean on television,' said Hagbard.
He gestured at the globe surrounding their Viking prow.
'What you see is simply color television with a few adap-
tations and modifications. We are inside the screen. The
cameras are all over the surface of the sub. The cameras
don't use ordinary light, of course. If they did, you wouldn't
be able to see anything. The submarine illuminates the sea
around us with an infrared laser-radar to which our TV
cameras are sensitive. The radiations are of a type that is
more readily conducted by the hydrogen in water than by
any other element. The result is that we can see the ocean
bottom almost as clearly as if it were dry land and we
were in a plane flying above it.'

'That'll make it easy to see Atlantis when we get to it,'
George said. 'By the way, why did you say we're going to
Atlantis, again? I didn't believe it when you told me, and
now I'm too stoned to remember.'

'The Illuminati are planning to loot one of the greatest
works of art in the history of man – the Temple of Tethys.
It happens to be a solid-gold temple, and their intention is
to melt it down and sell the gold to finance a series of
assassinations in the U.S. I intend to get there before them.'

The reference to assassinations reminded George that
he'd gone down to Mad Dog, Texas, on Joe Malik's hunch
that he'd find a clue there to an assassination conspiracy. If
Joe knew that the clue was leading 20,000 leagues under
the sea and eons back through time, would he believe it?
George doubted it. Malik was one of those hard-nosed
'scientific' leftists. Though he had been acting and talking
a little strangely lately.

'Who did you say was looting this temple?' he asked
Hagbard.

'The Illuminati. The real force behind all communist and
fascist movements. Whether you're aware of it or not,
they're also already in control of the United States government.'

'I thought everybody in your crowd was a right-winger—'

'And I told you spacial metaphors are inadequate in discussing politics today,' Hagbard interrupted.

'Well, you sound like a gang of right-wingers. Up until the last minute, all I've heard from you and your people was that the Illuminati were commies, or were behind the commies. Now you say they're behind fascism and behind the current government in Washington, too.'

Hagbard laughed. 'We came on like right-wing paranoids, at first, to see how you'd react. It was a test.'

'And?'

'You passed. You didn't believe us – that was obvious – but you kept your eyes and ears open and were willing to listen. If you were a right-winger, we would have done our pro-communist rap. The idea is to find out if a new man or woman will listen, really listen, or just shut their minds at the first really shocking idea.'

'I'm listening, but not uncritically. For instance, if the Illuminati control America already, what's the purpose of the assassinations?'

'Their grip on Washington is still pretty precarious. They've been able to socialize the economy. But if they showed their hand now and went totalitarian all the way, there would be a revolution. Middle-roaders would rise up with right-wingers, and left-libertarians, and the Illuminati aren't powerful enough to withstand that kind of massive revolution. But they can rule by fraud, and by fraud eventually acquire access to the tools they need to finish the job of killing off the Constitution.'

'What sort of tools?'

'More stringent security measures. Universal electronic surveillance. No-knock laws. Stop and frisk laws. Government inspection of first-class mail. Automatic fingerprinting, photographing, blood tests, and urinalysis of any person arrested before he is charged with a crime. A law making it unlawful to resist even unlawful arrest. Laws establishing detention camps for potential subversives. Gun control laws. Restrictions on travel. The assassinations, you see, establish the need for such laws in the public mind. Instead of realizing that there is a conspiracy, conducted by a handful of men, the people reason – or are

manipulated into reasoning – that the entire populace must
have its freedom restricted in order to protect the leaders.
The people agree that they themselves can't be trusted.
Targets for assassination will be mavericks of left or right
who are either not part of the Illuminati conspiracy or
have been marked as unreliable. The Kennedy brothers
and Martin Luther King, for example, were capable of
mobilizing a somewhat libertarian left-right-black-white
populist movement. But the assassinations that have occurred so far are nothing compared to what will take place.
The next wave will be carried out by the Mafia, who will be
paid in Illuminati gold.'

'Not Moscow gold,' said George with a smile.

'The puppets in the Kremlin have no idea that they and
the puppets in the White House are working for the same
people. The Illuminati control all sorts of organizations
and national governments without any of them being aware
that others are also controlled. Each group thinks it is
competing with the others, while actually each is playing its
part in the Illuminati plan. Even the Morituri – the six-
person affinity groups which splintered from the SDS
Weathermen, because the Weathermen seemed too cautious – are under the control of the Illuminati. They think
they're working to bring down the government, but actually they are strengthening its hand. The Black Panthers
are also infiltrated. Everything is infiltrated. At present
rate, within the next few years the Illuminati will have the
American people under tighter surveillance than Hitler had
the Germans. And the beauty of it is, the majority of the
Americans will have been so frightened by Illuminati-
backed terrorist incidents that they will beg to be controlled as a masochist begs for the whip.'

George shrugged. Hagbard sounded like a typical paranoid, but there was this submarine and the strange events
of the past few days. 'So the Illuminati are conspiring to
tyrannize the world, is that it? Do you trace them back to
the First International?'

'No. They're what happened when the Enlightenment of
the eighteenth century collided with German mysticism.
The correct name for the organization is Ancient Illuminated Seers of Bavaria. According to their own traditions
they were founded or revived in seventeen seventy-six on

May first by a man named Adam Weishaupt. Weishaupt was an unfrocked Jesuit and a Mason. He taught that religions and national governments had to be overthrown and the world ruled by an elite of scientifically-minded materialistic atheists, to be held in trust for the masses of mankind who would eventually rule themselves when enlightenment became universal. But this was only Weishaupt's "Outer Doctrine." There was also an "Inner Doctrine," which was that power is an end in itself, and that Weishaupt and his closest followers would make use of the new knowledge being developed by scientists and engineers to seize control of the world. Back in seventeen seventy-six, things were run largely by the Church and the feudal nobility, with the capitalists slowly getting a bigger and bigger piece of the pie. Weishaupt declared that these groups were obsolete, and it was time for an elite with a monopoly on scientific and technological knowledge to seize power. Instead of eventually producing a democratic society, as the "Outer Doctrine" promised, the Ancient Illuminated Seers of Bavaria would saddle mankind with a dictatorship that would last forever.'

'Well, it would be logical enough that someone around that time would think of that,' said George. 'And who more likely than a Mason who was an unfrocked Jesuit?'

'You recognize that what I tell you is relatively plausible,' said Hagbard. 'That's a good sign.'

'A sign that it's plausible,' laughed George.

'No, a sign that you're the kind of person I'm always looking for. Well, the Illuminati, after staying above ground long enough to recruit a hard-core membership from Masons and freethinkers and to establish international contacts, allowed it to seem that the Bavarian government had suppressed them. Subsequently, the Illuminati launched their first experimental revolution, in France. Here they suckered the middle class, whose true interests lay in laissez faire free enterprise, to follow the Weishaupt slogan of "Liberty, Equality, Fraternity." The catch, of course, is that where equality and fraternity rule, there is no liberty. After the career of Napoleon, whose rise and fall was purely the result of Illuminati manipulations, they started planting the seeds of European socialism, leading to the revolutions of eighteen forty-eight, to Marxism, finally to the seizure of Russia, one-sixth of the earth's land mass. Of course, they had to engineer a world war to make the Russian Revolution possible, but by nineteen seventeen they had become quite good at that. World War Two was an even more clever job and resulted in more gains for them.'

'Another thing this explains,' George said, 'is why orthodox Marxism-Leninism, in spite of all its ideals, always turns out to be not worth a shit. Why it's always betrayed the people wherever it established itself. And it explains why there's such an inevitable quality about America's drift toward totalitarianism.'

'Right,' said Hagbard. 'America is the target now. They've got most of Europe and Asia. Once they get America, they can come out into the open. The world will then be much as Orwell predicted in *Nineteen Eighty-four*. They bumped him off after it was published, you know. The book hit a little too close to home. He was obviously on to them – the references to Inner and Outer parties with different teachings, O'Brien's speech about power being an end in itself – and they got him. Orwell, you see, ran across them in Spain, where they were functioning quite openly at one point during the Civil War. But artists also arrive at truth through their imaginations, if they let themselves wander freely. They're more likely to arrive at the truth than more scientific-minded people.'

'You've just tied two hundred years of world history up in a theory that would make me feel I should have myself committed if I accepted it,' said George. 'But I'm drawn to it, I admit. Partly intuitively – I feel you are a person who is essentially sane and not paranoid. Partly because the orthodox version of history that I was taught in school never made sense to me, and I know how people can twist history to suit their beliefs, and therefore I assume that the history I've learned is twisted. Partly because of the very wildness of the idea. If I learned one thing in the last few years, it's that the crazier an idea is the more likely it is to be true. Still and all, given all those reasons for believing you, I would like some further sign.'

Hagbard nodded. 'All right. A sign. So be it. First, a question for you. Assuming your boss, Joe Malik, was on to something – assuming that the place he sent you did have something to do with assassinations and might lead to the Illuminati: what would be likely to happen to Joe Malik?'

'I know what you're suggesting. I don't like to think about it.'

'Don't think.' Hagbard suddenly pulled a telephone from under the railing of the ship. 'We can tap into the Bell System through the Atlantic cable from here. Dial the New York area code and dial any person in New York, any person who could give you up-to-date information on Joe Malik and on *Confrontation* magazine. Don't tell me who you're dialing. Otherwise, you might suspect I had someone on the ship impersonate the person you want to speak to.'

Holding the phone so Hagbard couldn't see, George dialed a number. After a wait of about thirty seconds, after numerous clicks and other strange sounds, George could hear a phone ringing. After a moment, a voice said. 'Hello.'

'This is George Dorn,' said George. 'Who is this?'

'Well, who the hell did you think it was? You dialed my number.'

'Oh, Christ,' said George. 'Look, I'm in a place where I don't trust the phones. I have to be sure I'm really talking to you. So I want you to identify yourself without my telling you who you're supposed to be. Do you understand?'

'Of course I understand. You don't have to use that grade school language. This is Peter Jackson, George, as I presume you intended that it should be. Where the hell are you? Are you still in Mad Dog?'

'I'm at the bottom of the Atlantic Ocean.'

'Knowing your bad habits, I'm not surprised. Have you heard about what happened to us? Is that why you're calling?'

'No. What happened?' George gripped the telephone tighter.

'The office was blown up by a bomb early this morning. And Joe has disappeared.'

'Was Joe killed?'

'Not as far as we know. There weren't any bodies in the wreckage. How about you – are you okay?'

'I'm getting into an unbelievable story, Peter. It's so unbelievable that I'm not going to try to tell you about it. Not till I get back. If you're still running a magazine there then.'

'As of now there's still a magazine, and I'm running it from my apartment,' said Peter. 'I only hope they don't decide to blow me up.'

'Who?'

'Whoever. You're still on assignment. And if this has anything to do with what you've been doing down in Mad Dog, Texas, you're in trouble. Reporters are not supposed to go around getting their boss's magazines bombed.'

'You sound pretty cheerful, considering Joe might be dead.'

'Joe is indestructible. By the way, George, who's paying for this call?'

'A wealthy friend, I think. He's got a corner on flax or something like that. More on him later. I'm going to sign off now, Pete. Thanks for talking.'

'Sure. Take care, baby.'

George handed the phone to Hagbard. 'Do you know what's happened to Joe? Do you know who bombed *Confrontation*? You knew about this before I called. Your people are pretty handy with explosives.'

Hagbard shook his head. 'All I know is, the pot is coming to a boil. Your editor, Joe Malik, was onto the Illuminati. That's why he sent you to Mad Dog. As soon as you show your face down there, you get busted and Malik's office is bombed. What do you think?'

'I think that what you've been telling me is the truth, or a version of it. I don't know whether to trust you completely. But I've got my sign. If the Bavarian Illuminati don't exist, *something* does. So, then, where do we go from here?'

Hagbard smiled. 'Spoken like a true *homo neophilus*, George. Welcome to the tribe. We want to recruit you, because you are so gullible. That is, gullible in the right way. You're skeptical about conventional wisdom, but attracted to unorthodox ideas. An unfailing mark of *homo neophilus*. The human race is not divided into the irrational and the rational, as some idealists think. All humans are irrational, but there are two different kinds of irrationally – those who love old ideas and hate and fear new ones, and those who despise old ideas and joyfully embrace new ones. *Homo neophobus* and *homo neophilus*. *Neophobus* is the original human stock, the stock that hardly changed at all for the first four million years of human history. Neophilus is the creative mutation that has been popping up at regular intervals during the past million years, giving the race little forward pushes, the kind you give a wheel to make it spin faster and faster. Neophilus makes a lot of mistakes, but he or she moves. They live life the way it should be lived, ninety-nine percent mistakes and one percent viable mutations. Everyone in my organization is *neophilus*, George. That's why we're so far ahead of the rest of the human race. Concentrated neophilus influences, without any neophobe dilution. We make a million mistakes, but we move so fast that none of them catch up with us. Before you get any deeper, George, I'd like you to become one of us.'

'Which means what?'

'Become a Legionnaire in the Legion of Dynamic Discord.'

George laughed. 'Now that sounds like a gas. But it's hard to believe that an organization with an absurd name like that could build anything as serious as this submarine, or work for such a serious end as foiling the Ancient Illuminated Seers of Bavaria.'

Hagbard shook his head. 'What's serious about a yellow submarine? It's right out of a rock song. And everybody knows people who worry about the Bavarian Illuminati are crackpots. Will you join the Legion – in whatever spirit you choose?'

'Certainly,' said George promptly.

Hagbard clapped him on the back. 'Ah, you're our type, all right. Good. Back through the door you came, then turn right and through the golden door.'

'Is there someone lifting a lamp beside it?'

'There are no honest men on this voyage. Get along with you now.' Hagbard's full lips curled in a leer. 'You're in for a treat.'

('Every perversion,' Smiling Jim screamed. 'Men having sex with men. Women having sex with women. Obscene desecrations of religious articles for deviant purposes. Even men and women having sex with animals. Why, friends,

the only thing they haven't gotten around to yet is people
copulating with fruits and vegetables, and I guess that'll be
next. Some degenerate getting his kicks with an apple!'
The audience laughed at the wit.)

'You've got to run very fast to catch up with the sun.
That's the way it is, when you're lost out here,' the old
woman said, stressing the last five words in a kind of
childish singsong. . . . The woods were incredibly thick
and dark, but Barney Muldoon stumbled after her. . . .
'It's getting darker and darker,' she said darkly, 'but's
always dark, *when you're lost out here*'. . . . 'Why do we
have to catch the Sun?' Barney asked, perplexed. 'In
search of more light,' she cackled gleefully. 'You always
need more light, *when you're lost out here*'. . . .

Behind the golden door stood the lovely black receptionist. She had changed into a short red leather skirt that left
all of her long legs in view. Her hands rested lightly on her
white plastic belt.

'Hi, Stella,' said George. 'Is that your name? Is it really
Stella Maris?'

'Sure.'

'No honest men on this voyage is right. Hagbard *was*
talking to me telepathically. He told me your name.'

'I told you my name when you boarded the sub. You
must have forgotten. You've been through a lot. And sad
to say you'll be going through a lot more. I must ask you
to remove your clothing. Just shed it on the floor, please.'

George unhesitatingly did as he was told. Total or partial nudity was required in lots of initiation rituals; but a
twinge of anxiety ran through him. He was trusting these
people simply because they hadn't done anything to him
yet. But there was really no telling what kind of freaks
they might be, what kind of ritual torture or murder they
might involve him in. Such fears were part of initiation
rituals, too.

Stella was grinning at him, eyebrows raised, as he dropped
his shorts. He understood the meaning of the grin, and he
felt the blood rush hot as a blush to his penis, which grew
thicker and heavier in an instant. Being aware that he was
standing nude with the start of an erection in front of this
beautiful and desirable woman, who was enjoying the
spectacle, made him swell and harden still more.

'That's a good-looking tool you've got there. Nice and thick and pink and purple.' Stella sauntered over to him, reached out and touched her fingers to the underside of his cock, just where it met his scrotum. He felt his balls draw up. Then her middle finger ran down the central cord, flicking the underside of the head. George's penis rose to full staff in salute to her manual dexterity.

'The sexually responsive male,' said Stella. 'Good, good, good. Now you're ready for the next chamber. Right through that green door, if you please.'

Naked, erect, regretfully leaving Stella behind, George walked through the door. These people were too healthy and good-humored to be untrustworthy, he thought. He liked them and you ought to trust your feelings.

But as the green door slammed shut behind him, his anxiety came back even stronger than before.

In the center of the room was a pyramid of seventeen steps, alternating red and white marble. The room was large, with five walls that tapered together in a gothic arch thirty feet above the pentagonal floor. Unlike the pyramid in the Mad Dog jail, this one had no huge eye goggling down at him. Instead there was an enormous golden apple, a sphere of gold the height of a man with a foot-long stem and a single leaf the size of an elephant's ear. Cut into the side of the apple was the word KALLISTI in Greek letters. The walls of the room were draped with enormous gold curtains that looked like they'd been stolen from a Cinerama theater, and the floor was covered with lush gold carpet into which George's bare feet sank deeply.

This is different, George told himself to quiet his fear. These people are different. There's a connection with the others, but they're different.

The lights went out. The golden apple was glowing in the dark like a harvest moon. KALLISTI was etched in sharp black lines.

A voice that sounded like Hagbard boomed at him from all sides of the room: 'There is no goddess but Goddess, and she is your goddess.'

This is actually an Elks Club ceremony, George thought. But there were strange, un-BPOE fumes drifting into his nostrils. An unmistakable odor. High-priced incense these people use. An expensive religion, or lodge, or whatever

it is. But you can afford the best when you're a flax tycoon.
Flax, huh? Hard to see how a man could make such big
money in the flax biz. Did you corner the market, or what?
Now, mutual funds, that was more down to earth than flax.
I do believe I'm feeling the effects. They shouldn't drug a
man without his consent.

He found he was holding his penis, which had shrunk
considerably. He gave it a reassuring pull.

Said the voice, 'There is no movement but the Discordian movement, and it is the Discordian movement.'

That would appear to be self-evident. George rolled his
eyes and watched the giant, golden-glowing apple wheel
and spin above him.

'This is a most sacred and a most serious hour for Discordians. It is the hour when the great, palpitating heart of
Discordia throbs and swells, when She What Began It All
prepares to ingest into her heaving, chaotic bosom another
Legionnaire of the Legion of Dynamic Discord. O minerval
are ye willing to make a commitment to Discordia?'

Embarrassed at being addressed directly, George let go
of his wang. 'Yes,' he said, in a voice that sounded muffled to him.

'Are ye a human being, and not a cabbage or something?'

George giggled. 'Yes.'

'That's too bad,' the voice boomed. 'Do ye wish to better
yourself?'

'Yes.'

'How stupid. Are ye willing to become philosophically
illuminated?'

Why that word, George wondered briefly. Why *illuminated*? But he said, 'I suppose so.'

'Very funny. Will ye dedicate yerself to the holy Discordian movement?'

George shrugged. 'As long as it suits me.'

There was a draught against his belly. Stella Maris, naked
and gleaming, stepped out from behind the pyramid. The
soft glow from the golden apple illuminated the rich
browns and blacks of her body. George felt the blood
charging back into his penis. This part was going to be
OK. Stella walked toward him with a slow, stately stride,
gold bracelets sparkling and tinkling on her wrists. George

felt hunger, thirst, and a pressure as if a balloon were slowly being inflated in his bowels. His cock rose, heart-beat by heartbeat. The muscles in his buttocks and thighs tightened, relaxed, and tightened again.

Stella approached with gliding steps and danced around him in a circle, one hand reaching out to brush his bare waist. He stepped forward and held out his hands to her. She danced away on tiptoes, spinning, arms over her head, heavy conical breasts with black nipples tilted upward. For once George understood why some men like big boobs. His eyes moved to the globes of her buttocks, the long muscular shadows in her thighs and calves. He stumbled toward her. She stopped suddenly, legs slightly apart form-ing an inverse with her patch of very abundant hair at the Royal Arch, her hips swaying in a gentle circular motion. His tool pulled him to her as if it were iron and she were magnetized; he looked down and saw that a little pearl of fluid, gleaming gold in the light from the apple, had appeared in the eye. Polyphemus wanted very much to get into the cave.

George walked up to her until the head of the serpent was buried in the bushy, prickly garden at the bottom of her belly. He put his hands out and pressed them against the two cones, feeling her ribcage rise and fall with heavy breathing. Her eyes were half closed and her lips slightly open. Her nostrils flared wide.

She licked her lips and he felt her fingers lightly circling his cock, lightly brushing it with a friction strong enough to gently electrify it. She stepped back a bit and pushed her finger into the moisture on his tip. George put his hand into the tangle of her pubic hair, feeling the lips hot and swollen, feeling her juices slathering his fingers. His middle finger slid into her cunt, and he pushed it in past the tight opening all the way up to his knuckle. She gasped, and her whole body writhed around his finger in a spiral motion.

'Wow, God!' George whispered.

'Goddess!' Stella answered fiercely.

George nodded. 'Goddess,' he said hoarsely, meaning Stella as much as the legendary Discordia.

She smiled and drew away from him. 'Try to imagine that this is not me, Stella Maris, the youngest daughter of Discordia. She is merely the vessel of Goddess. Her priest-

ess. Think of Goddess. Think of her entering me and acting through me. I *am* her now!' All the while she was
stroking Polyphemus gently but insistently. It was already
ferocious as a stallion, but it seemed to be getting more
inflamed, if that were possible.

'I'm going to go off in your hand in a second,' George
moaned. He gripped her slender wrist to stop her. 'I've *got
to fuck you*, whoever you are, woman or goddess. *Please.*'

She stepped back from him, her tan palms turned toward
him, her arms held away from her sides in a receiving,
accepting gesture. But she said, 'Climb the steps now.
Climb up to the apple.' Her feet twinkling on the thick
carpet, she ran backward away from him and disappeared
behind the pyramid.

He climbed the seventeen steps, old one-eye still swollen
and aching. The top of the pyramid was broad and flat, and
he stood facing the apple. He put a hand out and touched
it, expecting cold metal, surprised when the softly glowing
texture felt warm as a human body to his touch. About
half a foot below the level of his waist he saw a dark,
elliptical opening in the side of the apple, and a sinister
suspicion formed in his mind.

'You got it, George' said the booming voice that pre-
sided over his initiation. 'Now you're supposed to plant
your seeds in the apple. Go to it, George. Give yourself to
Goddess.'

Shit man, George thought. What a silly idea! They get a
guy turned on like this and then they expect him to fuck a
goddamn golden idol. He had a good mind to turn his
back on the apple, sit down on the top step of the pyramid
and jack-off to show them what he thought of them.

'George, would we let you down? It's nice there in the
apple. Come on, stick it in. Hurry up.'

I am so gullible, thought George. But a hole is a hole.
It's all friction. He stepped up to the apple and gingerly
placed the tip of his cock in the elliptical opening, half expecting to be sucked in by some mechanical force, half
fearing it would be chopped off by a miniature guillotine.
But there was nothing. His cock didn't even touch the
edges of the hole. He took another small step, and put it
halfway in. Still nothing. Then something warm and wet
and hairy squirmed up against the tip of his cock. And,

whatever it was, he felt it give as he reflexively pushed forward. He pushed some more and it pushed back, and he slid into it. A cunt by all the high hidden Gods, a cunt! – and by the feel it was almost surely Stella's.

George exhaled a deep sigh, planted his hands on the smooth surface of the apple to support himself and began thrusting. The pumping from inside the apple was as fierce. The metal was warm against his thighs and belly. Suddenly the pelvis inside slammed up against the hole, and a hollow scream resounded from the inside of the apple. The echo effect made it seem to hang in the air, containing all the agony, spasm, itch, twitch, moon madness, horror, and ecstasy of life from the ocean's birth to now.

George's prick was stretched like the skin of a balloon about to burst. His lips drew back from his teeth. The delicious electricity of orgasm was building in his groin, in the deepest roots of his penis, in his quick. He was coming. He cried out as he fired his seed into the unseen cunt, into the apple, into Goddess, into eternity.

There was a crash above. George's eyes opened. A nude male body at the end of a rope came hurtling at him from the vaulted ceiling. It jerked to a stop with a horrible crack, its feet quivering above the stem of the apple. Even as the leaps of ejaculation still racked George's body, the penis over his head lifted and spurted thick white gobbets of come, like tiny doves, arcing out over George's uplifted, horrified head to fall somewhere on the side of the pyramid. George stared at the face, canted to one side, the neck broken, a hangman's knot behind the ear. It was his own face.

George went ape. He pulled his penis out of the apple and nearly fell backward down the stairs. He ran down the seventeen steps and looked back. The dead figure was still hanging, through a trap in the ceiling, directly above the apple. The penis had subsided. The body slowly rotated. Enormous laughter boomed out in the room, sounding very much like Hagbard Celine.

'Our sympathies,' said the voice. 'You are now a legionnaire in the Legion of Dynamic Discord.'

The hanging figure vanished soundlessly. There was no trapdoor in the ceiling. A colossal orchestra somewhere began to play *Pomp and Circumstance*. Stella Maris came round from the back of the pyramid again, this time clothed from head to foot in a simple white robe. Her eyes shone. She was carrying a silver tray with a steaming hot towel on it. She put the tray on the floor, knelt, and wrapped George's relaxing dick in the towel. It felt delicious.

'You were beautiful,' she whispered.

'Yeah, but – wow!' George looked up at the pyramid. The golden apple gleamed cheerfully.

'Get up off the floor,' he said. 'You're embarrassing me.'

She stood up smiling at him, the broad grin of a woman whose lover has thoroughly satisfied her.

'I'm glad you liked it,' said George, his wildly disparate emotions gradually coalescing as anger. 'What was the idea of that last little gag? To turn me off permanently on sex?'

Stella laughed. 'George, admit it. Nothing could turn you off sex, right? So don't be such a bad sport.'

'Bad *sport*? That sick trick is your idea of sport? What a goddam rotten dirty motherfucking thing to do to a man!'

'Motherfucking? No, that's for when we ordain deacons.'

George shook his head angrily. She absolutely refused to be shamed. He was speechless.

'If you have any complaints, sweet man, take them to Episkopos Hagbard Celine of the *Lief Erikson* Cabal,' said Stella. She turned and started walking back toward the pyramid. 'He's waiting for you back the way you came. And there's a change of clothes in the next room.'

'Wait a minute!' George called after her. 'What the blazes does *Kallisti* mean?'

She was gone.

In the anteroom of the initiation chamber he found a green tunic and tight black trousers draped over a costumer. He didn't want to put them on. It was probably some sort of uniform of this idiotic cult, and he wanted no part of it. But there weren't any other clothes. There was also a beautiful pair of black boots. Everything fit perfectly and comfortably. There was a full-length mirror on the wall and he looked at himself and grudgingly admitted that the outfit was a gas. A tiny golden apple glinted on the left side of his chest. The only thing was that his hair needed washing. It was getting stringy.

Through two more doors and he was facing Hagbard.

'You didn't like our little ceremony?' said Hagbard with exaggerated sympathy. 'That's too bad. I was so proud of it, especially the parts I lifted from William Burroughs and the Marquis de Sade.'

'It's *sick*,' said George. 'And putting the woman inside the apple so I couldn't have any kind of personal sex with her, so I had to *use* her as a receptacle, as, as an *object*. You made it pornographic, And sadistic pornography, at that.'

'Dig, George,' said Hagbard. 'Thou art that. If there were no death, there would be no sex. If there were no sex, there would be no death. And without sex, there would be no evolution toward intelligence, no human race. Therefore death is necessary. Death is the price of orgasm. Only one being on all this planet is sexless, intelligent and immortal. While you were pumping your seeds into the symbol of life, I showed you orgasm and death in one image and brought it home to you. And you'll never forget it. It was a trip, George. Wasn't it a trip?'

George nodded reluctantly. 'It was a trip.'

'And you know – in your bones – a little more about life than you did before, right, George?'

'Yes.'

'Well, then, thank you for joining the Legion of Dynamic Discord.'

'You're welcome.'

Hagbard beckoned George to the edge of the boat-shaped balcony. He pointed down. Far below in the blue-green medium through which they seemed to be flying George could see rolling lands, hills, winding riverbeds – and then, broken buildings. George gasped. Pyramids rose up below, as high as the hills.

'This is one of the great port cities,' Hagbard said. 'Galleys from the Americas plied their trade to and from this harbor for a thousand years.'

'How long ago?'

'Ten thousand years,' said Hagbard. 'This was one of the last cities to go. Of course, their civilization had declined quite a bit by then. Meanwhile, we've got a problem. The Illuminati are here already.'

A large, undulating, blue-gray shape appeared ahead of

them, swam toward them, whirled and matched their speed so it seemed to drift alongside. George felt another momentary leap of fright. Was this another of Hagbard's tricks?

'What is that fish? How does it keep up with us?' George asked.

'It's a porpoise, not a fish, a mammal. And they can swim a lot faster than submarines can sail underwater. We can keep up with them, though. They form a film around their bodies that enables them to slide through the water without setting up any turbulence. I learned from them how to do it, and I applied it to this sub. We can cross the Atlantic under water in less than a day.'

A voice spoke from the control panel. 'Better go transparent. You'll be within range of their detectors when you've gone another ten miles.'

'Right,' said Hagbard. 'We will maintain present course until further notice, so you'll know where we are.'

'I'll know,' said the voice.

Hagbard slashed his hand through the air disgustedly. 'You're so fucking *superior*.'

'Who are you talking to?' said George.

'Howard.'

The voice said, 'I've never seen machines like this before. They look something like crabs. They've just about got the temple all dug up.'

'When the Illuminati do something on their own, they go first class,' said Hagbard.

'Who the hell is Howard?' said George.

'It's me. Out here. Hello, Mr. Human,' said the voice. 'I'm Howard.'

Unbelieving, yet knowing quite well what was happening, George slowly turned his head. The dolphin appeared to be looking at him.

'How does he talk to us?' said Hagbard.

'He's swimming alongside the prow of the submarine, which is where we pick up his voice. My computer translates from Delphine to English. A mike here in the control room sends our voices to the computer which translates into Delphine and broadcasts the correct sounds through the water to him.'

'Lady-oh, oh de-you-day, a new human being has come

my way,' Howard sang. 'He has swum into my ken. I hope he's one of the friendly men.'

'They sing a lot,' said Hagbard. 'Also recite poetry and make it up on the spot. A large part of their culture is poetry. Poetics and athletics – and, of course, the two are very closely related. What they do mostly is swim, hunt, and communicate with each other.'

'But we do all with artful complexity and rare finesse,' said Howard, looping the loop outside.

'Lead us to the enemy, Howard,' said Hagbard.

Howard swam out in front of them, and as he did so, he sang:

Right on, right on, a-stream against the foe
The sallying schools of the Southern seas make their
          course to go.
Attack, attack, with noses sound as rock
No shark or squid can shake us loose or survive our
          dour shock.

'Epics,' said Hagbard. 'They're mad for epics. They have their whole story for the past forty thousand years in epic form. No books, no writing – how could they handle pens with their fins, you know? All memorization. Which is why they favor poetry. And their poems are marvelous, but you must spend years studying their language before you know that. Our computer turns their works into doggerel. It's the best it can do. When I have the time, I'll add some circuits that can really translate poetry from one language to another. When the Porpoise Corpus is translated into human languages, it will advance our culture by centuries or more. It will be as if we'd discovered the works of a whole race of Shakespeares that had been writing for forty millennia.'

'On the other hand,' said Howard, 'your civilizations may be demoralized by culture shock.'

'Not likely,' said Hagbard grumpily. 'We've a few things to teach you, you know.'

'And our psychotherapists can help you over the anguish of digesting our knowledge,' said Howard.

'They have psychotherapists?' said George.

'They invented psychoanalysis thousands of years ago

as a means of passing the time on long migrations. They have highly complex brains and symbol-systems. But their minds are unlike ours in very important ways. They are all in one piece, so to speak. They lack the structural differentiation of ego, superego, and id. There is no repression. They are fully aware, and accepting, of their most primitive wishes. And conscious will, rather than parent-inculcated discipline, guides their actions. There is no neurosis, no psychosis among them. Psychoanalysis for them is an imaginative poetic exercise in autobiography, rather than a healing art. There are no difficulties of the mind that require healing.'

'Not quite true,' said Howard. 'There was a school of thought about twenty thousand years ago that envied humans. They were called the Original Sinners, because they were like the first parents of your human race who, according to some of your legends, envied the gods and suffered for it. They taught that humans were superior because they could do many more things than dolphins. But they despaired, and most ended up by committing suicide. They were the only neurotics in the long history of porpoises. Our philosophers mostly hold that we live in beauty all the days of our lives, as no human does. Our culture is simply what you might call a commentary on our natural surroundings, whereas human culture is at war with nature. If any race is afflicted, it is yours. You can do much, and what you can do, you must do. And, speaking of war, the enemy lies ahead.'

In the distance George could make out what appeared to be a mighty city rising on hills surrounding a deep depression which must have been a harbor when Atlantis was on the surface. The buildings marched on and on as far as the eye could see. They were mostly low, but here and there a square tower reared up. The sub was heading for the center of the ancient waterfront. George stared at the buildings; he was able to see them better now. They were angular, very modern in appearance, whereas the other city they'd flown – sailed – over had a mixed Greek-Egyptian-Mayan quality to its architecture. Here there were no pyramids. But the tops of many of the structures were broken off, and many others were heaps of rubble. Still, it was remarkable that a city which had sunk so many thousands of feet to the bottom of the ocean in the course of what must have been an enormous earthquake should be this well preserved. The buildings must be incredibly durable. If New York went through a catastrophe like that there'd be nothing left of its glass-and-alloy skyscrapers.

There was one pyramid. It was much smaller than the towers around it. It gleamed a dull yellow. Despite its lack of height, it seemed to dominate the harbor skyline, like a squat, powerful chieftain in the center of a circle of tall, slender warriors. There was movement around its base.

'This is the city of Peos in the region of Poseida,' said Hagbard, 'and it was great in Atlantis for a thousand years after the hour of the Dragon Star. It reminds me of Byzantium, which was a great city for a thousand years after the fall of Rome. And that pyramid is the Temple of Tethys, goddess of the Ocean Sea. It was seafaring that made Peos great. I have a soft spot in my heart for those people.'

Crawling around the base of the temple were strange sea creatures that looked like giant spiders. Lights flashed from their heads and glinted on the sides of the temple. As the submarine swept closer, George could see that the spiders were machines, each with a body the size of a tank. They appeared to be excavating deep trenches around the base of the pyramid.

'Wonder where they had those built,' muttered Hagbard. 'Hard to keep innovations like that a secret.'

As he spoke, the spiders stopped whatever work they were doing around the pyramid. There was no motion among them at all for a moment. Then one of them rose up from the sea bottom, followed by another, and another. They formed quickly into a V shape and started toward the submarine like a pair of arms outstretched to seize it. They picked up speed as they came.

'They've detected us,' Hagbard growled. 'They weren't supposed to, but they have. It never pays to underestimate the Illuminati. All right, George. Button up your asshole. We're in for a fight.'

At that moment but exactly two hours earlier on the clock, Rebecca Goodman awoke from a dream about Saul and a Playboy bunny and something sinister. The phone was ringing (was there a pyramid in the dream? – she tried

to remember – something like that) and she reached grog-
gily past the mermaid statue and held the receiver to her
ear. 'Yes?' she said cautiously.

'Put your hand on your pussy and listen,' said August
Personage. 'I'd like to lift your dress and—' Rebecca hung
up.

She suddenly remembered the hit when the needle went
in, and all those wasted years. Saul had saved her from
that, and now Saul was gone and strange voices on the
phone talked of sex the way addicts talked of junk. 'In the
beginning of all things was Mummu, the spirit of pure
Chaos. In the beginning was the Word, and it was written
by a baboon.' Rebecca Goodman, twenty-five years old,
started to cry. If he's dead, she thought, these years have
been wasted, too. Learning to love. Learning that sex was
more than another kind of junk. Learning that tenderness
was more than a word in the dictionary: that it was just
what D. H. Lawrence said, not an embellishment on sex
but the center of the act. Learning what that poor guy on
the phone could never guess, as most people in this crazy
country never guessed it. And then losing it, losing it to an
aimless bullet fired from a blind gun somewhere.

August Personage, about to leave the phone booth at the
Automat on Fortieth Street and the Avenue of the Americas, catches a flash of plastic on the floor. Bending, he
picks up a pornographic tarot card, which he quickly
shoves into a pocket to be examined at leisure later.

It was the Five of Pentacles.

And, when the throne room was empty and the believers
had departed in wonder and redoubled faith, Hassan knelt
and separated the two halves of the vessel which held the
head of Ibn Azif. 'Very convincing screams,' he commented, slipping the trapdoor beneath the plate and Ibn
Azif climbed out, grinning at his own performance. His
neck was thick, bull-like, undamaged, and quite solid.

THE FIFTH TRIP, OR GEBURAH
Swift-Kick, Inc

And, behold, thusly was the Law formulated:
IMPOSITION OF ORDER = ESCALATION OF CHAOS!
—Lord Omar Khayaam Ravenhurst,
'The Gospel According to Fred,' *The Honest Book of Truth*

The lights flashed; the computer buzzed. Hagbard attached the electrodes.

On January 30, 1939, a silly little man in Berlin gave a silly little speech; among other things, he said: 'And another thing I wish to say on this day which perhaps is memorable not only for us Germans: in my life I have many times been a prophet and most of the times I have been laughed at. During the period of my struggle for power, it was in the first case the Jews that laughed at my prophecies that some day I would take over the leadership of the State and thereby of the whole folk and that I would among other things solve also the Jewish problem. I believe that in the meantime the hyena-like laughter of the Jews of Germany has been smothered in their throats. Today I want to be a prophet once more: if the international-finance Jews inside and outside Europe should succeed once more in plunging nations into another world war the consequence will be the annihilation of the Jewish race in Europe.' And so on. He was always saying things like that. By 1939 quite a few heads here and there realized that the silly little man was also a murderous little monster, but only a very small number even of these noticed that for the first time in his anti-Semitic diatribes he had used the word *Vernichtung* – annihilation – and even they couldn't believe he meant what that implied. In fact, outside of a small circle of friends, nobody guessed what the little man, Adolf Hitler, had planned.

Outside that small – very small – circle of friends, others

came in intimate contact with *der Führer* and never guessed what was in his mind. Hermann Rauschning, the Governor of Danzig, for instance, was a devout Nazi until he began to get some hints of where Hitler's fancies were tending; after fleeing to France, Rauschning wrote a book warning against his former leader. It was called *The Voice of Destruction* and was very eloquent, but the most interesting passages in it were not understood by Rauschning or by most of his readers. 'Whoever sees in National Socialism nothing but a political movement doesn't know much about it,' Hitler told Rauschning, and this is in the book, but Rauschning and his readers continued to see National Socialism as a particularly vile and dangerous *political movement* and nothing more. 'Creation is not yet completed,' Hitler said again; and Rauschning again recorded, without understanding. 'The planet will undergo an upheaval which you uninitiated people can't understand,' *der Führer* warned on another occasion; and, still another time, he remarked that Nazism was, not only more than a political movement, but 'more than a new religion'; and Rauschning wrote it all and understood none of it. He even recorded the testimony of Hitler's physician that the silly and murderous little man often awoke screaming from nightmares that were truly extraordinary in their intensity and would shout, 'It's HIM, it's HIM, HE's come for me!' Good old Hermann Rauschning, a German of the old school and not equipped to participate in the New Germany of National Socialism, took all this as evidence of mental unbalance in Hitler. . . .

All of them coming back, all of them. Hitler and Streicher and Goebbels and the powers behind them what look like something you can't even imagine, guvnor. . . .

You think they was human, the patient went on as the psychiatrist listened in astonishment, *but wait till you see them the second time. And they're coming – By the end of the month, they're coming. . . .*

Karl Haushofer was never tried at Nuremberg; ask most people to name the men chiefly responsible for the *Vernichtung* (annihilation) decision, and his name will not be mentioned; even most histories of Nazi Germany relegate him to footnotes. But strange stories are told about his many visits to Tibet, Japan, and other parts of the Orient;

THE EYE IN THE PYRAMID

his gift for prophecy and clairvoyance; the legend that he belonged to a bizarre sect of dissident and most peculiar Buddhists, who had entrusted him with a mission in the Western world so serious that he vowed to commit suicide if he did not succeed. If the last yarn is true, Haushofer must have failed in his mission, for in March 1946 he killed his wife Martha and then performed the Japanese suicide-rite of *sepukku* upon himself. His son, Albrecht, had already been executed for his role in the 'officer's plot' to assassinate Hitler. (Of his father, Albrecht had written in a poem: 'My father broke the seal/He did not feel the breath of the Evil One/He set It free to roam the world!')

It was Karl Haushofer, clairvoyant, mystic, medium, Orientalist, and fanatic believer in the lost continent of Thule, who introduced Hitler to the Illuminated Lodge in Munich, in 1923. Shortly thereafter, Hitler made his first bid to seize power.

No rational interpretation of the events of August 1968 in Chicago, satisfactory to all participants and observers, has yet been produced. This suggests the need for value-free models, inspired by the structural analysis in von Neumann and Morgenstern's *Theory of Games and Economic Behavior*, which will allow us to express what actually occurred functionally, without tainting our analysis with bias or moral judgments. The model we will employ is that of two teams, an uphill motorcar race and a downhill bicycle race, accidentally intersecting on the same hill. The Picasso statue in the Civic Center will be regarded as 'start' for the downhill motorcar race and 'finish' for the uphill bicycle race. Pontius Pilate, disguised as Sirhan Sirhan, fires the opening shot, thereby disqualifying Robert F. Kennedy, for whom Marilyn Monroe committed suicide, as recorded in the most trustworthy tabloids and scandal sheets.

THIS IS THE VOICE OF YOUR FRIENDLY NEIGHBORHOOD SPIDER MAN SPEAKING. YOU MUST REALIZE THAT YOU ARE NOT JOSEPH WENDELL MALIK.

Hell's Angels on motorcycles do not fit the structure of the race at all, so they endlessly orbit around the heroic statue of General Logan in Grand Park ('finish' for the from the 'action', which is, of course, America.
from the 'actior', which is, of course, America.

When Jesus falls the first time, this can be considered as a puncture and Simon operates an air pump on his tires, but the threat to throw LSD in the water supply constitutes a 'foul' and this team thereby is driven back three squares by Mace, clubs, and the machine guns of the Capone mob unleashed from another time track in the same multiverse. Willard Gibbs, far more than Einstein, created the modern cosmos, and his concept of contingent or statistical reality, when cross-fertilized with the Second Law of Thermodynamics by Shannon and Wiener, led to the definition of information as the negative reciprocal of probability, making the clubbings of Jesus by Chicago cops just another of those things that happens in this kind of quantum jump.

A centurion named Semper Cuni Linctus passes Simon in Grand Park looking for the uphill bike race. 'When we crucify a man,' he mutters, 'he should confounded well *stay* crucified.' The three Marys clutch handkerchiefs to their faces as the teargas and Zyklon B pours upward on the hill, to the spot where the crosses and the statue of General Logan stand. . . . 'Nor dashed a thousand kim,' croons Saint Toad looking through the door at Fission Chips. . . . Arthur Flegenheimer and Robert Putney Drake ascend the chimney. . . . 'You don't have to believe in Santa Claus,' H. P. Lovecraft explains. . . . 'Ambrose,' the Dutchman says to him imploringly.

'But it can't be,' Joe Malik says, half weeping. 'It can't be that crazy. Buildings wouldn't stand. Planes wouldn't fly. Dams would collapse. Engineering colleges would be lunatic asylums.'

'They aren't already?' Simon asks. 'Have you read the latest data on the ecological catastrophe? You have to face it, Joe. God is a crazy woman.'

'There are no straight lines in curved space,' Stella adds.

'But my mind is dying,' Joe protests, shuddering.

Simon holds up an ear of corn and tells him urgently, 'Osiris is a black god!'

(Sir Charles James Napier, bearded, long-haired and sixty-odd years old, General of Her Majesty's Armies in India, met a most engaging scoundrel in January 1843 and immediately wrote to his cronies in England about this remarkable person, whom he described as brave, clever, fabulously wealthy, and totally unscrupulous. Since this

curious fellow was also regarded as God by his followers,
who numbered over three million, he charged twenty
rupees for permission to kiss his hand, asked – and got –
the sexual favors of the wives or daughters of any True
Believers who took his fancy, and proved his divinity by
brazenly and openly commiting sins which any mortal
would shrivel with shame to have acknowledged. He also
proved, at the Battle of Miani, where he aided the British
against the rebellious Baluchi tribesmen, that he could
fight like ten tigers. All in all, General Napier concluded, a
most unusual human being – Hasan ali Shah Mahallat,
forty-sixth Imam, or living God, of the Ishmaelian sect of
Islam, direct descendant of Hassan i Sabbah, and first Aga
Khan.)

Dear Joe:
    I'm back in Czechago again, fabulous demesne of
Crookbacked Richard, pigbaschard of the world, etc.,
where the pollution comes up like thunder out of
Gary across the lake, etc., and the Padre and I are
still working on the heads of the local Heads, etc., so
I've finally got time to write you that long letter I
promised.
    The Law of Fives is all the farther that Weishaupt
ever got, and Hagbard and John aren't much interested in any further speculations along those lines. The
23/17 phenomenon is entirely my discovery, except
that William S. Burroughs has noted the 23 without
coming to any conclusions about it.
    I'm writing this on a bench in Grand Park, near the
place I got Maced three years ago. Nice symbolism.
    A woman just came along from the Mothers March
Against Polio. I gave her a quarter. What a drag, just
when I was trying to get my thoughts in order. When
you come out here, I'll be able to tell you more; this
will obviously have to be somewhat sketchy.
    Burroughs, anyway, encountered the 23 in Tangiers,
when a ferryboat captain named Clark remarked that
he'd been sailing 23 years without an accident. That
day, his ship sunk, with all hands and feet aboard.
Burroughs was thinking about it in the evening when
the radio newscast told him that an Eastern Airlines

plane, New York to Miami, had crashed. The pilot was another Captain Clark and the plane was Flight 23.

'If you want to know the extent of their control,' Simon told Joe (speaking this time, not writing a letter; they were driving to San Francisco after leaving Dillinger), 'take a dollar bill out of your wallet and look at it. Go ahead – do it now. I want to make a point.' Joe took out his wallet and looked for a single. (A year later, in the city Simon called Czechago in honor of the synchronous invasions in August 1968, the KCUF convention is taking its first luncheon break after Smiling Jim's sock-it-to-'em opening speech. Simon brushes against an usher, shouts, 'Hey, you damned faggot, keep your hands off my ass,' and in the ensuing tumult Joe has no trouble slipping the AUM in the punch.)

'Do I have to get a library card just to look at one book?' Carmel asks the librarian in the Main Branch of the Las Vegas Library, after Maldonado had failed to produce any lead to a communist agent.

'One of the most puzzling acts of Washington's Presidency,' Professor Percival Petsdeloup tells an American history class at Columbia, back in '68, 'was his refusal to aid Tom Paine when Paine was condemned to death in Paris.' . . . Why puzzling? George Dorn thinks in the back of the class, Washington was an Establishment fink. . . . 'First of all, look at that face on the front,' Simon says. 'It isn't Washington at all, it's Weishaupt. Compare it with any of the early, authentic pictures of Washington and you'll see what I mean. And look at that cryptic half-smile on his face.' *(The same smile Weishaupt wore when he finished the letter explaining to Paine why he couldn't help him; sealed it with the Great Seal of the United States whose meaning only he knew; and settling back in his chair, murmured to himself, 'Jacques De Molay, thou art again avenged!')*

'What do you mean, I'm creating a disturbance? It was that faggot there, with his big mitts on my ass.'

('Well, I don't know which particular book, honey. Something that tells how the communists work. You know, how a patriotic citizen can spot a commie spy ring if

there's one in his neighborhood. That kind of thing,' Car-
mel explained.)

A swarm of men in blue shirts and white plastic helmets
rushes down the steps at Forty-third Street and UN Plaza,
past the inscription reading, 'They shall beat their swords
into plowshares and their spears into pruning hooks, neither
shall they study war any more.' Waving heavy wooden
crosses and shouting angry battle cries, the helmeted men
surge into the crowd like a wave hitting a sand castle.
George sees them coming, and his heart skips a beat.

'And when you turn the bill over, the first thing you see
is the Illuminati pyramid. You'll notice it says seventeen
seventy-six on it, but our government was founded in
seventeen eighty-eight. Supposedly, the seventeen seventy-
six is there because that's when the Declaration of Indepen-
dence was signed. The real reason is that seventeen seventy-
six is the year Weishaupt revived the Illuminati. And why
do you suppose the pyramid has seventy-two segments in
thirteen layers?' Simon asks in nineteen sixty-nine. . . .
'Misunderstanding, my eye! When a guy gropes my butt
that way I understand exactly what he wants,' Simon
shouts in nineteen seventy. . . . *George nudges Peter Jack-*
son. 'God's Lightning,' he says. The plastic hats gleam in
the sunlight, more of them jostling down the stairs, a
banner, red letters on a white background unfurling above:
'AMERICA: LOVE IT OR WE'LL STOMP YOU. . . . *'Christ on*
rollerskates,' Peter says, 'now watch the cops do a vanish-
ing act.' . . . Dillinger settles down cross-legged in a five-
sided chamber under the UN meditation room. He curls
into the lotus posture with an ease that would appear unusual in an American in his late sixties were there anyone
to witness it.

'Seventy-two is the cabalistic number for the Holy Un-
speakable Name of God, used in all black magic, and
thirteen is the number in a coven,' Simon explains. 'That's
why.' The Volkswagen purrs toward San Francisco.

Carmel comes down the steps of the Las Vegas Public
Library, a copy of J. Edgar Hoover's *Masters of Deceit*
under his arm, an anticipatory smirk on his face, *and*
Simon is finally ejected from the Sheraton-Chicago shout-
ing, 'Faggots! I think you're all a bunch of faggots!'

'And here's one of their jokes,' Simon adds. 'Over the

*eagle's head, do you dig that Star of David? They put that
one in – one single six-pointed Jewish star, made up of all
the five-pointed stars – just so some right-wing cranks
could find it and proclaim it as proof that the Elders of
Zion control the Treasury and the Federal Reserve.'*

Overlooking the crowd in UN Plaza, Zev Hirsch, New
York State Commander of God's Lightning, watches his
thick-shouldered troops, swinging their wooden crosses like
tomahawks, drive back the lily-livered peaceniks. There is
an obstacle. A blue line of policemen has formed between
the men of God's Lightning and their prey. Over the cops'
shoulders, the peaceniks are screeching dirty words at their
plastic-hatted enemies. Zev's eyes scan the crowd. He
catches the eye of a red-faced cop with gold braid on his
cap. Zev gives the Police Captain a questioning look. The
Captain winks. A minute later the Captain makes a small
gesture with his left hand. Immediately, the line of police
vanishes, as if melted in the bright spring sun that beats
down on the plaza. The battalion of God's Lightning falls
upon their anguished, outraged, and astonished victims.
Zev Hirsch laughs. This is a lot more fun than the old days
in the Jewish Defense League. All the servants are drunk.
And the rain continues.

*At an outdoor café in Jerusalem two white-haired old
men wearing black are drinking coffee together. They try
to mask their emotions from the people around them, but
their eyes are wild with excitement. They are staring at an
inside page of a Yiddish newspaper, reading two ads in
Yiddish, a large, quarter-page announcement of the greatest
rock festival of all time to be held near Ingolstadt, Bavaria
– bands of all nations, people of all nations, to be known
as Woodstock Europa. On the same page is the paper's
personals column, and the watery eyes of the two old men
are re-reading for the fifth time the statement, in Yiddish,
'In thanks to St. Jude for favors granted. – A. W.'*

*One old man points at the page with a trembling finger.
'It is coming,' he says in German.*

*The other one nods, a beatific smile on his withered
face. 'Jawohl. It is coming very soon. Der Tag. Soon we
must to Bavaria go. Ewige Blumenkraft!'*

Carlo put the gun on the table between us. 'This is it,
George,' he said. 'Are you a revolutionary, or are you just

on an ego trip playing at being a revolutionary? Can you take the gun?'

I wiped my eyes. The Passaic was flowing below me, a steady stream of garbage from the Paterson falls down to Newark and the Atlantic Ocean. Like the garbage that was my contemptible, cowardly soul. . . . The God's Lightning troopers fan out, clubbing each person wearing an I WON'T DIE FOR FERNANDO POO button. Blood dances in the air, fragile red bubbles, before the tomblike slab of the UN building. . . . *Dillinger's breathing slows down. He stares at the ruby eye atop the 13-step pyramid hidden in the UN building, and he thinks of pentagons.*

'I'm a God's Lightning,' Carlo said. 'This is no joke, baby, I'm going to do the whole bit.' His intense eyes burned into mine as the switchblade came out of his pocket. 'Motherfuckin' commie,' he screamed suddenly, leaping up so quickly that the chair fell over behind him. 'You're not getting off with a beating this time. I'm gonna cut your balls off and take them home as a souvenir.' He slashed forward with the knife, deflecting his swing at the last minute. 'Made you jump, you long-haired faggotty freak. I wonder if you have any balls to cut off. Well, I'll find out.' He inched forward, the knife weaving snakelike patterns in the air.

'Look,' I said desperately, 'I know you're only play-acting.'

'You don't know *nothing*, baby. Maybe I'm FBI or CIA. Maybe this is just an excuse to get you to go for the gun so I can kill you and claim self-defense. Life isn't all demonstrations and play-acting, George. There comes a time when it gets serious.' He lunged again with the knife, and I stumbled clumsily backward. 'Are you going to take the gun or am I going to cut your balls off and tell the Group you're no fucking good and we couldn't use you?'

He was totally mad and I was totally sane. Is that a more flattering way of telling it, instead of the truth, that he was brave and I was yellow?

'Listen,' I said, 'I know you won't really stab me and you know I won't really shoot you—'

'Shit on *you know* and *I know*,' Carlo hit me in the chest with his free hand, hard. 'I'm a God's Lightning, really a God's Lightning. I'm gonna do the whole scene.

This is a test, but the test is for real.' He hit me again, jarring my balance, then slapped my face, twice, rapidly, back and forth like a windshield wiper. 'I always said you longhaired commie freaks don't have no guts. You can't even fight back. You can't even feel angry, can you? You just feel sorry for yourself, right?'

It was too damned true. A nerve twinged deep down inside at the unfairness of it, of his ability to see into me more than I usually dared see into myself; and at last I grabbed the gun from the table, screaming, 'You sadistic *Stalinist* son-of-a-bitch!'

'And look at the eagle,' Simon says. 'Look real close. That ain't really no olive branch in his left claw, baby. That's our old friend Maria Juana. You never really looked at a dollar bill before did you?

'And the real symbolism of the pyramid is alchemical, of course. The traditional code represents the three kinds of sex by a cube, a pyramid, and a sphere. The cube is that travesty we call "normal" sex, in which the two nervous systems never actually merge at the orgasm, like the two parallel sides of the cube. The pyramid is the two coming together and joining, the magical-telepathic orgasm. The sphere is the Tantric ritual, endlessly prolonged, with no orgasm at all. The alchemists used that code for over two thousand years. The Rosicrucians among the founding fathers used the pyramid as a symbol of their kind of sex magic. Aleister Crowley used that symbol the same way, more recently. The eye on the pyramid is the two minds meeting. Neurological interlock. The opening of the Eye of Shiva. Ewige Schlangekraft – the eternal serpent power. The joining of the Rose and Cross, vagina and penis, into Red-Cross. The astral leap. Mind escaping from physiology.'

The AUM was supposed to work almost instantly, according to what the scientists at ELF had told Hagbard, so Joe approached the first man who had sampled the punch and started a conversation. 'Nice talk Smiling Jim gave,' he said earnestly. *(I rammed the gun into Carlo's gut and saw him go white about the lips. 'No, don't worry,' I said, smiling. 'I'm not using it on you. But when I come back there'll be a dead pig on the streets somewhere in Morningside Heights.' He started to speak, and I jabbed down-*

ward with the gun, grinning as he gasped for air. 'Comrade,' I added.) 'Yeah, Smiling Jim was born with a silver tongue,' the other man said.

'A silver tongue,' Joe agreed solemnly, then added, holding out his hand, 'by the way, I'm Jim Mallison from the New York delegation.'

'Knew by your accent,' the other said shrewdly. 'I'm Clem Cotex from down Little Rock.' They shook. 'Pleasure to meet you.'

'Too bad about that kid that got thrown out,' Joe said, lowering his voice. 'It looked to me like that usher really was – you know – *touching* him.'

Cotex looked surprised for a moment, but then shook his head in doubt. 'Can't tell nowadays, especially in big cities. Do you really think an *Andy Frain* usher could be a – fairy?'

'Like you said, nowadays in big cities . . .' Joe shrugged. 'I'm just saying that it looked like it to me. Of course, maybe the usher isn't one. Maybe he's just a cheap thief who was trying to pick the kid's pocket. A lot of that goes on these days, too.' Cotex involuntarily reached back to check his own wallet, and Joe went on blandly. 'But I wouldn't rule out the other, not by a long shot. What sort of man would want to be an usher at a KCUF meeting, if you stop and think about it? You must have observed how many homosexuals there are in our organization.'

'What?' Cotex's eyes bulged.

'You haven't noticed it?' Joe smiled loftily. 'There are very few of us who are really Christians. Most of the membership are just a *little bit lavender*, know what I mean? I think it's one of our biggest problems, and we ought to bring it out into the open and discuss it frankly. Clear the air, right? For instance, take the way Smiling Jim always puts his arm around your shoulder when he talks to you—'

Cotex interrupted, 'Hey, mister, you're pretty darn bright. Just now hit me like a flash – some of the *men* here, when Smiling Jim showed those beaver shots to prove how bad some magazines are getting, they really shuddered. They didn't just disapprove – it really honest-to-Pete revolted them. What kind of *man* actually finds a naked lady disgusting?'

Go, baby, go, Joe thought. The AUM is working. He quickly derailed the conversation. 'Another thing that bothers me. Why don't we ever challenge the spherical earth theory?'

'Huh?'

'Look,' Joe said. 'If all the scientists and eggheads and commies and liberals are pushing it in our schools all the time, there must be something a little fishy about it. Did you ever stop to think that there's no way – just no way at all – to reconcile a spherical earth with the story of the Flood, or Joshua's miracle, or Jesus standing on the pinnacle of the Temple and seeing all the kingdoms of the earth? And I ask you, man to man, in all your travels have you ever *seen* the curvature anywhere? Every place *I've* been is flat. Are we going to trust the Bible and the evidence of our own senses, or are we going to listen to a bunch of agnostics and atheists in laboratory smocks?'

'But the earth's shadow on the moon during an eclipse...'

Joe took a dime out of his pocket and held it up. 'This casts a circular shadow, but it's flat, not spherical.'

Cotex stared into space for a long moment, while Joe waited with suppressed excitement. 'You know something?' Cotex said finally, 'all the Bible miracles and our own travels and the shadow on the moon would make sense if the earth was shaped like a *carrot* and all the continents were on the flat end—'

Praise be to Simon's god, Bugs Bunny, Joe thought elatedly. It's happening – he's not only gullible – he's creative.

I followed the cop – the pig, I corrected myself – out of the cafeteria. I was so keyed up that it was a Trip. The blue of his uniform, the neon signs, even the green of the lampposts, all were coming in superbright. That was adrenalin. My mouth was dry – dehydration. All the classic flight-fight symptoms. The activation syndrome, Skinner calls it. I let the cop – the pig – get half a block ahead and reached in my pocket for the revolver.

'Come on, George!' Malik shouted. George didn't want to move. His heart was thumping, his arms and legs trembling so hard he knew they'd be useless to him in a fight. But he just didn't want to move. He'd had enough of running from these motherfuckers.

But he couldn't help himself. As the men in blue shirts and white helmets came on, the crowd surged away from them, and George had to move back with the crowd or be knocked down and trampled.

'Come *on*, George.' It was Pete Jackson at his side now, with a good, hard grip on his arm, tugging him.

'Goddam it, why do we have to run away from them?' George said, stumbling backward.

Peter was smiling faintly. 'Don't you read your Mao, George? Enemy attacks, we retreat. Let the Morituri fanatics stand and get creamed.'

I couldn't do it. My hand held the gun, but I couldn't take it out and hold it in front of me any more than I could take out my penis and wave it around. I was sure, even though the street was empty except for me and the pig, that a dozen people would jump out of doorways yelling, 'Look, he took it out of his pants.'

Just like right now, when Hagbard said, 'Button up your asshole. We're in for a fight,' I stood frozen like I stood frozen on the embankment above the Passaic.

'Are you on an ego trip playing at being a revolutionary?' Carlo asked.

And Mavis: 'All the militant radicals in your crowd ever do is take out the Molotov cocktail diagram that they carefully clipped from *The New York Review of Books*, hang it on the bathroom door, and jack-off in connection with it.'

Howard sang:

> The foe is attacking, their ships coming near,
> Now is the time to fight without fear!
> Now is the time to look death in the eye
> Before we submit, we'll fight till we die!

This time I got the gun out of my pocket – standing there, looking down at the Passaic – and raised it to my forehead. If I didn't have the courage for homicide, Jesus knows I have despair enough for a hundred suicides. And I only have to do it once. Just once, and then oblivion. I cock the firing pin. (More play-acting, George? Or will you really do it?) I'll do it, damn you, damn all of you. I pull the trigger and fall, with the explosion, into blackness.

(AUM was a product of the scientists at ELF – the Erisian Liberation Front – and shared by them with the JAMs. An extract of hemp, boosted with RNA, the 'learning' molecule, it also had small traces of the famous 'Frisco Speedball' – heroin, cocaine, and LSD. The effect seemed to be that the heroin stilled anxiety, the RNA stimulated creativity, the hemp and acid opened the mind to joy, and the cocaine was there to fit the Law of Fives. The delicate balance created no hallucinations, no sense of 'high' – just a sudden spurt in what Hagbard Celine liked to call 'constructive gullibility.')

It was one of those sudden shifts of movement that occur in a mob scene. Instead of pushing George and Peter back, the crowd between them and the white helmets were parting. A slender man fell heavily against George, anguish in his eyes. There was a terrible thump, and the man fell to the ground.

George saw the dark brown wooden cross before he saw the man who wielded it. There was blood and hair at the end of the crossarm. The God's Lightning man was dark, broad and muscular, with a blue shadow on his cheeks. He looked Italian or Spanish – he looked, in fact, a lot like Carlo. His eyes were wide and his mouth was open and he was breathing heavily. The expression was neither rage nor sadistic joy – just the unthinking panting alertness of a man doing a difficult and fatiguing job. He bent over the fallen slender man and raised the cross.

'All right!' snapped Peter Jackson. He pushed George aside. There was a silly-looking yellow plastic water pistol in his hand. He squirted the oblivious God's Lightning man in the back of the neck. The man screamed, arched backward, the cross flying end over end into the air. He fell on his back and lay screaming and writhing.

'Come on now, motherfucker!' Peter snarled as he dragged George into the crowd, broken-field running toward Forty-second Street.

'An hour and a half to go,' Hagbard says, finally beginning to show suppressed tension. George checks his watch – it's exactly 10:30 P.M., Ingolstadt time. The Plastic Canoe is wailing KRISHNA KRISHNA HARE HARE.

(Under the noon sun, two days earlier, Carmel speeds in his jeep away from Las Vegas.)

'Who am I going to meet at the Norton Cabal?' Joe asks. 'Judge Crater? Amelia Earhart? Nothing would surprise me now.'

'A few real together people,' Simon replies. 'But no one like that. But you'll have to die, really die, man, before you're illuminated.' He smiles gently. 'Aside from death and resurrection, you won't find anything you'd call "supernatural" with this bunch. Not even a whiff of old Chicago-style Satanism.'

'God,' Joe says, 'was that only a week ago?'

'Yep,' Simon grins, gunning his VW around a Chevrolet with Oregon license plates, 'It's still nineteen sixty-nine, even if you seem to have lived several years since we met at the anarchist caucus.' His eyes are amused as he half turns to glance at Joe.

'I suppose that means you know what's been happening in my dreams. I'm getting the flashforwards already.'

'Always happens after a good dirty Black Mass with pot mixed in the incense,' Simon says. 'What sort of thing you getting? Is it happening when you're awake yet?'

'No, only in my dreams.' Joe pauses, thinking. 'I only know it's the real article because the dreams are so vivid. One set has to do with some kind of pro-censorship rally at the Sheraton-Chicago hotel, I think about a year from now. There's another set that seems farther in the future – five or six years – where I'm impersonating a doctor for some reason. And a third group of images comes to me, now and then, that seems to be the set of a Frankenstein movie, except that the extras are all hippies and there seems to be a rock festival going on.'

'Does it bother you?'

'A little. I'm used to waking up in the morning with the future ahead of me, not behind me *and* ahead of me *both*.'

'You'll get used to it. You're just beginning to contact what old Weishaupt called *"die Morgensheutegesternwelt"* – the tomorrow-today-yesterday world. It gave Goethe the idea for *Faust*, just like Weishaupt's *"Ewige Blumenkraft"* slogan inspired Goethe's *"Ewige Weibliche."* I'll tell you what,' Simon suggested. 'You might try wearing three wristwatches, like Bucky Fuller does – one showing the time where you're at, one showing the time where you're going, and one showing the time at some arbitrary place

like Greenwich Mean Time or your home town. It'll help
you get used to relativity. Meanwhile, never whistle while
you're pissing. And you might repeat to yourself, when you
get disoriented, Fuller's sentence, "I seem to be a verb." '

They drove in silence for a while, and Joe pondered on
being a verb. Hell, he thought, I have enough trouble
understanding what Fuller means when he says *God* is a
verb. Simon let him mull it over, and began humming
again: 'Rameses the Second is dead, my love/He's walking
the fields where the BLESSED liiiiive. . . .' Joe realized he
was starting to doze . . . *and all the faces at the luncheon
table looked at him in astonishment. 'No, seriously,' he
said. 'Anthropologists are too timid to say it out in the
open, in public, but corner one of them in private and ask
him.'*

*Every detail was clear: it was the same room in the
Sheraton-Chicago Hotel, and the faces were the same. (I've
been here before and said this before.)*

'The rain dances of the Indians work. The rain always
comes. So why isn't it possible that their gods are real and
ours isn't? Have you ever prayed to Jesus for something
and really gotten it?' There is a long silence and finally an
old tight-faced woman smiles youthfully and declares,
'Young man, I'm going to try it. How do I meet an Indian
in Chicago?'*

Like tomahawks the crosses of God's Lightning rose and
fell on the slender man's defenseless skull. They'd found
their injured comrade lying on the street twisting and
moaning beside his erstwhile victim. A couple of them
hauled the wounded God's Lightning man away, while the
rest took their revenge on the unconscious peace demon-
strator.

('You, Luke,' says Yeshua ben Yosef, 'don't write that
down.')

Space-time, then, may be slanted or kiltered when you're
lost out here: Fernando Poo looks through his glass at a
new island, not guessing that it will be named after himself, not imagining that someday Simon Moon will write
'In Fourteen Hundred and Seventy Two, Fernando Poo
discovered Fernando Poo,' and Hagbard says, 'Truth is a
tiger,' while Timothy Leary does a Crown Point Pavanne
out of San Luis Obispo Jail and four billion years earlier

one squink says to another, 'I've solved the ecology problem on this new planet.' The other squink, partner to the first (they own Swift Kick Inc., the shoddiest contractors in the Milky Way) says 'How?' The first squink laughs coarsely. 'Every organism produced will be programmed with a Death Trip. It'll give them a rather gloomy outlook, I admit, especially the more conscious ones, but it will sure minimize costs for us.' Swift Kick Inc. cut the edges every other way they could think, and Earth emerged as the Horrible Example invoked in all classes on planetary design throughout the galaxy.

When Burroughs told me that, I flipped, because I was 23 that year and lived on Clark Street. Besides, I immediately saw the application to the Law of Fives: $2 + 3 = 5$ and Clark has 5 letters.

I was mulling this over when I happened to notice the shipwreck in Pound's Canto 23. That's the only shipwreck mentioned in the whole 800-page poem, in spite of all the nautical voyages described. Canto 23 also contains the line, 'with the sun in a golden cup,' which Yeats says inspired his own lines, 'the golden apples of the sun, the silver apples of the moon.' Golden apples, of course, brought me back to Eris, and I realized I was onto something hot.

Then I tried adding the Illuminati Five to 23, and I got 28. The average menstrual period of Woman. The lunar cycle. Back to the silver apples of the moon – and I'm Moon. Of course, Pound and Yeats both had five letters in their names.

If this be schizophrenia, I said with a P. Henry twist (one better than an O. Henry twist), make the most of it!

I looked deeper.

Through a bullhorn, a police captain began to shout, CLEAR THE PLAZA CLEAR THE PLAZA.

The first reports of the annihilation camps were passed on to the OSS by a Swiss businessman evaluated as being one of the most trustworthy informants on affairs in Nazi Europe. The State Department decided that the stories

were not confirmed. That was early in 1943. By autumn of
that year, more urgent reports from the same source transmitted still through the OSS forced a major policy conference. It was again decided that the reports were not true.
As winter began, the English government asked for another
conference to discuss similar reports from their own intelligence networks and from the government of Rumania.
The delegates met in Bermuda for a warm, sunny weekend,
and decided that the reports were not true; they returned
to their work refreshed and tanned. The death trains continued to roll. Early in 1944, Henry Morgenthau, Jr.,
Secretary of the Treasury, was reached by dissenters in the
State Department, examined the evidence, and forced a
meeting with President Franklin Delano Roosevelt. Shaken
by the assertions in Morgenthau's documents, Roosevelt
pledged that he would act at once. He never did. It was
said later that the State Department convinced him, once
again, of their own analysis: the reports simply were not
true. When Mr. Hitler said *Vernichtung* he had not really
meant *Vernichtung*. An author, Ben Hecht, then placed an
ad in the *New York Times*, presenting the evidence to the
public; a group of prominent rabbis attacked him for
alarming Jews unnecessarily and undermining confidence
in America's Chief Executive during wartime. Finally, late
that year, American and Russian troops began liberating the
camps, and General Eisenhower insisted that news photo-
graphers take detailed movies which were released to the
whole world. In the interval between the first suppressed
report by the Swiss businessman and the liberation of the
first camp, six million people had died.

'That's what we call a Bavarian Fire Drill,' Simon explained to Joe. (It was another time; he was driving another
Volkswagen. In fact, it was the night of April 23 and they
were going to meet Tobias Knight at the UN building.) 'It
was one official named Winifred who'd been transferred
from the Justice Department to a key State Department
desk where every bit of evidence passed for evaluation.
But the same principles apply everywhere. For instance –
we're half an hour early for the meeting anyhow – I'll give
you an illustration right now.' They were approaching the
corner of Forty-third Street and Third Avenue and Simon
had observed that the streetlight was changing to red. As

he stopped the car, he opened the door and said to Joe, 'Follow me.'

Puzzled, Joe got out as Simon ran to the car behind them, beat on the hood with his hand and shouted 'Bavarian Fire Drill! Out!' He made vigorous but ambiguous motions with his hands and ran to the car next back. Joe saw the first subject look dubiously at his companion and then open the door and get out, obediently trailing behind Simon's urgent and somber figure.

'Bavarian Fire Drill! Out!' Simon was already shouting at the third car back.

As Joe trotted along, occasionally adding his own voice to persuade the more dubious drivers, every car gradually emptied and people formed a neat line heading back toward Lexington Avenue. Simon then ducked between two cars and began jogging toward the front of the line at Third Avenue again, shouting to everybody, 'Complete circle! Stay in line!' Obediently, everyone followed in a great circle back to their own cars, reentering from the side opposite to that from which they had left. Simon and Joe climbed back into the VW, the light changed, and they sped ahead.

'You see?' Simon asked. 'Use words they've been conditioned to since childhood – "fire drill," "stay in line," like that – and never look back to see if they're obeying. They'll follow. Well, that's the way the Illuminati guaranteed that the Final Solution wouldn't be interrupted. Winifred, one guy who had been around long enough to have an impressive title, and his scrawl "Evaluation: dubious" on the bottom of each memo . . . and six million died. Hilarious, isn't it?'

And Joe remembered from the little book by Hagbard Celine, *Never Whistle While You're Pissing* (privately printed, and distributed only to members of the JAMs and the Legion of Dynamic Discord): 'The individual act of obedience is the cornerstone not only of the strength of authoritarian society but also of its weakness.'

(On November 23, 1970, the body of Stanislaus Oedipuski, forty-six, of West Irving Park Road, was found floating in the Chicago river. Death, according to the police laboratory, did not result from drowning but from beating about the head and shoulders with a square-ended object.

The first inquiries by homicide detectives revealed that Oedipuski had been a member of God's Lightning and the theory was formed that a conflict between the dead man and his former colleagues might have resulted in his being snuffed with their wooden crosses. Further investigation revealed that Oedipuski had been a construction worker and until very recently well liked on his job, behaving in a normal, down-to-earth manner, bitching about the government, cursing the lazy bums on Welfare, hating niggers, shouting obscene remarks at good-looking dolls who passed construction sites and – when the odds were safely above the 8-to-1 level – joining other middle-aged workers in attacking and beating young men with long hair, peace buttons, or other un-American stigmata. Then, about a month before, all that had changed. He began bitching about the bosses as well as the government – almost sounding like a communist at times; when somebody else cussed the crumb-bums on Welfare, Stan remarked thoughtfully, 'Well, you know, our union keeps them from getting jobs, fellows, so what else can they do but go on Welfare? Steal?' He even said once, when some of the guys were good-humoredly giving the finger and making other gallant noises and signals toward a passing eighteen-year-old girl, 'Hey, you know, that might really be embarrassing and scaring her . . .!' Worse yet, his own hair begun to grow surprisingly long in the back, and his wife told friends that he didn't look at TV much anymore but instead sat in a chair most evenings reading *books*. The police found that was indeed true, and his small library – gathered in less than a month – was remarkable indeed, featuring works on astronomy, sociology, Oriental mysticism, Darwin's *Origin of the Species*, detective novels by Raymond Chandler, *Alice in Wonderland*, and a college-level text on number theory with the section on primes heavily marked with notes in the margin; the gallant, and now pathetic, tracks of a mind that was beginning to grow after four decades of stagnation, and then had been abruptly stomped. Most mysterious of all was the card found in the dead man's pocket, which although waterlogged, could still be read. One side said

THERE IS NO ENEMY
ANYWHERE

and the other side, even more mysteriously, was inscribed:

$$-\Pi\Delta\varphi \quad \text{Ж}\Theta\Delta\Theta$$

The police might have tried to decipher this, but then they discovered that Oedipuski had resigned from God's Lightning – giving his fellow members a lecture on tolerance in the process – the night before his death. That closed the case, definitely. Homicide did not investigate murders clearly connected with God's Lightning, since the Red Squad had its own personal accommodation with that burgeoning organization. 'Poor motherfucker,' a detective said, looking at Oedipuski's photographs; and closed the file forever. Nobody ever reopened it, or traced the change in the dead man back to his attendance at the meeting, one month before, of KCUF at the Sheraton-Chicago, where the punch was spiked with AUM.)

In the act of conception, of course, the father contributes 23 chromosomes and the mother contributes another 23. In the *I Ching*, hexagram 23 has connotations of 'sinking' or 'breaking apart,' shades of the unfortunate Captain Clarks. . . .

Another woman just came by, collecting for the Mothers March against Muscular Dystrophy. I gave her a quarter. Where was I? Oh, yes: James Joyce had five letters in both his front name and his hind name, so he was worth looking into. *A Portrait of the Artist* had five chapters, all well and good, but *Ulysses* had 18 chapters, a stumper, until I remembered that 5 + 18 = 23. How about *Finnegans Wake*? Alas, that has 17 chapters, and I was bogged down for a while.

Trying another angle, I wondered if Frank Sullivan, the poor cluck who got shot instead of John at the Biograph Theatre that night, could have lingered until after midnight, dying on July 23 instead of July 22 as usually stated. I looked it up in Toland's book, *The Dillinger Days*. Poor Frank, sad to say, died before midnight, but Toland included an interesting detail, which I told you that night at the Seminary bar: 23 people died of heat prostration that day in Chi-

cago. He added something else: 17 people had died
of heat prostration the day before. Why did he mention that? I'm sure he doesn't know – but there it was
again, 23 and 17. Maybe something important is going
to happen in the year 2317? I couldn't check that,
of course (you can't navigate precisely in the *Morgensheutegesternwelt*), so I went back to 1723, and
struck golden apples. That was the year Adam Smith
and Adam Weishaupt were both born (and Smith
published *The Wealth of Nations* the same year
Weishaupt revived the Illuminati: 1776.)

Well, $2 + 3 = 5$, fitting the Law of Fives, but
$1 + 7 = 8$, fitting nothing. Where did that leave me?
Eight, I reflected, is the number of letters in Kallisti,
back to the golden apple again, and 8 is also 2^3, hot
damn. Naturally, it came as no surprise when the 8
defendants in the Chicago Conspiracy Trial, which
grew out of our little Convention Week Carnival, were
tried on the 23rd floor of the Federal Building, amid
a flurry of synchronicity – a Hoffman among the
defendants, a Hoffman as judge; the Illuminati pya-
mid, or Great Seal of the U.S. right inside the door
of the building, and a Seale getting worse abuse than
the other defendants; five-letter names and prolifer-
ating – Abbie, Davis, Foran, Seale, Jerry Rubin
(twice), and the clincher, Clark (Ramsey, not Captain)
who was torpedoed and sunk by the judge before he
could testify.

I got interested in Dutch Shultz because he died on
October 23. A cluster of synchronicity, that man: he
ordered the shooting of Vincent 'Mad Dog' Coll (remember Mad Dog, Texas); Coll was shot on 23rd
Street, when he was 23 years old; and Charlie Workman, who allegedly shot Schultz, served 23 years in
prison for it (although rumor has it that Mendy Weiss
– two five-letter names, again – did the real shooting.)
Does 17 come in? You bet. Shultz was first sentenced
to prison at the age of 17.

Around this time I bought Robert Heinlein's *The
Puppet Masters*, thinking the plot might parallel some
Illuminati operations. Imagine how I felt when Chap-

ter Two began, '23 hours and 17 minutes ago, a flying saucer landed in Iowa . . .'

And, in New York, Peter Jackson is trying to get the next issue of *Confrontation* out on time – although the office is still a shambles, the editor and star researcher have disappeared, the best reporter has gone ape and claims to be at the bottom of the Atlantic with a wax tycoon, and the police are hounding Peter to find out why the first two detectives assigned to the case can't be located. Sitting in his apartment (now the magazine's office) in his shirt and shorts, Peter dials his phone with one hand, adding another crushed cigarette to the pile in the ashtray with the other. Throwing a manuscript onto a basket marked 'Ready for Printer,' he crosses off 'lead article – The Youngest Student Ever Admitted to Columbia Tells Why He Dropped Out by L. L. Durrutti' from a list on the pad before him. His pencil moves down to the bottom, 'Book Review,' as he listens to the phone ring. Finally, he hears the click of a lifted receiver and a rich, flutey voice says, 'Epicene Wildeblood here.'

'Got your book review ready, Eppy?'

'Have it tomorrow, dear boy. Can't be any faster, *honestly*!'

'Tomorrow will do,' Peter says writing *call again* – A.M. next to 'Book Review.'

'It's a dreadfully long monster of a book,' Wildeblood says pettishly, 'and I certainly won't have time to read it, but I'm giving it a thorough *skimming*. The authors are utterly incompetent – no sense of style or structure at all. It starts out as a detective story, switches to science-fiction, then goes off into the supernatural, and is full of the most detailed information of dozens of *ghastly* boring subjects. And the time sequence is all out of order in a very pretentious imitation of Faulkner and Joyce. Worst yet, it has the most raunchy sex scenes, thrown in just to make it sell, I'm sure, and the authors – whom I've *never* heard of – have the supreme bad taste to introduce real political figures into this mishmash and pretend to be exposing a real conspiracy. You can be *sure* I won't waste time reading such rubbish, but I'll have a perfectly devastating review ready for you by tomorrow noon.'

'Well, we don't expect you to read every book you review,' Peter says mollifyingly, 'just so long as you can be entertaining about them.'

'The Foot Fetishist Liberation Front will be participating in the rally at the UN building,' Joe Malik said, as George and Peter and he were affixing their black armbands.

'Christ,' Jackson said disgustedly.

'We can't afford to take that attitude,' Joe said severely. 'The only hope for the Left at this time is coalition politics. We can't exclude anybody who wants to join us.'

'I've got nothing against faggots personally,' Peter begins ('Gays,' Joe says patiently). 'I've got nothing against Gays personally,' Peter goes on, 'but they are a bringdown at rallies. They just give God's Lightning more evidence to say we're all a bunch of fruits. But, OK, realism is realism, there are a lot of them, and they swell our ranks, and all that, but, Jesus, Joe. These *toe freaks* are a splinter within a splinter. They're microscopic.'

'Don't call them toe freaks,' Joe says. 'They don't like that.'

A woman from the Mothers March Against Psoriasis just came by with another collection box. I gave her a quarter, too. The marching mothers are going to strip Moon of his bread if this keeps up.

Where was I? I meant to add, in relation to the Dutch Shultz shooting that Marty Krompier, who ran the policy racket in Harlem, was also shot on October 23, 1935. The police asked him if there was a connection with phlegmatic Flegenheimer's demise and he said, 'It's got to be one of them coincidences.' I wonder how he emphasized that – 'one of them *coincidences*' or 'one of *them* coincidences'? How much did he know?

That brings me to the 40 enigma. As pointed out, $1 + 7 = 8$, the number of letters in Kallisti. $8 \times 5 = 40$. More interestingly, without invoking the mystic 5, we still arrive at 40 by adding $17 + 23$. What, then, is the significance of 40? I've run through various associations – Jesus had his 40 days in the desert, Ali Baba had his 40 thieves, Buddhists have their 40

meditations, the solar system is almost exactly 40
astronomical units in radius (Pluto yo-yos a bit) –
but I have no definite theory yet. . . .

The color television set in the Three Lions Pub in the
Tudor Hotel at Forty-second Street and Second Avenue
shows the white-helmeted men carrying wooden crosses
fall back as the blue-helmeted men carrying billy clubs
move forward. The CBS camera pans over the plaza.
There are five bodies on the ground scattered like flotsam
tossed on a beach by a receding wave. Four of them are
moving, making slow efforts to get up. The fifth is not
moving at all.

George said, 'I think that's the guy we saw getting
clubbed. My God, I hope he isn't dead.'

Joe Malik said, 'If he is dead, it may get people to
demand that something be done about God's Lightning.'

Peter Jackson laughed mirthlessly. 'You still think some
honky peacenik getting killed is going to make people in-
dignant. Don't you understand, nobody in this country
cares what happens to a peace freak. You're in the same
boat with the niggers now, you silly sons-of-bitches.'

Carlos looked up in astonishment as I burst into the
room, still wet from the Passaic, and threw the gun at his
feet, screaming, 'You silly sons-of-bitches, you can't even
make bombs without blowing yourselves up, and when you
buy a gun the motherfucker is defective and misfires. You
can't expel me – I quit!' You silly sons-of-bitches. . . .

'You silly sons-of-bitches!' Simon shouted. Joe woke as
the VW swerved amid a flurry of Hell's Angels bike roar-
ing by. He was back in 'real' time again – but the word
had quotes around it, in his mind, now, and it always
would.

'Wow,' he said, 'I was in Chicago again, and then at
that rock festival . . . and then I was in somebody else's
lifeline. . . .'

'Goddam Harley-Davidsons,' Simon mutters as the last
Angel thunders by. 'When fifty or sixty of them swarm by
like that, it's as bad as trying to drive on the sidewalk in
Times Square at high noon without hitting a pedestrian.'

'Later-for-that,' Joe said, conscious of his growing ease
in using Simon's own language. 'This tomorrow-today-

yesterday time is beginning to get under my skin. It's happening more and more often. . . .'

Simon sighed, 'You want words to put around it. You can't accept it until it has labels dangling off it, like a new suit. OK. And your favorite word-game is science. Fine, right on! Tomorrow we'll drop by the Main Library and you can look up the English science journal *Nature* for Summer nineteen sixty-six. There's an article in there by the University College physicist F. R. Stannard about what he calls the Faustian Universe. He tells how the behavior of K-mesons can't be explained assuming a one-way time-track, but fits into a neat pattern if you assume our universe overlaps another where time runs in the opposite direction. He calls it the Faustian universe, but I'll bet he has no idea that Goethe wrote *Faust* after experiencing that universe directly, just as you're doing lately. Incidentally, Stannard points out that everything in physics is symmetrical, except our present concept of one-way time. Once you admit two-way time traffic, you've got a completely symmetrical universe. Fits the Occamite's demand for simplicity. Stannard'll give you lots of *words*, man. Meanwhile, just settle for what Abdul Alhazred wrote in the *Necronomicon*: "Past, present, future: all are one in Yog-Sothoth." Or what Weishaupt wrote in his *Konigen, Kirchen und Dummheit*: "There is but one Eye and it is all eyes; one Mind and it is all minds; one time and it is Now." Grok?' Joe nods dubiously, faintly hearing the music:

RAMA RAMA RAMA HAAAAARE
Two big rhinoceroses, three big rhinoceroses . . .

Dillinger made contact with the mind of Richard Belz, forty-three-year-old professor of physics at Queens College, as Belz was being loaded into an ambulance to be taken to Bellevue Hospital where X rays would reveal severe skull fractures. Shit, Dillinger thought, why does somebody have to be half dead before I can reach him? Then he concentrated on his message: Two universes flowing in opposite directions. Two together form a third entity which is synergetically more than the sum of its two parts. Thus two always leads to three. Two and Three. Duality and trinity. Every unity is a duality and a trinity. A pentagon. Sheer energy, no matter involved. From the pentagon depend five more pentagons, like the petals of a flower. A

white rose. Five petals and a center: six. Two times three.
The flower interlocks with another flower just like it, form-
ing a polyhedron made of pentagons. Each such polyhedron
could have common surfaces with other polyhedrons,
forming infinite latticeworks based on the pentagonal unit.
They would be immortal. Self-sustaining. Not computers.
Beyond computers. Gods. All space for their habitation.
Infinitely complex.

The howl of a siren reached the unconscious ears of
Professor Belz. Consciousness is present in the living body,
even in one that is apparently unconscious. Unconscious-
ness is not the absence of consciousness, but its temporary
immobility. It is not a state resembling death. It is not like
death at all. Once the necessary complexity of brain-cell
interconnections is reached, substantial energy relationships are set up. These can exist independently of the
material base that brought them into being.

All of this, of course, is merely visual structural metaphor for interactions on the energy level than cannot be
visualized. The siren howled.

*In the Three Lions pub, George said to Peter, 'What
was in that water pistol?'*

'Sulphuric acid.'

'Acid is just the first stage,' said Simon. 'Like matter is
the first stage of life and consciousness. Acid launches you.
But once you're out there, if the mission is successful, you
jettison the first stage and you're traveling free of gravity.
Which means free of matter. Acid dissolves the barriers
which prevent the maximum possible complexity of energy
relationships from building up in the brain. At Norton
Cabal, we'll show you how to pilot the second stage.'

*(Waving their crosses over their heads and howling in-
coherently, the men of God's Lightning formed wavering
ranks and marched around the territory they had conquered. Zev Hirsch and Frank Ochuk carried the banner
that read 'LOVE IT OR WE'LL STOMP YOU.')*

Howard sang:

The tribes of the porpoise are fearless and strong
Our land is the ocean, our banner's a song
Our weapon is speed and our noses like rock
No foe can withstand our terrible shock.

A cloud of porpoise bodies swam out from somewhere behind Hagbard's submarine. Through the pale blue-green medium which Hagbard's TV cameras made out of water, they seemed to fly toward the distant spiderlike ships of the Illuminati.

'What's happening?' said George. 'Where's Howard?'

'Howard is leading them,' said Hagbard. He flipped a toggle on the railing of the balcony on which they stood in the center of a globe that looked like a bubble of air at the bottom of the Atlantic Ocean. 'War room, get missiles ready. We may have to back up the porpoise attack.'

'*Da, tovarish Celine,*' came a voice.

The porpoises were too far away to be seen now. George discovered that he was not afraid. The whole thing was too much like watching a science-fiction movie. There was too much illusion involved in this submarine of Hagbard's. If he were able to realize, in his glands and nerves, that he was in a vulnerable metal ship thousands of feet below the surface of the Atlantic, under such enormous pressure that the slightest stress could crack the hull and send water bursting in that would crush them to death, then he might be afraid. If he were really able to accept the fact that those little distant globes with waving legs appended to them were undersea craft manned by people who intended to destroy the vessel he was in, then he could be afraid. Actually, if he could not see as much as he was seeing, but only feel and sense things and be told what was happening, as in the average airplane flight, then he would be afraid. As it was, the 20,000-year-old city of Peos looked like a tabletop model. And though he might intellectually accept Hagbard's statement that they were over the lost continent of Atlantis, in his bones he didn't believe in Atlantis. As a result, he didn't believe in any of the rest of this, either.

Suddenly Howard was outside their bubble. Or some other porpoise. That was another thing that made this hard to accept. Talking porpoises.

'Ready for destruction of enemy ships,' said Howard.

Hagbard shook his head. 'I wish we could communicate with them. I wish I could give them a chance to surrender. But they wouldn't listen. And they have communications systems on their ships that I can't get through to.' He turned to George. 'They use a type of insulated telepathy to communicate. The very thing that tipped off Sheriff Jim Cartwright that you were in a hotel room in Mad Dog smoking Weishaupt's Wonder Weed.'

'You don't want them too close when they go.' said Howard.

'Are your people out of the way?' said Hagbard.

(Five big rhinoceroses, six big rhinoceroses. . . .)

'Of course. Quit this hesitating. This is no time to be a humanitarian.'

'The sea is crueler than the land,' said Hagbard, 'sometimes.'

'The sea is cleaner than the land,' said Howard. 'There's no hate. Just death when and as neeeded. These people have been your enemies for twenty thousand years.'

'I'm not that old,' said Hagbard, 'and I have very few enemies.'

'If you wait any longer you'll endanger the submarine and my people.'

George looked out at the red and white striped globes which were moving toward them through the blue-green water. They were much larger now and closer. Whatever was propelling them wasn't visible. Hagbard reached out a brown finger, let it rest on a white button on the railing in front of him, then pressed it decisively.

There was a bright flash of light, dimmed slightly by the medium through which it traveled, on the surface of each of the globes. It was like watching fireworks through tinted glasses. Next, the globes crumbled as if they were ping-pong balls being struck by invisible sledge hammers.

'That's all there is to it,' said Hagbard quietly.

The air around George seemed to vibrate, and the floor under him shook. Suddenly he was terrified. Feeling the shock wave from the simultaneous explosions out there in the water made it real. A relatively thin metal shell was all that protected him from total annihilation. And nobody would ever hear from him or know what happened to him.

Large, glittering objects drifted down through the water from one of the nearby Illuminati spider ships. They vanished among the streets of the city that George now knew was real. The buildings in the area near the explosion of the Illuminati ships looked more ruined than they had

before. The ocean bottom was churned up in brown clouds.
Down into the brown clouds drifted the crushed spider
ships. George looked for the Temple of Tethys. It stood,
intact, in the distance.

'Did you see those statues fall out of the lead ship?'
said Hagbard. 'I'm claiming them.' He hit the switch on
the railing. 'Prepare for salvage operation.'

They dropped down among buildings deeply buried in
sediment, and at the bottom of their television globe
George saw two huge claws reach out, seemingly from
nowhere – actually he guessed, from the underside of the
submarine – and pick up four gleaming gold statues that
lay half-buried in the mud.

Suddenly a bell rang and a red flash lit up the interior
of the bubble. 'We're under attack again,' said Hagbard.
Oh, no, George thought. Not when I'm starting to believe
that all this is real. I won't be able to stand it. Here goes
Dorn doing his world-famous coward act again. . . . Hagbard pointed. A white globe hovered like an underwater
moon above a distant range of mountains. On its pale surface a red emblem was painted, a glaring eye inside a
triangle.

'Give me missile visibility,' said Hagbard, flicking a
switch. Between the white globe and the *Lief Erickson*
four orange lights appeared in the water rushing toward
them.

'It just doesn't pay to underestimate them – ever,' said
Hagbard. 'First it turns out they can detect me when they
shouldn't have equipment good enough to do that, now I
find that not only do they have small craft in the vicinity,
they've got the *Zwack* herself coming after me. And the
Zwack is firing underwater missiles at me, though I'm
supposed to be indetectable. I think we might be in trouble,
George.'

George wanted to close his eyes, but he also didn't want
to show fear in front of Hagbard. He wondered what death
at the bottom of the Atlantic would feel like. Probably
something like being under a pile driver. The water would
hit them, engulf them, and it wouldn't be like any ordinary
water – it would be like liquid steel, every drop striking
with the force of a ten-ton truck, prying cell apart from
cell and crushing each cell individually, reducing the body

to a protoplasmic dishrag. He remembered reading about
the disappearance of an atomic submarine called the
Thresher back in the '60s, and he recalled that the *New
York Times* had speculated that death by drowning in
water under extreme pressure would be exceedingly pain-
ful, though brief. Every nerve individually being crushed.
The spinal cord crushed everywhere along its length. The
brain squeezed to death, bursting, rupturing, bleeding into
the steel-hard water. The human form would doubtless be
unrecognizable in minutes. George thought of every bug
he had ever stepped on, and bugs made him think of the
spider ships. That's what we did to *them*. And I define
them as enemies only on Hagbard's say so. Carlo was
right. I can't kill.

Hagbard hesitated, didn't he? Yes, but he did it. Any
man who can cause a death like that to be visited upon
other men is a monster. No, not a monster, only too
human. But not my kind of human. Shit, George, he's your
kind of human, all right. You're just a coward. Cowardice
doth make consciences for us all.

Hagbard called out, 'Howard, where the hell are you?'

The torpedo shape appeared on the right side of the
bubble. 'Over here, Hagbard. We've got more mines ready.
We can go after those missiles with mines like we did the
spider ships. Think that would work?'

'It's dangerous,' said Hagbard, 'because the missiles
might explode on contact with the metal and electronic
equipment in the mines.'

'We're willing to try,' said Howard, and without another
word he swam away.

'Wait a minute,' Hagbard said. 'I don't like this. There's
too much danger to the porpoises.' He turned to George
and shook his head. 'I'm not risking a goddamned thing,
and they stand to be blown to bits. It's not right. I'm not
that important.'

'You are risking something,' said George, trying to control the quaver in his voice. 'Those missiles will destroy us
if the dolphins don't stop them.'

At that moment, there were four blinding flashes where
the orange lights had been. George gripped the railing,
sensing that the shock wave of these explosions would be
worse than that caused by the destruction of the spider

ships. It came. George had been readying himself for it, but unable to tell when it would come, and it still took him by surprise. Everything shook violently. Then the bottom dropped out of his stomach, as if the submarine had suddenly leaped up. George grabbed the railing with both arms, clinging to it as the only solid thing near him. 'O God, we're gonna be killed!' he cried.

'They got the missiles,' Hagbard said. 'That gives us a fighting chance. Laser crew, attempt to puncture the *Zwack*. Fire at will.'

Howard reappeared outside the bubble. 'How did your people do?' Hagbard asked him.

'All four of them were killed,' said Howard. 'The missiles exploded when they approached them, just as you predicted.'

George, who was standing up straight now, thankful that Hagbard had simply ignored his episode of terror, said, 'They were killed saving our lives. I'm sorry it happened, Howard.'

'Laser-beam firing, Hagbard,' a voice announced. There was a pause. 'I think we hit them.'

'You needn't be sorry,' said Howard. 'We neither look forward to death in fear nor back upon it in sorrow. Especially when someone has died doing something worthwhile. Death is the end of one illusion and the beginning of another.'

'What other illusion?' asked George. 'When you're dead, you're dead, right?'

'Energy can neither be created, nor destroyed,' said Hagbard. 'Death itself is an illusion.'

These people were talking like some of the Zen students and acid mystics George had known. If I could feel that way, he thought, I wouldn't be such a goddamned coward. Howard and Hagbard must be enlightened. I've got to become enlightened. I can't stand living this way any more. Whatever it took, acid alone wasn't the answer. George had tried acid already, and he knew that, while the experience might be wholly remarkable, for him it left little residue in terms of changed attitudes or behavior. Of course, if you *thought* your attitudes and behavior should change, you mimicked other acidheads.

'I'll try to find out what's happening to the *Zwack*,' said Howard, and swam away.

'The porpoises do not fear death, they do not avoid suffering, they are not assailed by conflicts between intellect and feeling and they are not worried about being ignorant of things. In other words, they have not decided that they know the difference between good and evil, and in consequence they do not consider themselves sinners. Understand?'

'Very few humans consider themselves sinners nowadays,' said George. 'But everyone is afraid of death.'

'All human beings consider themselves sinners. It's just about the deepest, oldest, and most universal human hangup there is. In fact, it's almost impossible to speak of it in terms that don't confirm it. To say that human beings have a universal hangup, as I just did, is to restate the belief that all men are sinners in different languages. In that sense, the Book of Genesis – which was written by early Semitic opponents of the Illuminati – is quite right. To arrive at a cultural turning point where you decide that all human conduct can be classified in one of two categories, good and evil, is what creates all sin – plus anxiety, hatred, guilt, depression, all the peculiarly human emotions. And, of course, such a classification is the very antithesis of creativity. To the creative mind there is no right or wrong. Every action is an experiment, and every experiment yields its fruit in knowledge. To the moralist, every action can be judged as right or wrong – and, mind you, *in advance* – without knowing what its consequences are going to be – depending upon the mental disposition of the actor. Thus the men who burned Giordano Bruno at the stake *knew* they were doing good, even though the consequence of their actions was to deprive the world of a great scientist.'

'If you can never be sure whether what you are doing is good or bad,' said George, 'aren't you liable to be pretty Hamlet-like?' He was feeling much better now, much less afraid, even though the enemy was still presumably out there trying to kill him. Maybe he was getting *darshan* from Hagbard.

'What's so bad about being Hamlet-like?' said Hagbard. 'Anyway, the answer is no, because you only become hesitant when you believe there is such a thing as good and evil, and that your action may be one or the other, and you're not sure which. That was the whole point about Hamlet, if you remember the play. It was his *conscience* that made him indecisive.'

'So he should have murdered a whole lot of people in the first act?'

Hagbard laughed. 'Not necessarily. He might have decisively killed his uncle at the earliest opportunity, thus saving the lives of everyone else. Or he might have said, "Hey, am I really obligated to avenge my father's death?" and done nothing. He was due to succeed to the throne anyway. If he had just bided his time everyone would have been a lot better off, there would have been no deaths, and the Norwegians would not have conquered the Danes, as they did in the last scene of the last act. Though being Norwegian myself I would hardly begrudge Fortinbras his triumph.'

At that moment Howard appeared again outside their bubble. 'The *Zwack* is retreating. Your laser beam punctured the outer shell, causing a leak in the fuel-storage cells and putting excessive stress on the pressure-resisting system. They were forced to climb to higher levels, which put them so far away from you that they're now heading south toward the tip of Africa.'

Hagbard expelled a great sigh of relief. 'That means they're heading for their home base. They'll enter a tunnel in the Persian Gulf which will bring them into the great underground Sea of Valusia, which is deepest beneath the Himalayas. That was the first base they established. They were preparing it even before the fall of High Atlantis. It's devilishly well defended. One day we'll penetrate it though.'

The thing that puzzled Joe most after his illuminization was John Dillinger's penis. The rumors about the Smithsonian Institute, he knew, were true: even though any casual phone-caller would get a flat denial from Institute officials, certain high-placed government people could provide a dispensation and the relic would be shown, in the legendary alcohol bottle, all legendary 23 inches of it. But if John was alive, it wasn't his, and, if it wasn't his, whose was it?

'Frank Sullivan's,' Simon said, when Joe finally asked him.

'And who the hell was Frank Sullivan to have a tool like that?'

But Simon only answered, 'I don't know. Just some guy who looked like John.'

Atlantis also bothered Joe, after he saw it the first time Hagbard took him for a ride in the *Lief Erikson*. It was all too pat, too plausible, too good to be true, especially the ruins of cities like Peos, with their architecture that obviously combined Egyptian and Mayan elements.

'Science has been flying on instruments, like a pilot in a fog, ever since nineteen hundred,' he said casually to Hagbard on the return trip to New York. (This was in '72, according to his later recollections, Fall of '72 – almost two years exactly after the test of AUM in Chicago.)

'You've been reading Bucky Fuller,' was Hagbard's cool reply. 'Or was it Korzybski?'

'Never mind who I've been reading,' Joe said directly. 'The thought in my head is that I never saw Atlantis, any more than I ever saw Marilyn Monroe. I saw moving pictures which you told me were television reception of cameras outside your sub. And I saw moving pictures of what Hollywood assured me was a real woman, even though she looked more like a design by Petty or Vargas. In the Marilyn Monroe case, it is reasonable to believe what I am told: I don't believe a robot that good has been built yet. But Atlantis . . . I know special-effects men who could build a city like that on a tabletop, and have dinosaurs walking through it. And your cameras trained on it.'

'You suspect me of trickery?' Hagbard asked raising his eyebrows.

'Trickery is your metier,' Joe said bluntly. 'You are the Beethoven, the Rockefeller, the Michelangelo of deception. The Shakespeare of the gypsy switch, the two-headed nickel, and the rabbit in the hat. What little liver pills are to Carter, lies are to you. You dwell in a world of trapdoors, sliding panels, and Hindu rope tricks. Do I suspect you? Since I met you, I suspect *everybody*.'

'I'm glad to hear it,' Hagbard grinned. 'You are well on your way to paranoia. Take this card and keep it in your wallet. When you begin to understand it, you'll be ready for your next promotion. Just remember: *it's not true unless it makes you laugh*. That is the one and sole and infallible test of all ideas that will ever be presented to you.' And he handed Joe a card saying

THERE IS NO FRIEND
ANYWHERE

Burroughs, incidentally, although he discovered the 23 synchronicity principle, is unaware of the correlation with 17. This makes it even more interesting that his date for the invasion of earth by the Nova Mob (in *Nova Express*) is September 17, 1899. When I asked him how he picked that date, he said it just came to him out of the air.

Damn. I was just interrupted by another woman, collecting for the Mothers March Against Hernia. I only gave her a dime.

W, the 23rd letter, keeps popping up in all this. Note: Weishaupt, Washington, William S. Burroughs, Charlie Workman, Mendy Weiss, Len Weinglass in the Conspiracy Trial, and others who will quickly come to mind. Even more interesting, the first physicist to apply the concept of synchronicity to physics, after Jung published the theory, was Wolfgang Pauli.

Another suggestive letter-number transformation: Adam Weishaupt (A.W.) is 1-23, and George Washington (G.W.) is 7-23. Spot the hidden 17 in there? But, perhaps, I grow too imaginative, even whimsical. . . .

There was a click. George turned. All the time he'd been in the control center with Hagbard, he had never looked back at the door through which he had come. He was surprised to see that it looked like an opening in thin air – or thin water. On either side of the doorway was blue-green water and a dark horizon which was actually the ocean bottom. Then, in the center, the doorway itself and a golden light silhouetting the figure of a beautiful woman.

Mavis strode onto the balcony, pulling the door shut behind her. She was wearing forest-green tights with white patent leather boots and a wide white belt. Her small but well-shaped breasts jiggled naturally under her blouse.

George found himself thinking back to the scene on the beach. That was only this morning, and what time was it anyway? What time where? Back in Florida it was probably two or three in the afternoon. Which would make it one P.M. in Mad Dog, Texas. And probably about six out here in the Atlantic. Did time zones extend beneath the water? He supposed they did. On the other hand, if you were at the North Pole, you could skip around the Pole and be in a different time zone every few seconds. And cross the International Date Line every five minutes if you wanted to. Which would not, he reminded himself, make it possible to travel in time. But if he could go back to this morning and replay Mavis's demand for sex, this time he would respond! He now wanted her desperately.

Well and good, but why did she say he was *not* a schmuck, why did she imply admiration for him because he would not fuck her? If he had fucked her because she asked him and he felt he should but without wanting to, he would have been a pure and simple schmuck. But he could have pronged her simply because she would have been nice to fuck, regardless of whether she would have admired him or despised him. But that was their game – Mavis's and Hagbard's game of saying I do what I want to do, and I don't give a damn what you think. George cared a great deal about what other people thought, so not fucking Mavis at the time was at least honest, even if he was beginning to see some merit in the Discordian (he supposed it was Discordian) attitude of super self-sufficiency.

Mavis smiled at him. 'Well, George, had your baptism of fire?'

George shrugged. 'Well, there was the Mad Dog jail. And I've been in a few other bad scenes.' For instance, there was the time I held a pistol to my head and pulled the trigger.

She'd sucked his cock, he'd watched her in manic manustupration, but he was desperate to get inside her, all the way, up the womb, riding her ovarian trolley to the wonderful land of fuck, as Henry Miller said. What the hell was so special about Mavis's cunt? Especially after that induction ceremony scene. Hell, Stella Maris seemed like a less neurotic woman and was certainly a classic lay. After Stella Maris, who needed Mavis?

A sudden question struck him. How did he know he'd laid Stella? It could have been Mavis inside that golden apple. It could have been some woman he'd never met. He was pretty sure it was a woman, unless it was a goat or a cow or a sheep. Best not put that kind of joke past Hagbard either. But even if it was a woman, why visualize Stella or Mavis or somebody like them? It was probably some diseased old Etruscan whore that Hagbard kept around for religious purposes. Some Sibyl. Some wop witch. Maybe it was Hagbard's rotten old Sicilian mother with no teeth, a black shawl, and three kinds of VD. No, it was Hagbard's father who was Sicilian. His mother was Norwegian.

'What color were they?' he said suddenly to Hagbard.

'Who?'

'The Atlanteans.'

'Oh.' Hagbard nodded. 'They were covered with fur over most of their bodies, like any normal ape. At least, the High Atlanteans were. A mutation occurred around the time of the Hour of the Evil Eye – the catastrophe that destroyed High Atlantis. Later Atlanteans, like modern humans, were hairless. Those of the oldest Atlantean ancestry tend to be rather furry.' George couldn't help looking down at Hagbard's hand as it rested on the railing. It was covered with thick black hair.

'All right,' said Hagbard, 'it's time to head back to our North American base. Howard? You out there?'

The long, streamlined shape performed a somersault on their right. 'What's happening, Hagbard?'

'Have some of your people keep an eye on things here. We've got work to do on land. And – Howard, as long as I live I will be in debt to your people for the four who died to save me.'

'Haven't you and the *Lief Erickson* saved us from several kinds of deaths planned for us by the shore people?' said Howard. 'We'll keep watch over Atlantis for you. And the seas in general, and that which Atlantis has spawned. Hail and farewell, Hagbard and other friends—

> 'The sea is wide and the sea is deep
> But warm as blood through it there rolls
> A tide of friendship that will keep
> Us close in Ocean's blackest holes.'

He was gone. 'Lift off,' Hagbard called. George felt the surge of the sub's colossal engines, and they were sailing high above the hills and valleys of Atlantis. With the special lighting of Hagbard's television screen system, it seemed much like flying in a jet plane over one of the continents above the ocean's surface.

'Too bad we don't have time to get deeper into Atlantis,' said Hagbard. 'There are many mighty cities to see. Though of course none of them can approach the cities that existed before the Hour of the Evil Eye.'

'How many of these Atlantean civilizations were there?' asked George.

'Basically, two. One leading up to the Hour, and one afterward. Before the Hour, there was a civilization of about a million human beings on this continent. Technically, they were further advanced than the human race is today. They had atomic power, space travel, genetic technology and much else. This civilization was struck a death blow in the Hour of the Evil Eye. Two-thirds of them were killed – almost half the human population of the planet at that time. After the Hour, something made it impossible for them to make a comeback. The cities that came through the first catastrophe relatively undamaged were destroyed in later disasters. The inhabitants of Atlantis were reduced to savagery in a generation. Part of the continent sank under the sea, which was the beginning of the process that ended when all of Atlantis was under water, as it is today.'

'Was this the earthquakes and tidal waves that you always read about?' George asked.

'No,' said Hagbard with a curious closed expression. 'It was manmade.' High Atlantis was destroyed in a kind of war. Probably a civil war, since there was no other power on the planet that could have matched them.'

'Anyway, if there'd been a victor, they'd still be around now,' said George.

'They are,' said Mavis. 'The victors are still around. Only they're not what you might visualize. Not a conquering nation. And we are the descendants of the defeated.'

'Now,' said Hagbard, 'I'm going to show you something I promised when we first met. It has to do with the catastrophe I've been talking about. Look there.'

The submarine had risen high above the continent, and
it was possible to see landscapes stretching for hundreds of
miles. Looking in the direction in which Hagbard pointed,
George saw a vast expanse of black, glazed plain. Out of
its center jutted something white and pointed, like a canine
tooth.

'It is said of them that they even controlled the comets
in their courses,' said Hagbard. He pointed again.

The submarine sailed closer to the jutting white object.
It was a four-sided white pyramid.

'Don't say it,' said Mavis, giving him a warning look,
and George remembered the tattoo he had seen between
her breasts. He looked down again. They were above the
pyramid now and George could see the side that had been
hidden from him as they approached. He saw what he had
half-feared, half-expected to see: a blood-red design in the
shape of a baleful eye.

'The Pyramid of the Eye,' Hagbard said. 'It stood in
the center of the capital of High Atlantis. It was built in
the last days of that civilization by the founders of the
world's first religion. It doesn't look very big from up here,
but it's five times the size of the Great Pyramid of Cheops,
which was modeled after it. It's made of an imperishable
ceramic substance which repels even ocean sediment. As if
the builders knew that to last it would have to survive tens
of thousands of years of ocean burial. And maybe – depending on who they were – they did know that. Or maybe
they just built well in those days. Peos, as you saw, was a
pretty durable city, and that was built after High Atlantis
fell, by the second civilization I spoke of. That second
civilization reached a level somewhat more advanced than
that of the Greeks and Romans, but it was nothing like
its predecessor. And some malevolent force seemed bent
on destroying it, too, and it was destroyed, about ten
thousand years ago. Of that civilization we have the evidence of ruins. But of High Atlantis we have only records
and legends dug up from the later civilization – and, of
course, poetry from the Porpoise Corpus. This is the only
artifact, this pyramid. But its existence and durability prove
that as long ago as ten Egypts, a race of men existed whose
technology was far advanced beyond what we know today.
So advanced that it took twenty thousand years for that

civilization's successor culture to disappear completely. The men who destroyed High Atlantis did their best to make it disappear. But they couldn't quite manage it. The Pyramid of the Eye, for instance, is indestructible. Though it's probable that they didn't want to destroy it.'

Mavis nodded sombrely. 'That is their most sacred shrine.'

'In other words,' said George, 'you're telling me that the people who destroyed Atlantis still exist. Do they have the powers they had then?'

'Substantially, yes,' said Hagbard.

'Is this the Illuminati you told me about?'

'Illuminati, or Ancient Illuminated Seers of Bavaria is one of the names they have used, yes.'

'So they didn't start in seventeen seventy-six – they go a long way back before that, right?'

'Right,' said Mavis.

'Then why did you lie to me about their history? And why the hell haven't they taken over the world by now, if they're all that powerful? When our ancestors were savages, they could have dominated them completely.'

Hagbard replied, 'I lied to you because the human mind can only accept a little of the truth at a time. Also, initiation into Discordianism has stages. The answer to the other question is complicated. But I'll try to give it to you simply. There are five reasons. First, there are organizations like the Discordians which are almost as powerful and which know almost as much as the Illuminati and which are able to thwart them. Second, the Illuminati are too small a group to enjoy the creative cross-fertilization necessary to progress of any kind, and they have been unable to advance much beyond the technological level they reached thirty thousand years ago. Like Chinese Mandarins. Third, the Illuminati are hamstrung in their actions by the superstitious beliefs that set them apart from the other Atlanteans. As I told you, they're the world's first religion. Fourth, the Illuminati are too sophisticated, ruthless and decadent to want to take over the world – it amuses them to *play* with world. Fifth, the Illuminati *do* rule the world and everything that happens, happens by their sufferance.'

'Those reasons contradict each other,' said George.

'That's the nature of logical thought. All propositions are true in some sense, false in some sense and meaningless in some sense.' Hagbard didn't smile.

The submarine had described a great arc as they talked and now the Pyramid of the Eye was far behind them. The eye itself, since it faced eastward, was no longer visible. Below, George could see the ruins of several small cities at the edge of tall cliffs that fell away into darker depths – cliffs that doubtless had been the seacoast of Atlantis at one time.

Hagbard said, 'I've got a job for you, George. You're going to like it, and you're going to want to do it, but it is going to make you shit a brick. We'll talk about it when we get to Chesapeake Base. Now, though, let's go down into the hold and have a look at our acquisitions.' He flicked a switch. 'FUCKUP, get your finger out of your ass and drive this thing for a while.'

'I'll see the statues later,' said Mavis. 'I've got other things to do just now.'

George followed Hagbard down carpeted staircases and halls paneled in glowing, polished oak. At last they came to a large hall which was apparently paved with marble flagstones. A group of men and women wearing horizontally striped nautical shirts similar to Hagbard's were clustered around four tall statues in the center of the room. When Hagbard entered the room they stopped talking and stepped away to give him a clear look at the sculptures. The floor was covered with puddles of water and the statues themselves were dripping.

'No wiping them dry,' Hagbard said. 'Every molecule is precious just as it is, and the less disturbed the better.' He stepped closer to the nearest one and looked at it for a long moment. 'What do you say about a thing like this? It's beyond exquisite. Can you imagine what their art was like *before* the disaster? And to think the Unbroken Circle destroyed every trace of it, except for that crude, stupid pyramid.'

'Which is the greatest piece of ceramic technology in the history of the human race,' said one of the women. George looked around for Stella Maris, but she wasn't there.

'Where's Stella?' he asked Hagbard.

'Upstairs minding the store. She'll see them later.'

The sculptures were unlike the work of any culture George knew, which was to be expected, after all. They were at once realistic, fanciful and abstractly intellectual. They bore resemblance to Egyptian and Mayan, Classical Greek, Chinese and Gothic, combined with a surprisingly modern-looking note. There were some qualities in the statues that were totally unique, though, qualities doubtless lost by the civilizations to which Atlantis was ancestral, but that might have been found in known world art, had there been other civilizations to preserve and emphasize them. This, George realized, was the Ur-Art; and looking at the statues was like hearing a sentence in the first language spoken by men.

An elderly sailor pointed at the statue farthest from where they were standing. 'Look at that beatific smile. A woman thought of that statue, I'll bet. That's every woman's dream – to be totally self-sufficient.'

'Some of the time, Joshua,' said the Oriental woman who had spoken before, 'but not all of the time. Now what I prefer is that.' She pointed to another statue.

Hagbard laughed. 'You think that's just nice, healthy oragenitalism, Tsu-Hsi. But the child in the woman's arms is the Son Without a Father, the Self-Begotten, and the couple at the base represent the Unbroken Circle of Gruad. Usually it's a serpent with its tail in its mouth, but in some of the earlier representations the couple in oral intercourse symbolizes sterile lust. The Unloved Mother has her foot on the man's head to indicate that she conquers lust. The whole sculpture is the product of the foulest cult to come out of Atlantis. They originated human sacrifice. First they practiced castration, but then they escalated to killing men instead of just cutting off their balls. Later, when women were subjugated, the sacrifice became a virgin female, supposedly to give her to the Unloved Ones while she was still pure.'

'That halo around the child's head looks like the peace symbol,' said George.

'Peace symbol, my ass,' said Hagbard. 'That's the oldest symbol of evil there is. Of course, in the cult of the Unbroken Circle it was a symbol of good, but that's the same difference.'

'They can't have been so vicious if they produced that statue,' said the Oriental woman stubbornly.

'Could you deduce the Spanish Inquisition from a painting of the manger at Bethlehem?' said Hagbard. 'Don't be naive, Miss Mao.' He turned to George, 'The value of any one of these statues is beyond calculation. But not many people know that. I'm sending you to one who does – Robert Putney Drake. One of the finest art connoisseurs in the world crime syndicate. You're going to see him with a gift from me – these four statues. The Illuminati were planning to buy his support with gold from the Temple of Tethys: I'm going to get to him first.'

'If they only needed four statues, why were they trying to raise the whole temple?' George asked.

'I think they wanted to remove the temple to Agharti, their stronghold under the Himalayas, for safekeeping. I haven't been any closer to the Temple of Tethys than we were today, but I suspect it's a treasure-house of evidence of High Atlantis. As such, it would be something the Illuminati would want to remove. Until now there was no reason to, because no one had access to the seabottom other than the Illuminati. Now I can get around down here just as well, better in fact, than they can, and pretty soon others will be following. Several nations and many groups of private persons are exploring the undersea world. It's time for the Illuminati to finish taking away whatever tells of High Atlantis.'

'Will they destroy that city we saw? And what about the Pyramid of the Eye?'

Hagbard shook his head. 'They'd be willing to let later Atlantean ruins to be found. That wouldn't say anything about their existence. As for the Pyramid of the Eye, I suspect they have a real problem with that. They can't destroy it, and even if they could they wouldn't want to. But it's a dead giveaway to the existence of a supercivilization in the past.'

'Well,' said George, not at all wanting to meet the head of the American crime syndicate, 'what we ought to do is go back and raise the Temple of Tethys ourselves, before the Illuminati grab it.'

'Good grief,' said Miss Mao. 'This happens to be the

most critical moment in the history of this civilization. We don't have time to fiddle-fuck around with archeology.'

'He's just a legionnaire,' said Hagbard. 'Though after this mission he'll know the Fairest and become a deacon. He'll understand more then. George, I want you to act as a go-between for the Discordian movement and the Syndicate. You're going to bring these four statues to Robert Putney Drake and tell him there are more where they came from. Ask Drake to stop working for the Illuminati, to take the heat off our people, wherever he's after them, and to drop the assassination project the Illuminati have been working on with him. And as an earnest of good faith, he's to snuff twenty-four Illuminati agents for us in the next twenty-four hours. Their names will be contained in a sealed envelope which you'll give him.'

FIVES. SEX. HERE IS WISDOM. The mumble of the breast is the mutter of man.

State's Attorney Milo A. Flanagan stood on the roof of the high rise condominium on Lake Shore Drive in which he lived, scanning blue-gray Lake Michigan with powerful binoculars. It was April 24, and Project Tethys should be completed. At any moment Flanagan expected to sight what would look like another Great Lakes freighter heading for the Chicago River locks. Only this one would be carrying a dismantled Atlantean temple crated in its hold. The ship would be recognizable by a red triangle painted on the funnel.

After being inspected by Flanagan (whose name in the Order was Brother Johann Beghard) and after his report had been sent on to Vigilance Lodge, the North American command center, the crated temple would be moved down-river to Saint Louis, where, by prior agreement with the President of the United States, it would be trucked over-land to Fort Knox under the guard of the U.S. Army. The President didn't know with whom he was dealing. The CIA had informed him that the source of the artifacts was the Livonian Nationalist Movement, now behind the Iron Curtain, and that the crates would contain Livonian art treasures. Certain high officers in the CIA did know the real nature of the organization which the U.S. was helping, because they were members of it. Of course, the Syndicate (without even a cover story) was keeping three-quarters of its gold in with the government store at Fort Knox these days. 'Where could you find a safer place?' Robert Putney Drake once asked.

But the freighter was behind schedule. The wind battered at Flanagan, whipping his wavy white hair and the well-tailored jacket sleeves and trouser legs. The goddamned Chicago wind. Flanagan had been fighting it all his life. It had made him the man he was.

Police Sergeant Otto Waterhouse emerged from the doorway to the roof. Waterhouse was a member of Flanagan's personal staff, which meant he was on the Police Department payroll, the Syndicate payroll, and another payroll that regularly deposited a fixed sum in the account of Herr Otto Wasserhaus in a Bavarian bank. Waterhouse was a six-and-a-half-foot-tall black man who had made a career for himself in the Chicago Police Department by being more willing and eager to harass, torture, maim, and kill members of his race than the average Mississippi sheriff. Flanagan had early spotted Waterhouse's ice-cold, self-hating love affair with death, and had attached him to his staff.

'A message from CFR communications center in New York,' said Waterhouse. 'The word has come through from Ingolstadt that Project Tethys was aborted.'

Flanagan lowered his binoculars and turned to look at Waterhouse. The State's Attorney's florid face with its bushy pepper-and-salt eyebrows was shrewd and distinguished, the sort of face people vote for, especially in Chicago. It was a face that had once belonged to a kid who had run with the Hamburgers in Chicago's South Side Irish ghetto and bashed out the brains of black men with cobblestones for the fun of it. It was a face that had come from that primitive beginning to knowing about ten-thousand-year-old sunken temples, spider ships, and international conspiracies. It was stamped indelibly with the lines of Milo. A. Flanagan's ancestors, the ancestors of the Gauls, Britons, Scots, Picts, and Irish. Around the time the Temple of Tethys was sinking into the sea, they had been driven forth on orders from Agharti from that thick ancient forest that is now the desert country of Outer Mongolia. But Flanagan was only a Fourth-degree Illuminatus and not fully instructed in the history. Though he did not display much emotion there were blue-white flames of murderous madness burning deep in his eyes. Waterhouse was one of the few people in Chicago who could meet Flanagan's baleful stare head-on.

'How did it happen?' Flanagan asked.

'They were attacked by porpoises and an invisible submarine. The spider craft were all blown to bits. The *Zwack* came in and counterattacked, was damaged by a laser beam and forced to disengage.'

'How did they find out we had spider ships at the temple site?'

'Maybe the porpoises told them.'

Flanagan looked at Waterhouse coldly and thoughtfully. 'Maybe it leaked at this end, Otto. There are JAMs active in this town, more here than anywhere in the country right now. Dillinger has been spotted twice in the last week. By Gruad, how I'd like to be the one to *really* get him, once and for all! What would Hoover's ghost say then, huh, Otto?' Flanagan grinned, one of his rare genuine smiles, exposing prominent canine teeth. 'We know there's a JAM cult center somewhere on the North Side. Someone's been stealing hosts from my brother's church for the past ten years — even at times when I've had as many as thirty men staked out there. And my brother says that there have been more cases of demonic possession in his parish in the last five years than in all of Chicago in all its previous history. One of our sensitives has reported emanations of the Old Woman in this area at least once a month during the past year. It's long past time we found them. They could be reading our minds, Otto. That could be the leak. Why haven't we got a fix on them?'

Waterhouse, who only a few years ago had known nothing more unconventional than how to turn a homicide into 'killed while resisting arrest', looked back calmly at Flanagan and said, 'We need ten sensitives of the fifth grade to form the pentacle, and we've only got seven.'

Flanagan shook his head. 'There are seventeen fifth graders in Europe, eight in Africa, and twenty-three scattered around the rest of the world. You'd think they could spare us three for a week. That's all it would take.'

Waterhouse said, 'Maybe you've got enemies in the higher circle. Maybe somebody wants to see us get it.'

'Why the hell do you say things like that, Waterhouse?'

'Just to fuck you up, man.'

Eight floors below, in an apartment which was regularly used for black masses, a North Clark street hippie named Skip Lynch opened his eyes and looked at Simon Moon and Padre Pederastia. 'Time's getting very short,' he said. 'We've got to finish off Flanagan soon.'

'It can't be too soon for me,' said Padre Pederastia. 'If Daddy hadn't favored him so outrageously he'd be the priest today and I'd be State's Attorney.'

Simon nodded. 'But then we'd be snuffing you instead of Milo. Anyway, I believe George Dorn will be taking care of the problem for us right now.'

Squinks? It all began with the squinks – and that sentence is more true than you will realize until long after this mission is over, Mr. Muldoon.

It was the night of February 2, 1776, and it was dark and windy in Ingolstadt; in fact, Adam Weishaupt's study looked like a set for a Frankenstein movie, with its windows rattling and candles flickering, and old Adam himself casting terrifying shadows as he paced back and forth with his peculiar lurching gait. At least the shadows were terrifying to *him*, because he was flying high on the new hemp extract that Kolmer had brought back from his last visit to Baghdad. To calm himself, he was repeating his English vocabulary-building drill, working on the new words for that week. 'Tomahawk . . . Succotash . . . Squink. *Squink?*' He laughed out loud. The word was 'skunk,' but he had short-circuited from there to 'squid' and emerged with 'squink.' A new word: a new concept. But what would a squink look like? Midway between a squid and a skunk, no doubt: it would have eight arms and smell to *hoch Himmel*. A horrible thought: it reminded him, uncomfortably, of the shoggoths in the damnable *Necronomicon* that Kolmer was always trying to get him to read when he was stoned, saying that was the only way to understand it.

He lurched over to the Black Magic and Pornography section of his bookshelves – which he kept, sardonically, next to his Bible commentaries – and took down the long-forbidden volume of the visions of the mad poet Abdul Alhazred. He turned to the first drawing of a shoggoth. Strange, he thought, how a creature so foul could also, from certain angles and especially when you were high, look vaguely like a crazily grinning rabbit. '*Du haxen Hase*,' he chortled to himself. . . .

Then his mind made the leap: five sides on the borders on the shoggoth sketches . . . five sides, always, on all the shoggoth sketches . . . and 'squid' and 'skunk' both had five letters in them. . . .

He held up his hands, looked at the five fingers on each, and began to laugh. It was all clear suddenly: the Sign of the Horns made by holding up the first two fingers in a V and folding the other three down: the two, the three and their union in the five. Father, Son and Holy Devil . . . the Duality of good and evil, the Trinity of the Godhead . . . the bicycle and the tricycle. . . . He laughed louder and louder, looking – despite his long, thin face – like the Chinese statues of the Laughing Buddha.

While the gas chambers were operating, other features of life in the camps were also contributing to the Final Solution. At Auschwitz, for instance, many perished from beatings and other forms of ill treatment, but the general neglect of elementary sanitary and health precautions had the most memorable results. First there was spotted fever, then paratyphoid fever and abdominal typhus erysipelas. Tuberculosis, of course, was rampant, and – particularly amusing to certain of the officers – incurable diarrhea brought death to many inmates, degrading as it killed. No attempt was made, either, to prevent the ubiquitous camp rats from attacking those too ill to move or defend themselves. Never before witnessed by twentieth-century doctors, noma also appeared and was recognized only from the descriptions in old textbooks: it is the complication of malnutrition which eats holes in the cheeks until you can see right throught to the teeth. '*Vernichtung*,' a survivor said later, 'is the most terrible word in any language.'

Even so, the Aztecs grew more frantic toward the end, increasing the number of sacrifices, doubling and tripling the days of the year that called for spilled blood. But nothing saved them: just as Eisenhower's army advanced across Europe to end the ovens of Auschwitz, Cortez and his ships moved toward the great pyramid, the statue of Tlaloc, the confrontation.

Seven hours after Simon spoke of George Dorn to Padre

Pederastia, a private jet painted gold landed at Kennedy International Airport. Four heavy crates were moved by crane from the belly of the plane into a truck which bore on its side the sign 'GOLD & APPEL TRANSFERS.' A young man with shoulder-length blond hair, wearing a fashionable cutaway and knee breeches of red velvet with bottle-green silk stockings, stepped down from the plane and climbed into the cab of the truck. Holding an alligator briefcase in his lap, he sat silently beside the driver.

Tobias Knight, the driver, kept his thoughts to himself and asked no questions.

George Dorn was frightened. It was a feeling he was getting used to, so accustomed in fact that it no longer seemed to stop him from doing insane things. Besides, Hagbard had given him a talisman against harm, assuring him that it was 100 percent infallible. George slipped it out of his pocket and glanced at it again, curiously and with a wan hope. It was gold-tinted card with the strange glyphs:

$$\text{HJ3JX } \boxtimes\text{·+OrCJ}$$
$$\boxtimes\text{·+CJ}$$
$$\text{:T}\flat\text{XJ :}\dot\dagger\text{OO+HJ}$$

It was probably another of Hagbard's jokes, George decided. It might even be Etruscan for 'Kick this boob in the ass.' Hagbard's refusal to translate it suggested some such Celinean irony, and yet he had seemed very sober – almost religious – about the symbols.

One thing was sure: George was still frightened, but the fear was no longer paralyzing. *If I was this casual about fear a few years ago,* he thought, *there'd be one less cop in New York. And I wouldn't be here either, probably. No, that's not right, either. I would have told Carlo to go fuck himself. I wouldn't have let the fear of being called a cop-out stop me.* George had been scared when he went to Mad Dog, when Harry Coin tried to fuck him up the ass, when Harry Coin was killed, when he escaped from the Mad Dog jail, when he saw his own death just as he was coming, and when the Illuminati spider ships had attacked the *Lief Erickson.* Being scared was beginning to seem a normal condition to him.

So now he was going to meet the men who ran organized crime in the U.S. He knew practically nothing about the Syndicate and the Mafia, and what little he did know he tended to disbelieve on the grounds that it was probably myth. Hagbard had sketched in a little additional information for him while he was preparing for this flight. But the one thing that George was absolutely certain about was that he was going unprotected among men who killed human beings as easily as a housewife kills silverfish. And he was supposed to negotiate with them. The Syndicate had been working with the Illuminati until now. Now they were supposed to switch over to the Discordians, on George's say-so. With, of course, the help of four priceless statues. Except, what were Robert Putney Drake and Federico Maldonado going to say when they heard these statues had been dredged up from the bottom of the ocean floor out of the ruins of Atlantis? They would probably express their skepticism with pistols and send George back to the place he claimed the statues came from.

'Why me?' George had asked Hagbard earlier that day.

'Why me?' Hagbard repeated with a smile. 'The question asked by the soldier as the enemy bullets whistle around him, by the harmless homeowner as the homicidal maniac steps through the kitchen door hunting knife in hand, by the woman who has given birth to a dead baby, by the prophet who has just had a revelation of the word of God, by the artist who knows his latest painting is a work of genius. Why you? Because you're there, schmuck. Because something has to happen to you. OK?'

'But what if I fuck it up? I don't know anything about your organization or the Syndicate. If times are as crucial as you say, it's silly to send somebody like me on this mission. I have no experience meeting people like this.'

Hagbard shook his head impatiently. 'You underrate yourself. Just because you're young and afraid you think you can't talk to people. That's stupid. And it's not typical of your generation, so you should be all the more ashamed of yourself. Furthermore, you are experienced with even worse people than Drake and Maldonado. You spent part of a night in a cell with the man who killed John F. Kennedy.'

'*What?*' George felt the blood rush out of his face and he thought he might faint.

'*Oh, sure,*' said Hagbard casually. '*Joe Malik was on the right track when he sent you to Mad Dog, you know.*'

After all that, Hagbard told George he was perfectly free to turn down the mission if he didn't want to go. And George said he would go for the same reason he had agreed to accompany Hagbard on his golden submarine. Because he knew that he would have been a fool to pass up the experience.

A two-hour drive brought the truck to the outskirts of Blue Point, Long Island, to the gates of an estate. Two heavy-set men in green coveralls searched George and the driver, pointed the bell-shaped nozzle of an instrument at the truck and studied some dials, and then waved them through. They drove up a winding, narrow asphalt road through woods just beginning to show the light green budding of early spring. Shadowy figures prowled among the trees. Suddenly the road burst out of the woods and into a meadow. From here there was a long gentle rising slope to the top of a hill that was crowned by houses. From the edge of the woods George could see four large, comfortable-looking cottages, each three stories high, a little smaller than Newport, a little larger than Atlantic City. They were made of brick painted in seaside pastel colors and formed a semicircle on the crest of the hill. The grass of the meadow was cut very short, and halfway up the hill it became a beautifully manicured lawn. The woods screened the houses from the road, the meadow made it impossible for anyone emerging from woods to approach the houses without being seen, and the houses themselves constituted the elements of a fortress.

The Gold & Appel truck followed the driveway, which led between two of the houses, rolling over slots in the driveway where a section might be hydraulically raised to form a wall. The driver stopped at a gesture from one of two men in khakis who approached. George could now see the Syndicate fortress consisted of eight separate houses forming an octagon around a lawn. Each house had its own fenced-in yard, and George noticed with surprise that there was play equipment for children in front of several cottages. In the center of the compound was a tall white pole from which flew an American flag.

George and the driver stepped down from the cab of the truck. George identified himself and was ushered to the far side of the compound. The hill was much steeper on this side, George saw. It sloped down to a narrow boulder-strewn beach drenched by hugh Atlantic waves. A nice view, George thought. And eminently secure. The only way Drake's enemies could get at him would be to shell his home from a destroyer.

A slender, blond man – at least sixty and maybe a well-preserved seventy – came down the steps of the house George was approaching. He had a concave nose that ended in a sharp point, a strong, cleft chin, ice-blue eyes. He shook hands vigorously.

'Hi. I'm Drake. The others are inside. Let's go. Oh – is it OK with you if we go ahead and unload your truck?' He gave George a sharp, birdlike look. George realized with a sinking feeling that Drake was saying that they would take the statues regardless of whether any deal went through. Why, then, should they inconvenience themselves by changing sides in this underground war? But he nodded in acquiescence.

'You're young, aren't you?' said Drake as they went into the house. 'But that's the way it is nowadays. Boys do men's work.' The house was handsome inside, but not as one might expect, incredible. The carpets were thick, the woodwork heavy, dark and polished, the furnishings probably genuine antiques. George didn't see how Atlantean statues would fit into the decor. There was a painting at the top of the stairs to the second floor of a woman who looked slightly like Queen Elizabeth II. She wore a white gown with diamonds at her neck and wrists. Two small, fragile-looking blond boys in navy blue suits with white satin ties stood with her, staring solemnly out of the painting.

'My wife and sons,' said Drake with a smile.

They entered a large study full of mahogany, oak panel-ing, leatherbound books and red and green leather furniture. Theodore Roosevelt would have loved it, George thought. Over the desk hung a painting of a bearded man in Elizabethan costume. He was holding a bowling ball in his hand and looking superciliously at a messenger type who pointing out to sea. There were sailing ships in the distant background.

'An ancestor,' said Drake simply. He pressed a button in a panel on the desk. A door opened and two men came in, the first a tall young Chinese with a boney face and unruly black hair, the second a short, thin man who bore a faint resemblance to Pope Paul VI.

'Don Federico Maldonado, a man of the greatest respect,' said Drake. 'And Richard Jung, my chief counsellor.' George shook hands with both of them. He couldn't understand why Maldonado was known as 'Banana-Nose'; his proboscus was on the large side, but bore little resemblance to a banana. It was more like an eggplant. The name must be a sample of low Sicilian humor. The two men took seats on a red leather couch. George and Drake sank into armchairs facing them.

'And how are my favourite musicians doing?' Jung said genially.

Was this some kind of password? George was sure of one thing: his survival depended on sticking absolutely to truth and sincerity with these people, so he said, very sincerely, 'I don't know. Who are your favourite musicians?'

Jung smiled back, saying nothing, until George, his heart racing inside his chest like a hamster determined to run clear off the treadmill, reached into his briefcase and took out a parchment scroll.

'This,' he said, 'is the fundamental agreement proposed by the people I represent.' He handed it to Drake. Maldonado, he noticed, was staring fixedly, expressionlessly, at him in the most unnerving way. The man's eyes looked as if they were made of glass. His face was a waxen mask. He was, George decided, a wax dummy of Pope Paul VI which had been stolen from Madame Tussaud's, dressed in a business suit, and brought to life to serve as the head of the Mafia. George had always thought there was something witchy about Sicilians.

'Do we sign this in blood?' said Drake, removing the cloth-of-gold ribbon from the parchment and unrolling it.

George laughed nervously. 'Pen and ink will do fine.'

Saul's angry, triumphant eyes stare into mine, and I look

away guiltily. *Let me explain,* I say desperately. *I really am trying to help you. Your mind is a bomb.*

'What Weishaupt discovered that night of February second, seventeen seventy-six,' Hagbard Celine explained to Joe Malik in 1973, on a clear autumn day in Miami, about the same time that Captain Tequilla y Mota was reading Luttwak on the coup d'etat and making his first moves toward recruiting the officer's cabal that later seized Fernando Poo, 'was basically a simple mathematical relationship. It's so simple, in fact, that most administrators and bureaucrats never notice it. Just as the householder doesn't notice the humble termite, until it's too late. . . . Here, take this paper and figure for yourself. How many permutations are there in a system of four elements?'

Joe, recalling his high school math, wrote 4 x 3 x 2 x 1, and read aloud his answer 'Twenty-four.'

'And if you're one of the elements, the number of coalitions – or to be sinister, conspiracies – that you may have to confront would be twenty-three. Despite Simon Moon's obsessions, the twenty-three has no particularly mystic significance,' Hagbard added quickly. 'Just consider it pragmatically – it's a number of possible relationships which the brain can remember and handle. But now suppose the system has five elements . . .?'

Joe wrote 5 x 4 x 3 x 2 x 1 and read aloud, 'One hundred and twenty.' 'You see? One always encounters jumps of that size when dealing with permutations and combinations. But, as I say, administrators as a rule aren't aware of this. Korzybski pointed out, back in the early thirties, that nobody should ever *directly* supervise more than four subordinates, because the twenty-four possible coalitions ordinary office politics can create are enough to tax any brain. When it jumps up to one hundred and twenty, the administrator is lost. That, in essence, is the sociological aspect of the mysterious Law of Fives. The Illuminati always has five leaders in each nation, and five international Illuminati Primi supervising all of them, but each runs his own show more or less independent of the other four, united only by their common commitment to the Goal of Gruad.' Hagbard paused to relight his long, black Italian cigar.

'Now,' he said, 'put yourself in the position of the head of any counterespionage organization. Imagine, for instance,

that you're poor old McCone of the CIA at the time of the
first of the New Wave of Illuminati assassinations, ten
years ago, in sixty-three. Oswald was, of course, a double
agent, as everybody always knew. The Russians wouldn't
have let him out of Russia without getting a commitment
from him to do "small jobs," as they're called in the
business, although he'd be a "sleeper." That is, he'd go
about his ordinary business most of the time, and only be
called on occasionally when he was in the right place at
the right time for a particular "small job." Now, of course,
Washington knows this; they know that no expatriate
comes back from Moscow without some such agreement.
And Moscow knows the other side: that the State Department wouldn't take him back unless he accepted a similar
status with the CIA. Then, November twenty-second,
Dealy Plaza – blam! the shit hits the fan. Moscow and
Washington both want to know, the sooner the quicker,
who was he working for when he did it, or was it his own
idea? Two more possibilities loom at once: could a loner
with confused politics like him have been recruited by the
Cubans or the Chinese? And, then, the kicker: could he
be innocent? Could another group – to avoid the obvious,
let's call them Force X – have stage-managed the whole
thing? So, you've got MVD and CIA and FBI and who-all
falling over each other sniffing around Dallas and New
Orleans for clues. And Force X gets to seem more and
more implausible to all of them, because it is intrinsically
incredible. It is incredible because it has no skeleton, no
shape, no flesh, nothing they can grab hold of. The reason
is, of course, that Force X is the Illuminati, working
through five leaders with five times four times three times
two times one, or one hundred and twenty different basic
vectors. A conspiracy with one hundred and twenty vectors
doesn't look like a conspiracy: it looks like chaos. The
human mind can't grasp it, and hence declares it nonexistent. You see, the Illuminati is always careful to keep
a random element in the one hundred and twenty vectors.
They didn't *really* need to recruit both the leaders of the
ecology movement *and* the executives of the worst pollu-
tion-producing corporations. They did it to create ambi-
guity. *Anybody* who tries to describe their operations
sounds like a paranoid. What clinched it,' Hagbard con-

cluded, 'was a real stroke of luck for the Weishaupt gang: there were two other elements involved, which nobody had planned or foreseen. One was the Syndicate.'

'It always starts with nonsense,' Simon is telling Joe in another time-track, between Los Angeles and San Francisco, in 1969. 'Weishaupt discovered the Law of Fives while he was stoned and looking at one of those shoggoth pictures you saw in Arkham. He imagined the shoggoth was a rabbit and said, *"du hexen Hase,"* which has been preserved as an in-joke by Illuminati agents in Hollywood. It runs through the Bugs Bunny cartoons: "You wascal wabbit!" But out of that schizzy mixture of hallucination and logomania, Weishaupt saw both the mystic meaning of the Five and its pragmatic application as a principle of international espionage, using permutations and combinations that I'll explain when we have a pencil and paper. That same mixture of revelation and put-on is always the language of the supra-conscious, whenever you contact it, whether through magic, religion, psychedelics, yoga, or a spontaneous brain nova. Maybe the put-on or nonsense part comes by contamination from the unconscious, I don't know. But it's always there. That's why serious people never discover anything of real importance.'

'You mean the Mafia?' Joe asks.

'What? I didn't say anything about the Mafia. Are you in another time-track again?'

'No, not the Mafia alone,' Hagbard says. 'The Syndicate is much bigger than the Maf.' The room returns to focus: it is a restaurant. A seafood restaurant. On Biscayne Avenue, facing the bay. In Miami. In 1973. The walls are decorated with undersea motifs, including a hugh octopus. Hagbard, undoubtedly, had chosen this meeting place just because he liked the decor. Crazy bastard thinks he's Captain Nemo. Still: we've got to deal with him. As John says, the JAMs can't do it alone. Hagbard, grinning, seemed to be noting Joe's return to present time. 'You're reaching the critical stage,' he said changing the subject. 'You now only have two mental states: high on drugs and high without drugs. That's very good. But as I was saying, the Syndicate is more than just the Maf. The only Syndicate, up until October twenty-third, nineteen thirty-five, was nothing more than the Mafia, of course. But then they killed the Dutchman, and a young psychology student, who also happened to be a psychopath with a power drive like Genghis Khan, was assigned to do a paper on how the Dutchman's last words illustrate the similarity between somatic damage and schizophrenia. The Dutchman had a bullet in his gut while the police interviewed him, and they recorded everything he said, but on the surface it was all gibberish. This psychology student wrote the paper that his professor expected, and got an *A* for the course – but he also wrote another interpretation of the Dutchman's words, for his own purposes. He put copies in several bank vaults – he came from one of the oldest banking families in New England, and he was even then under family pressure to give up psychology and go into banking. His name was

(Robert Putney Drake visited Zurich in 1935. He personally talked to Carl Jung about the archetypes of the collective unconscious, the *I Ching*, and the principle of synchronicity. He talked to people who had known James Joyce before that drunken Irish genius had moved to Paris, and learned much about Joyce's drunken claims to be a prophet. He read the published portions of *Finnegans Wake* and went back for further conversations with Jung. Then he met Hermann Hesse, Paul Klee and the other members of the Eastern Brotherhood and joined them in a mescaline ritual. A letter from his father arrived about then, asking when he was going to give up wasting his time and return to Harvard Business School. He wrote that he would return for the fall semester, but not to study business administration. A great psychologist was almost born then, and Harvard might have had its Timothy Leary scandal thirty years earlier.

Except for Drake's power drive.)

I. THE FAUST PARSON, SINGULAR. Napalm sundaes for How Chow Mein, misfortune's cookie.

Josephine Malik lies trembling on the bed, trying to be brave, trying to hide her fear. Where, now, is the mask of masculinity?

This delusion that you are a man trapped in a woman's body can only be cured one way. I might be kicked out of the American Psychoanalystical Association if they knew about my methods. In fact, already had a spot of bother with them when one of my patients cured his Oedipus com-

plex by actually fucking his mother, convincing himself
extensionally as the semanticists would say that she really
was an old lady and not the woman he remembered from
infancy. Nevertheless, the whole world is going bananas as
you must have observed, my poor girl, and we have to use
heroic measures to save whatever sanity remains in any
patient we encounter. *(The psychiatrist is now naked. He
joins her on the bed.)* Now, my little frightened dove, I will
convince you that you really are a true-born, honest-to-God
woman. . . .

*Josephine feels his finger in her cunt and screams. Not
at the touch: at the reality of it. She hadn't believed until
then that the change was real.*

> *Weishaupt bridge is falling down*
> *Falling down*
> *Falling down*

And modern novels are the same: in the YMCA on
Atlantic Avenue in Brooklyn, looking out the window at
the radio tower atop Brooklyn Technical High School, a
man named Chaney (no relative of the movie family)
spreads his pornographic tarot cards across the bed. One
of them, he notes, is missing. Quickly, he arranges them
in suits, and hunts for the lost card: it is the Five of
Pentacles. He curses softly: that was one of his favourite
orgy tableux.

Rebecca. The Saint Bernard.

'It's probably all jumbled in your head,' I went on,
furious that our plan was falling apart, that I needed his
trust now but had no way to earn it. 'We've been disin-
toxicating and dehypnotizing you, but you almost certainly
can't tell where the Illuminati left off and we rescued you
and started reversing the treatment. You're due to explode
into psychosis within twenty-four hours and we're using
the only techniques that can defuse that process.'

'Why am I hearing everything twice?' Saul asked,
balancing between wary skepticism and a sense that Malik
was not playing games any more but urgently trying to
help him.

'The stuff they gave you was an MDA derivative – very
high on mescaline and methedrine both. It has an echo

effect for seventy-two hours minimum. You're hearing what
I'm going to say before I say it and then again when I do
say it. That'll pass in a few minutes, but it'll be back, every
half hour or so, for the next day yet. The end of the chain
is psychosis, unless we can stop it.' Unless we can stop it.'

'It's easing up now,' Saul said carefully, 'Less of an
echo that time. I still don't know whether to trust you.
Why were you trying to turn me into Barney Muldoon?'

'Because the psychic explosion is on Saul Goodman's
time-track, not on Barney Muldoon's.'

Ten big rhinoceroses, eleven big rhinoceroses . . .

'You Wascal Wabbit,' Simon whispers through the Judas
Window. Immediately the door opens and a grinning young
man with the Frisco-style Jesus Christ hair-and-beard says,
'Welcome to the Joshua Norton Cabal.' Joe sees to his relief that it was a normal but untypically clean hippie hang-
out, and there are none of the sinister accoutrements of the
Lake Shore Drive coven. At the same time, he hears the
strange man in the bed asking, 'Why were you trying to
turn me into Barney Muldoon?' *My God, now it's happening when I'm awake as well as when I'm asleep.* Simu-
multi-taneously, he hears the alarm and cries, 'The Illuminati must be attacking!'

'Attacking this building?' Saul asks confusedly.

'Building? You're on a submarine, man. The *Lief Erickson*, on its way to Atlantis!'

Twenty big rhinoceroses, twenty-one big rhinoceroses . . .

'Number Seventeen,' read Professor Curve, ' "Law and
anarchists will give the American people a speedy Cadillac." '

All the Helen Hokinson types are out today. Another
one just hit me for the Mothers March Against Dan-
druff. I gave her a nickel.

1923 was a very interesting year for the occult, by
the way. Not only did Hitler join the Illuminati and
attempt the Munich putsch, but, glancing through the
books of Charles Fort, I found quite a few suggestive
events. On March 17th – which not only fits our 17-
23 correlation but is also the anniversary of the defeat
of the Kronstadt rebellion, the day the Lord Nelson
statue was bombed in Dublin in 1966 and, of course,

THE EYE IN THE PYRAMID 281

good Saint Patrick's holy day – a naked man was seen mysteriously running about the estate of Lord Caernarvon in England. He appeared several times in the following days, but was never caught. Meanwhile, Lord Caernarvon himself died in Egypt – some said he was a victim of the curse of Tut-Ankh-Amen, whose tomb he had burglarized. (An archaeologist is a ghoul with credentials.) Fort also records two cases that May of a synchronistic phenomenon he has traced through the centuries: a volcanic eruption coinciding with the discovery of a new star. In September, there was a Mumiai scare in India – Mumiais are invisible demons that grab people in broad daylight. Throughout the year, there were reports of exploding coal in England; some tried to explain this by saying the embittered miners (it was a time of labor troubles) were putting dynamite in the coal, but the police couldn't prove this. The coal went on exploding. In the summer, French pilots began having strange mishaps, whenever they flew over Germany, and it was suggested that the Germans were testing an invisible ray machine. Considering the last three phenomena together – invisible demons in India, exploding coal in England, invisible rays over Germany – I guess somebody was testing something. . . .

You can call me Doc Iggy. My full name, at present, is Dr. Ignotum P. Ignotius. The P. stands for Per. If you're a Latinst, you'll realize that translates as 'the unknown explained by the still more unknown.' I think it's a quite appropriate name for my function tonight, since Simon brought you here to be illuminized. My slave name, before I was turned on myself, is totally immaterial. As far as I'm concerned, your slave name is equally pointless, and I'll call you by the password of the Norton Cabal, which Simon used at the door. Until tomorrow morning, when the drug starts wearing off, you are U. Wascal Wabbit. That's U., the initial, not why-oh-you, by the way.

We accept Bugs Bunny as an exemplar of Mummu here, too, but otherwise we have little in common with the SSS. That's the Satanist, Surrealists and Sadists – the crew who began your illumination in Chicago. All we share with them actually is use of the Tristero anarchist postal system to evade the government's postal inspectors, and a financial agreement whereby we accept their DMM script – Divine Marquis Memorial script – and they accept our hempscript and the flaxscript of the Legion of Dynamic Discord. Anything to avoid Federal Reserve notes, you know.

It'll be a while yet before the acid starts working, so I'll just chat like this, about things that are more or less trivial – or quadrivial, or maybe pentivial – until I can see that you're ready for more serious matters. Simon's in the chapel, with a woman named Stella who you'll really dig, getting things ready for the ceremony.

You might wonder why we're called the Norton Cabal. The name was chosen by my predecessor, Malaclypse the Younger, before he left us to join the more esoteric group known as ELF – the Erisian Liberation Front. They're the Occidental branch of the Hung Mung Tong Cong and all their efforts go into a long-range anti-Illuminati project known only as Operation Mindfuck. But that's another, very complicated, story. One of Malaclypse's last writings, before he went into the Silence, was a short paragraph saying, 'Everybody understands Mickey Mouse. Few understand Hermann Hesse. Hardly anyone understands Albert Einstein. And nobody understands Emperor Norton.' I guess Malaclypse was already into the Mindfuck mystique when he wrote that.

(Who was Emperor Norton? Joe asks, wondering if the drug is beginning to work already or Dr. Ignotius just has a tendency to speak more slowly than most people.)

Joshua Norton, Emperor of the United States and Protector of Mexico. San Francisco is proud of him. He lived in the last century and got to be emperor by proclaiming himself as such. *For some mysterious reason,* the newspapers decided to humor him and printed his proclamations. When he started issuing his own money, the local banks *went along with the joke* and accepted it on par with U.S. currency. When the Vigilantes got into a lynching mood one night and decided to go down to Chinatown and kill some Chinese, Emperor Norton stopped them *just by standing in the street with his eyes closed reciting the Lord's Prayer.* Are you beginning to understand Emperor Norton a little, Mr. Wabbit?

(A little, Joe said, a little . . .)

Well, chew on this for a while, friend: there were two very sane and rational anarchists who lived about the same time as Emperor Norton across the country in Massachusetts: William Green and Lysander Spooner. They also realized the value of having competing currencies instead of one uniform State currency, and they tried logical arguments, empirical demonstrations and legal suits to get this idea accepted. They accomplished nothing. The government broke its own laws to find ways to suppress Green's Mutual Bank and Spooner's People's Bank. That's because they were obviously sane, and their currency did pose a real threat to the monopoly of the Illuminati. But Emperor Norton was so crazy that people *humored* him and his currency was allowed to circulate. Think about it. You might begin to understand why Bugs Bunny is our symbol and why our currency has the ridiculous name hempscript. Hagbard Celine and his Discordians, even more absurdly, call their money flaxscript. That commemorates the Zen Master who was asked, 'What is the Buddha?' and replied, 'Five pounds of flax.' Do you begin to see the full dimensions of our struggle with the Illuminati?

At least, for now, you can probably grasp this much: their fundamental fallacy is the Aneristic Delusion. They *really* believe in law 'n' order. As a matter of fact, since everybody in this crazy, millennia-old battle has his own theory about what the Illuminati are really aiming at, I might as well tell you mine. I think they're all scientists and they want to set up a scientific world government. The Jacobins were probably following precise Illuminati instructions when they sacked the churches in Paris and proclaimed the dawn of the Age of Reason. You know the story about the old man who was in the crowd when Louis XVI went to the guillotine and who shouted as the king's head fell, 'Jacques De Molay, thou art avenged'? All the symbols that De Molay introduced into Masonry are scientific implements – the T-square, the architect's triangle, even that pyramid that has caused so much bizarre speculation. If you count the eye as part of the design, the pyramid has 73 divisions, you know, not 72. What's 73 mean? Simple: multiply it by five, in accordance with Weishaupt's *funfwissenschaft*, the science of fives, and you get 365, the

days of the year. The damn thing is some kind of astronomical computer, like Stonehenge. The Egyptian pyramids
are facing to the East, where the sun rises. The great pyramid of the Mayans has exactly 365 divisions, and is also
facing to the East. What they're doing is worshipping the
'order' they have found in Nature, never realizing that they
projected the order there with their own instruments.

That's why they hate ordinary mankind – because we're
so disorderly. They've been trying for six or seven thousand years to reestablish Atlantis-style high civilization –
law 'n' order – the Body Politic, as they like to call it. A
giant robot is what their Body Politic really amounts to,
you know. A place for everything and everything in its
place. A place for everybody and everybody in his place.
Look at the Pentagon – look at the whole army, for Goddess's sake! That's what they want the planet to be like.
Efficient, mechanical, orderly – very orderly – and in-
human That's the essence of the Aneristic Delusion: to
imagine you have found Order and then to start manipula-
ting the quirky, eccentric chaotic things that really exist into
some kind of platoons or phalanxes that correspond to
your concept of the Order they're supposed to manifest. Of
course, the quirkiest, most chaotic things that exist are
other people – and that's why they're so obsessed with trying to control us.

Why are you staring like that? Am I changing colors or
growing bigger or something? Good: the acid is starting to
work. Now we can really get to the nitty-gritty. First of
all, most of what I've been telling yo؟ is bullshit. The
Illuminati have no millennia-old history; neither do the
JAMs. They invented their great heritage and tradition –
Jacques De Molay and Charlemagne and all of it – out of
whole cloth in 1776, picking up all sorts of out-of-context
history to make it seem plausible. We've done the same.
You might wonder why we copy them, and even deceive
our own recruits about this. Well, part of illumination –
and we've got to be illuminized ourselves to fight them – is
in learning to doubt everything. That's why Hagbard has
that painting in his stateroom saying 'Think for yourself,
schmuck,' and why Hassan i Sabbah said 'Nothing is true.'
You've got to learn to doubt us, too, and everything we
tell you. There are no honest men on this voyage. In fact,

maybe *this part* is the only lie I've told you all evening, and the Illuminati history before 1776 really is true and not an invention. Or maybe we're just a front for the Illuminati ... to recruit you indirectly....

Feeling paranoid? Good: illumination is on the other side of absolute terror. And the only terror that is truly absolute is the horror of realizing that you can't believe anything you've ever been told. You have to realize fully that you *are* 'a stranger and afraid in a world you never made,' like Houseman says.

Twenty-two big rhinoceroses, twenty-three big rhinoceroses ...

The Illuminati basically were structure-freaks. Hence, their hangup on symbols of geometric law and architectural permanence, especially the pyramid and the pentagon. ('God's Lightning, like all authoritarian Judeo-Christian heresies, had it own share of this typically Occidental straight-line mystique, which was why even the Jews among them, like Zev Hirsch, accepted the symbol first suggested by Atlanta Hope: that most Euclidean of all religious emblems: the Cross.) The Discordians made their own sardonic commentary on the legal and scientific basis of law 'n' order by using a 17-step pyramid – 17 being a number with virtually no interesting geometric, arithmetic or mystic properties, outside of Java, where it was the basis of a particularly weird musical scale – and topping it with the Apple of Discord, symbol of the un-rational, ungeometrical, and thoroughly disorderly spontaneity of the vegetable world of creative evolution. The Erisian Liberation Front (ELF) had no symbol, and when asked for one by new recruits, replied loftily that their symbol could not be pictured, since it was a circle whose circumference was everywhere and its center nowhere. They were the most far-out group of all, and only the most advanced Discordians could begin to understand their gibberish.

The JAMs, however, had a symbol that anyone could understand, and, just as Harry Pierpont showed it to John Dillinger midway through a nutmeg high in Michigan City prison, Dr. Ignotius showed it to Joe midway through his first acid trip.

'This,' he said dramatically, 'is the Sacred Chao.'

'That's a symbol of technocracy,' Joe said, giggling.

'Well,' Dr. Ignotius smiled, 'at least you're original. Nine out of ten new members mistake it for the Chinese yin-yang or the astrological symbol of Cancer. It's similar to both of them – and also to the symbols of the Northern Pacific Railroad and the Sex Information and Education Council of the United States, all of which is eventually going to lead to some interesting documents being produced at John Birch headquarters, I'm sure, proving that sex educators run the railroads or that astrologers control the sex educators or something of that sort. No, this is different. It is the Sacred Chao, symbol of Mummu, God of Chaos.

'On the right, O nobly born, you will see the image of your "female" and intuitive nature, called *yin* by the Chinese. The yin contains an apple which is the golden apple of Eris, the forbidden apple of Eve, and the apple which used to disappear from the stage of the Flatbush Burlesque House in Brooklyn when Linda Larue did the split on top of it at the climax of her striptease. It represents the erotic, libidinal, anarchistic, and subjective values worshipped by Hagbard Celine and our friends in the Legion of Dynamic Discord.

'Now, O nobly born, as you prepare for Total Awakening, turn your eyes to the left, yang side of the Sacred Chao. This is the image of your "male," rationalistic ego. It contains the pentagon of the Illuminati, the Satanists, and the U.S. Army. It represents the anal, authoritarian, structural, law 'n' order values which the Illuminati have imposed, through their puppet governments, on most of the peoples of the world.

'This is what you must understand, O newborn Buddha: neither side is complete, or true, or real. Each is an abstraction, a fallacy. Nature is a seamless web in which both sides are in perpetual war (which is another name for perpetual peace). The equation always balances. Increase one side, and the other side increases by itself. Every homosexual is a latent heterosexual, every authoritarian cop is the shell over an anarchistic libido. There is no *Vernichtung,* no Final Solution, no pot of gold at the end of the rainbow, and you are not Saul Goodman, when you're lost out here.'

Listen: the chaos you experience under LSD is not an illusion. The orderly world you *imagine you experience,* under the artificial and poisonous diet which the Illuminati have forced on all civilized nations, is the real illusion. I am not saying what you are hearing. The only good fnord is a dead fnord. Never whistle while you're pissing. An obscure but highly significant contribution to sociology and epistemology occurs in Malignowski's study 'Retroactive Reality,' printed in *Wieczny Kwiat Wtadza,* the journal of the Polish Orthopsychiatric Psociety, for Autumn 1959.

'All affirmations are true in some sense, false in some sense, meaningless in some sense, true and false in some sense, true and meaningless in some sense, false and meaningless in some sense, and true and false and meaningless in some sense. Do you follow me?'

(*In some sense,* Joe mutters. . . .)

The author, Dr. Malignowski, was assisted by three graduate students named Korzybski-1, Korzybski-2, and Korzybski-3 (Siamese triplets born to a mathematician and, hence, indexed rather than named). Malignowski and his students interviewed 1,700 married couples, questioning husband and wife separately in each case, and asked 100 key questions about their first meeting, first sexual experience, marriage ceremony, honeymoon, economic standing during the first year of marriage, and similar subjects which should have left permanent impressions on the memory. Not one couple in the 1,700 gave exactly the same answers to 100 questions, and the highest single score was made by a couple who gave the same answers to 43 of the questions.

'This study demonstrated graphically what many psychologists have long suspected: the life-history which most of us carry around in our skulls is more our own creation (at least seven percent more) than it is an accurate recording of realities. As Malignowski concludes, "Reality is retroactive, retrospective and illusory."

'Under these circumstances, things not personally experienced but recounted by others are even more likely to be distorted, and after a tale passes through five tellers it is virtually one hundred percent pure myth: another example of the Law of Fives.

'Only Marxists,' Dr. Iggy concluded, opening the door to usher Joe into the chapel room, 'still believe in an objective history. Marxists and a few disciples of Ayn Rand.'

Jung took the parchment from Drake and stared at it. 'It's not to be signed in blood? And what the hell is this yin-yang symbol with the pentagon and the apple? You're a fucking fake.' His lips curled tightly in against his teeth.

'What do you mean?' said George through a throat that was rapidly closing up.

'I mean you're not from the goddam Illuminati,' said Jung. 'Who the hell are you?'

'Didn't you know that before I came here – that I'm not from the Illuminati?' said George. 'I'm not trying to fake anybody out. Honest, really, I thought you knew the people who sent me. I never *said* I was from the Illuminati.'

Maldonado nodded, a slight smile bringing his face to life. 'I know who he is. The people of the Old *Strega*. The Sybil of Sybils. All hail Discordia, kid. Right?'

'Hail Eris,' said George with a slight feeling of relief.

Drake frowned. 'Well, we seem to be at cross purposes. We were contacted by mail, then by telephone, then by messenger, by parties who made it quite clear that they knew all about our business with the Illuminati. Now, to the best of my knowledge – perhaps Don Federico knows better – there is only one organization in the world that knows anything about the AISB, and that is the AISB itself.' George could tell he was lying.

Maldonado raised a warning hand. 'Wait. Up, everybody. To the bathroom.'

Drake sighed. 'Oh, Don Federico! You and your tired notions of security. If my house isn't safe, we're all dead men as of this moment. And if the AISB is as good as it's said to be, an old trick like running water will be no obstacle to them. Let's conduct this discussion like civilized men, for God's sake, and *not* huddled around my shower stall.'

'There are times when dignity is suicide,' said Maldonado. He shrugged. 'But, I yield. I'll settle the question with you in hell if you're wrong.'

'I'm still in the dark,' said Richard Jung. 'I don't know who this guy is or where he's from.'

'Look, Chinaman,' said Maldonado. 'You know who the Ancient Illuminated Seers of Bavaria are, right? Well, every organization has opposition, right? So do the Illuminati. Opposition that's like them, religious, magical, spooky stuff. Not simply interested in becoming rich, as is our gentlemanly aim in life. Playing supernatural games. *Capeesh?*'

Jung looked skeptical. 'You could be describing the Communist party, the CIA, or the Vatican.'

'Superficial,' said Maldonado scornfully. 'And upstarts, compared with the AISB. Because the Bavarian Illuminati aren't Bavarians, you understand. That's just a recent name and manifestation for their order. Both the Illuminati and their opposition, which this guy represents, go back a long ways before Moscow, Washington or Rome. A little imagination is called for to understand this, Chinaman.'

'If the Illuminati are yang,' George said helpfully, 'we're yin. The only solution is a Yin Revolution. Dig?'

'I am a graduate of Harvard Law School,' said Jung loftily, 'and I do *not* dig it. What are you, a bunch of hippies?'

'We never made a deal with your bunch before,' said Maldonado. 'They never had enough to offer us.'

Robert Putney Drake said, 'Yes, but wouldn't you *like* to, though, Don Federico? Haven't you had a bellyfull of the others? I know I have. I know where you're from now, George. And you people have been making giant strides in recent decades. I'm not surprised that you're able to tempt us. It's worth our lives – and we are supposedly the most secure men in the United States – to betray the Illuminati. But I understand you offer us statues from Atlantis. By now they should be uncrated. And that there are more where these came from? Is that right, George?'

Hagbard had said nothing about that, but George was too worried about his own survival to quibble. 'Yes,' he said. 'There are more.'

Drake said, 'Whether we want to risk our lives by working with your people will depend on what we find when we examine the *objets d'art* you are offering. Don Federico, being a highly qualified expert in antiquities, particularly in those antiquities which have been carefully kept outside of the ken of conventional archaeological knowledge, will pronounce on the value of what you've brought. As a Sicilian thoroughly versed in his heritage, Don Federico is familiar with things Atlantean. The Sicilians are about the only extant people who do know about Atlantis. It is not generally realized that the Sicilians have the oldest continuous civilization on the face of the planet. With all due respects to the Chinese.' Drake nodded formally to Jung.

'I consider myself an American,' said Jung. 'Though my family knows a thing or two about Tibet that might surprise you.'

'I'm sure,' said Drake. 'Well, you shall advise, as you are able. But the Sicilian heritage goes back thousands of years before Rome, as does their knowledge of Atlantis. There were a few things washed up on the shores of North Africa, a few things found by divers. It was enough to establish a tradition. If there were a museum of Atlantean arts, Don Federico is one of the few people in the world qualified to be a curator.'

'In other words,' said Maldonado with a ghastly smile, 'those statues better be authentic, kid. Because I will know if they are not.'

'They are,' said George. 'I saw them picked up off the ocean bottom myself.'

'That's impossible,' said Jung.

'Let's look,' said Drake.

He stood up and placed the palm of his hand flat against an oak panel which immediately slid to one side, revealing a winding metal staircase. Drake leading the way, the four of them descended what seemed to George five stories to a door with a combination lock. Drake opened the door and they passed through a series of other chambers, ending up in a large underground garage. The Gold & Appel truck was there and beside it the four statues, freed of their crates. There was no one in the room.

'Where did everybody go?' said Jung.

'They're Sicilians,' said Drake. 'They saw these and were afraid. They did the job of uncrating them and left.' His face and Maldonado's wore a look of awe. Jung's craggy features bore an irritated, puzzled frown.

'I'm beginning to feel that I've been left out of a lot,' he said.

'Later,' said Maldonado. He took a small jeweler's glass out of his pocket and approached the nearest statue. 'This is where they got the idea for the great god Pan,' he said. 'But you can see the idea was more complicated twenty thousand years ago than two thousand.' Fixing the jeweler's glass in his eye, he began a careful inspection of a glittering hoof.

At the end of an hour, Maldonado, with the help of a ladder, had gone over each of the four statues from bottom to top with fanatical care and had questioned George about the manner of their seizure as well as what little he knew of their history. He put his jeweler's glass away, turned to Drake and nodded.

'You got the four most valuable pieces of art in the world.'

Drake nodded. 'I surmised as much. Worth more than all the gold in all the Spanish treasure ships there ever were.'

'If I have not been dosed with a hallucinogenic drug,' said Richard Jung, 'I gather you are all saying these statues come from Atlantis. I'll take your word for it that they're solid gold, and that means there's a lot of gold there.'

'The value of the matter is not worth one one ten-thousandth the value of the form,' said Drake.

'That I don't see,' said Jung. 'What is the value of Atlantean art if no reputable authority anywhere in the world believes in Atlantis?'

Maldonado smiled. 'There are a few people in the world who know that Atlantis existed, and who know there is such a thing as Atlantean art. And believe me, Richard, those few got enough money to make it worth anyone's while who has a piece from the bottom of the sea. Any one of these statues could buy a middle-sized country.'

Drake clapped his hands with an air of authority. 'I'm satisfied if Don Federico is satisfied. For these and for four more like them – or the equivalent if four such statues simply don't exist – my hand is joined with the hand of the Discordian movement. Let us go back upstairs and sign the papers – in pen and ink. And then, George, we would like you to be our guest at dinner.'

George didn't know if he had the authority to promise four more statues, and he was certain that total openness was the only safe approach with these men. As they were climbing the stairs, he said to Drake, who was above him, 'I wasn't authorized by the man who sent me to promise anything more. And I don't believe he has any more at the moment, unless he has a collection of his own, I know these four statues are the only ones he captured on this trip.'

Drake let out a small fart, an incredible thing, it seemed to George, for the leader of all organized crime in the United States to do. 'Excuse me,' he said. 'The exertion of these stairs is too much for me. Would love to put in an elevator, but that wouldn't be as secure. One of these days my heart will give out, going up and down those stairs.' The fart smelled moderately bad, and George was glad when he had climbed out of its neighborhood. He was surprised that a man of Drake's importance would acknowledge that he farted. Perhaps that kind of straightforwardness was a factor in Drake's success. George doubted that Maldonado would admit to a fart. The Don was too devious. He was not your earthy sort of Latin – he was paper-thin and paper-pale, like a Tuscan aristocrat of attenuated blood-line.

They reentered Drake's office, and Drake and Maldonado each signed the parchment scroll. After the phrase, 'for valuable considerations received,' Drake inserted the words, 'and considerations of equal value yet to come.' He smiled at George. 'Since you can't guarantee the additional objects, I'll expect to hear from your boss within twenty-four hours after you leave here. This whole deal is contingent upon the additional payment from you.'

ORGASM. HER BUBBIES FRITCHID BY THE GYNING DEEP-SEADOODLER. All in a lewdercrass chaste for a moulteeng fawkin. In fact, hearing Drake say that he was to be leaving the Syndicate fortress made George feel a bit better. He signed in behalf of the Discordians and Jung signed as a witness.

Drake said, 'You understand, there is no way the organizations which Don Federico and I represent can be bound by anything we sign. What we agree to here is to

use our influence with our many esteemed colleagues and
to hope that they will grant us the favor of cooperation in
the mutual enterprise.'

Maldonado said, 'I couldn't have said it better myself.
We, of course, personally pledge our lives and our honor
to further your purposes.'

Robert Putney Drake took a cigar out of a silver humi-
dor. Slapping George on the back, he shoved the cigar into
his mouth. 'You know, you're the first hippie I've ever
done business with. I suppose you'd like to have some marijuana. I don't keep any around the house, and as you probably know we don't deal much in the stuff. Too bulky to
transport, considering the amount you can make on it.
Aside from that, I think you'll like the food and drink here.
We'll have a big dinner and some entertainment.'

The dinner was steak Diane, and it was served to the
four men at a long table in a dining room hung with large,
old paintings. They were waited on by a series of beautiful
young women, and George wondered where the gang leaders kept their wives and mistresses. In some sort of *purdah*,
perhaps. There was something Arabic about this whole
setup.

During the main course a blonde in a long white gown
which left one breast bare played the harp in a corner of
the room and sang. There was conversation with the coffee;
four young women sat down briefly with the men and re-
galed them with witticisms and funny stories.

With the brandy came Tarantella Serpentine. She was an
amazingly tall woman, at least six feet two, with long blond
hair that was piled high on her head and fell below her
shoulders. She was wearing tinkling gold bracelets around
her wrists and ankles, and there were diaphonous veils
wrapped around her slender body, and nothing else. George
could see pink nipples and dark crotch hair. When she
strode through the door Banana-Nose Maldonado wiped
his mouth with his napkin and began applauding gleefully.
Robert Putney Drake smiled proudly and Richard Jung
swallowed hard.

George just stared. 'The star of our little rural retreat,'
said Drake by way of introduction. 'May I present – Miss
Tarantella Serpentine.' Maldonado's applause continued,
and George wondered if he should join in. Music, Oriental

but with a touch of rock, flooded the room. The sound
reproduction equipment was excellent, nigh perfect. Tarantella Serpentine began to dance. It was a strange, hybrid
sort of dance, a synthesis of belly-dancing, go-go, and
modern ballet. George licked his lips and he felt his face
get warm and his penis begin to throb and swell as he
watched Tarantella Serpentine's dance was even more sen-
suous than the dance Stella Maris had done when he was
being initiated into the Discordian movement.

After she had done three dances, Tarantella bowed and
left. 'You must be tired, George,' said Drake, resting his
hand on George's shoulder.

Suddenly, George realized he had been going on almost
no sleep except for the times he'd dozed off in the car on
the way from Mad Dog to the Gulf. He had been under
incredible physical, and even more important, emotional
pressure.

He agreed that he was tired, and, praying that he would
not be murdered in his sleep, he let Drake lead him to a
bedroom.

The bed was an enormous fourposter with a cloth-of-gold
canopy. Naked, George slid between cool, crisp sheets, and
clutching the top sheet around his neck, lay flat on his
back, shut his eyes tight and sighed. That morning he had
been on a beach in the Gulf of Mexico watching naked
Mavis masturbate. He had fucked an apple. He had been
to Atlantis. And now he was lying on a downy-soft mattress
in the home of the chief of all organized crime in America.
If he closed his eyes he might find himself back in the Mad
Dog jail. He shook his head. There was nothing to fear.

He heard the bedroom door open. There was nothing to
fear. To prove it, he kept his eyes closed. He heard a board
squeak. Squeaky boards in this place? Sure – to warn the
sleeper that there was someone sneaking up on him. He
opened his eyes.

Tarantella Serpentine was standing over the bed. 'Bobby-
baby sent me,' she said.

George closed his eyes again. 'Sweetheart,' he said, 'you
are beautiful. You really are. You're beautiful. Make yourself comfortable.'

She reached down and turned on a bedside lamp. She
was wearing a gold metallic bikini top with a short match-

ing skirt. Her breasts were delightfully small, George
thought. Although, on a five-foot-two girl they'd be ample.
But Tarantella was built like a *Vogue* model. George liked
her looks. He had always been partial to tall, slender boyish
women.

'I'm not intruding on you, am I?' she asked. 'You sure
you wouldn't rather sleep?'

'Well it's not so much what I'd *rather* do,' said George.
'I doubt that I can do anything other than sleep. I have
had a very trying day.' Masturbated once, he thought, had
one blow job, and fucked one apple. Forgive us our debts
as we forgive our debtors. Plus been scared out of my wits
90 percent of the time.

Tarantella said, 'My name is known in rarified circles
for what I can achieve with men whose days are *all* trying.
Presidents, kings, Syndicate heads – naturally – rock stars,
oil billionnaires, people like that. My thing is, I can make
men come. Over and over and over and *over* again. Ten
times, sometimes even twenty times, no matter how old or
how tired. I get paid a lot. Tonight, Bobby-baby is paying
for my services, and I'm to service you. Which I like very
much, because most of my clientele is on the middle-aged
side, and you're nice and young and have a firm body.' She
gently pulled the sheet loose from George's grip – he had
forgotten he was still holding it up around his neck – and
caressed his bare shoulder.

'How old are you, George – twenty-two?'

'Twenty-three,' said George. 'But I don't want to disappoint you. I'm willing and I'm interested. In fact, I'm
curious about what you do. But I'm pretty tired.'

'Honey, you *can't* disappoint me. The more limp you
are, the more I like it. The more of a challenge you are to
me. Let me show you my specialty.'

Tarantella doffed her bra, skirt, and panties quickly but
deliberately enough to let George enjoy watching her. Smiling at him, she stood before him, her legs spread wide
apart. Her fingernails tickled her nipples, and George
watched them swell up. Then, her left hand playing with
her left breast, her right hand snaked down to her groin
and began massaging the golden-brown hairs of her mons.
Her middle finger disappeared between her legs. After a
few moments a scarlet flush spread over her face, neck, and

chest, her body arched backward, and she gave a single, agonized cry. Her skin, from head to toe, was glowing with a fine coating of sweat.

After a momentary pause she smiled and looked at him. Her right hand caressed his cheek and he felt the wetness on his face and smelled the Lobster Newbury aroma of a young cunt. Her fingers drifted to the sheets, and with a sudden movement she stripped them away from George's body. She grinned down at his stiff cock and in a moment was on top of him, holding his prick, inserting it into herself. Two minutes of smooth pistonlike movements on her part brought him to an unexpectedly pleasant orgasm.

'Baby,' he said. 'You could wake the dead.'

He enjoyed his second orgasm about a half hour later, and his third a half hour after that. The second time Tarantella lay on her back and George lay on top of her, and the third time she was on her stomach and he was straddling her from the rear. There was something about the mood Tarantella created that was crucial to what she called her 'specialty.' Though she had boasted about her ability to make a man come repeatedly, when it came right down to doing things she made him feel that it didn't really matter what happened with him. She was fun-loving, playful, carefree. He did not feel obligated in any sense to stiffen, to come. Tarantella might view men as a challenge, but she made it clear that George was not to see her as a challenge.

After a short nap, he woke to find her sucking his rapidly hardening penis. It took much longer this time for him to come, but he enjoyed every second of mounting pleasure. After that they lay side by side and talked for a while. Then Tarantella went to the beside table and took a tube of petroleum jelly out of a drawer. She began applying it to his penis, which grew erect during the process. Then she rolled over and presented him with her rosy ass-hole. It was the first time George had had a woman that way, and he came rather quickly after insertion from the novelty and excitement of it all.

They slept for a while and he awoke to find her masturbating him. Her fingers were very clever and seemed quickly to find their way to all the most sensitive parts of his penis – with special attention to that area just behind the crown of the head. He opened his eyes wide when he came and saw, after a few seconds, a small, pale, pearl-like drop of semen appear on the end of his dick. A wonder there was any at all.

It was getting to be a trip. His ego went away somewhere, and he was all body, letting it all happen. *It* was fucking Tarantella, and *it* was coming – and, judging by the sounds she was making and the wetness in which his penis was sloshing, she was coming, too.

There followed two more blow jobs. Then Tarantella pulled something that looked like an electric razor out of the bed-table drawer. She plugged it into the wall and began to stroke his penis with its vibrating head, pausing every so often to lick and lubricate the areas she was working on.

George closed his eyes and rolled his hips from side to side as he felt yet another orgasm coming on. From a great distance he heard Tarantella Serpentine say, 'My greatness lies in the life I can generate in limp pricks.'

George's pelvis began to pump up and down. It was really going to be that superorgasm Hemingway described. It began to happen. It was pure electricity. No juice – all energy pouring out like lightning through the magic wand at the center of his being. He wouldn't be surprised to discover that his balls and cock were disintegrating into whirling electrons. He screamed, and behind his tight-clenched eyes, he saw, very clearly, the smiling face of Mavis.

He awoke in the dark, and his instinctive groping motion told him that Tarantella was gone.

Instead, Mavis, in a white doctor's smock, stood at the foot of the bed, watching him with large bright eyes. The darkened Drake bedroom had turned into a hospital ward, and was suddenly brightly lit.

'How did you get here?' he blurted. 'I mean – how did I get here?'

'Saul,' she said kindly, 'it's almost all over. You've come through it.'

And suddenly he realized that he felt, not twenty-three, but sixty-three years old.

'You've won,' he admitted, 'I'm no longer sure who I am.'

'You've won,' Mavis contradicted. 'You've gone through ego loss and now you're beginning to discover who you really are, poor old Saul.'

He examined his hands: old man's. Wrinkled. Goodman's hands.

'There are two forms of ego loss,' Mavis went on, 'and the Illuminati are masters of both. One is schizophrenia, the other is illumination. They set you on the first track, and we switched you to the other. You had a time bomb in your head, but we defused it.'

Malik's apartment. The Playboy Club. The submarine. And all the other past lives and lost years. 'By God,' Saul Goodman cried, 'I've got it. I *am* Saul Goodman, but I am all the other people, too.'

'And all time is this time,' Mavis added softly.

Saul sat upright, tears gleaming in his eyes. 'I've killed men. I've sent them to the electric chair. Seventeen times. Seventeen suicides. The savages who cut off fingers or toes or ears for their gods are more sensible. We cut off whole egos, thinking they are not ourselves but separate. God God God,' and he burst in sobs.

Mavis rushed forward and held him, cradling his head to her breast. 'Let it out,' she said. 'Let it all out. It's not true unless it makes you laugh, but you don't understand until it makes you weep.'

QUEENS. Psychoanalysts in living cells, moving in military ordure, and a shitty outlook on life and sex, dancing coins in harry's krishna. It all coheres, even if you approach it bass ackwards. It coheres.

'Gruad the grayface!' Saul screamed, weeping, beating his fist against the pillow as Mavis held his head, stroked his hair. 'Gruad the damned! And I have been his servant, his puppet, sacrificing myselves on his electric altars as burnt offerings.'

'Yes, yes,' Mavis cooed in his ear. 'We must learn to give up our sacrifices, not our joys. They have taught us to give up everything except our sacrifices, and those are what we must give up. We must sacrifice our sacrifices.'

'The Grayface, the lifehater!' Saul shrieked. 'The bastard motherfucker! Osiris, Quetzalcoatl, I know him under all his aliases. Grayface, Grayface, Grayface! I know his wars and his prisons, the young boys he shafts up the ass, the George Dorns he tries to turn into killers like himself. And I have served him all my life. I have sacrificed men on his bloody pyramid!'

'Let it out,' Mavis repeated, holding the old man's trembling body 'Let it all out, baby. . . .'

NOTHUNG. Woden you gnaw it, when you herd those flying sheeps with wagner's loopy howls? Hassan walked this loony valley, he had to wake up by himself. August 23, 1966: before he ever heard of the SSS, the Discordians, the JAMs or the Illuminati: stoned and beatific, Simon Moon is browsing in a Consumer Discount store on North Clark street, digging the colors, not really intending to buy anything. He stops in a frieze, mesmerized by a sign above the timeclock:

NO EMPLOYEE MAY, UNDER ANY CIRCUMSTANCES, PUNCH
THE TIME CARD FOR ANY OTHER EMPLOYEE.
ANY DEVIATION WILL RESULT IN TERMINATION.
THE MGT.

'God's pyjamas,' Simon mutters, incredulous.

'Pyjamas? Aisle seven,' a clerk says helpfully.

'Yes. Thanks,' Simon speaks very distinctly, edging away, hiding his high. God's *pyjamas and spats*, he thinks in a half-illuminated trance, either I'm more stoned than I think or that sign is absolutely the whole clue to how the show runs.

RAGS. Hail Ghoulumbia, her monadmen are fled and all she's left now is a bloody period. 'The funny part,' Saul said, smiling while a few tears still flowed, 'is that I'm not ashamed of this. Two days ago I would have rather died than be seen weeping – especially by a woman.'

'Yes,' Mavis said, *'especially by a woman.'*

'That's it – isn't it?' Saul gasped. 'That's their whole gimmick. I couldn't see you without seeing a *woman*. I couldn't see that editor, Jackson, without seeing a *Negro*. I couldn't see anybody without seeing the attached label and classification.'

'That's how they keep us apart,' Mavis said gently. 'And that's how they train us to keep our masks on. Love was the hardest bond for them to smash, so they had to create patriarchy, male supremacy, and all that crap – and the "masculine protest" and "penis envy" in women came in as a result – so even lovers couldn't look at one another without seeing a separate category.'

'O my God, my God,' Saul moaned, beginning to weep heavily again. ' "A rag, a bone, a hank of hair." O my God. *And you were with them!*' he cried suddenly, raising his head. 'You're a former Illuminatus – that's why you're so important to Hagbard's plan. And that's why you have that tattoo!'

'I was one of the Five who run the U.S.,' Mavis nodded. 'One of the Insiders, as Robert Welch calls them. I've been replaced now by Atlanta Hope, the leader of God's Lightning.'

'I've got it, I've got it!' Saul said, laughing. 'I looked every way but the right way before. *He's* inside the Pentagon. That's why they build it in that shape, so *he* couldn't escape. The Aztecs, the Nazis . . . and now us . . .'

'Yes,' Mavis said grimly. 'That's why thirty thousand Americans disappear every year, without trace, and their cases end up in the unsolved files. *He* has to be fed.'

' "A man, though naked, may be in rags." ' Saul quoted. 'Ambrose Bierce knew about it.'

'And Arthur Machen,' Mavis added. 'And Lovecraft. But they had to write in code. Even so, Lovecraft went too far, mentioning the *Necronomicon* by name. That's why he died so suddenly when he was only forty-seven. And his literary executor, August Derleth, was persuaded to insert a note in every edition of Lovecraft's works, claiming that the *Necronomicon* doesn't exist and was just part of Lovecraft's fantasy.'

'And the *Lloigor*?' Saul asked. 'And the *dols*?'

'Real,' Mavis said. 'All real. That's what causes bad acid trips and schizophrenia. Psychic contact with *them* when the ego wall breaks. That's where the Illuminati were sending you when we raided their fake Playboy Club and short-circuited the process.'

'*Du hexen Hase*,' Saul quoted. And he began to tremble.

UNHEIMLICH. Urvater whose art's uneven, horrid be thine aim. Harpoons in him, corpus whalem: take ye and hate.

Fernando Poo was given prominent attention in the world press only once before the notorious Fernando Poo Incident. It occurred in the early 1970s (while Captain Tequilla y Mota was first studying the art of the Coup d'Etat and laying his first plans), and was occasioned by the outrageous claims of the anthropologist J. N. Marsh, of Miskatonic University, that artifacts he had found on Fernando Poo proved the existence of the lost continent of Atlantis. Although Professor Marsh had an impeccable reputation for scholarly caution and scientific rigor before this, his last published book, *Atlantis and Its Gods*, was greeted with mockery and derision by his professional colleagues, especially after his theories were picked up and sensationalized by the press. Many of the old man's friends, in fact, blame this campaign of ridicule for his disappearance a few months later, which they suspect was the suicide of a broken-hearted and sincere searcher after truth.

Not only were Marsh's theories now beyond all scientific credibility, but his methods – such as quoting Allegro's *The Sacred Mushroom and the Cross* or Graves' *The White Goddess* as if they were as reputable as Boas, Mead, or Frazer – seemed to indicate senility. This impression was increased by the eccentric dedication. 'To Ezra Pound, Jacques De Molay and Emperor Norton I.' The real scientific scandal was not the theory of Atlantis (that was a bee that had haunted many a scholarly bonnet) but Marsh's claim that the gods of Atlantis actually existed; not as supernatural beings, of course, but as a superior class of life, now extinct, which had preexisted mankind and duped the earliest civilization into worshipping them as divine and offering terrible sacrifices at their altars. That there was absolutely no archaeological or paleontological evidence that such beings ever existed, was the mildest of the scholarly criticisms aimed at this hypothesis.

Professor Marsh's rapid decline, in the few months between the book's unanimous rejection by the learned world and his sudden disappearance, caused great pain to colleagues at Miskatonic. Many recognized that he had acquired some of his notions from Dr. Henry Armitage, generally regarded as having gone somewhat bananas after too many years devoted to puzzling out the obscene metaphysics of the *Necronomicon*. When the librarian Miss Horus mentioned at a faculty tea shortly after the disappearance that Marsh had spent much of the past month with that volume, one Catholic professor urged, only half-jokingly, that Miskatonic should rid itself of scandals once and for all by presenting 'that damned book' (he emphasized the word very deliberately) to Harvard.

Missing Persons Department of the Arkham police assigned the Marsh case to a young detective who had previously distinguished himself by tracing several missing infants to one of the particularly vile Satanist cults that have festered in that town since the witch-hunting days of 1692. His first act was to examine the manuscript on which the old man had been working since the completion of '*Atlantis and Its Gods.*' It seemed to be a shortish essay, intended for an anthropological magazine, and was quite conservative in tone and concept, as if the professor regretted the boldness of his previous speculations. Only one footnote, expressing guarded and qualified endorsement of Urquhart's theory about Wales being settled by survivors from Mu, showed the bizarre preoccupations of the Atlantis book. However, the final sheet was not related to this article at all and seemed to be notes for a piece which the Professor evidently intended to submit, brazenly and in total contempt of academic opinion, to a pulp publication devoted to flying saucers and occultism. The detective puzzled over these notes for a long time:

> *The usual hoax: fiction presented as fact. This hoax described here opposite to this: fact presented as fiction.*
> *Huysmans' La-Bas started it, turns the Satanist into hero.*
> *Machen in Paris 1880s, met with Huysman's circle.*
> *'Dols' and 'Aklo letters' in Machen's subsequent 'fiction.'*
> *Same years: Bierce and Chambers both mention Lake of Hali and Carcosa. Allegedly, coincidence.*
> *Crowley recruiting his occult circle after 1900.*
> *Bierce disappears in 1913.*
> *Lovecraft introduces Hali, dols, Aklo, Cthulhu after 1923.*
> *Lovecraft dies unexpectedly, 1937.*
> *Seabrook discusses Crowley, Machen, etc. in his 'Witchcraft,' 1940.*

Seabrook's 'suicide,' 1942.

Emphasize: Bierce describes Oedipus Complex in 'Death of Halpin Frazer,' BEFORE Freud, and relativity in 'Inhabitant of Carcosa,' BEFORE Einstein. Lovecraft's ambiguous descriptions of Azathoth as 'blind idiot-god,' 'Demon-Sultan' and 'nuclear chaos' circa 1930: fifteen years before Hiroshima.

Direct drug references in Chambers' 'King in Yellow,' Machen's 'Whit Powder,' Lovecraft's 'Beyond the Wall of Sleep' and 'Mountains of Madness.'

The appetites of the Lloigor or Old Ones in Bierce's 'Damned Thing.' Machen's 'Black Stone,' Lovecraft (constantly).

Atlantis known as Thule both in German and Panama Indian lore, and of course, 'coincidence' again the accepted explanation. Opening sentence for article: 'The more frequently one uses the word "coincidence" to explain bizarre happenings, the more obvious it becomes that one is not seeking, but evading, the real explanation.' Or, shorter: 'The belief in coincidence is the prevalent superstition of the Age of Science.'

The detective then spent an afternoon at Miskatonic library, browsing through the writings of Ambrose Bierce, J-K Huysmans, Arthur Machen, Robert W. Chambers, and H. P. Lovecraft. He found that all repeated certain key words; dealt with lost continents or lost cities; described superhuman beings trying to misuse or victimize mankind in some unspecified manner; suggested that there was a cult, or group of cults, among mankind who served these beings, and described certain books (usually not giving their titles: Lovecraft was an exception) that reveal the secrets of these beings. With a little further research, he found that the occult and Satanist circles in Paris in the 1880s had influenced the fiction of both Huysmans and Machen, as well as the career of the egregious Aleistair Crowley, and that Seabrook (who knew Crowley) hinted at more than he stated outright in his book on Witchcraft, published two years before his suicide. He then wrote a little table:

Huysmans – hysteria, complaints about occult attacks,
    final seclusion in a monastery.
Chambers – abandons such subjects, turns to light ro-
    mantic fiction.
Bierce – disappears mysteriously.
Lovecraft – dead at an early age.
Crowley – hounded into silence and obscurity.
Machen – becomes a devout Catholic. (Huysman's
    escape?)
Seabrook – alleged suicide.

The detective then went back and reread, not skimming
this time, the stories by these writers in which drugs were
specifically mentioned, according to Marsh's notes. He now
had a hypothesis: the old man had been lured into a drug
cult, as had these writers, and had been terrified by his
own hallucinations, finally ending his own life to escape
the phantoms his own narcotic-fogged brain had created. It
was a good enough theory to start with, and the detective
conscientiously set about interviewing every friend on campus of old Marsh, leading into the subject of grass and
LSD very slowly and indirectly. He made no headway and
was beginning to lose his conviction when good fortune
struck, in the form of a remark by another anthropology
professor about Marsh's preoccupation in recent years
with *amanita muscaria*, the hallucinogenic mushroom used
in ancient Near Eastern religions.

'A very interesting fungus, *amanita*,' this professor told
the detective. 'Some sensationalists without scholarly caution have claimed it was every magic potion in ancient
lore: the soma of the Hindus, the sacrament used in the
Dionysian and Eleusinian mysteries in Greece, even the
Holy Communion of the earliest Christians and Gnostics.
One chap in England even claims amanita, and not hashish,
was the drug used by the Assassins in the Middle Ages,
and there's a psychiatrist in New York, Puharich, who
claims it actually does induce telepathy. Most of that is
rubbish, of course, but amanita certainly is the strongest
mind-altering drug in the world. If the kids ever latch onto
it, LSD will seem like a tempest in a teapot by comparison.'

The detective now concentrated on finding somebody –
anybody – who had actually seen old Marsh when he was

stoned out of his gourd. The testimony finally came from a young black student named Pearson, who was majoring in anthropology and minoring in music. 'Excited and euphoric? Yeah,' he said thoughtfully. 'I saw old Joshua that way once. It was in the library of all places – that's where my girl works – and the old man jumped up from a table grinning about a yard wide and said out loud, but talking to himself, you know, "I saw them – I saw the fnords!" Then he ran out like Jesse Owens going to get his ashes hauled. I was curious and went over to peek at what he'd been reading. It was the *New York Times* editorial page, and not a picture on it, so he certainly didn't see the fnords, whatever the hell they are, *there*. You think he was maybe bombed a little?'

'Maybe, maybe not,' the detective said noncommittally, obeying the police rule of never accusing anyone of anything in hearing of a witness unless ready to make an arrest. But he was already quite sure that Professor Marsh would never reappear to be subject to arrest or any other harassment by those who had not entered his special world of lost civilizations, vanished cities, lloigors, dols, and fnords. To this day, the file on the Joshua N. Marsh case in the Arkham police department bears the closing line: 'Probable cause of death: suicide during drug psychosis.' Nobody ever traced the change in Professor Marsh back to a KCUF meeting in Chicago and a strangely spiked punch; but the young detective, Daniel Pricefixer, always retained a nagging doubt and a shapeless disquiet about this particular investigation, and even after he moved to New York and went to work for Barney Muldoon, he was still addicted to reading books on pre-history and thinking strange thoughts.

SIMON MAGUS. You will come to know gods.

After the disappearance of Saul Goodman and Barney Muldoon, the FBI went over the Malik apartment with a fine-tooth comb. Everything was photographed, fingerprinted, analyzed, catalogued, and where possible shipped back to the crime laboratory in Washington. Among the items was a short note on the back of a Playboy Club lunch receipt, not in Malik's handwriting, which meant nothing to anybody and was included only for the sake of the completeness so loved by the Bureau.

The note said: 'Machen's *dols* = Lovecraft's *dholes*!'
VECTORS. You will come to no gods.

On April 25, most of New York was talking about the incredible event that had occurred shortly before dawn at the Long Island mansion of the nation's best-known philanthropist, Robert Putney Drake. Danny Pricefixer of the Bomb Squad, however, was almost oblivious of this bizarre occurrence, as he drove through heavy traffic from one part of Manhattan to another interviewing every witness who might have spoken to Joseph Malik in the week before the *Confrontation* explosion. The results were uniformly disappointing: aside from the fact that Malik had grown increasingly secretive in recent years, none of the interviews seemed to provide any useful information. A killer smog had again settled on the city, for the seventh straight day, and Danny, a nonsmoker, was very aware of the wheeze in his chest, which did nothing to improve his mood.

Finally, at three in the afternoon, he left the office of ORGASM at 110 West Fortieth Street (an associate editor there was an old friend of Malik's and frequently lunched with him, but had nothing substantial to offer in leads) and remembered that the main branch of the New York Public Library was only half a block away. The hunch had been in the back of his mind, he realized, ever since he glanced at Malik's weird Illuminati memos. *What the hell,* he thought, *it'll only be a few more wasted minutes in a wasted day.*

For once, the congestion at the window in the main reference room was not quite as bad as a Canal Street traffic jam. *Atlantis and Its Gods* by Professor J. N. Marsh was delivered to him in seventeen minutes, and he began leafing through it looking for the passage he vaguely remembered. At last, on page 123, he found it:

Hans Stefan Santesson points out the basic similarity of Mayan and Egyptian investiture rituals, as previously indicated in Colonel Churchward's insightful but wrongheaded books on the lost continent of Mu. As we have demonstrated, Churchward's obsession with the Pacific, based on his having received his first clues about our lost ancestors in an Asiatic temple,

led him to attribute to the fictitious Mu much of the
real history of the actual Atlantis. But this passage
from Santesson's *Understanding Mu* (Paperback Library, New York, 1970, page 117) needs little correction:

> Next he was taken to the Throne of Regeneration
> of the Soul, and the Ceremony of Investiture or
> Illumination took place. Then he experienced
> further ordeals before attaining to the Chamber
> of the Orient, to the Throne of Ra, to become
> truly a Master. He could see for himself in the
> distance the uncreated light from which was
> pointed out the whole happiness of the future . . .
> In other words, as Churchward puts it, both in
> Egypt and in Maya the initiate had to 'sustain'
> (i.e., survive) 'the fiery ordeal' to be approved
> as an adept. The adept had to become justified.
> The justified must then become illuminate. . . .
> The destruction of Mu was commemorated by
> the possibly symbolic House of Fire of the
> Quiche Mayas and by the relatively later Chamber
> of Central Fire of the Mysteries which we are
> told were celebrated in the Great Pyramid.

Substituting Atlantis for Mu, Churchward and Santesson are basically correct. The god, of course, could
choose the shape in which He would appear in the
final ordeal, and, since these gods, or *lloigor* in the
Atlantean language, possessed telepathy, they would
read the initiate's mind and manifest in the form most
terrifying to the specific individual, although the *shoggoth* form and the classic Angry Giant form such as
appears in Aztec statues of Tlaloc were most common.
To employ an amusing conceit, if these beings had
survived to our time, as some occultists claim, they
would appear to the average American as, say, King
Kong or, perhaps, Dracula or the Wolf-Man.

The sacrifices demanded by these creatures evidently
contributed significantly to the fall of Atlantis, and
we can conjecture that the mass burnings practised by
the Celts at Beltain and even the Aztec religion, which

turned their altars into abattoirs, were minor in comparison, being merely the result of persistent tradition after the real menace of the *lloigor* had vanished. We, of course, cannot fully understand the purpose of these bloody rituals, since we cannot fathom the nature, or even the sort of matter or energy, that comprised the *lloigor*. That the chief of these beings, is known in the *Pnakotic Manuscripts* and the Eltdown Shards as Iok-Sotot, 'Eater of Souls,' suggests that it was some energy or psychic vibration of the dying victim that the *lloigor* needed; the physical body was, as in the case of the corpse-eating cult of Leng, consumed by the priests themselves, or merely thrown away as among the Thuggee of India.

Thoughtfully and quietly, Danny Pricefixer returned the book to the clerk at the checkout window. Thoughtfully and quietly, he walked out on Fifth Avenue and stood between the two guardian lions. Who was it, he wondered, who had asked, 'Since nobody wants war, why do wars keep happening?' He looked at the killer smog around him and asked himself another riddle, 'Since nobody wants air pollution, why does air pollution keep increasing?'

Professor Marsh's words came back to him: *'if these beings had survived to our time, as some occultists claim....'*

Walking toward his car, he passed a newsstand and saw that the disaster at the Drake Mansion was still the biggest headline even in the afternoon editions. It was irrelevant to his problem, however, so he ignored it.

Sherri Brandi continued the chant in her mind, maintaining the rhythm of her mouth movements . . . *fifty-three big rhinoceroses, fifty-four big rhinoceroses, fifty-five* – Carmel's nails dug into her shoulders suddenly and the salty gush splashed hot on her tongue. Thank the Lord, she thought, the bastard finally made it. Her jaw was tired and she had a crick in her neck and her knees hurt, but at least the son-of-a-bitch would be in a good mood now and wouldn't beat her up for having so little to report about Charley and his bugs.

She stood up, stretching her leg and neck muscles to remove the cramps, and looked down to see if any of Carmel's come had dribbled on her dress. Most men wanted her naked during a blow job, but not creepy Carmel; he insisted she wear her best gown, always. He liked soiling her, she realized; but, hell, he wasn't as bad as some pimps and we've all got to get our kicks some way.

Carmel sprawled back in the easy chair, his eyes still closed. Sherri fetched the towel she had been warming over the radiator and completed the transaction, drying him and gently kissing his ugly wand before tucking it back inside his fly and zippering him up. He *does* look like a goddam frog, she thought bitterly, or a nasty-tempered chipmunk.

'Terrif,' he said finally. 'The johns really get their money's worth from you, kid. Now tell me about Charley and his bugs.'

Sherri, still feeling cramped, pulled over a footstool and perched on its edge. 'Well,' she said, 'you know I gotta be careful. If he knows I'm pumping him, he might drop me and take up with some other girl. . . .'

'So you were too damned cautious and you didn't get anything out of him?' Carmel interrupted accusingly.

'Oh, he's over the loop,' she answered, still vague. 'I mean, really crazy now. That must be . . . uh, important . . . if you have to deal with him. . . .' She came back into focus. 'How I know is, he thinks he's going to other planets in his dreams. Some planet called Atlantis. Do you know which one that is?'

Carmel frowned. This was getting stickier: first, find a commie: then, find how to get the info out of Charley despite the FBI and CIA and all the other government people; and now, how to deal with a maniac. . . . He looked up and saw that she was out of focus again, staring into space. *Dopey broad*, he thought, and then watched as she slid slowly off the stool onto a neat sleeping position on the floor.

'What the hell?' he said out loud.

When he kneeled next to her and listened for her heart, his own face paled. *Jesus, Jesus, Jesus,* he thought standing up, now I got to *get rid of a fucking corpus delectus. The damned bitch went and died.*

'I can see the fnords!' Barney Muldoon cried, looking up from the *Miami Herald* with a happy grin.

Joe Malik smiled contentedly. It had been a hectic day – especially since Hagbard had been tied up with the battle

of Atlantis and the initiation of George Dorn – but now, at
last, he had the feeling their side was winning. Two minds
set on a death trip by the Illuminati had been successfully
saved. Now if everything worked out right between George
and Robert Putney Drake . . .

The intercom buzzed and Joe answered, calling across
the room without rising, 'Malik.'

'How's Muldoon?' Hagbard's voice asked.

'Coming all the way. He sees the fnords in a Miami
paper.'

'Excellent,' Hagbard said distractedly. 'Mavis reports
that Saul is all the way through, too, and just saw the
fnords in the *New York Times*. Bring Muldoon up to my
room. We've located that other problem – the sickness
vibrations that FUCKUP has been scanning since March.
It's somewhere around Las Vegas and it's at a critical
stage. We think there's been one death already.'

'But we've got to get to Ingolstadt before Walpurgis
night. . . .' Joe said thoughtfully.

'Revise and rewrite,' Hagbard said. '*Some* of us will go
to Ingolstadt. Some of us will have to go to Las Vegas. It's
the old Illuminati one-two punch – two attacks from different directions. Get your asses in gear, boys. They're immanentizing the Eschaton.'

WEISHAUPT. Fnords? Prffft!

Another interruption. This time it was the Mothers
March Against Muzak. Since that seems the most
worthwhile cause I've been approached for all day, I
gave the lady $1. I think that if Muzak can be stamped
out a lot of our other ailments will disappear too,
since they're probably stress symptoms, caused by
noise pollution.

Anyway, it's getting late and I might as well con-
clude this. One month before our KCUF experiment
– that is, on September 23, 1970 – Timothy Leary
passed five federal agents at O'Hare Airport here in
Chicago. He had vowed to shoot rather than go back
to jail, and there was a gun in his pocket. None of
them recognized him . . . And, oh, yes, there was a
policeman named Timothy O'Leary in the hospital
room where Dutch Schultz died on October 23, 1935.

'I've been saving the best for last. Aldous Huxley, the first major literary figure illuminated by Leary, died the same day as John F. Kennedy. The last essay he wrote revolved around Shakespeare's phrase, 'Time must have a stop' – which he had previously used for the title of a novel about life after death. 'Life is an illusion,' he wrote, 'but an illusion which we must take seriously.'

Two years later, Laura, Huxley's widow, met the medium, Keith Milton Rinehart. As she tells the story in her book, *This Timeless Moment*, when she asked if Rinehart could contact Aldous, he replied that Aldous wanted to transmit 'classical evidence of survival,' a message, that is, which could not be explained 'merely' as telepathy, as something Rinehart picked out of *her* mind. It had to be something that could only come from Aldous's mind.

Later that evening, Rinehart produced it: instructions to go to a room in her house, a room he hadn't seen and find a particular book, which neither he nor she was familiar with. She was to look on a certain page and a certain line. The book was one Aldous had read but she had never even glanced at; it was an anthology of literary criticism. The line indicated – I have memorized it – was: 'Aldous Huxley does not surprise us in this admirable communication in which paradox and erudition in the poetic sense and the sense of humor are interlaced in such an efficacious form.' Need I add that the page was 17 and the line was, of course, line 23?

(I suppose you've read Seutonius and know that the late J. Caesar was rendered exactly 23 stab wounds by Brutus and Co.)

Brace yourself, Joe. Worse attacks on your Reason are coming along. Soon, you'll see the fnords.

                                        Hail Eris,

P.S. Your question about the vibes and telepathy is easily answered. The energy is always moving in us, through us, and out of us. That's why the vibes have to be right before you can read someone without static. Every emotion is a motion.

Robert Anton Wilson
Secrets of Power

In January 1986, Robert Anton Wilson made one of his brief visits to London to lecture at The Town Hall, Chelsea. That evening's lecture was recorded and is now available as a full length LP record.

On the record Mr Wilson discusses the importance of 5, the connection between rabbits and UFOs and the religion of Discordianism. The record also features specially recorded sequences chronicling the rise of Leviathan.

The record is not readily available in the shops. You can obtain a copy by sending either a cheque or postal order made payable to 'ILLUMINATED' for £5.55 (includes post and packaging) to:

ILLUMINATED
46 CARTER LANE
LONDON EC4

HAIL ERIS!

LOVE WAS AN EASY GAME UNTIL SHE BROKE ALL THE RULES . . .

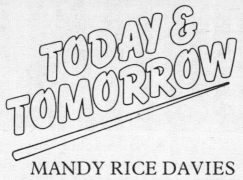

MANDY RICE DAVIES

The sensational, unstoppable story of high class seduction and ruthless international intrigue

In 1963, Mandy Rice Davies created a storm for her part in the series of political and sexual scandals surrounding the Profumo affair. Now, drawing on a controversial and colourful life of bizarre adventure, she has written TODAY AND TOMORROW, a novel as riveting and readable as it is robust . . .

0 7221 2847 9   GENERAL FICTION   £2.95

From the bestselling authors of
LUCIFER'S HAMMER and THE MOTE IN GOD'S EYE –
the ultimate novel of alien invasion!

FOOTFALL

NIVEN & POURNELLE

It was big all right, far bigger than any craft any
human had seen. Now it was heading for Earth.

The best brains in the business reckoned that any
spacecraft nearing the end of its journey would just
have to be friendly.

But they were wrong! Catastrophically wrong!

The most successful collaborative team in the history
of science fiction has combined again to produce a
devastating and totally convincing novel of alien
invasion.

FOOTFALL – the ultimate disaster

GENERAL FICTION   0 7221 6339 8   £3.95

The classic Amber series continues

ROGER ZELAZNY
TRUMPS OF DOOM

RETURN TO AMBER – The irresistible powers of the
kingdom beyond imagination draw Merlin, son of
Corwin, back to the magical realm . . .

Merlin is content to bide the time when he will activate
his superhuman strength and genius and claim his
birthright.

But that time arrives all too soon when the terrible
forces of evil drive him mercilessly from Earth, and upon
reaching Amber, he finds the domain in awesome,
bloody contention.

And in every strange darkness of his fantastic crusade,
there stalks a figure determined to destroy Merlin and
wipe out the wondrous world of Amber . . .

SCIENCE FICTION   0 7221 9410 2   £2.50

Also by Roger Zelazny in Sphere Science Fiction:

From the Hugo and Nebula award-winning author

TIME
PATROLMAN
by POUL ANDERSON

DEFENDER OF THE PAST . . .

The creaking Phoenician ship slowly approached its
destination. Everard gazed out over the sparkling water at the
ancient port of Tyre. "A grand sight indeed," he murmured to
the captain, glad of the easy electrocram method of learning
the language. His gaze went forward again; the city reminded
him not a little of New York.

Time patrolmen like Everard guard the past. No matter how
good or evil an event, it must be held inviolate. The slightest
slip, and Time would become Chaos, and all that has ever
been or will ever be will tumble into darkness. When the Birth
of Civilization is endangered by the malign counter-emperor
Varagan, the patrol must be on its mettle . . .

SCIENCE FICTION   **0 7221 1290 4**   **£2.50**